UPENDED

UPENDED

a novel by
AMANDA KABAK

Published in the United States by Brain Mill Press.
Print ISBN 978-1-948559-57-7
EPUB ISBN 978-1-948559-60-7
MOBI ISBN 978-1-948559-58-4
PDF ISBN 978-1-948559-59-1

www.brainmillpress.com

For Anna, as always.

UPENDED

CHAPTER 1

LOVE WHAT YOU DO, AND YOU'LL NEVER WORK A DAY IN YOUR life. Madeline Sawyer lived by that adage, but after three years of helming a start-up, the doing eclipsed the loving, and she had to moonlight as a prospector to excavate moments of delight from her daily grind. She and her business partner, Joe MacKenzie, took turns staving off existential despair by reminding each other that the shit work overflowing their inboxes was actually the steaming, fragrant proof of Mindful Management's success.

Madeline was a trailblazer, evangelist, cheerleader, and all-around role model. Along with Joe, she mentored companies in advanced management techniques with a deliciously devious approach. In a Trojan horse of progress, they leveraged the allure of ferocious productivity and competitive advantage to lay the groundwork for inclusion. Despite the trendiness of this goal, their marketing materials addressed more measurable benefits because, in business, quality was nothing without quantification. But measurement meant data, and data meant reports, and generating reports meant the necessity of reminding herself that she loved what she did.

UPENDED

She worked sixty- or seventy-hour weeks, holidays, Sundays, and occasional midnights, when something innocuous—unidentified, even—woke her from fitful sleep. She worked through blizzards and heat waves and perfect New England fall afternoons when the air was crystal and the trees neon. And for the last ten months, she'd gone into her office every Saturday after having breakfast with her brother, Ethan. She'd been keeping an eye on him since he'd moved to town because she was his big sister and she loved him, though sometimes that was as complicated as loving what she did.

Madeline regularly exhausted her deep reserves of patience at work and couldn't abide waiting for food, so they met at a diner scruffy enough not to be busy during prime brunch hour. The East-Side Eatery had probably been classic twenty years before, but its chrome had lost its luster, shadows of griddle smoke and grease stained the white tile behind the line cook, and the ceiling fans turned at a desultory tempo. Even the customers looked rough around the edges, including Ethan. She spotted him in their usual booth through the diner's window, mug of coffee stapled to his lip. He wasn't much of a morning person, and though it was already ten o'clock, she appreciated his effort.

She opened the door of the restaurant into a savory-sweet humidity that obliterated the early April chill and threaded her way past Formica-topped tables to Ethan. "That coffee smells good." She bounced onto the springy bench across from him, shrugging off her powder blue fleece in the process.

Ethan stopped drinking long enough to say, "Elixir of the gods." In addition to a thick flannel shirt and jeans, he wore the aggressive slouch and droopy eyes of a hangover, and her love for him became simple.

Darla, their regular waitress and a tank of a woman, lumbered up to the table with a pot of coffee and poured Madeline a cup. "Morning, Doll, what'll it be today?" Her voice was rough with decades of cigarettes. At their first breakfast here, they had assumed Darla's legendary gruffness marbled all the way through her like fat in Kobe beef. Yet within a month, Madeline had charmed her into slinging these small endearments along with their hash browns.

"Sausage, egg, and extra cheese on wheat toast. Oh"—she put a hand on Darla's formidable forearm—"and a side of fruit, please."

Darla turned to Ethan. "And you?"

"What, no Doll or Honey or Sugar?" Ethan offered his cup for a refill.

"Please. You're the sour to your sister's sweet."

"At least I've got a vital role in our relationship. Can I have the number five with bacon and eggs scrambled hard?"

"Gotcha. Cottage cheese and fruit coming up." She squeaked off toward the kitchen.

Madeline leaned across the table. "She likes you. And she's single. Didn't she say it's been eight years since she divorced her rat bastard of a husband?"

"She's a hundred and ten."

"You think anyone over forty is a hundred and ten."

"Yeah, and you're toeing the line."

She sat back and wagged a finger at him. "I've still got five years."

"Pretty soon you're going to be ordering that cottage cheese plate and lecturing me about my cholesterol."

"You know, Darla's right. You're not only sour but as scruffy as this diner. Really, Ethan, that so-called beard has to go."

He stretched out his hand. "Okay. Truce." They shook.

They talked easily about nothing while sipping coffee and settling in: the slow start to spring, random (and hilarious) things they'd overheard on the bus or the T, seasonal allergies, and the upcoming marathon, which ran right by Mindful Management's office in Brookline's Coolidge Corner. Once their food came, they lapsed into a companionable prandial quiet, but Madeline's mind expanded into the conversational vacuum, latching on to the one topic they most definitely weren't discussing—their father's death. Ethan had arrived in Boston not long after the funeral, and he'd seemed a bit lost ever since. Still, she resolved not to bring it

3

up; Ethan could get prickly about their father, not that Madeline's relationship with the man had been all shits and giggles.

Under Ethan's flannel, Madeline glimpsed a T-shirt sporting the logo of the coffee shop where he worked as a barista. For years, he'd been serving espresso and baked goods at a long string of stores to support his less lucrative life as a musician, but he hadn't been making much music lately, which was another topic she decided not to broach. She nodded at his chest. "Do you have a shift after this?"

"Noon to close. Practically the worst shift ever—all college kids who sit around for hours and don't tip." He finished his coffee. "Do *you* have a shift?" It was sarcastic and serious at the same time. When she rolled her eyes, he said, "Don't you know that the winters up here are meant for hibernation, not putting on the consulting afterburners?"

"If only. I would totally hibernate if I didn't wake up at the slightest provocation."

He put down his fork. "You know what I mean." The dark way his eyebrows pulled together contrasted with the comic relief of his flyaway hair and challenged beard. The love in his judgment warmed (and exhausted) her.

"Believe me, Joe and I are working on it. Neither of us wants to flounder in these fucking hours, but that's the nature of a start-up. Like how playing gigs until midnight and getting up for a six a.m. shift at the coffee shop is the nature of what you do. Everything's got a cost, right?"

He shrugged. "At least musicians get laid."

"Oh, really? Because from where I sit, you're the one musician who's taken a vow of chastity."

"What, you think I make a habit of detailing my sex life to my big sister?"

She wrinkled her nose. "Who said I wanted details?"

He speared a wedge of pancake and dragged it through a pool of syrup. His smile bloomed slowly but was infectious despite its mystery. "Speaking of details, where'd you get those books of lezzie porn you left behind when you went to college? Because I totally didn't read all of them cover to cover, and they weren't unbelievably steamy."

Her smile faltered a little. "It's called erotica, and they weren't all like that. The bookstore on Walnut would special order anything you wanted and not tell the whole universe about it."

"Damn, you were a ballsy one. I genuflect to your guts." He bowed low over the table, and she laughed. But then he said, "Sheesh, Maddy, what happened to you? Are you even gay anymore, or have they revoked your membership? You and Joe should tie the knot already."

Madeline's internal barometer rose with that low blow, but she kept a lid on her pique. "Yes, I'm still gay, thank you very much."

"Well, you could've fooled me. The Mad Hatter has gone all mainstream. Ten to one you haven't been with anyone since Jane. Sure, she was blazing hot, but six years? Forget turning straight; you're practically a nun."

"It's been three years, not that it's any of your business. Not even three years. Besides, I've been a little busy."

"Meaning you work like a dog."

"Hey, what happened to our stay-off-each-other's-ass policy?"

He shrugged. "You started it."

"I started it? What are you, eleven?" She reviewed their conversation to see where it had gone off the rails, but it was useless. What did it matter who started it (though Ethan had)? Madeline could get on his case about countless things: his grooming, his aimlessness, the twelve credits between him and a college degree, or his misplaced animosity toward their father, but she merely said, "Consider your point made."

"Come on, Hat Trick. I was just giving you a hard time. That's my job as a younger brother."

"And it's a job you clearly take very seriously."

"As opposed to my real job, you mean?"

"I didn't say that." She pulled the last grapes from a decimated stem and dug around in her purse. "Speaking of jobs, I should get to work." She pulled money from her wallet and dropped it on the table—enough to cover both their breakfasts, which was an act of mild aggression she knew would annoy him.

"Maddy."

She got up. "It's fine. Really. Let's just quit while we're ahead." Or at least only a little behind.

DESPITE CLOCKING SIXTY-EIGHT HOURS OF WORK SINCE THAT breakfast, Madeline had failed to shake Ethan's words. In between meetings and reports and research, she was plagued by thoughts of Jane, her father, and Ethan: various kinds of family in various states of existence. While Ethan had anointed Madeline's ex "Sister Jane," her father hadn't referred to her at all—at least not in relation to Madeline. To him, Madeline was a businesswoman, an entrepreneur, a professional success story straight out of the Arizona desert, but not a lesbian. He'd known she was gay for twenty years, but he'd been adept at not acknowledging it.

Friday night, she stood at her kitchen counter, eating lo mein right from the carton with splintery chopsticks. She'd made it as far as kicking off her heels and untucking her blouse, but inside her business suit, she crawled with dissatisfaction, a helpless regret, and overwhelming disgust at the state of her apartment. When she'd moved in a couple years before, she'd had enough shelves for her books, but now hundreds of volumes crowded windowsills, end tables, and even half the couch. Normally, one of them would croon to her with distraction, beckon with the smell of tree pulp, caress her fingertips with the sharp yet delicate edges of its pages, but tonight, they massed like a menacing hoard.

Madeline Mismanagement, she thought, then tried immediately to unthink it. It was what Jane had called Madeline's company near the end of their relationship. Jane hadn't been a neat freak by any measure, but this mess would have driven her around the bend. For the seven years they'd lived together, the majority of Madeline's library had been incarcerated in the spare bedroom, with a select few volumes released for good behavior to one stuffed but orderly bookcase in the living room. Faced with the unsavory devolution of this apartment and its mirror image at work, Madeline couldn't help but admit that this...hoarding (she made herself think the word) was a way to fill the void Jane had left.

"Don't," Madeline told herself.

Yes, okay, she worked like a dog, which was something that had drawn her father closer and pushed Jane away as if her job were the focal point of a zero-sum game of love, but that was reality, life, which maybe Ethan was still too young to comprehend in an appropriately fatalistic way. But Madeline had almost a decade on her brother, and fatalistic was a pale approximation of what she felt. Her empty takeout container did nothing but foretell the rest of this empty evening and the empty weekend beyond—except for their weekly breakfast that was fated to turn contentious. She dumped the dregs of her dinner in the trash and swore without much force. What was there to do?

A FEW HOURS LATER, MADELINE WAS IMMERSED IN A SHIFTING, swirling fray of women on the dance floor at Club True in Central Square. It was lesbian night, and she wove among small groups or pairs of women, grounding herself with the momentary brush of her fingers against a bicep here, a wrist there. The music was loud and driving, and after a couple drinks, the thump of bass filled her chest, its delicious vibrations dislodging her thoughts.

She danced for over an hour, taking breaks only to cool down and survey the scene from among women loitering at the bar or in wallflower-like positions around the main room. Being here was a great and perilous escape from her life but also an inadvertent and probably ill-advised surrender to her memories of Jane. When they would go out dancing before Mindful Management, Jane would steal the show every time. Why not? She was six feet tall and blond with a body that made no secret of the hours she spent on the volleyball court—first as a top-ranked college player, then on the U.S. national team. She exuded strength and confidence and total control on the dance floor, and Madeline was perfectly happy to dance in her shadow.

Tonight, Madeline was moderately successful at shrugging off the solo nature of this expedition and just *moving*—at least until the alcohol in her system and the heat of the bodies around her heterodyned into an irrepressible inferno. Her deep-V T-shirt clung to her shoulder blades and lower back, and she eased toward a darkly inviting corner, which, she discovered almost too late, was occupied by an otherwise-occupied couple.

"Shit," she said, but the word was swallowed up by music, and she backtracked, sliding over to the bar even though she didn't need another drink. Then again, another drink might impair her enough to stop seeing bits of Jane all over the club—hands here, neck there, shoulders way across the room.

She claimed an empty stool next to a woman redolent with ill-advised patchouli, ordered a shot, and dipped her head, blotting sweat from her hairline and upper lip with the hem of her T-shirt. When she heard her name, she straightened up with a surprised jolt, turning away from that noxious perfume and toward the voice.

It took a moment for familiarity to snap into recognition, but when it did, Madeline smiled. "Hey, I know you." Zoe Doolittle was an acquaintance from a Jamaica Plain café they both frequented, where they'd historically made small talk more with the proprietor than with each other. But their proximity had led to Zoe doing graphic design work for Mindful Management, and they even had a meeting on the books for Monday, not that Madeline should be thinking about work. "It's good to see you. Have you been here before?" She said the words in a half shout so Zoe could hear.

"Just once." Zoe indicated the dance floor with a tilt of her head, her small, stylish glasses catching the lights behind them. "I saw you out there. You can really move."

"I wouldn't say that." Despite years of studying Jane, Madeline had never approached her ex's prowess. "I'm so out of shape I'm sweating like an absolute pig." Her drink came, and she swallowed half of it. Its blooming warmth pushed up against the inside of her skin, meeting the press of the club's heat.

Zoe gazed at her with a directness she'd never shown before—not at the café or in the conference rooms at IDK Designs, where she worked. But now, in the darkness with this thick atmosphere of music and energy, the rules between them shifted. Zoe leaned closer than she needed to and laid her hand next to Madeline's on the bar. Her dark hair was especially wild, the top exuberant over sides and back shaved tight to her scalp. In the dim light and with some whiskey in her, Zoe felt like a tantalizing stranger. When Madeline had left her apartment, all she'd wanted was to misplace her loneliness in a venue crowded with life instead of books, but Zoe's suddenly clear interest was...interesting.

Madeline said, "Wanna dance?"

"I'm not much of a dancer."

Jane had described dancing as a controlled relinquishing of control, an astute observation that explained why some people didn't like it. Madeline told herself to forget about Jane and held out her hand. "Come on. It'll be okay."

"I've been compared to Frankenstein's monster."

"I doubt that's accurate, but if it is, it's probably pretty cute." Madeline finished her drink and gave Zoe a smile she hoped looked as flirtatious as it felt.

When Zoe finally let Madeline lead her to the edge of the dance floor, she held her arms out in front of her like Mary Shelley's creation, which made them both laugh. Zoe's jeans were fitted, and the sleeves of her oxford shirt were rolled to her elbows, revealing delicate forearms in an appealing combination of feminine and butch. Madeline's last drink settled in her knees, and she embraced the looseness and succumbed to rhythm and movement, laying a palm on Zoe's arm one moment and her shoulder the next, trying to infect her admittedly stiff body with the beat. Madeline was fairly drunk and happy enough not to think, but thinking was a lot like breathing, so she wondered how long Zoe had been alone, why she was alone, and if she went out like this often.

Madeline took in Zoe's dark eyes behind her glasses, the dimple high on her left cheek, the way the soft curves of her smile contrasted with the sharpness of her collarbones visible in the open neck of her shirt. They drifted closer, Madeline not sure if she was merely complicit in the movement or the one driving their proximity. Zoe's face, visible in stark snapshots from a slow strobe light, was a mix of concentration and bright pleasure. Madeline felt blissfully outside her own life, outside everything but this loud, hot moment of here and now—at least until Zoe snagged her hand and pulled her away from the other dancers toward that previously occupied dark corner. Oh, Madeline thought with a clarity that belied the alcohol in her system, this isn't a good idea. "I don't think—"

But her voice was lost in the music, and Zoe's kiss was brief, exploratory. It neither flooded Madeline with desire nor made her want to pull away. Zoe's next kiss was more serious, paired with a hand that fluttered at Madeline's waist. Madeline extricated herself, stepping back for a clear view of Zoe, whose mouth transformed into a frown so comprehensive it tugged at Madeline even more than her attraction. Now that was a frown she totally got, but she shouted over the music, "I've had too much to drink. Really." Madeline squeezed Zoe's shoulder and looked at her until she looked back. "I'm not saying no. I'm not. Will you call me?"

Zoe nodded, and Madeline kissed her on the cheek. "I'm serious. Call me," she said again before making her way through music and lighting and heat and dancing women. Outside the club lay the deafening quiet of a spring night. The air had gone clammy-cool, which sobered her a notch and made her realize just how drunk she was. Tomorrow's breakfast with Ethan was going to be a disaster.

It was just after one, which gave her plenty of time to catch the T home—a long ride that would further delay the inevitable. The cotton of quiet in her ears and her fuzzed inebriation made the walk to the station and the subsequent subway ride go by in thick, slow motion. She let the familiar rocking of the train lull her into a stupor.

She got off the T at Green Street, thinking ahead to a shower and the deep, dreamless sleep alcohol sometimes facilitated. She crossed Washington Street and sighed at the half mile and big hill that stood between her and her apartment. Her ears had recovered from the onslaught of music at the club, and her walk was accompanied by the low swish of intermittent traffic on the Arborway and the hum of a nearby transformer. She trudged ahead, thinking only about water and sleep, until a scraping footstep very close by shot a ribbon of adrenaline through her.

Before she could even turn around and look for its source, someone grabbed her arms and slammed her against the building next to her, the force knocking breath clear from her lungs. The hands clamped down even harder, and she still couldn't breathe when the side of the building rushed at her again.

CHAPTER 2

JOE MACKENZIE SAT IN HIS CRAMPED BUT FUNCTIONAL KITCHEN, eating oatmeal and perusing the latest *Harvard Business Review*. He devoted the first hour of every day to reading in a fruitless attempt to keep up with Madeline, who could seemingly slip a book under her pillow at night and wake with it memorized. He savored this time of quiet contemplation and percolating neurons that had become indelibly associated with the earthy smell of Colombian coffee. A ray of sunshine graced the table like a cosmic nod of affirmation, prompting a Pavlovian feeling of content.

Only faint birdsong marred his apartment's hush, so when the phone rang, it startled him into sloshing a splash of coffee onto the glossy pages of his magazine. He mopped up the mess while he answered, which was enough of a distraction that he couldn't quite get who the caller was and what they wanted. When they identified themselves again, his mouth went dry. The emergency room at Beth Israel hospital? It was his daughter. It had to be his daughter, though Katie shouldn't be anywhere near there, was out in Belmont with her mother. Then, finally, he heard Madeline's name and stopped panicking long enough to listen.

That pocket of calm collapsed when he hung up, and he reeled around his apartment, changing into the first clothes he could find, then searching for wallet and keys, socks and shoes, visiting his bedroom three different times in scattered inefficiency. Madeline would say he was in a lather, and she'd be right. She'd advise him to pull himself together, but she was always better at crisis management than he was.

It seemed impossible to be this old—forty-three, already—without ever having rushed to the hospital, not for sliced finger or broken bone or gallbladder. Not even for Katie's birth, which he and his ex-wife had organized to death, just like everything else in their marriage. Hurrying to Madeline was involuntary, necessary. She'd been viciously beaten, found unconscious in an alleyway, and was in serious condition. But not dead, definitely not dead. There'd be no rush if she were dead. The words rang like a mantra.

After a short, reckless drive from Brookline to Beth Israel, he parked his sedan in the wrong structure and hustled through two buildings before arriving at the ER intake desk, where the nurse seemed intent on not understanding what he wanted. Madeline would extend her considerable empathy and conjecture that the nurse was probably tired the end of her shift, but Joe didn't care. He needed to be understood, so he relaxed his hands and shoulders and neck, took a steadying breath, and started over: Madeline Sawyer, business partner, emergency contact, assault. This time his words filtered through, and an orderly led him past curtained areas and gurneys and empty IV stands into the bowels of the department. The light was otherworldly, and his ears kept catching on short snippets of urgent conversation he couldn't quite understand.

Suddenly, there she was, a bandaged blur in observation. Stable now but still unconscious. The orderly withdrew, and Joe sank onto a beige plastic chair under a rack of monitors, his shoulder brushing wires that disappeared beneath Madeline's hospital gown. He watched the spiked line of her heartbeat while steeling himself to take a good look at her.

UPENDED

An IV snaked down to her forearm; though its end was hidden under a wide piece of tape, Joe couldn't help imagining its needle resting deep in her vein, which was a thought harrowing in its minute specificity. He stood and turned his attention to her face, but the trauma there set up an ache in his thighs. Her nose was bulbous, and discoloration fanned out to her eyes. A split through her left eyebrow was bisected with a butterfly bandage, and a large gauze pad covered her forehead and right temple. The whole right side of her face was a big abraded bruise, but her lips affected him the most. They were swollen, cut in multiple places, raw with trauma at the corners and under her nose. Madeline's mouth was the root of her expressiveness. Her smile radiated warmth, friendliness, and camaraderie and evoked a beauty she didn't quite have, not with a mouth so full of Chiclet-sized teeth that they were in a perpetual brawl for position.

She called them Chiclets, not Joe, was always upfront and matter-of-fact about things others might find unattractive about her: not just those teeth but eyes that were set too close together and indecisive hair—not long, not short, not straight, not curly, not blond, not brown. She didn't seem bothered by these supposed deficiencies, and when she smiled and her light brown eyes crinkled at the corners, her warm cheer eclipsed every other impression. After four years of working together, Madeline was just...Madeline, a disembodied spirit of optimism, elbow grease, and intuitive ingenuity. At least until now.

The nurse had told him that along with the damage to Madeline's face, several of her ribs and two fingers were broken, and she had severe sprains in her shoulder and left knee. During his freshman year in college, Joe had gotten into a fistfight over something monumentally stupid, and the single punch he'd taken had exploded with such pain he couldn't fathom the horror of Madeline's beating, how it must've unfolded over a sickening sequence of intolerable instances. Why would someone do this?

He brushed his fingers over Madeline's hands, each thumbnail chewed ragged at one corner. His heart rate slowed to match the

14

one he saw on the monitor, and in the face of this almost end of theirs, he couldn't help but think about their beginning—a whirlwind that had started when they'd run into each other at a management seminar in Copley Square. They had worked together before he'd left State Street a few years earlier, and he'd found her eminently capable, not to mention had been intrigued by the leggy blonde she'd always brought to company holiday parties, a woman whose intimidating height and obvious strength were wonderfully offset by the tender way she gazed at Madeline and held her hand.

Joe had heard from former coworkers about the division-wide management training Madeline was spearheading, so he made a point to intercept her between sessions. After some brief chitchat, he asked, "Why are you attending and not presenting?"

"State Street's footing the bill, so I thought I'd see what they're peddling." She glanced around at who was within earshot and went on in a low voice. "It's a racket. It's supposed to be guru-level, but there's nothing new in it."

"Certainly nothing like what I've heard you're trying to do these days."

They watched people filing into a session behind them, and Madeline made a face. "They're selling leftovers in new shrink-wrapped packaging."

"Let's play hooky. Coffee?" Joe asked. She agreed, and they drifted to the nearest Starbucks, where they sat with their drinks at a counter against the window. Under free-form jazz crooning from the speaker above them, he said, as sarcastically as he could, "Isn't the packaging all that matters?"

"So jaded. True but jaded." She sipped her coffee, watching people flow past on the sidewalk in the sharp fall sunshine. "I'll bet you good money the place you're working at now had someone come in and do a buzzword blitz."

"Sure. I was a 'Logical Inventor.'"

She rolled her eyes. "Exactly. It was useless, right? Just like this seminar." She made a disgusted face, her lips twisted to the side and down in a crooked frown. But after another drink of coffee, her expression changed again into a sly smile. "Are you thinking what I'm thinking?"

"That we're in the wrong racket?"

She laid her hand on his arm, stopping him in the middle of raising his cup to his mouth. "Everyone goes about this ass backwards. Buzzword blitzes don't work. Joe, here, is a logical inventor, whatever the fuck that means, and this generic, useless handbook says I should approach him in X way. But what about context? What about Joe as a person? His patterns and preferences, whether he's more productive in the morning or the afternoon, if he's buying a house or his dog just died."

"Or if he got a divorce."

"Or if he got a divorce." She shifted to face him more fully. "You got a divorce?" She squeezed his forearm.

"Yes, but it's fine. Go on. Joe as a person."

"Right." She took her hand away. "What I mean is that getting better at managing people isn't about ignoring complexity. It's about recognizing the incredible benefit of complexity and knowing how to work with it."

"That would require a long-term partnership."

Madeline made a loud dinging sound, startling a man who was halfway out the shop's door. "Ongoing training. On-site embedding. Real working sessions. Programs tailored for specific teams and goals."

"Boutique, high-end consulting for the truly committed."

She grinned and said, "*Exactly*," poking him in the chest at the same time.

He felt an explosion of purpose while they discussed how a consulting business like that might work. While Madeline spoke theoretically, Joe itched to print up business cards and have client meetings, to be driving his own destiny as surely as he hadn't been since his divorce. This was just the thing to fill his long, empty hours in the evenings and weekends without Katie.

He doubled down on market research and case studies, presenting his findings to Madeline for her feedback—and to try to infect her with his determination. She was analytical and encouraging and intuited his thoughts like she was reading the printed book of his mind. The more they dug into the idea, the more convinced he became that he couldn't do this without her. They were the perfect team for this.

Through sheer force of will (and Madeline's inability to deny her deep well of ideas and enthusiasm), he converted her to his righteous cause, and they eventually sat across a desk from their lawyer to sign official partnership papers. Madeline pulled a cigar-sized pen from her briefcase and smiled at his look. "I know, right? My dad gave it to me when I got my MBA. Maybe he thought the degree wasn't enough, and I still required something phallic to be successful. I mean, look at this thing." She waggled it in front of his face. "You'll be glad to know he sees this company like you do: an opportunity to shine. To break ground. Even though the whole thing is a little too psychological for his comfort, I swear he'd be asking to join us if he weren't across the country. Not that I would ever let that happen—I shiver at the thought. Still, it's nice that we have this connection now, so I thought he'd appreciate my using this pen today instead of just on his birthday cards."

This closeness between Madeline and her father was a shining signpost that they were on the right path. Mindful Management was all about strengthening relationships, and it was showing results before they'd even officially started. The months of work to get to this point had been nothing less than a return to life for Joe, and it was a life that promised to be full of sparkling connection.

WHEN MADELINE WOKE UP, JOE THOUGHT THE WORDLESS SOUNDS she made were from the next partition over, where there'd been a woman talking fast and loud between bouts of vomiting. But her slurred and unintelligible voice eventually coalesced into something well-known, and he stood quickly, clutching the plastic bed rail. "Madeline. It's Joe. I'm here."

UPENDED

She lifted a hand to her temple and glanced at the arm attached to it, the splinted fingers, the IV tube taped to the soft white of her skin. She looked at Joe but appeared not to see him. Her gaze circled the room once, then again, before she closed her eyes and cried.

He pushed the call button and held her good hand in both of his. She squeezed his fingers in weak pulses. A nurse answered via the intercom, and Joe said, "She's awake. She's— she's awake, okay?"

"Someone will be right in."

Joe had seen Madeline cry only once, about a year after they'd started out, and that had been tears of frustration over a tenaciously recalcitrant client—a short, violent cloudburst accompanying choked swearing they'd both laughed about later. This bore no relation to that. Her face, neck, and cheeks grew red and blotchy. Her mouth, already so painful looking, twisted with her sobs, but it was the hoarseness in her keening that made Joe's eyes tear up in response.

A nurse came in, moved Joe out of the way, and talked to Madeline in soothing tones while taking her blood pressure. A doctor arrived, crowding Joe out into the hall. Someone took him by the arm and directed him to a chair, asking him if there were someone else they could call. He dropped down, his legs weak, his breath knocked out of him.

After a while, a policeman walked past him into Madeline's room.

CHAPTER 3

WHEN ETHAN SAWYER HAD MOVED FROM AUSTIN TO BOSTON (there was a song in there somewhere), Maddy had orchestrated the hell out of their weekly breakfasts: finding the diner, picking the time, schlepping across town from Jamaica Plain, all of which felt decidedly managerial. It wasn't as if she took attendance, but the thought of her sitting alone in a blue Naugahyde booth, eating a sausage-egg-and-cheese sandwich with her nose in a book or magazine, *handling* his not being there, was enough to compel him out of bed.

This morning, the April sun was ineffective against the chill in the air, and he strode faster to stay warm, the effort freeing him from the last clinging fingers of sleep. Truthfully, he was drawn along more by the thought of bacon than his sister. As much as Ethan liked Maddy, her kind of success was maximally unappealing. A Harvard MBA and endless days in business drag, blah-blahing through one long progression of meetings? No, thank you. Five years before, he'd had a vision at his mother's funeral that foretold the futility of his almost–poli sci degree, that said drop out and leave that shit to Maddy. And why not, given how good she was at it, how she always knew the just-right way to spin an awful truth?

At the diner, he settled into their usual booth, which was somehow always available. Ethan figured Maddy's sheer force of will repelled people from it even from clear across town. He sipped his way through a mug of coffee while waiting for her, but she didn't appear before he tipped the last swallow into his mouth from the thick ceramic vessel. He was contemplating calling her when Darla appeared with the pot of coffee he swore was welded to her hand.

"Where's your sister? That doll. Is she mad at you or just sick of your ugly mug?"

Ethan said, "I'll have you know that I'm a hot commodity among certain ladies."

"The blind ones?"

"You're a riot."

"If you stopped masquerading as a derelict, I might believe you."

He fingered his patchy beard. "Duly noted."

"Do you want to order now or wait for Madeline?"

He checked the time again. "I have to go to work soon, so how about that cottage cheese and fruit you're always threatening me with?"

"So, your usual, then?"

"That's the one. Extra bacon."

She refilled his mug and left him alone to gaze out the window, where a plastic bag and some wadded paper tumbleweeded down the sidewalk in the still-wintery light. Maybe Maddy was mad at him since he'd admittedly been a bit of an ass at their last breakfast, but wasn't the best defense a good offense? Any week now, she'd be bringing up their dad, and he did not want to get into it, not one little bit. Yes, the man had died, and Ethan had moved up here, but despite Maddy's ardent belief, those two incidents were a textbook example of correlation without causation. He would do just about anything to avoid that conversation, including the razzle-dazzle of a bald-faced lie.

Maddy had an inexplicable compulsion to honesty, so every time he lied to her, he was sure she knew. If she didn't call him on it, which she often didn't, he felt the full weight of their nine-year age difference. Each and every time, he was convinced that her going along with his lie was some kind of super-adult ploy that was supposed to work on him like steamed broccoli or vigorous exercise.

Even so, while he waited for her, he concocted a story about a local folk goddess, Danika Miller, making hints the night before about him opening for her at some gigs. The best lies contained a grain of truth, and this one qualified. He had actually played at an open mic at Fuel, the shop where he jerked coffee most days. It had been packed and so hot sweat had made his shirt its bitch by the end of his two songs and their lukewarm reception. Though Danika Miller had been there, the truth was she hadn't been talking to him when she'd said that opening act bit. Sure, she'd been talking around him, hadn't specifically excluded him, but "hint" was a deception of the highest order.

A year ago, opening for Danika Miller would've been a serious step down for him despite her wide smile, easy between-song banter, and dark hair that smelled like almonds and honey. Back in Austin, his band had been headliners, had two albums under their belt, and had amassed a certain local following, including a girl who eyed Ethan in a decidedly rabid way. That he hadn't played any gigs (or even written any songs) since moving here was nothing more than coincidence.

His breakfast arrived without Maddy, and he called her but was sent right to voice mail. Even if she were pissed at him for last week, he couldn't believe she would go in for this passive-aggressive bullshit. He shoveled some eggs into his mouth and called Mindful Management's office. Where else could she possibly be? Mindful Management. What a repulsively well-meaning name. No one answered, though he kept his finger poised over the disconnect button in case Joe picked up.

UPENDED

He wolfed down his breakfast while contemplating his next move. She could be working over at Joe's place, but no way was Ethan going to call there to find out. All Ethan had done the week before was to try to provide some well-needed perspective: all work and no play makes Maddy a dull girl. It was only the truth. Maybe she'd actually listened to him and had gone out the night before and tied one on—or even gotten lucky, which would be an added bonus. If she met someone, she might actually relax about these breakfasts, and he could start sleeping in again. Win-win.

Darla snuck up on him, her white waitress shoes carrying her stealthily across the linoleum for once. "She stood you up, huh?"

"It appears that way."

"What'd you do?"

He pushed his empty plate away. "I didn't do anything, thank you very much. Why is everything my fault, anyway? Seriously. I'm twenty-six years old. I don't need my big sister to babysit me."

"Mm-hmm. Next week, then?"

He rubbed his cheek through his beard. "Unless there's a new world order."

"If there is, hopefully it's the one where I win the lottery." Darla laid down the check.

He paid and called Maddy again while he walked to the bus stop. No dice. Imagining her hungover made him feel a little better while he rode the 89 bus to Davis Square. Once there, he crossed a couple streets and passed a few shops before arriving at Fuel, where he flung open the front door and spied Nettie behind the register. "Help has arrived!"

She clapped and whooped. Nettie reminded Ethan of the best parts of white bread—pale and comforting with an aura of softness, though she also scooped ice cream at the J.P. Licks down the street and had guns of steel (or at least *a* gun of steel). Once, she claimed she could fell a horse with a single blow from her scooping arm. A horse! During the frequent shifts they shared, one of their favorite pastimes was talking about how old they were, especially in the

22

face of gaggles of Tufts University students loitering over cold remnants of foam in their large latte cups.

The phone rang, cutting off Nettie's applause. "Aw, really?" she said but answered. "Fuel, this is Nettie. How can I help you?" She turned away from Ethan, but he heard her murmur, "Yes, I remember. Seven o'clock...I know I forgot last time...Okay...Okay. I'll remember, I promise." It was The Boyfriend; he could tell by her apologetic tone.

Nettie wasn't the sharpest, most confident person in general, but while she'd been known to emerge, pink-cheeked, from behind her blond curtain of hair with Ethan, she was maddeningly subservient around The Boyfriend. While she okayed a few more times, Ethan clocked in and straightened chairs at the dozen tables in the shop. The place was decorated with license plates and street signs, trying for a gas station/road trip feel, but the people who hung out here were too glued to their laptops to notice.

Nettie hung up the phone. "Sorry."

Ethan grunted.

"I just...he just...Oh, never mind."

"That guy."

"Don't. I know you don't like him." She still had the phone in her grip. "But you don't understand."

"Ah, yes, the Ethan Sawyer refrain." He made himself laugh. Nettie didn't laugh with him, but she relaxed enough to pass a pinch of hair between her nose and mouth, which made his frustration melt into ready affection. "This is me officially butting out."

"This is me officially pretending none of that happened." She put the phone back on its cradle, but it rang again, making her flinch. After she answered, her face got serious but not uncertain, like when it was The Boyfriend. She extended the phone toward him. "It's your sister's business partner."

UPENDED

THOUGH ETHAN HAD CALLED A RIDE TO THE ER, HE FELT WINDED when a nurse led him back to Maddy. He was desperate to see her except when he remembered Joe's words on the phone, which made blood roar in his ears and sweat dampen the armpits of his Fuel-issued T-shirt. Maddy attacked? Jesus *Christ*. So far, the words had only bounced around the top layer of his consciousness, but when he saw Joe sitting outside a curtained room, they became dense with reality. Joe's blue button-down was rumpled and open at the collar, and his hair was everywhere; he looked nothing like the put together, clenched-ass dude Ethan knew and most definitely didn't love. Ethan had always considered him a Maddy wannabe—seriously professional but without the compensating balance of her outlaw undercurrent and trash mouth—but now he cut a sympathetic figure.

Ethan said, "Can I? Is she—"

"The police are talking to her." Joe got up. "Sit."

He wanted to refuse, but his knees felt like water, and his chest was hot and pounding.

"Put your head down."

He did and breathed in and out until he started to feel ridiculous, hunched over like this. "When she didn't show up to breakfast this morning, I thought...I don't know what I thought. Nothing like this, though."

"She's going to be okay."

His head snapped up. "Don't do that. Don't fucking manage me." He put his head back down and breathed some more before looking at Joe again. "Did he rape her?"

Joe said, "I don't know. They just said 'assault.' We shouldn't imagine the worst. All I know is that a runner found her this morning, and they think she'd been out there for a while."

"Now, hey, wait a second. How long have you been here? And why are you here, anyway? *I'm* her brother." It was so much easier to be angry than afraid.

24

"I'm in her phone as her emergency contact." He held up a baggie with the phone and a fold of money. "They found it with her."

"And, what, it took you this long to think of calling me? What the hell?"

"I had other things on my mind. It's not personal."

Ethan laughed but couldn't think of anything else to say, which surely eroded the credibility of his outrage. Damn Maddy—didn't trust him to have his shit together in an emergency, and Joe knew it. Ethan had always suspected Joe thought he was a fuckup, but now it was confirmed.

They fell silent, and he thought about what Joe had said on the phone: she'd been naked. *Jeans down around her ankles.* Maddy was right: he was in no way prepared for this. When he got up and leaned against a narrow strip of wall to the side of the curtain, Joe didn't take the vacated chair, and the petty fury Ethan felt was a relief. "You can go home. I got it from here."

"I'm staying."

"What, protecting your investment? Your precious, precious company?"

"What do you mean by that?" Joe crossed his arms in an admirably fierce pose.

Ethan shrank back even though he had a good six inches (and way too many pounds) on the guy. "Nothing. Forget it. Stay if you want."

Joe ducked his chin to his chest. The hair at the top of his head was thinning, which sparked a pale and stupid superiority in Ethan. "I love your sister. I'd be here even if we weren't partners."

"Hey, I've known her twenty years longer than you. Zits and social outcast and all. We're tight."

"I'm not going to get into a pissing contest over this."

"Oh, right. 'Mediation and understanding.'"

Joe dropped his arms and finally took the empty seat. "Madeline's too good to say it, but you really need to grow up."

Ethan blew out a stream of air, letting that barb go without a response—not that he had a ready one. He leaned heavily against the wall, settling into this impossible waiting. Nurses and doctors trickled past, having murmured conversations. The air was sharp with disinfectant and a kind of ozone-laced plastic essence. He felt unpleasantly cocooned despite being in the middle of a hallway.

After a while, Joe sighed. "Patience may be a virtue, but it's not one of mine."

"That sure sounded rehearsed."

"Usually it puts people at ease." He shrugged.

"People are dumbasses."

"In general, I totally agree with you."

"I'll bet your clients would love to hear that."

"You think they're not aware? If everyone thought they knew what they were doing, we'd be out of business." He nodded to the curtain. "Besides, I'm not the real people person; Madeline is. She can connect with practically anyone."

This "gift" of hers had driven Ethan nuts as a kid. In the afternoons they spent together after school, she invariably found ways to...if not explain, then at least justify classmates who'd shoved her into lockers hours earlier for being a dyke. Back then, he'd always wished she'd possessed hidden ninja skills to unleash on her tormentors, but instead of getting even, Maddy extended a standard, jumbo-sized benefit of the doubt to everyone—most especially him (he had to admit), over and over again.

When he realized he was thinking about her in the past tense, he rubbed his beard and his eyes. "Thank God you don't go in for platitudes, though at least they pass the time."

"What, like things'll be better in the morning?"

"Yeah, or, you know, she's in good hands now."

"We're only given what we can handle."

Ethan said, "Everything happens for a reason."

"I've never understood that one, but what doesn't kill us makes us stronger."

They both looked down at the linoleum, which shone dully. Ethan said, "Maddy was already plenty strong."

The cops emerged, whispering, weighed down by badges and serious expressions, and a nurse was saying they would move Maddy to a room upstairs once the transfer was in the system. When they shuffled into the curtained area, Ethan absorbed himself with the nurse, who brought to mind Darla at the diner, though the only resemblance was her chunky, on-your-feet-all-day shoes. Still, anything to avoid looking at Maddy.

That face, the ripe bruised one at the head of the bed, was not his sister's. This was the wrong person. A huge misunderstanding. And yet, when the nurse left and his gaze was drawn back to the bed again, he recognized Maddy beneath the swollen awfulness. His chest constricted with the inescapable reality of what had happened to her and of how much he would give to have this bandaged person in front of him not be his sister.

Joe hustled to her, but Ethen hung back to reconcile himself to the full extent of the situation. Maddy said something to Joe, a murmur Ethan couldn't hear, but then she held out her mangled hand to Ethan and said his name in a wobbly, hoarse voice. He eased closer. The cuts on her lips were crusty and red, both her eyes were blackened, and he hesitated before reaching out and taking her hand. Even with the splinted fingers, her grip was fierce, which was somehow terrifying.

"Madeline," Joe said.

"I need to talk to my brother." She looked at Ethan as if she were trying to see beneath his skin, but her squint and frown told him she couldn't focus.

"Sure, of course," Joe said, "I just want you to know I'm here. Whatever you need."

"I really need to talk to Ethan." She cleared her throat with a wince. "Alone."

Joe appeared poised to argue but turned and walked to the curtain. His face was red under the indistinct darkness of stubble. "I'll see about your transfer."

UPENDED

When Joe slipped outside, Madeline pulled Ethan closer, tugging at his hand until he was practically in bed with her. He meant to wait until she said something, but he blurted out, "Did he rape you? Did he?"

"I shouldn't have been walking there alone. Not so late."

"I'm going to kill the sick son of a bitch." Ethan tried to pull back and look at her, but she held him tight, her mouth close to his ear.

"He didn't rape me. He tried to. He meant to, but he couldn't— He couldn't, and then he—" The last word came out squeezed, and Ethan's throat tightened in response. She clamped down on his hand. "I lied to the police," she said almost inaudibly. "I told them I was at the office, that I was sober. I didn't tell them what he said to me. I told them I didn't know him, that it was random. And I *don't* know him. But he hated me so much, Ethan. He tried to kill me. He meant to kill me, I think. He hated me so much."

CHAPTER 4

SHE COULDN'T BREATHE, WHICH WAS A PANIC SO PRESSING everything else was a jumble: the grinding pain of rough bricks against her face, the cold touch of a dumpster next to her, words as searing as the tearing in her shoulder. "...dyke. You fucking dyke." His hands tightened on her arms. He was going to throw her against the wall again like it was nothing, like she was a handful of trash. Just one breath. If she could just get one breath. She tried to force air into her paralyzed chest and jerked awake, her lungs full to bursting under a hospital gown wet with sweat. Lightning bolts of pain shot from her ribs and head, narrowing her already clouded vision.

She breathed shallowly while orienting herself. She was in the hospital. It was night. She was warm. Hot, actually. He was *not* here. She closed her eyes, but behind her lids lurked that brick wall and the rest of the alleyway. She opened them again. While waiting for her heart to exhaust that rush of adrenaline, she glanced around the room, taking in the shadowed TV in a corner near the ceiling, the plastic rails of her bed, and IV bags hanging above her, their tubes a tangle of snaking tentacles in the dim, greenish light.

Where was Ethan? He'd been there when a refreshed dose of painkillers had made sleep irresistible. She searched for a slumped figure in one of the chairs, listened for the gurgley snoring she remembered from his childhood. Nothing. Trembling started up at her fingertips and amplified through her arms. Her neck tightened and teeth chattered, shaking loose tears and setting off a renewed throbbing of her ribs.

You cunt. You useless dyke. You're so fucking dead, she heard again and again, unable to turn it off. She tried to drown it out with something else, anything else—as long as it meant safety and calm. Jane. She remembered Jane's long, strong arms wrapped around her at night, the heaviness of a muscled thigh draped over hers. "You're trapped," Jane would whisper. "I've got you now."

"Oh no," Madeline would say. "Whatever am I going to do?"

"Be mine forever.

THE NEXT TIME SHE WOKE, CLAWING HER WAY FROM THE SAME nightmarish memory, a strangled whoop escaped her before she could clamp her lips together. She opened her eyes, saw a person-shaped blur above her, and finished the cry she'd just chopped off.

"Madeline, hey. It's okay."

She focused enough to recognize Joe and glanced around. "What time is it? Where's Ethan?" She tried to take a deep breath, then swore and squeezed a forearm against her side at the answering flare of pain from her ribs.

Joe dragged a chair close to the bed and sat down. "It's early. Relax. Don't worry about anything."

She shook her head despite the bruised stiffness of her neck, her eyes welling up at her helplessness in the face of that dream. Joe took her good hand and squeezed it, but his touch was tight and uncomfortable. He was projecting intense calm and reasonableness, clearly trying to pull her back from going completely out of her mind, and she slid her hand from his to stop him. What was the point?

He asked, "Are you in pain?"

"It's in layers. Diffuse, then sharp, then throbbing. They told me a ligament in my knee is torn, but they don't want to operate on it until my head is right from the concussion." As if her head would ever be right again.

"You have enough medication, though? Is there someone I need to talk to—"

"I'm okay."

"It's no trouble. Everyone needs an advocate in these places. Have they offered you a counselor?"

She closed her eyes, which was the closest she could get to walking away from his concern.

"Too much?"

She held up her thumb and forefinger an inch apart.

"Sorry. I'll back off—at least for now. I make no promises about tomorrow. But, hey, I have books with me. And your sweatshirt from work. *And* an extra-large bag of pizza-flavored Combos."

She opened her eyes and saw him rummaging around in a small lavender backpack that had to be Katie's. He sported one of the green Mindful Management polo shirts he'd had made and that he wore like a uniform on weekends. Ordinarily she'd love a handful (or five) of Combos, but her head pounded and jaw ached; crunching those cylindrical bastards would push her right over the edge. "The concussion did something to my vision. They say it's temporary, but I can't read right now. Have you been in touch with Ethan? Do you know when he's coming by this morning?"

"He hasn't called. Didn't he stay with you last night? Someone should have been here." He made a rumbling sound of disapproval. "I'm going to have to—"

"Forget it. Never mind." They sat in momentary quiet, serenaded by the ebb and flow of hospital background noise. Though her head and ribs and knee and fingers pounded in symphony with her heavy pulse, though she was nowhere in the vicinity of rational sense, this was Joe next to her, and work was a shining beacon of distraction. "I'm going to be behind on client deliverables pretty much immediately."

He let out a startled blurt of laughter. "Madeline. Seriously. That's the last thing you should be worrying about. It shouldn't even be on the list of things to worry about. Besides, isn't expecting the unexpected a rule somewhere? If it isn't, it should be."

"This goes way beyond unexpected."

"You know what I mean." He folded her sweatshirt and rested it on top of the backpack.

"But what are we going to tell clients?"

He gave her a very long, very priestly look. "Beth already made calls to the folks you have meetings scheduled with Monday and Tuesday." Their uber-admin. Calendar gatekeeper. "She said she was admirably vague."

"What does that mean?"

"Just that you've been indisposed and have to reschedule at some later date yet to be determined."

"Did she tell anyone where I am? I mean at this hospital?"

"I'm sure she didn't, but why?" He leaned closer, and even with her faulty vision, she could see he hadn't slept the night before—his eyes were sunken and bloodshot. "Are you okay? Is there something you're not telling me?"

Something? There were hundreds of things, and they piled up in her throat, making it doubly hard to breathe. She couldn't seem to tell anyone about the fucking dyke comment, not even Ethan, who had asked multiple times the night before. Maybe he'd left because she'd so adamantly refused to talk about it. "How could I possibly be okay?" she said to herself as much as Joe. "No one can know where I am. *No one.*" She had doctor's orders to try to stay calm, and now she knew why—all her injuries were agitated, making sweat rise on her forehead and upper lip. "Does Beth know what happened?"

"Of course she knows. What was I supposed to tell her?"

When Madeline had dismissed Joe the day before, she'd told him the assault hadn't tipped into rape, not technically, and while the sag of relief in his face and shoulders was understandable, it made her wonder. Would her assailant have beaten her if her lesbianism hadn't disgusted him into impotence? Would she feel the same fractured way without broken ribs and fingers, sprung ligaments and stretched tendons?

"Madeline?"

He had attacked her closer to the T than her house, which meant he didn't know where she lived—or not exactly, not even if he'd searched through her pockets, not with that old address on her driver's license, the place she'd lived with Jane. And he'd be crazy to track her down here to finish the job. To silence her, not that she was talking. Shit like that only happened in the movies, right? But how could he know she was a fucking dyke without knowing *her*? Her sexuality was neither a secret nor immediately obvious. Had he seen her at Club True? But then why did he grab her miles away in Jamaica Plain? How could he have when she was positive he hadn't been on the train with her? Did he work at one of her clients? Had she walked past him in some gray-carpeted hallway and not noticed? Or had he seen that stupid video of a talk she'd done at TEDx in Brookline the year before where she'd used herself and her brother as examples? The video had gone as viral as any talk on that topic could, with a few thousand watching it. Did her coming out so blithely ignite his rage? Her uncertainty fizzed inside her.

"Madeline." Joe touched her arm. She jumped and hissed at her ribs. He said, "I've got this. Don't worry about anything, anything at all. You just..."

"I just what? What do I do?"

"Heal up. Rest. Take all the time you need."

Joe had to say this because nothing else was possible to say, but broken bones were one thing. Everything else was everything else. He didn't know about "fucking dyke," about the lies to the police she hadn't even meant to tell. She'd been confused, in pain, had gotten tripped up on a detail early in the recounting, then got even more flustered when pressed for clarification. Talking hurt her face, her mouth. Remembering hurt her head, and what were the police going to do, anyway? Especially if she told them she'd been drinking, that she'd been fresh from kissing a woman in that club? What were they going to do when they'd never helped her friends in college, the ones harassed or attacked for being gay, for being women?

While she sat with Joe, not talking, drowsiness collected behind her eyes until she slipped them closed for a moment. There she was, against the cold brick wall, and there he was, his face shadowed and ominous, indecipherable, and she woke with a jerk.

Pain stampeded through her, and she said, "Fuck, fuck," through gritted teeth. Joe watched her, his face broken open. She'd never seen him like this before, a kaleidoscope of the familiar (sleep deprivation, worry, concentration) but with an undercurrent of something else she couldn't place. "I can't identify him. I don't know anything," she said, but its truth only made her lies scrabble around inside her.

"I know. That's to be expected. It's not your fault."

She shook her head, cautiously this time, but it still hurt. "What does it matter? We're all culpable. We're all fucked."

"I'm not even going to answer that. Give it time. Stop trying to figure it out. It can't be figured out. It's irrational, random."

But was it really? She pressed a hand against her head. "Just don't tell me it's going to be okay. I don't want to hear it, not when I don't believe it."

"What do you want me to say?"

She turned away from him toward the ceiling, which was wonderfully featureless, absolutely unconcerned. "Nothing."

"Do you want me to leave?"

The thought of being alone triggered a spasm of fear that made her grope for his hand. "No. Stay." His fingers were warm and solid, and for the time being, he seemed content with quiet. The last time she'd been called a fucking dyke was also the last time she'd been physically assaulted. In high school, girls had dragged her from the locker room to out behind the school, where they'd dumped her on the hot asphalt and kicked her silly, cracking a rib or two, raising deep contusions on her belly and back—anywhere that wouldn't show unless Madeline showed someone, which they all knew she wouldn't. She'd been in pain for weeks, and no one had asked about it but Ethan, whom she'd protected from the truth with her silence.

Where the hell was he? She longed for the easy, transparent affection he'd given her during her high school years in Arizona, when he'd sat with her after school, not saying all the right things. As if to underscore their differences, Joe said, "It's going to be okay." He couldn't help saying it. It was no one's fault.

CHAPTER 5

ETHAN HADN'T MEANT TO LEAVE MADDY IN THE LURCH WHEN he'd slipped out of her hospital room the night before. She'd been rumbling out broken-nose snores, and he'd needed a change of clothes and a shower. A few hours of shut-eye. He'd told himself he would be back before she woke up. Very first thing in the morning. He was going to step up for sure, which meant trying to recognize Maddy inside this new, beaten-to-a-pulp version of her, but in the end, he was too afraid. He knew that leaving her hanging at the hospital was infinitely worse than standing her up at breakfast, but his shame couldn't touch his fear, and he went straight from bed to Fuel.

Nettie was behind the register, counting coins from the tip jar. "Hey! I didn't know if you'd be in today. What happened? How is she?"

Better to ask Joe, who Ethan suspected was with his sister, doing what needed to be done. "I don't know. Horrible? She's horrible."

"What happened? Was it an accident?"

He brushed past her to the back. "Forget it."

"Hey." She followed him through the swinging door. "What's going on?"

He could still feel The Mad Hatter's maniacal grip on his hand when she'd pulled him close, and he wondered if maybe she wouldn't want him to tell Nettie. But Nettie was maybe his best friend anywhere, and what was he supposed to say with her standing right in front of him? Not only that, but how would he survive not telling anyone? "Some guy beat the living shit out of her."

Nettie's face emerged from behind her hair, her eyes wide, the light catching her crystal blue irises. "Is she okay?"

"No, she's absolutely not okay." He wanted to tell Nettie everything, but everything was too much. Everything would include not only how the razor-thin miracle of the creep's faulty plumbing had saved Maddy from being raped but also that he'd meant to kill her because of it. If Ethan got into that, he would also have to divulge her lies to the police, which loomed larger in his mind than any potential danger she might be in from the perp still being out there. No one was going to attack her in the hospital, let alone a guy who couldn't even get it up in the moment, but the lie was so strange, so completely out of character, that he'd latched on to it even though it induced a knock-kneed, schoolgirl fear. At least that fear had boundaries he could wrap his arms around, unlike the idea of Maddy dead. "She's not like I've told you. Or not all like that. The Harvard degrees and suits and everything. She's...I don't know. Special."

Nettie pulled him into an awkward, spastic hug. "When you took that call, your face went so white I thought you might pass out. She'll be okay, especially with your help. I'm kind of surprised you're even here. I was getting psyched up to handle the afternoon rush alone."

He pulled away from this reminder of his cowardice. "When have I ever left you in the lurch?"

"Uh." She cast her eyes up in an innocent look.

"Don't answer that."

37

"But seriously, why aren't you with her? I can handle things here."

He rubbed a hand across his eyes and tugged hard at his beard. "Who's to say I wasn't there all night and this morning?"

"Were you?"

"Of course!" The lie felt like both relief and bondage. "You know we're close. But I can still manage to annoy her."

Nettie hauled off and punched him on the shoulder with her scooping arm, which stung like a bitch. "What's wrong with you? Don't you know you're supposed to be nice to people in the hospital?"

"Maddy wouldn't recognize me without a little animosity."

She softened. "Yeah. I wouldn't know anything about that."

"It's part of my charm."

From out front, someone called, "Yo, can I get some service?"

"Yeah, one second," Nettie yelled. It was strange how such a normally unassuming woman could project like a motherfucker. She looked at him and sighed. "I better go 'service' this guy."

"I'll be out in a minute."

"Don't rush." She took a step toward the swinging door and another. Her moves were slow, reluctant, and Ethan wished she would tell the customer to piss off and run away with him. But she ducked her head, pushed through the door, and left him alone.

"Fuuuck." The word rode on a long stream of breath. He leaned back against a tall baker's rack holding extra bottles of syrup and bundles of napkins. Metal shelves pressed thin lines of coolness onto his back through his T-shirt. Fear knitted itself around his bones until he felt fused to the rack, too heavy to do anything but stand and listen to Nettie's pleasant customer service murmurs out front. He longed to be next to her, beset by nothing more onerous than having to explain for the thousandth time the difference between a cortado and a macchiato, but he couldn't face her if he didn't at least call Maddy.

Despite his sister's early childhood influence on him, Ethan had no trouble stretching (or even obliterating) the truth. But

Maddy...well, when she came out in high school, people thought her carpet-munching desires were the most perverted thing about her when, really, it was her obsession with honesty.

As far as Ethan could tell, her avoidance of falsification was driven neither by morality nor religious instruction; she just couldn't seem to help it. It was woven into her DNA. The only thing that saved her from the fallout of this horrible, antisocial habit was her mastery of tact, but even so, she at most skirted honesty with silence. Sure, she had a concussion and broken bones, but plaster and bruising and abrasions weren't what made the extent of her injuries real. No, the lie was somehow even more concrete and made his muscles seize up and sweat pool at the waistband of his boxer shorts.

He fished his phone out of his pocket. He found the number for Beth Israel and dialed it. He asked the operator for Madeline Sawyer. He waited while the phone in her hospital room rang.

Joe answered.

Ethan choked down a clot of embarrassment and identified himself. "Can you put Maddy on?"

"She's sleeping."

"No, she's not. She's the lightest sleeper the world has ever known. I'm sure the phone woke her."

"I'm telling you, she's asleep," Joe said in a whisper.

"And I'm telling you she's faking it." Why wouldn't she, now that she played fast and loose with the truth?

"She's heavily medicated, Ethan. Where have you been, anyway? She waited for you all morning."

Thank God for anger. Though shame was no match for fear, anger trumped it handily, and this allowed Ethan to become a little more himself. He tugged at his beard. "Got called into work. Coffee staffing emergency. Listen, have the cops been by today?"

"No. I doubt they have much to report about the investigation yet."

"I know that. I just— I wanted to know if they questioned her again."

39

UPENDED

"They were in with her a long time yesterday."

"Forget it. I have to run. My coworker's out front alone, dealing with the post-lunch rush. Tell Maddy I'll see her soon."

He hung up, his heart pounding. He needed to talk to Maddy. She always knew what to do, even if he usually didn't want to hear it. But she was sleeping. Or "sleeping." Besides, he realized he might be in a better position than she was to figure out how to handle things, which was a scary thought that led directly to the inescapable fact that without Maddy, he was alone. Really and truly alone. A shiver rippled through him, and in an effort to deny it, he pried himself from the rack behind him and fled through the swinging door to Nettie.

CHAPTER 6

ON THE WEEKENDS JOE DIDN'T HAVE KATIE, HE DROVE OUT TO Belmont for Sunday night dinner with his daughter; his ex-wife, Bridget; and Darrin, the replacement husband, a grotesquely well-meaning high-level software engineer. This grand, hybrid-family, everybody-respect-each-other experiment was mostly successful but exhausting, and by the time he left the hospital in the early evening he was already late and in no mood. He would've called to beg off, but after the whole day with Madeline, he was hungry and disturbed and wanted, more than anything, to drink in the restorative sight of his daughter. She answered the door after he rang the bell, holding a drumstick in one hand, dark pigtails sprouting like horns. "Where have you been?"

"Hey, Ladybug." He kissed her on the crown of her head, avoiding the greasy drumstick, and followed her down a wide, wallpapered hallway to the kitchen. "Sorry I'm late, but maybe your food should stay on your plate the next time you answer the door."

"Party pooper."

"Does your mother let chicken near her suits?"

"Party pooper. Were you working?" she asked, both knowing and not knowing what she said. What did a seven-year-old know about the particulars of work? But given his hours, Bridget's position as a partner at a large law firm, and Darrin's home office brimming with computer equipment, she was steeped in the concept.

"Yeah, I was working," he said when they arrived at the kitchen. Bridget and Darrin had bought and redone this house while living together in momentary sin before their wedding, and everything about it was four or five times larger than his apartment. The kitchen was painted a cheerful green and sported white marble countertops still pristine after five years. Joe had to admit it was comfortable and welcoming, especially with a large reclaimed wood table, four cushioned swivel chairs, and the savory smell of dinner, which made his mouth water.

Katie took her seat with a theatrical jump that spun it around twice, and Bridget asked, "Client emergency? On a Sunday?" She held a fork in one hand and glanced up at him from beneath a short, severe haircut that highlighted her cheekbones and gave her a predatory look he suspected played some small part in her success as a trial lawyer.

"You could say that." He sat, avoiding her gaze.

"It's always something, isn't it?" Darrin passed Joe a platter of chicken and containers of sides. Takeout, of course, because who of them had time to cook?

Joe said, "My clients tell me the tech sector's insane these days. 'Palpable talent drought' was the phrase one of them used."

As he hoped, that got Darrin talking, which gave Joe time to put his plate together and sink into the sight of Katie. The curls in her dark hair were loosening more with each year, just like his had, taking with them the common indistinctions of early childhood. She looked more like a fully formed, individual person every day, which evoked a pang of wistfulness. With the sharp accuracy of cliché, time flew by. And yet, some things held steady, like the fact that, despite the industrious way she gnawed at her drumstick, she was going to leave it full of meat, which he'd finish for her. This glimpse of daily normalcy reminded him to be here, now, to savor his time with Katie and not think about Madeline or the sorry state of their sales pipeline that he'd reviewed while she'd been sleeping—and she *had* been sleeping, despite what Ethan had said.

Darrin rambled on. "One or two recruiters contact me every week. Mostly with junk, but they keep coming. And from all over, not just Boston."

"Are you thinking of changing jobs?"

He shook his head, light from the overhead fixture glinting off the metal frames of his glasses. "We've gotten pretty busy lately, but I can't beat the flexibility of being home for Katie when I need to."

Around a big mouthful of mashed potatoes, Katie said, "He made me apples and peanut butter after school today. No peel."

"Did he also remind you not to talk with your mouth full?" Joe asked.

"Yes." The word squeaked out from between lips squeezed nearly shut. She chewed rapidly and made an audible gulp. "I got to read in his office today, but sometimes he's on a call, and he gets too loud to concentrate. Just like you, Dad."

"Yeah. I'm always on calls, aren't I? Except when we go sailing in the summer. Then it's just you and me. It's almost warm enough now."

"We should all go together," she said.

"Maybe, Ladybug."

Throughout this exchange, Darrin diced up his green beans with surgical precision, seemingly preoccupied, and Joe inwardly heaved a sigh. Was he thrilled that Darrin saw Katie every day and knew how she preferred her afternoon snacks? Of course not. But what was the alternative? From the huge body of anecdotal evidence he'd gathered since his divorce, Joe knew they were doing better than most.

UPENDED

He wasn't even bothered that Darrin had won over Bridget despite his stereotypical geekiness—glasses, a pallor part hereditary and part computer dungeon, and a chest that flirted with the adjective "sunken." Joe always felt virile in comparison: hairy chested, thick armed, and strong featured despite a persistent swivel-chair potbelly and hair that, admittedly, started farther back on his forehead than it used to. But he and Bridget had been terrible together, and he couldn't begrudge her this better match.

They passed the rest of the meal with talk about school and soccer practice and the book series Katie was plowing through—a series Madeline had recommended. Ever since Katie had started reading, books had been the point of contact between his daughter and his business partner. He liked to joke that Katie had inherited her bookworm tendency from Madeline.

Joe imagined Madeline here with them, perched in a chair squeezed between him and Bridget. When the two women had talked before, Joe never figured in their conversations, even if he was hanging with Katie just a few feet away. He'd overheard them chat about business, about the perils of being a woman in various professional situations, or about where they'd bought the best blouses or shoes.

If Madeline were here tonight, she'd twiddle her fingers on the wood tabletop and draw Darrin out about nuances of software development before relating them to their one tech client, Pinskey. He imagined her telling a story about them or another client, fully animated, her hand warm on his arm. The real, tactile component of that last thought bobbed him back to the surface of now, of here, of the ultimately impenetrable divide between this family and Madeline, of the sometimes yawning gap between *himself* and this family. This was Katie's family, in all its patchwork glory; Joe's family was something else entirely, made up more of wish and will than blood.

After Joe had picked Katie's drumstick clean and she'd excused herself to read the latest installment of her series, Bridget dropped a crumpled napkin on her plate and quoted him. "'You could say that?'"

It took a moment for him match those words to his earlier ones. "I really hate when you do that."

"So, not a client emergency?"

"No, not a client. Madeline."

"Is she okay?" When Bridget was concerned, her brow creased in thin, horizontal lines, and her fingers played over her lower lip as if assuring herself she was still in possession of all her parts.

"She was...in an accident." Bridget's chin edged up at that inadvertent hesitation, and Joe continued on to erase it from her memory. "A bad car accident. Yesterday. She's in the hospital, pretty banged up, but she's going to be okay." Only when he was in the position of actually lying for Madeline did he feel the deep strangeness of her demand for secrecy. He would never broadcast unnecessary details to clients, but wanting to keep the truth from Beth—or Bridget—wasn't like Madeline at all. He thought of her obvious fear, her flare of anger and helplessness, her fragility. What could he do except whatever she asked?

Darrin said, "That's terrible. Was anyone else hurt?"

"I don't really know all the details." He assumed his best matter-of-fact expression, bland and neutral, the face he wore when observing a meeting—or enduring a potential client's rejection. "They'll keep her in the hospital for another couple days, but she'll need a little more time before getting back to work."

Bridget gave Darrin an indecipherable married-couple look, and he got up and started clearing dishes. She asked, "How're your clients going to be with that?"

Joe stacked his plate on top of Katie's and shrugged. "Probably both annoyed and understanding. Beth's going to have to pull some miracles out of the calendar, but that's nothing new. Life, right? Besides, Madeline's been spending a lot of her time managing the software project, so she doesn't have quite as many meetings on the books as usual."

Bridget hummed. Her hums were rich with meaning but notoriously hard to translate. This one could mean she knew the accident was a lie, or maybe it was about the company still being so small. More likely, though, it was a general comment on the software project that was supposed to automate Mindful Management's methodology and that Bridget had once called "the mythical cash cow" in a moment of brutal candor she'd later apologized for.

She lowered her voice so Joe could barely hear her over the water Darrin was running in the sink. "How're you guys doing? Did you hear back about those two contracts?"

Though he loathed admitting any failures to Bridget, he said, "We lost the Bates and Gambel bid. I'm still waiting on Grasshopper Enterprises, which would be the more important win, anyway." The Bates email had come in very late on Friday, after Madeline had left for the day, and he had no idea how he was going to break the news to her. Now was clearly not the time for revelations; he'd spent much of the day wondering when Madeline was going to tell him what she'd been doing out so late that night. Not that it mattered. But it *was* strange.

Bridget interrupted that thought. "How badly do you need it?"

"We're fine, Bridget. We'll be fine. I know what I'm doing."

She raised her hands in surrender. "Does Madeline have someone to look after her when she's out of the hospital? Didn't you say her brother's in town now?"

"She can stay at my place. Hers is a third-floor walk-up, which will be unmanageable, given that her knee was cantaloupe-sized when she got to the hospital. Torn ligament."

"And you've discussed this with her?" For years, Bridget had insisted her questions were just questions, but her delivery dripped with purpose. It was unintentional, she claimed, and blaming her for it was like ostracizing a woman for a mean resting face, which Bridget truthfully didn't have.

"Bridget, really. I'm not on trial here."

"I hate when you say that."

He smiled, knowing she wouldn't ask him anything else. "Madeline's my partner. My friend. I'm going to help her however I can, and she and I will work it out."

Bridget sat back. "I trust you absolutely to do the best by her. I know you two are close."

"Well, yes. We work together most of our waking hours."

"You don't seem to notice that I'm not arguing with you. I'm glad you guys have each other."

Joe sagged in his chair and propped his head on his hand, his polo shirt pulling against his bicep. "Sometimes I miss when we were afraid to rock the boat with each other. It was suffocating but pleasant in a way."

She shrugged her right shoulder. "We were miserable."

"There's that. I spent four years not opening my mouth for fear of sending the whole thing tumbling down."

"For two smart people, we were pretty stupid." She tilted her head up a notch, and the overhead light turned her dark brown eyes into twin chocolate disks while she appraised him. "You need to get some sleep. When's the last time you took a day off?"

He sighed. "Believe me, we're working on it."

"I'd tell you to work harder, but I don't think that's possible."

HOURS AFTER JOE HAD LEFT BRIDGET AND KATIE, HE SAT AT HIS dining room table and trolled Mindful Management's bottom line. It barely qualified as "fine." Fine, in fact, was pushing it, and if they didn't get the Grasshopper contract, fine would be wishful thinking. The software project Madeline had been spearheading for the last year—that mythical cash cow—was currently much more porcine than bovine and had consumed all their cash reserves. Madeline had managed it brilliantly, which was why she was running it, not him, but with their consulting capacity impaired and now losing the Bates contract...

UPENDED

The software had been his idea, a stroke of genius he'd had on one of the many nights they'd worked in their respective offices late into the evening. He'd been hunched toward his monitor, trying to ignore the growling of his stomach, when he heard the now-familiar sound of a stack of journals and books in Madeline's office losing their fight with gravity.

She said, "Mother fucking piece of shit," in a staid, conversational tone. Anyone who thought a trash mouth and sunny demeanor were incompatible had never met Madeline.

"Everything okay?"

"Yes." Then, "I mean, no. How'd it get this late?"

"They say time flies when you're having fun."

"Is that what we're doing?" He heard her get up and swear again when she stumbled over something. She appeared in his doorway, leaning against the jamb. "And when's the last time anyone used that phrase non-sarcastically? Unsarcastically?"

"Anti-sarcastically."

"With reverse sarcasm."

"As intended."

She made a dismissive hiss. "Always the straight man."

"Would we work so well together if I weren't?"

"Probably not." She sighed. "Did you ever consider there was a reason no one else does this?"

"There are a million reasons no one else does this."

"Yeah, and one of them is compiling these meeting summaries." Their services weren't cheap, and hard data indicating success was the only way to convince CEOs to keep paying their bills. Madeline sat across from him in an exaggerated slouch, one arm flung across the back of the chair. "Data entry." She fake shivered. "A terrible byproduct of an otherwise brilliant approach."

Joe sat up and leaned forward.

"Oh, no," she said. "You have an idea."

"Since when is that a bad thing?"

"Since your last idea led directly to me doing data entry at seven o'clock at night. Have I mentioned how much I hate data entry?"

"This is the first I've heard of it. I'm absolutely shocked." That got her to smile, and he grinned back and raised an index finger. "What would you say if this idea got you *out* of the data entry business?"

"I'm listening."

He opened his mouth but closed it again. "No, an idea of this magnitude requires adequate time to express. Zaftigs?" He named the Jewish deli across the street. "Or do you have plans?" he asked, though he probably didn't have to. Ever since Madeline had split with Jane, she rarely had anything keeping her from working late.

"Patty melt, and I'm going to need extra cheese based on the look on your face."

An hour later, they sat at their conference table, a solid-wood eight-seater Joe had paid too much for, given how few clients came by their office. Amid empty takeout containers and wadded napkins, they digested their food and Joe's proposal: a custom software suite to facilitate automation, analytics, and eventual self-service of the Mindful Management methodology. Or, in other words, there's an app for that. Madeline wasn't nearly as enthusiastic as he'd hoped.

Not only was she not smiling, but her gaze traveled around the room, touching on whiteboards, the display monitor, and the windows into the rest of the office without settling anywhere—a sure sign of dissatisfaction. Joe tried a different tactic. "You can't tell me you actually enjoy being a stenographer at all these meetings, gathering data, marking down every interruption or negative statement."

"Or instance of praise or confirmation."

"Madeline 'Bright Side' Sawyer. We could hire interns for the dirty work we spend most of our time doing, or we can make use of all those cell phones always sitting out on conference room tables."

"I hate those phones."

"But what if they could record and do the first level of analysis of the meeting transcripts? We could gather five times as many inputs. Ten! And charge exorbitant rates for our personal insights and action plans."

"I like the sound of exorbitant rates. And providing more value." Madeline sat up from the half-reclined position she'd slid into after demolishing her patty melt. "But the self-service bit? I didn't get into this to become a product salesman."

"When it takes off, we'll hire someone to do that for us. We're spending too much time at client meetings, which leaves us only nights and weekends to do the important work. Have you ever calculated what our hourly pay actually ends up being?"

"I've been afraid to."

"Save yourself the anguish. This isn't sustainable. Can we fix it without hiring a bunch more consultants or seriously automating?"

She picked at a blob of cheddar that had melted from her sandwich onto the bottom of its container. "Maybe...just don't ask me how." But then she slowly smiled. "Total non sequitur: at my last meeting at Pinskey, Sergei asked me out." Her eyes cast upward. "He did it before anyone even left the room after the meeting. It was so Sergei. His lack of empathy is fascinating. Not even just empathy but situational awareness in general. 'Hey, Madeline,'" she said, mimicking Sergei's thick Russian accent. She squinted in an approximation of his sleepy, hooded eyes. "'Let's you and me get a drink together.'"

Joe laughed. "And you said, what, that he wasn't your type?"

"In retrospect, that might have been the best approach, but I made the mistake of trying to be professional and telling him thanks but no thanks, which I hoped would end it. But while I'm attempting that, people are fleeing the conference room, total mass exodus. He says, 'What, are you married or something?'"

"Oh my God."

"We get into this twenty questions thing about why I won't have a drink with him. All sorts of diplomacy on my end, believe me. Anyway, I finally say, 'Sergei, listen. I'm a lesbian.' And he looks at me with that super analytical expression he gets and says, 'Well. Interesting. Okay.' Then I tell him the meeting was much more energetic than usual, which was good. And he says, 'Okay, thank you,' and leaves before I even have a chance to put my things together. The meeting *was* good, by the way. Huge improvement in participation rates, and the data shows it."

Joe couldn't think of a single thing to say.

"There's no app that would fix Sergei." She pushed her dinner container away in emphasis.

"So, in other words, that was the most sequitur non sequitur, ever."

"You could say that."

He squared himself to the table, pressing his palms against its surface. "How about this. I'll be the product salesman, and you'll be our CCO—Chief Consulting Officer."

She smiled, bright and wide, her whole face lifting with it. "I love it. My dad would have loved it." Her smile faded a notch, but before Joe could say anything comforting regarding her father's recent death, Madeline went on. "As awkward and bizarre as that whole Sergei interaction was, it was the best thing all week. Maybe all month. You know, sometimes I think I should go crazy butch and see what kind of reactions I'd get. Talk about broadening horizons."

"Or you could just wear a fake wedding ring."

Joe knew that was the wrong thing to say even before Madeline's gaze dropped to the table, and her fingers stopped the slow, drumming wave they'd been beating this whole time. "You know me; I've never been at all closeted, but man, it was easier when I was with Jane. It's shocking how many people still believe a lesbian can't be at all feminine. But when I could just slip Jane's name or 'she' into the conversation, that was that. Subtle but clear. But to up and say, 'Yo, I'm a big dyke,' in a meeting of ten guys and one Indian woman is hugely disruptive."

"Everyone makes assumptions. Hell, I've lost track of the number of people who think I was a male model when I was younger." A statement like that would usually be rewarded with a hearty fake laugh, but she only half smiled, and her eyes were still downcast. He put joking aside and said, "Madeline Sawyer, CCO and Founder, Mindful Management."

She laughed. "God, your voice even sounded embossed. Who wouldn't want that on their business card? Okay, okay. I'm in, you persistent bastard, but I'm going to fight you on scope the whole time. There are things a piece of software shouldn't even try to do."

He reached his hand across the table. "Agreed. Believe me, you won't regret it."

They shook, and she said, "I'd better not."

CHAPTER 7

MADELINE FELT LIKE ABSOLUTE SHIT. THE DOCTOR HAD STEPPED down her pain medication, and although it was nice not to slip into a nightmarish near coma every few hours, moving made everything hurt. At the same time, *not* moving was its own special torture. Inside that incarcerated stillness teemed variations of fear and regret she couldn't help but relentlessly catalog.

Why had she let her memories get the best of her that night? Madeline fucking Mismanagement. If she'd buried those itching wounds, if she'd forced herself to find solace in a book, or if she'd just let herself be miserable with old, old longing for Jane...or if she'd gone out and danced away her frustrations without that ill-advised tangling of tongues or the drinking to excess...or what if she'd merely taken a car home? All those variations led to so many unknowns, but maybe the attack had been inevitable, and the only possible variations were the ones she was making now—her lie to the police, her shortness with Joe, her drive for secrecy. But even this could be foretold somewhere so the only thing left to do was to wait for what would happen next.

UPENDED

In the midst of this fruitless conjecturing, her phone buzzed at regular intervals, beating itself against the laminated wood grain of her bedside table in the urgent rhythm of Monday morning. It taunted her with a cache of work-related distractions she was in no state to take advantage of. She picked up her phone and turned it over and over, thinking of calling Ethan but mostly fantasizing about punching in Jane's number, which, though expunged from her contacts, blinked like neon in her memory. She would come, wouldn't she? If she knew?

Madeline squirmed at her idiocy, which set off a chain reaction of pain: shoulder, ribs, knee, then back up to her jaw and head. Stupid. And yet pain had the most wonderful side effect of making her able, for those moments, to forget to be afraid, to be in disbelief, to feel guilty, to be undone.

When the pain subsided, she tried to escape the helplessness that remained by unlocking her phone and flipping through emails and calls, thinking maybe Ethan had left word, whether excuse or promise. He hadn't, but the new voice mail she had, back from Saturday morning, made her blood shrink from her skin.

"Madeline, hi. It's Zoe. I was thinking that maybe you were sober now—duh, of course you're sober now—and that maybe we could get dinner tonight or brunch tomorrow if you want to be more casual. Any kind of activity, really, as long as it's not eating while sitting next to each other at Rosemary's. Anyway, you're probably not only sober but busy working. Call me back, okay?"

The attack had bled backward through that night, turning everything that had led up to it dark and disturbing in retrospect, a shadowy vortex that sucked Zoe in and entwined her with the fear that lurked in Madeline's bone marrow like leukemia. How could she possibly see Zoe and not recall the reverberation of his blows, the hot searing of his words? She couldn't. She listened to the message once more and deleted it.

She was still clutching the phone when Ethan appeared in her doorway late in the morning, a sudden, hulking, mouth-breathing apparition that scared the living shit out of her. She couldn't empty

54

her lungs until he moved into the room and became undeniably Ethan, tugging at his ratty-ass beard, his face pale and eyebrows pinched. His hand drifted down to his chest, resting momentarily on his heart. He squinted at her, then her phone. "Tell me you're not doing business on that thing."

"No. I was..." She put it aside. "Nothing."

"Well, you look like crap." He dropped down on a chair next to the bed.

"And that's surprising?"

"No, it's—"

She tried and failed to sit up. "Where the fuck have you been?"

"Now, hey, listen. I know you...Just because I..." He looked anywhere but at her, his leg jiggling. "I mean, seriously, Maddy." The longer he took to answer, the more a helpless anger overtook her receding fear. He squeezed his lips shut and made a production of breathing loudly through flared nostrils. "I was scared out of my wits, okay?"

Inside her ire was an immense weariness, but inside *that* was a comfort so old and dear it was worn threadbare. There it was: a quietness that existed nowhere else in nature except when she was here and he was there, and the full weight of their wordless history rested between them. Her eyes spilled tears even though it didn't feel like she was crying, and she wiped them away with the heels of her hands.

"I brought you something." He leaned forward to dig around in a backpack at his feet and handed her a crinkled brown bag with a grease stain at the bottom corner. "Grilled cheese from the diner. Hopefully it's still at least a little warm."

She opened the bag's folded-over top and took a deep huff of savory cheesiness, ignoring the stab of pain it caused. "Now I'm *really* mad you didn't come by yesterday." She unwrapped the sandwich and bit off a corner. "Oh, the butter." She took another bite. "Cheddar, jack, and Swiss, of all things. Genius." It was barely over room temperature, and her molars ached when chewing the toasted crust, but she didn't care. The combination of Ethan and cheese sated something in her deep, lizard brain, and for a few miracle minutes, she could just breathe and chew and occasionally blink and leave it at that.

He said, "I don't know how many of these you made for me growing up."

"One every school day for, what, three years? American cheese slices and Butternut white bread. And not that 'whole grain' white bread nonsense."

She was still a few bites shy of finishing—her fingers bright with butter—when Ethan asked, "How're you feeling, anyway? Do they still have you on the good stuff?"

"I'm...surviving, but it's much worse than last time," she said without thinking.

"What last time?"

"They took me off the hard drugs yesterday."

"What do you mean last time?" His leg started jiggling again, the denim of his jeans swishing against the chair.

The remaining corner of the sandwich, with its crunchy crust and even a bit of charred cheese, was the perfect bite, but it was suddenly unappealing. She shoved it in the bag and crumpled the brown paper around it.

Ethan said, "Hey, you're the one who brought it up."

He was right, and if she still couldn't find it in herself to tell him everything about the attack, exposing this other long-ago event was at least something—however poor a substitute. "My senior year in high school, the girls in my class gave me some spring-fever hazing in the parking lot behind the locker room. Kicked me, mostly. I'm pretty sure they cracked a rib. It hurt to breathe for a while."

There he went with that beard again, rubbing and pulling at it as if it were a genie-filled lamp. "I can't believe I don't remember that."

"I didn't broadcast my condition."

"What'd you tell Mom and Dad?"

"Nothing. They never asked."

His leg went still, and he planted his hands on the faded denim of his thighs. Even his breathing went low, inaudible. "You mean nothing happened to those bitches?"

She should've kept this to herself. "It was a long time ago."

"There's no statute of limitations on 'what the fucks.'" His voice rose in both pitch and volume.

"Let's just drop it."

"You brought it up."

She turned to him, her whole upper body wincing at the movement. "Drop. It."

He screwed up his face like the seven-year-old he used to be, the one who ate those grilled cheese sandwiches and kept her perfect company during interminable high school afternoons. The way he'd eased the pain of being a social pariah made her soften to him now—at least a little.

She said, "I didn't mean that—or at least the tone. I'm not mad at you, but I've got enough on my mind without that memory." As if she hadn't been thinking about it for days. He sat forward in the chair, but before he could say anything, she added, "Even though I brought it up."

But Ethan wasn't having any of it. "It's not right, Maddy."

"A lot of things aren't right." She'd had every intention of telling him about what her attacker had said—a secret that ate away at her but also felt too privately horrible to share. But after this reaction, she buried it back down; she didn't want to talk about it, and he had enough to handle already.

He slammed himself back in his seat, sending it squealing a couple inches across the linoleum. His sigh was rough, theatrical, and he forced a hand through his already disheveled hair. "Where's your boyfriend, anyway? I expected him to be attached to your hip."

Madeline rolled her eyes, a move that flirted with the boundary of her pain. "I don't know what your beef is with Joe, but knock it off."

"He's like you but without the good parts. A little insipid. Offensively well-meaning."

Why, today of all days, was Ethan not content to sit and be quiet with her? Still, in a small, hard scoop of her mind, she knew what he meant.

He went on. "At the hospital, on Saturday, he told me he loved you."

"Well, I love him, too."

"I think he meant, you know, *looove*."

"You're on crack. We're business partners, and he's the most professional person I know. And I'm gay. *And* I'm not even his type. He played it off well, but he was googly-eyed over Jane."

Ethan laughed. "Who wasn't?"

She glared at him.

His eyebrows went up, and his eyes got all innocent-wide. "I'm just saying. You're the one who wanted the subject changed."

"Not to one guaranteed to piss me off."

"It's better than the alternative."

"And what's that?"

"I don't know. Talking about what really happened? Or about your complete disregard for the truth when it might actually matter?"

Though she'd been yearning for the comfortable appeasement she'd always gotten from Ethan, this needling animation and the antagonistic feeling it stirred in her weren't entirely unpleasant. Even so, she dodged the sliver of truth in his words. "Ethan, there's a bigger picture here."

"Is there? Is there, really? Because your withholding valuable information from the police is a pretty damn big picture to me."

"You think you know something, but you don't."

"Have you thought about trying to explain instead of writing me off as a total idiot?"

"There's nothing to explain!" She wrapped an arm around her chest to contain the pain her outburst caused and continued in a hoarse whisper. "When the police were questioning me, they kept pushing like they were looking to trip me up or something, like there were right and wrong things to say. And there were, clearly, but I was...I'd just been attacked, for fuck's sake. If they were like that about my saying the wrong thing because I was flustered, how do you think they'd take what I had to say once they knew how much I'd had to drink that night? Huh? You don't know, Ethan. You just don't. You live in this fantasy world where cops actually do something about attacks like this, where they find the guy, but I could lay the God's honest truth at their feet, and nothing would be any different."

His hands gripped the armrests of his chair. "Maddy, I'm telling you—"

A knock on the open door to her room cut him off. Detective Henderson stood in the doorway. "Am I interrupting something?"

Madeline froze so completely the very air in her lungs solidified. How long had he been there? What had he heard? Ethan looked plenty panicked himself, his gaze clearly locked on the badge clipped to the detective's belt, but he pulled it together enough to say, "Nah, just your typical sibling disagreement. It's how we show our love."

She sat up with no small effort. "This is my brother, Ethan. Ethan, this is Detective Henderson, the one assigned to my case."

The detective was young and fit with a blond brush cut, nothing near the rumpled coffee-and-donuts stereotype. He crossed the room and shook Ethan's hand. "Good to meet you. I need to ask your sister a few questions if that's okay."

Ethan shifted in his seat to a position that made him look weighty and permanent, feet planted and arms crossed. "I'll stay right here."

"Good. Fine." The detective dragged a spare chair around to the other side of Madeline's bed, close enough so she could smell the woody scent of his aftershave. He made small talk, asking how she doing, commenting about the hospital food, but all the while, Madeline couldn't stop remembering being a one-woman crime scene, the squirming intimacy of having her nails scraped, the

UPENDED

pull of a comb through her tangled hair, the minefield she had to traverse to find the just-right answers to this man's questions, the vertiginous disorientation of what had happened, of the somehow possible impossibility of it all. Recalling it now made her skin crawl and jump, made her expect to see that hooded figure appear before her, made her want to cringe in front of anticipated blows.

The detective said, "If you're up for it, I wanted to clarify a couple points in your statement." She nodded. "You said you were coming home from work. Late night, huh?"

"We're a start-up, so pretty much every night is late."

Ethan barked a nervous-sounding laugh. "She's not kidding. They're crazy."

"And you took the Green Line in to, what, Copley, to change to the Orange Line?"

"It's faster than the alternative."

"Do you always take the T to and from work?"

Ethan said, "Maddy's one of those people who pays through the nose for a car she never drives. She claims the train gives her time to read."

The detective went on in this vein for a while, digging into that imaginary late-night commute and the other riders on the train or on the platform, all the while flipping through his notebook, which was similar to the ones Joe used despite his recent obsession with technology. "During the attack, do you remember him saying anything to you?"

"I..." She squinted as if sifting through memories.

"Take your time. Anything at all would be helpful."

"Maybe he told me to shut up? He just grabbed me and hit me. Or, you know, pushed me against a wall. Not pushed. *Flung.* It was so fast and hard I didn't have time to make a sound, so would he have said that? I remember his breathing, though. Rough and loud. Kind of wheezy."

Detective Henderson wrote quickly, as if taking dictation. Madeline kept her focus on his pen and thick fingers, which were dusted with hair. She couldn't look at his face and didn't dare glance at Ethan. She kept her hands clasped together to hide her trembling.

"And you never got a good look at him? Said he stayed behind you the whole time?"

"Mostly. After he hit me, I couldn't see very well. I still can't, really. And it was dark, and I— It was dark."

"We're still waiting for all the physical evidence to be processed—there's a backlog at the lab. We don't have any concrete leads right now, but given that he intended to rape you, we can assume he's a repeat offender. Though that makes him more dangerous in general, multiple attacks can help identify and catch him. Unfortunately, we haven't seen an incident with similar characteristics in the area. The details don't line up."

He asked a few more questions about timeline and anything else she could remember—odors or sounds or glimpses of anything (his shoes maybe), until she raised her hand with the broken fingers and pressed at her temple as if her head hurt, which it did, of course.

The detective took the hint and stood. "Thanks for your time, Ms. Sawyer. I'll keep you up to date on our progress. Ethan," he said, "Good to meet you. Take care of your sister."

"Yeah. Will do."

Then he was gone. Ethan got up and checked the hallway in both directions before sitting back down. "Was any of your statement not bullshit? The details don't line up because they're the wrong details. Did you not hear the man?"

"I don't know why I tell you anything."

"It must be your hyperactive moral compass cracking under the strain."

"This idea of me you have—"

"It's not my idea. It's *yours*, and you know it."

Madeline turned away from him. "Ethan. Really, you have no clue."

"Then educate me. And while you're at it, why don't you tell me what you were doing out so late alone. Because you sure as hell weren't at work. Not at one in the morning. Not with 'how much' you'd had to drink."

"Did you just say I was asking for it?"

"Fuck you," he said, his face twisted and red. "I would *never* do that, and you know it!"

Her throat closed up at the hot anger in his words and the shame at what she'd said to provoke it. "It was...I went to a club. I should've gotten a ride home, but the T was still running. Forget telling the cops that I was drunk, how do you think they'd take it if they knew I was kissing a woman in that club right before I left? What do you think would go through their heads after that?"

She pushed the heel of her hand against her forehead, creating a point of focus that might pull her from this precipice of panic. Almost losing it now felt too much like being out there that night, so she ground flesh against flesh until the undeniable reality of that dull pain grounded her. "He meant to kill me. You can't understand that, and the cops can't do the first thing about it."

"You're right. I can't understand, and I don't know what to do about that. But isn't telling them everything the best way to nail the bastard?"

"Stop." Distress percolated up from her gut.

"You let those bitches in high school get away with what they did to you, and you're doing the same thing now. It doesn't make any sense."

She felt the swirling, twisted illogic of her fear unfurl within her. "Maybe he thinks I'm dead, and we should leave it at that. If I tell the police the truth now, who knows what'll happen? What if they can't prove it and he gets away? What then?"

Ethan looked at her askance, his face turned away and his eyes narrowed, his fingers moving slowly against his mustache, and Madeline felt her strangeness to him—sudden and complete—echoed in herself. She covered her eyes with her hand to block the sight and whatever words he was poised to say. She was untethered, drifting free of rationality and control, yet, at the same time, certain that she'd done the only thing she could.

"This isn't right," he said. "It's not right, Maddy."

"I don't care!"

He got up and walked around the end of her bed to the door. "I need some air. Do you need anything? I need some air," he said again and left. With his bag, Madeline realized. That liar. That little—

But before she could finish this damning thought, tears roared up in her, and she was crying hard, her arms wrapped around her ribs to keep herself from ripping apart while she gasped for breath. Air was necessity and enemy all at once, contradictory like everything else.

CHAPTER 8

Zoe Doolittle commandeered a four-top booth at Rosemary's Kitchen on Monday night, littering the dark wood table with laptop and paper and phone, ready to pretend, when Madeline arrived, that business was the first thing on her mind. Ha. Business was buried far beneath that kiss, not to mention the searing embarrassment of her subsequent fumbling voice mail or the fact that Madeline hadn't called back—not to plan a date or to cancel this meeting that Zoe had been stupidly happy to accommodate. Not that Madeline would cancel because of that kiss; she was way too professional for that. What a disaster.

Rosemary's, located in the heart of Centre Street in Jamaica Plain, served timeless fare flagrant in its disregard for the latest health trends or allergens. Meatloaf, chicken and dumplings, lasagna, and mac and cheese were the perennial stars of Rosemary's menu, and regulars like Zoe (and Madeline) indulged in them at least once a week. It was a clubhouse for the culinarily challenged: warmly lit and aromatic like a kitchen on Thanksgiving, bubbling with conversation and grounded by a certain feeling of relaxation, of *home*. Rosemary herself was the embodiment of all this. She was gray-haired but spry and always dressed in a skirt, tennis shoes with white socks, and a button-up shirt more than a little wilted from the kitchen's heat. She was always, always glad to see you—and not just because you were paying her for the privilege. She was about the best surrogate mother Zoe could ask for.

Rosemary had come by to say hi, full of surprise that Zoe hadn't taken her usual place at the counter. When Zoe filled her in on the meeting, as businesslike as possible, Rosemary's face got bright and smiley (or brighter and more smiley than it usually was), and she made a small production of tiptoeing back behind the register. Zoe hadn't told Rosemary about her crush on Madeline in so many words and certainly hadn't filled her in on the kiss, but the woman had intuition honed through two children and years of unrelenting customer service.

To put Rosemary's watchful eye out of her mind, Zoe went over her notes for the meeting and made sure her few questions were neatly organized and to the point. It was useless busywork, but Zoe didn't want Madeline to catch her checking out social media or other mindless sites on her phone when she arrived. If she were going to arrive.

A half hour after Zoe got settled, when the growling of her stomach began to rival the background music, she ordered the spinach lasagna from the capable but busy guy who serviced the dining room tables. She savored the dish, hogging the booth with stubborn tenacity even though the place was so full the last group of three that came in were forced to sit at the counter between the dining room and kitchen, one of them smack-dab on Zoe's stool.

She was still toying with her last bites when Rosemary came over with a pitcher of water and leaned her hip against the booth's edge. "Madeline get held up?"

"I don't know. I guess she's not coming."

"What do you mean you don't know? Hasn't she called? Or either of you *texted*?" she asked with the kind of emphasis she reserved for anything with the faintest whiff of the newfangled about it.

"No." Zoe shoveled in the last of her lasagna.

"Zoe Doolittle." Yes, surrogate mother in all ways. "This isn't like Madeline, and you know it. You need to call her." She punctuated her point with a sloshing gesture of the water pitcher and walked back to the counter. Halfway there, without turning around, her voice sliced through the café's murmur. "Call her, Zoe."

Rosemary had a way of being both warm and commanding, and Zoe found herself dragging her phone to where her plate had been and considering her options. Out of habit and for a small comfort, she ran her fingers over the shorn hair at the back of her head, a short, velvety fuzz that was hard to resist touching. Rosemary watched her from across the small, crowded dining room, and Zoe gave in and dialed.

After several rings, when she was sure the call was going to go to voice mail, Madeline answered. "Ethan? Is that you?" Her breath roared across the connection in short, rapid bursts.

Who was Ethan? Hadn't she seen her caller ID? Could Zoe hang up and pretend this hadn't happened? But she said, "Hi. No, it's Zoe."

"What? Zoe?" Madeline's voice was loud and followed immediately by that breathing again. Was she running? Maybe to get here?

"Yeah. We were supposed to meet at Rosemary's tonight?"

The connection went very quiet. Zoe waited with her hand pressed against the table, its skin pale, a stubborn hangnail marring her middle finger. After a long while, Madeline said, "Zoe. And it's Monday."

"Uh...hey, why don't we reschedule?"

She heard a rustle, then a gasp. What in the world was Madeline doing? "Shit," Madeline said, "*For fuck's sake.* I'm such a mess."

"It's okay. I know you're crazy busy. I was just getting worried, so..."

"What time is it, anyway? This fucking sleeping, that dream. Sorry. I'm sorry."

"We should talk later. About work," she added stupidly. After waiting all weekend for Madeline to call, Zoe now wanted nothing more than to get off the phone. A hiss of breath filled her ear, ending with a strangled moan. "And, you know, don't feel bad. I had lasagna to keep me company. I mean, who am I kidding? I probably would've been here anyway."

"I'm sorry. About everything. But I can't— Joe didn't know about this meeting to cancel it. I'm not— I can't—" The words were rushed, breathless.

"Are you all right?" Dumb question, but still.

This time Madeline went so quiet Zoe could hear background noises, like someone was talking over an intercom. Where in the world was she? Zoe held the phone tight to her ear, as if that would help her intuit Madeline's situation. Finally, Madeline said, "No, I'm not all right. Not at all." She coughed, then gasped. "I can't talk to you. I have to go. I'm sorry. I'm sorry."

She hung up before Zoe could respond, which left her too flustered to do anything except shove her stuff in a bag, slide out of the booth, and hurry to the door.

"What'd she say?" Rosemary asked from behind the register.

Zoe made herself shrug. "She's sick, I guess. I'll catch you later." She pushed through the door, chilled by Madeline's voice, those long pauses, and the strangeness of her breathing, especially when it had caught in those sharp gasps. Zoe had overheard a statistically significant number of Madeline's conversations over the last year, played aural witness to her being direct and curious, very occasionally vulgar, but mostly undeniably forthright. In almost every respect, the woman Zoe had just spoken to was a completely different person.

But what did she know? A year of hearsay plus recent premeeting chitchat plus a kiss that Madeline clearly regretted in no way qualified Zoe as an expert. She didn't even know who this Ethan guy was. But anyone could tell that Madeline had sounded beside herself, wrecked, in some kind of serious trouble. Zoe's imagination ran more than a little wild, trying to match the sounds she'd heard to scenarios that might cause them, spiraling all the way to some kind of illicit sex or drug activity before she reeled herself back in.

Madeline was so smart and capable she could handle whatever was going on by herself—or with *Ethan*. Zoe shook off a feeling of helpless doom while she walked to the apartment off Centre Street she shared with Troy, her best friend and family function rent-a-date. They'd been to so many weddings and christenings together that relatives on both sides either (a) assumed they were already married or (b) grilled them about when they were going to be next down the aisle.

They'd lived in this apartment for the last few years, pooling money for rent, small appliances, and even the odd piece of art, like the landscape watercolor hanging in the foyer. Her glance lingered on the green of its weathered mountains and the faded denim of its sky before she followed a fragrant trace of dissipated shower steam and spicy aftershave to the bathroom. Troy was in front of the fogged-up mirror, working product into his hair. He ducked his head to see her in a patch of clear glass. "You look...*put together*." It was both compliment and judgment and made her glance down at her ironed shirt and tidy slacks that had coordinated well with her favorite oxfords, which she'd kicked off at the front door. "How was the date— I mean *meeting?*"

"That wasn't even funny the first three times."

"What was her excuse for not calling you back this weekend?" He pushed his short blond hair one way then another. He was tall and broad in the shoulders but skinny, sporting knife-edge cheekbones on his dear face.

She sat on the closed toilet seat and placed her feet along the diagonal pattern of the old back-and-white tile floor. "Can I say I don't want to talk about it without having you jump to all sorts of conclusions?"

"Highly doubtful. How do I look?"

"Irresistible, as always. She didn't show up."

He stopped messing with his hair and turned to her. "No."

Zoe was primed to tell him every detail about the strange phone call but suddenly didn't want to. "There was some kind of mix-up, and she apologized like twenty times."

"Did she mention *the kiss*?" He arched one eyebrow.

"It was a short conversation. All business."

"Did you at least reschedule?"

"Sure, of course."

"I will look forward to getting all the gory details then." He strode down the hall, still talking. "Your mom called me to remind us of your cousin's wedding next weekend. Apparently you didn't answer when she called you. Imagine that."

It had been wedding season for the last three years straight, a run set to climax with her younger sister Kimberly's nuptials in July. Zoe made a noise of disgust and followed Troy to the living room. "As if we'd forget. I have to go dress shopping or she'll give me that look."

"I don't envy getting any of Adele's looks, but what specific look is this?"

"Oh, you know. The I-raised-you-better-than-to-wear-the-same-dress-so-many-times-that-people-start-to-talk look."

"Ah, yes. That one." He slipped a slim bundle of money, ID, and credit cards in one pocket and the keys to their apartment in the other. Minimal cargo so as not to ruin the lines of his skinny jeans. She loved him so much she forgave this habitual vanity.

She said, "You have no idea. All you men need to do is change what tie you wear, and you're all set."

"Are you angling to get me to go shopping with you?"

She perched on the arm of their couch. "Yes, please. You know those fluorescent-lit dressing rooms make me feel like the undead."

He looked at her then, really looked, his baby blues flicking between her left and right eyes in rapid succession. He sighed and stepped closer. "I know you don't think I'm serious about us marrying, but I am. We're good together, as partners, which is way

UPENDED

more than I can say about all the other couples we've witnessed committing their lives to each other."

"You've made all your arguments before."

"Because I keep thinking that one of these days you'll listen."

"My disagreeing with you doesn't mean I'm not listening."

When they got serious like this, Zoe felt their intimacy most profoundly: bare feet, Sunday morning paper and breakfast, daily routines of dinner and laundry. It wasn't just the pull of warm, familiar company but their stockpile of shared experiences. But still. He leaned his forehead against hers, bending low to reach. "Come out to dinner with me and the guys. Celebrate Monday being over."

"I ate at Rosemary's."

"You can get a drink. Or three."

"Being the only dyke in a group of five fags isn't the unbounded delight you imagine it to be."

He straightened back up. "You need to get out."

"I was just out on Friday, and look how that went. Besides, if I get out more, maybe I'll meet someone and fall in love, and your plan of us in wedded bliss will go straight down the tubes."

She regretted her flip tone when he walked away to the foyer, saying, "Who said anything about love? You girls always confuse the subject, and look what happens—one kiss, and I have to suffer through a weekend of abject pining."

"I wasn't pining abjectly."

"Please." He found his loafers and slipped them on. "You and I know that forever-after love is a load of crap. Free yourself from the hetero-tyranny of that slow death and be with me. You know you want to. Who better to commit to than your best friend?"

She smiled. "Hetero-tyranny? That's a new one."

"I'll convince you yet. But for now I'll call later to check on you."

"Don't call me. Just have a good time. Be safe."

Then he was gone, and Zoe fell back onto the couch. Yes, with both their families, they were so deep in the closet that suffocating on off-season coats was a real danger, but Troy was smoking

70

crack to think they should make their act real. He pretended to be straight at work, too, keeping a picture of her at his desk for reasons Zoe couldn't completely comprehend, given that he was an accountant at one of those scary multinational corporations, not in the military or anything. Besides, she hated that picture, looked snub-nosed and round cheeked, not to mention alarmingly young. Not that it mattered since the whole thing was fake.

And yet, the idea of putting substance under their deceits had a certain perverse appeal. At least she wouldn't be alone. But did he actually not believe he'd find a man he wanted more than sex with? She swore he secretly imagined the two of them in some kind of commune—he with his love and she with hers, everyone in tight collusion, their abnormal private lives clear only behind closed doors.

Adele would love that. Whatever looked good. Having Troy around took the heat off Zoe for her other "questionable" traits, not the least of which was her art degree. Funny that she could be a determined black sheep about that but not want to rock the boat by coming out. Well, not rock, but capsize. Six years before, when she'd given up being straight and had broken things off with her (very real) fiancé, Sebastian, her family's reaction had been dicey enough even without the full truth surfacing. While she was thankful that this act she and Troy perpetuated enabled a sustainable equilibrium, when he pushed her about marriage, she wondered what they were doing.

This was not the 1950s. Lesbians were all over the place. Hell, in Massachusetts, she'd been able to marry another woman for *ages*. Besides, she didn't even like most of her family all that much. The problem was that, somehow, she still managed to love them, especially Kimberly, who was the straight-arrow, chip-off-the-old-block check to Zoe's deviant balance. Kimmy thought too highly of Zoe for the avant-garde life she thought Zoe lived—and the attractive men she'd kept company with. Going to her wedding with Troy was the cherry on that fabricated sundae, but Zoe didn't like cherries much—especially not this one.

UPENDED

She pulled a pillow under her head. Now that Troy and his gentle pressure were gone for the night, the apartment was quiet outside the rattling of the fridge and the moan of plumbing from the floor above, but Zoe couldn't relax. So many lies, and now she was lying to Troy, too? Damn Madeline. She couldn't shake her unease about that call despite telling herself it was probably nothing. So Madeline had missed a meeting. People missed meetings all the time. Zoe hadn't been stood up, no matter Troy's take on the situation. But Madeline hadn't called her over the weekend, which also meant Zoe needed to let go of the kiss and this crush and its attendant fantasies. If she wanted to exercise her imagination, she should get her brushes and oils out from their box under her bed and paint something. Instead, she found the remote between two cushions and flipped on the TV.

CHAPTER 9

IN PREPARATION FOR HOSTING A CONVALESCING MADELINE, JOE bought extra pillows and blankets and spent way too long at The Body Shop, assaulting his nose with bath salts and shampoos to find the right, soothing scent. He made sure his Tylenol was topped off and procured three different kinds of floss and toothbrushes. He made late-night and early-morning runs to the grocery, stocking a cabinet full of Madeline's favorite comfort foods: chips and wasabi almonds and all manner of processed cheese conveyances along with a case of seltzer water to wash them down.

Yet, despite all that activity—or because of it—he couldn't stop dwelling on Bridget's comment about him and Madeline. The words she'd used, "do the best by her," weren't nefarious or suggestive in the least, but they were as heavy with subtext as her expressive hums. She had made a point of saying what didn't need to be said. Why wouldn't he do everything he could for Madeline? How could he possibly leave her in Ethan's care after he'd run out on her at the hospital? Maybe Joe was reading too much into it, but weren't a lawyer's words like a surgeon's scalpel: delicate, precise, and deliberate?

UPENDED

This teasing, ultimately useless train of thought dogged him right to the moment on Thursday afternoon when he helped Madeline into his car at Beth Israel. Though she was uncharacteristically quiet, having her so close convinced him he'd gone down this rabbit hole of crazy because he'd been missing her regular steadying force. He'd come to rely on her in ways he'd only recently discovered, and not just in business matters. Not even mostly in business matters. She'd become his guiding light in humor and perspective, and her keen insight into the intractability of human nature had seeped into his bones. Over the years, he'd shed many of his previous insecurities simply by acknowledging and accepting his many flaws instead of twisting himself up in useless denials.

He took sidewise glances at her as she gazed out the windshield, biting at a corner of her thumbnail, lost inside herself. Her face was still a colorful map of pain, with reddish-yellow bruising around her nose and eyes, a crosshatch of scabbed scrapes along her cheek and chin, and stitches near her hairline that had cooled from angry to merely annoyed. She closed her eyes, took a deep breath, and winced. It was a veritable minefield under her skin—and surely in her skull.

"Glad to be out of the hospital?" he asked to try to pull her out of whatever she was contemplating.

She moved her head in a half nod. "I watched some TV out of desperation. It was both better than I remembered and terrifying at the same time. When I was waiting for my discharge this morning, I was thinking about how strangely familiar the whole hospital routine had become."

"We're adaptable creatures. If we weren't, our business would be doomed."

"To a degree." She pressed on her eyebrows, her fingers sliding along one then the other. "I was just thinking about how the baseline of our experiences slowly evolves with everything we go through. Sooner or later. Whether we want it to or not." She pulled the seatbelt away from her chest and let it reel back before she said, "Yes, I'm glad to be out of the hospital, but..."

He finished her thought in his mind. Being well enough to get discharged did nothing at all to erase the horrific thing that had landed her there in the first place. "It seems like you should've watched more TV and done less thinking."

"You're probably right."

Joe turned into his building's garage, a claustrophobic concrete bunker studded with square columns whispering sweet nothings to unsuspecting bumpers and car doors. He eased in between his neighbors' cars and pulled the parking brake. "Let me help you out. The elevator's around the corner there."

"I can do it."

"Or you can let me help."

"Or I can let you help."

He walked around to her side, cursing how tight these parking spaces were. With Madeline's left knee in a rigid brace and her shoulder lacking range of motion from its sprain, helping her turn in the seat so her legs protruded out of the car was a trial. Surprisingly, she laughed (maybe for the first time since the attack). "How many management consultants does it take to change a light bulb?"

"More than you can afford," he answered. When she was finally in position, he leaned down. "Put your arms around me, and I'll help you up. I've got one of your crutches right here."

When her arms snaked around his neck, a slide show of dreamlike images flooded his mind: him slipping his arms under her legs and behind her back; the warm snugness of holding her in a tender embrace; sweeping her out of the car and to his apartment, her feet never touching the ground. But the mirage evaporated as suddenly as it had materialized, spitting him back into this awkward moment of staggering and jimmying between his car and the next, then finally getting into the open with a crutch under one of her arms and his shoulders supporting her other side.

He blinked a few times, dispelling any lingering madness. "Okay. Ready?"

In answer, Madeline crutch-hopped forward, pulling Joe along with her. After a few steps, they settled into a vague rhythm, Joe attempting to steady her without putting any pressure on her ribs, which was impossible. Her breathing was uneven, her waist was soft and curved beneath his fingers, and a tremor started up in his arm. It propagated through nerves and sinew to his brain, where it was transformed into the urge to pull Madeline to him and feel the length of her against his side all the way down through hip and thigh, all the way up to his chest, his shoulder, where she'd rest her head.

He was shocked into stillness.

Madeline glanced between him and the elevator, which was still a few feet away. Without a word, she reached out with her crutch and used its rubber tip to push the up button, a move she counterbalanced by shifting more of her weight onto Joe's shoulders. The intensity of his tremor increased, threatening to undo him, and to stop it, he said, "You okay?"

"You look like I should ask you the same thing."

"I'm fine. Everything's fine. When I go out for food later, I can run by your apartment and pick up whatever you need."

"Ethan's bringing some things by tomorrow."

"And you think he'll show up?"

The look she gave him was both hard and tired, a frowning resignation. "That's it. I'm calling a moratorium. Neither of you is allowed to talk about the other. But since you asked, yes, he came by the hospital yesterday."

They boarded the elevator in a shuffle and rose through the building, the small space amplifying Madeline's breathing, which was heavy with effort, each inhale ending in a hitch. This rough rush of air echoed in Joe's ears, and with every breath, the warmth of her body dissolved something inside him. He gazed down the ripped neck of her sweatshirt at a delicate collarbone and felt a reverberating desire to touch her leg under the soft drape of the scrubs she'd inherited at the hospital.

He jerked away, forcing Madeline to take a quick hop to stay with him.

She said, "Seriously, what's wrong with you?"

"Nothing. I'm fine. Too much coffee." This was *Madeline*. Madeline Sawyer, his business partner, a woman previously defined by her smile, the sound of her laugh, the imprint of her stub-nailed fingers on his arm. Not the smooth line of her neck or the electric hairs along her forearm. Bridget's voice echoed in him, her tone now quite clear.

Inside the apartment, he helped Madeline ease down onto the couch—a deep, microfiber affair he'd surely have to rescue her from later—and excused himself to the kitchen, ostensibly to get her a glass of water but mostly to get himself a grip. He stood in the refrigerator's cool white light and surveyed its contents without really seeing any of them, not that there was much to see. Condiments. Always too many condiments. Still, he felt clarity trickle back to him and wanted more than anything to laugh at himself and shake off this silliness the way Madeline would— by brutal identification followed by a dose of perspective and laughter.

She'd say something like, *Did you hear me mangle those stats in the middle of the presentation? At least I didn't call their company by the wrong name. We can hope they were distracted by my ravishing beauty too much to notice. Ha-ha.* Perspective was important, yes, but when things got difficult, when uncertainty rose to eclipse everything else, perspective vanished first. Having Madeline in his arms like that, so close after nearly losing her, made the losing momentarily more real than the having, and now his perspective was shot.

From the living room, she said, "Thanks for taking me in. Being here...I feel safe."

He closed the refrigerator door and leaned back against it.

UPENDED

"It's always so tidy here. My apartment, well, you know. Jane's everything-in-its-place attitude never quite rubbed off on me."

Jane. Right.

"I don't suppose you have any Cheetos."

"Do I have Cheetos? Do *I* have Cheetos?" He opened the Madeline cabinet, as he'd come to think of it, which bulged with brightly colored, individually packaged junk food. He ignored the distinct possibility that this stock could be construed as over the top, snagged three snack packs of Cheetos, and walked to the living room doorway. "Do I have Cheetos?" He shook the bags in triumph.

"Oh, man, you're the best. Dare I ask if there's any seltzer in the house?" She was so small against his couch, but her faint smile was delightful.

"Do I have seltzer?" he said and laughed, feeling the heaviness of the last week lift from his lungs.

MUCH LATER, JOE LAY IN BED AND LISTENED TO THE QUIET apartment, wondering if Madeline were asleep. He'd left her in Katie's bedroom hours before, propped up against most of the available pillows in the house, reading by the light of the bedside lamp—a garish clown holding a glowing red balloon that Katie loved but he found disturbing. The lamp had a matching night-light, and he obsessed about it now, how weirdly powerful it was and how he should've turned it off when he'd said good night to Madeline.

He couldn't shake the desire to do something about it. If he could be sure she was sleeping, he could open the door to her room just wide enough to fit his arm inside and feel around for the light. He could picture the small switch at its base, feel the slight pressure needed to flip it, hear the tiny snap it would make.

But what if she weren't asleep (or was as light a sleeper as Ethan had implied), and she caught him coming in her room like that?

Surely she'd sense the longing that had crept back under the cover of darkness to lurk behind his eyelids, at the back of his throat, next to his spleen, but he didn't know how to banish it, couldn't find either laughter or perspective. It was as if their history was this soft, faded thing that the violence of her attack had ripped apart, exposing a blurry alternate reality it had previously obscured. Or alternate *unreality*. Just as Madeline's injuries would heal, the tears in the fabric between them would knit themselves closed over time, and these unsettling, wildly inappropriate feelings would be gone. He just had to be patient and ride it out.

But time passed in thick ribbons of hesitation, and he lay in paralyzed indecision about the night-light until the whoop of a scream across the hall scared him right to his feet. He barged through two doors and into Madeline's room, propelled by the same primordial response Katie's infrequent nightmares always summoned. The brightness of the clown lamp made him blink uncontrollably, and he laid his hands on her shoulders (gently, gently), then ran them down her arms to her hands, where he squeezed her palms, trying to coax the wildness from her wide eyes.

She breathed hard and fast through her nose, making little grunts of pain with each inhale. Eventually she closed her eyes, her respiration grew slower and easier, and she took her good hand from Joe, pressed it against her ribs, and let out a shaky sigh.

"I'm sorry," she said. "I tried to stay awake. I should've told you about the dreams."

"Don't."

She nodded, the back of one hand resting against her forehead like a woozy damsel in distress.

When his heart dropped back from his esophagus, he said, "Sometimes it makes Katie feel better to tell me about it."

"What's the use? It's not like it'll make it less real." She pressed her lips together and pushed them one way then the other. They were still roughed up and bruised looking, and Joe wondered if what she was doing hurt. "I'm not used to sleeping like this. It's an abyss until the dream wakes me. Too asleep then too awake. All those years with Jane, I never minded waking up all the time because it was to her. But when it's just me..." Her fingers played along the tape still bridging her nose. Her gaze fixed on the ceiling, and she spoke in a rush, the words laced with venom and fluent in a way that indicated they had been festering. "Fucking Ethan. He shouldn't have gotten on my case like that, but he was right. I hate when he's right about me, how he sees these things about me I work so hard to ignore. That squirrely little fink. All I wanted to do was forget about it, and the whole thing was so desperately stupid. I didn't want to tell you, disappoint you."

Joe had no idea what she was talking about, what Ethan had seen in her, and what stupid thing Madeline thought she'd done, but Madeline was rigid and radiating a prickliness he'd learned long ago not to try to engage. He tried a small de-escalation. "You didn't do anything wrong."

"I do wrong things all the time."

"Well, in this case, you're in the clear." Because she was. No matter what he might not know, what she hadn't told him, he was sure about that.

She sighed, and her shoulders dropped down. "Maybe, but Ethan reminded me that when we were kids, I used food as a bribe for him to spend time with me. I would do anything to keep from being stuck with the stupid shit in my head, which was, you know, nothing other than *reality*."

Reality. Right. Joe settled on the floor next to the bed, his back against the nightstand, his ugly feet stretched out toward the door. "Bribe?" he asked, ignoring everything else.

"Not in so many words, but yeah." She shifted, and the grunt it elicited mingled with a creak of the bed.

"Need your medicine?"

"No. The pain's...easy I guess. Easier than thinking about what happened—or even all the things I think about to avoid thinking about what happened. Did you know that between when I got to Harvard and when Jane left me, I wasn't single for more than six weeks at a time? Over those fourteen years, I was alone maybe nine months. *Maybe.* There's something wrong with me."

"You're fine. You're better than fine. What do you think about my killing this stadium lighting?"

"Don't change the subject."

"What subject? The one where there's nothing wrong with you?"

"You have a distinct incentive to appease me."

"Madeline, you're spectacular beyond measure, and nothing you say can dissuade me of that."

"I'm sure I can come up with something."

"Listen to me." He reached up to capture her hand in his. "You've been through a terrible trauma and are still on pretty good painkillers. Now is not the time to pass judgment about anything. Take my divorce attorney's advice: don't make any major decisions for at least three months. Following it meant I didn't get the '67 MG convertible I've always wanted, but he was absolutely right."

She squeezed his hand, just like she'd done at the hospital after she woke. Joe felt it all the way to his sternum. "You're a good friend."

He wanted to tell her about losing the Bates contract, let her into the company's failing finances, to have no secrets between them again, but the thumping of his heart and the pull of her fingers convinced him that a great number of things were better left unsaid. He'd get them out of this tight spot, she'd recover, and they would be best friends and business partners again.

He said, "I'll stay here until you're asleep."

Her hand slipped out of his, drifted up his arm, and squeezed his shoulder. "Thanks, Joe. Tell me what Katie's reading, if you want. Anything to distract me."

He turned off the clown lamp, sat back in the strong glow of the night-light, and dug up the last plot summary Katie had given him and Bridget and Darrin over that dinner in Belmont—four days ago that now felt like months. He spun it out, adding details he

UPENDED

remembered from other books until Madeline's breath deepened into sleep and stayed there awhile. Even then, it was a long time before he could make himself get up on stiff legs and leave her, unplugging the night-light from the wall on the way out.

CHAPTER 10

MADELINE DIDN'T KNOW WHICH WAS WORSE, JOE'S STIFLING concern and relentless positivity or the hamster wheel of her own thoughts that got her nowhere but tangled up and exhausted. As convinced as she was that she didn't know her attacker, she couldn't shake the suspicion that he knew her. But if he knew her, why did he attack her where he did? How did he know she was going to be there at that time? She was practically never out that late, let alone on the T. She reviewed her memories of that night for any hint of angry observation or men the same size and shape of her attacker. White. Tall. Strong but soft. Jeans and a dark jacket. Or maybe a sweatshirt. But both her train and the platform at Central Square had been nearly barren. Maybe he didn't know her and just thought all women were dykes—or considered that the worst possible insult, below bitch, below whore, below even inanimate and universally reviled trash. Despite that hope, she'd contacted her landlord to ask him to change the locks to the building and on her front door for whenever she could face going back home.

UPENDED

When all trains of thought related to her attacker were exhausted, the hamster wheel reversed, and she obsessed about lying to Joe and Ethan and the police, each in different measure, and about the impulse she felt—however irrational, however puzzling, however potentially hurtful—to hoard the details of the attack. Her lies were a buzzing atmospheric disturbance, charging the air and shifting the tides. Lying, she was reminded, was not just the lie itself but all the living with it you had to do afterward.

MONDAY MORNING, NINE DAYS AFTER THE ATTACK, MADELINE reclined on Joe's couch with a pillow under her knee and a laptop open on her thighs. She was acutely aware of her workout shorts and somewhat funky sweatshirt in the face of their admin, Beth, who sat on the love seat. Even here, in this most relaxed environment, with Madeline practically in pajamas, Beth looked like a fashion plate.

She'd been with them for a year and a half, working eight to two before taking off to write the great American novel, which she never discussed, and no one was allowed to read. She was disciplined and appropriately bossy, and no matter how many times Joe and Madeline told her that casual attire was fine, she always arrived with her hair and makeup just so, her shirts and trousers pressed to screaming, her earrings coordinated with her bracelets.

When alone with Madeline, Joe attributed many of Beth's traits to her divorce, which had been the epitome of acrimonious, but Madeline suspected that his tendency to see manifestations of divorce everywhere was itself a manifestation of his own. Then again, what did she know? She and Jane had been together longer than Joe and Bridget, but children and lawyers (and men) changed things.

While Beth typed up notes from the last agenda item, Madeline surreptitiously sniffed herself. She'd run one bath while Joe was

84

out, and once she'd managed to situate herself in the claw-foot tub, it had been quite pleasant, especially when she'd slid down until her ears were underwater and the apartment, with its unfamiliar, startling noises, was muted. But she slipped while climbing out and cracked her head so hard her vision had faded to a fuzzed gray. She sat in the draining tub, regaining her senses, sure that Joe was going to catch her in this state but too scared to move. She hadn't chanced the bath or shower again, and she smelled stale and felt scummy.

"Okay," Beth said. "Next item: Madeline still has a few client meetings on the calendar this Thursday and Friday. Do you want me to cancel them?"

"Yes," Joe said, right when Madeline said, "No."

Beth glanced between them.

"Yes," he said.

Madeline craned her neck to see him where he sat on the recliner behind her left shoulder. "Um, I'm right here."

She was reminded that Joe was a practiced poker player and had the ability to assume an expression pleasant and vague enough that it could mean everything or anything or nothing. He said, "That's why I'm saying we have to cancel those meetings. You still can't get around."

"They're not for three days, and the ribs are healing."

"They won't keep healing if you push it. Besides, with your shoulder—"

"Getting to a couple client meetings is hardly pushing it."

"Madeline, no."

She shifted to see him better, trying to hide her discomfort at the movement. His poker face had turned decidedly priestly, and the thought of him exercising patience over her was maddening. "You're not the boss here. Or at least not the only one."

He shifted his position, eliciting a squeak from the recliner's dark leather. "Your face; it's still so bruised."

Though she tried not to look at herself in the bathroom mirror, she knew every detail of her current disfigurement. Even so, she couldn't let this conversation go. "People have accidents," she said but was met with silence. "You know what I mean. They come to meetings with walking casts, slings, bandages. Who's to say I didn't hurt myself hiking the Himalayas?"

"Give it another week. Just until the bruising and scabs are gone and you can get around without...you know."

She waited.

"Without looking like it hurts you so much," Joe said but went on in a hurry. "You've said it yourself—minimizing distractions is one of the most important management tactics. 'We're all children waiting for the next shiny thing,' right?"

"Don't throw my words back at me."

"I'm just saying that those meetings won't be productive if the clients are distracted by your injuries."

"Don't you think I'd be able to dismiss them and get us to move on?"

"No," Joe said. "I don't." He folded his arms across his chest as a period to the end of that damning sentence.

Beth said, "Listen, that's a great thing. People trust you not to lie to them. Joe, not so much."

Madeline relaxed back with a physical relief she tried not to show. "Fine, cancel the meetings. Am I allowed to use the phone or can they"—she waved her fingers in the air—"sense injuries in my voice? You know what? Forget it. Clear my schedule through the summer, and I'll work on my tan."

"Someone's cranky," Beth said. "Did you not get one of the cookies I brought? They're still in the kitchen, I think."

What good would a fucking cookie do? The placation Beth jokingly offered made anger percolate in Madeline's gut, which was both surprising and strangely comforting. Wasn't she supposed to be angry? Furious at what had happened and at the circumstances she found herself in? She couldn't even bathe herself without an element of danger! Being broken under Joe's watchful eye was bad enough, but things wouldn't be better when she went home. Home. What a joke. Not only would the scene of the crime be a mere half mile away, but her apartment was nothing more than a few rooms of her shit that were supposed to be temporary. Most of the time her anger lurked far below the surface like a deep-sea leviathan, where, despite her best efforts, it fed on slights and inequity and ignorance. But now the placid waters of her psyche were disturbed, and all sorts of unsavory emotions were stirred up to the surface.

She remembered where she was and Beth's offer. Right. A fucking cookie. She let out a pent-up breath that had set up an ache under her ribs. "Are there any with nuts? Or sea salt?"

"Let me see what they gave us." Beth put her laptop aside and went to the kitchen, her heels rapping on the hardwood floor.

Madeline turned to Joe, ignoring the ache in her ribs. "You don't make decisions for me."

"I'm not—"

"Just say 'okay' and we can talk."

"Okay," he said, which allowed her anger to retreat but not fully disarm. He leaned forward, his hands on his knees, one of them clutching a steno pad like Detective Henderson. "I'm not used to us disagreeing. Believe me, I'm not trying to control you. I'm making things up as I go along."

"You *are* trying to control me but probably for good reason." She dropped her voice to a whisper. "I see how you look at me, like I'm about to slit my wrists or something, but I'm not. I'm trying to understand what happened. Put it in a place that isn't absolutely everywhere."

"Do you really think it can be understood?"

Beth came back in, paper bag of cookies and plates in hand. "Chocolate chip, sugar, and oatmeal raisin."

She and Joe watched Madeline, who rolled her eyes in surrender. "Where are we with the Bates and Grasshopper contracts?"

Beth put the cookies on the coffee table within Madeline's reach, and Joe said, "We lost Bates and are still waiting on Grasshopper."

A long blink of surprise showed on Beth's face before she busied herself getting settled in the love seat with her laptop. The news, and the matter-of-fact way Joe delivered it, *was* surprising, but Madeline couldn't fathom why Beth felt the need to hide it—or at least try to. "Do we know why Bates didn't go with us? Was it cost? And what's taking Grasshopper so long to decide? They should've gotten back to us at least a week ago. Do I need to call them?"

"I've got it under control." He leaned forward to snag the oatmeal raisin cookie.

"I'm just saying that when the process drags out, our win percentage drops way off. Death by committee."

"I'm on it," he said.

Madeline wanted to excavate past Joe's adamant verbal blockade, but she also wanted not to seem irrational and reactionary, so she shook her finger at their admin and said, "Beth, the man's on it. Stop riding him, already."

Beth smiled. "Okay, so Joe's *on* the contracts, and Madeline apparently *didn't* want a cookie after all." She paused and peered at them over tortoiseshell glasses maybe a little too chunky and young for her, though Madeline wasn't quite sure how old she actually was. "Next. There's a big red reminder on the calendar in a week that our next payment to Pinskey is due. Is that still right? Are we on schedule, or should I move the reminder? Or, wait, have they invoiced us, and I don't know about it?"

Madeline said, "We're a little behind. The project's waiting on a meeting I missed with the design firm last week."

Joe said, "We'll get them paid. Don't worry."

She watched him chew his cookie, muscles bunching and relaxing under his five-o'clock shadow even though it was only 1:30. He looked back at her steadily, and she thought she might actually be going insane, that maybe Ethan was right about the state of her moral compass because playing fast and loose with her own truth now made her see subterfuge everywhere.

She said, "I wasn't worried, but should I be?"

"No, definitely not."

Beth cleared her throat. "Listen, not to interrupt, but am I moving that date or leaving it as is?"

Madeline said, "I'll forward you the invoice when I get it."

"Gotcha."

Joe said, "Madeline, will you send it to me instead of Beth? I want to pass it by the accountant to see if we should treat it differently from the rest of our expenses."

"Why would it be different from any other service?"

"I don't know. That's why we have an accountant."

"We haven't sent them any of the other invoices for review."

"I just want to see this one. Dot some i's."

Having Beth around had never inhibited Madeline before, but now she stopped herself from digging into Joe about this nonsensical idea. Or about why he was being so uncharacteristically...manly. Excessively decisive. Then again, maybe she was imagining this—or the irritating, puzzling extent of it. She reminded herself that *she* was the altered one, not him, which meant this was likely more her problem than his.

The buzzer for the building's front door rang, short-circuiting the fruitless cycle of these thoughts. For the last several days, this sound had heralded the arrival of food, but after a glance at her computer screen to check the time, she said, "It's Ethan. Since he had the afternoon off, I asked him to bring over some more of my things."

A gust of sighs greeted her brother's name. Joe said, "I could've gone by your place."

"You do enough already. Besides, the landlord changed the locks for me, so the keys you have won't work. Is someone going to let him in?"

When Joe disappeared down the hall to the front door, Beth slipped her computer into her tote bag. "I think that about wraps it up."

"I agree."

She ran her hands down the sleeves of her blouse, smoothing them and straightening their seams. "Listen, I wanted to apologize for not calling or coming by. I know it's inexcusable, but—"

"It's fine. Don't worry about it."

"No, you were in need, and I bailed—and after the two of you have been nothing but kind to me. I should've returned the favor, but I bailed instead."

Madeline shut her laptop and pressed her hands against its cover. Reassuring Beth was the last thing she had energy for, and how could she do it with any sincerity, anyway? But she dredged up a small slice of truth. "Beth, this totally blows, but there's no way you can help except to keep things running and write the shit out of your novel."

Beth gathered her things and got up, avoiding Madeline's gaze. "Yeah, but listen. I was mugged when I lived in New York. I was young. Before-I-got-married young. Really, it was nothing, just a swiped purse and a skinned knee, but I was petrified for months. *Months.* And when Joe told me about you, I felt it all over again, which is silly. Then I thought about what you went through, *you*, who have been such a rock for me, and I was afraid of seeing you...It was unforgivably selfish. I should've made you carry pepper spray. Why didn't I make you carry pepper spray?"

Madeline reached out and captured her arm. "Believe me, pepper spray wouldn't have helped."

"But you'll carry it from now on?"

She held up an approximation of the Girl Scout salute. "From now on. On my honor. But, you know, there *is* something you can do for me."

"Anything."

"Let me read your book. I have nothing but time since Joe's got me on lockdown."

Beth laughed. "Nice try. When it's ready, okay? You'll be the first."

"Is it ever going to be ready?"

"That remains to be seen. And about Joe...you know he's got mother hen tendencies, and you gave us quite a scare. He'll calm down. Anyway, I'll come by again soon and talk to you sooner," she said and left.

In this transient solitude between business and her brother, Madeline wondered how clearly Beth could see the ruined part of her, which started just below the surface of her assaulted skin and ran right through to her core. If it had taken Beth months to recover from her relatively minor run-in with violence, what did that mean for Madeline? Would anything get rid of this infection, or would she have to amputate herself piece by piece?

CHAPTER 11

ETHAN HAD LEFT MADDY'S CAR PARKED IN A RED ZONE, ASSUMING she wasn't jonesing to visit with him. He wondered why she hadn't sent Joe to pick up her new keys and these additional supplies, but he wasn't complaining. He had errands to run and was thankful to have her car for the afternoon. He stepped out of the elevator, holding a plastic bag of her things in each hand, and saw Joe and Beth deep in conversation down the hall. He swore under his breath. The last thing he needed was a run-in with these two. Why hadn't Maddy mentioned they were going to be here? He crept closer while trying to remain invisible.

Beth was saying, "We heard about Bates over a week ago, and now you're not telling her about Grasshopper?"

"There's still a chance I can turn it around. Besides, she would worry."

"*Should* she worry? Should I?"

"No. And no. But she's just so..."

Despite his ardent wish not to call attention to himself, Ethan asked, "She's so what?"

Beth eyed him from head to toe, and Joe crossed his arms, which reminded Ethan of school-day dreams of being naked and unprepared. Finally, Beth said, "Not herself."

He laughed. "Believe me, you have no idea."

"What does that mean?" Joe and Beth both asked.

A swell of equal parts pride and fear rose in him at what he knew and they didn't. "Nothing. Forget it. Sister-brother confidentiality." He shimmied between them and the smooth tan wall of the hallway.

Joe moved closer as if to stop Ethan. "If you know something that would help, you need to tell me."

Ethan quickstepped by. "I don't *need* to do anything. Besides, I'm here, aren't I? You don't have a monopoly on this."

"Oh, you're here, are you? What about at two in the morning when she has a nightmare?"

He shook his head. "Dude, you know no guy has gotten close to her like that."

Joe's mouth hung open a little while Beth's pressed into a line so hard and sharp it stung just looking at it. Ethan nearly missed that she was directing this devil gaze at Joe instead of him.

He took the opportunity to slip fully past them to the apartment door that had been left ajar. "She's inside? Great." He stomped down the hallway within and found The Mad Hatter lounging on a big, cushy couch, looking like someone should be feeding her grapes right from the stem—at least until he saw her face, which resembled hamburger gone bad around the edges, sickly green and yellow.

Just like at the hospital, the only thing he could do when faced with gory reality was to pretend she was the sister he'd always known. He dropped the plastic bags at her feet and jerked his thumb at the front door. "Those two don't like me at all."

"It's the facial hair." She twiddled her fingers against her chin as if he didn't know what she was talking about.

"What've you been telling them about me?"

"Nothing. Just the truth."

93

UPENDED

"There's the truth and there's the truth. There's whether you were at your office or a club and there's 'Ethan dropped out of school for no good reason' or 'Ethan up and quit his band.' Nuance, you know?"

Joe appeared from the hallway. "Hey. What's going on here?"

"Nothing," Ethan said, shamed at his aggressive yet whiny tone.

"Madeline?" Joe asked.

Maddy's face scrunched and twisted as if she'd bitten into an egg sandwich and encountered a big piece of shell. "It's between me and Ethan."

Joe raised his hands then dropped them back to his sides while Ethan gave a small internal cheer. Yet despite Maddy's show of solidarity, he couldn't keep himself from a last lick, saying, "I don't randomly quit things." This shut everyone up long enough that he noticed cookies on the coffee table. "Are these up for grabs?" He swiped one before anyone answered, took a bite, and said to Maddy, "Your one plant is dead, and I was too afraid to open your fridge."

"Thanks. The plant was dead already."

"I should've known. The landlord's charging you three hundred bucks for the locks, which I told him was highway robbery, but he made two sets of keys for you, so I didn't rough him up too much."

"I appreciate that."

He liked how they were both pretending Joe wasn't there. "Also, I kind of had my eyes closed when I packed stuff from your underwear drawer, so you get what you get."

"Understood."

"I put a couple books from your nightstand in the other bag. One day that pile's going to fall and smother you in your sleep." That, along with the roughing-up comment, was almost certainly the wrong thing to say, but when pretending to be normal, overdoing it was easy.

"I'll keep that in mind," Maddy said, and he mostly loved her again.

94

He stood there a moment, trapped between these two, not sure if he was supposed to stay or go. Things between him and Maddy had been...not so great since he'd run out on her at the hospital. He'd come by here with some clothes and face cream packaged in a heavy-bottomed glass jar like really good booze, but other than that, they'd shared only short, businesslike phone calls. He didn't like how guarded and quiet her voice was during those chats and was always relieved when they hung up, but Joe's holier-than-thou attitude made him decide to stay awhile and risk getting Maddy's car ticketed or towed. He took a load off on the love seat and asked her, "You're still having nightmares?"

She tilted her head back and leveled a look at Joe, who said, "Just because you asked me not to help you doesn't mean I stopped noticing."

"So I have dreams. Big deal."

Joe said, "Did the counselor at the hospital refer you to someone or maybe recommend a support group?"

"I doubt sitting in a support group will suddenly cure my nightmares. Or erase my memory."

Maddy's ears were pink at their tips, trending toward fire-engine red. They were a barometer of her mood, and Ethan used to thrill at provoking her into this state. Their little exchange hadn't seemed like enough to prime this pump of anger, and he wondered what had gone down before his arrival. Since Maddy was only ever rash or stupid when she was angry, Ethan thought it might be wise to diffuse the situation. He said, "Where'd you guys get these cookies? They're, like, ten times better than what we sell at Fuel."

She shot him a modified version of the eggshell look but shrugged. "Beth brought them."

"Well, this one is excellent."

Joe finally sat down. "How's your music?" His tone was pleasant enough, but it felt like a trap.

"Fine."

"Are you in a band up here? Madeline told me a little about your group down in Austin. Even played your album in the office. Good stuff."

Ethan glanced over at Maddy to see if she saw through this nice-nice act, but she was too busy frowning in a painful-looking way and examining her fingernails. "Yeah, she was one of the ten people who bought it."

Maddy said, "That's not true. You guys were doing really well."

Joe asked, "What happened?"

"Nothing," Ethan said. "Bands break up all the time."

"Our dad died," Maddy said.

"That had nothing to do with it."

She tilted her head in an all-knowing way. "I can see when you're lying."

"Oh, yeah? I guess I won't confess to the last ten times I totally bullshitted you." He looked at Joe, not waiting for Maddy's reaction. "Bands are like families. When things go wrong, they go really wrong."

Joe leaned forward. "I know firsthand how complicated family can be, and maybe, right now, you should go a little easier on Madeline."

Maddy sat up fast, huffed out a whoosh of breath, and fell back against the pillows. "Don't," she said with the same hard tone that, when used on Ethan, carried the full weight of her considerable non-parental sway over him. "It's not your place to tell him how he should and shouldn't treat me."

"I'm just saying—"

"I know *exactly* what you're just saying. You're just saying that I'm broken and incapable, and it might be true, but it's crap at the same time. I'm still capable of thought, you know." She tapped her head with way more force than necessary, making Ethan wince. "I'm still the person you hounded to build this business with you."

"Hounded? You were as excited as I was. Of course you're the same person, but to deny what's happened and how it affected you—"

"What do you want me to do? Torture myself with it all day?" Her voice had started to go shrill, which was never a good sign. "Be a nice little helpless package for you to take care of?"

When Joe spoke, his voice dripped with low calm. "You need help, and I'm trying to give it."

Oh, man, he should *not* have said that. Sure enough, the fire-engine red of Maddy's ears spread to her neck, and her eyes got bright in a dangerous way. "I don't want help." Her voice shook. "I don't want help, Joe. I'm perfectly capable of— I know how— Do I look like I want your help?"

The impending carnage was fascinating in such a horrifying way Ethan knew he should step in, but that might make him Maddy's target.

"You look like someone who *needs* help, at least temporarily."

"I'm not talking about getting up from this couch. I'm talking about the kid-glove shit, the holding my hand in the middle of the night, the deciding for me, the the the—"

Joe blinked at each of the the's, and Ethan got up. "I think that maybe we should all simmer down." That was so much something his father would have said that Maddy's gaze finally moved off Joe to spotlight Ethan. He tried to shrug off its intensity. "I'm just saying."

She said, "You came in my car, right? Where are you parked?"

"A block over."

"Bring it around. You're taking me home."

Joe said, "That's ridiculous! Absolutely not."

Ethan totally agreed but held his tongue.

Maddy sat up with a grimace. "You," she said to Joe, "have no say in the matter."

"Be reasonable. You can't make it up and down those stairs, and you'd be all alone."

At Joe's father-knows-best tone, Ethan rallied to the misguided cause. "Hey buddy, she's got me." He asked Maddy, "Do you have stuff here you want to take with you?"

"The bedroom down the hall to the left." She swung her legs off the couch with visible effort.

"Are you nuts?" Joe said.

Probably, Ethan thought, but he went down the hall anyway. He could hear Joe talking to Maddy, who was surely way beyond listening. Snippets came to him while he shoved clothes into a bag. "...know you're upset...have some dinner and talk...I'm sorry, I am."

Maddy still hadn't softened when he returned to the living room, which might be a new anger record for her. "Let's go. I can take this"—she indicated a bulging briefcase—"if you get everything else."

"How about I come back up for the stuff?"

"Okay," she said, though he could tell she was in no mood to acquiesce.

He went over to help her off the couch, and she draped an arm over his shoulder like she was going to tweak him in the ribs or whisper a secret in his ear. She leaned on him, and though they managed to get out of the living room and to the front door relatively quickly, he still had enough time to come to his senses. "You sure?"

"Hell, yes."

"'Cause he's right about the stairs. I got winded going up them."

"I don't care."

He helped her down to the sidewalk and ran to retrieve the car. Once he got her settled in the passenger seat, which was far from the easiest task, he buzzed Joe's apartment, half expecting not to be let in. But then he was upstairs, and Joe was waiting for him in the hallway, flushed and frowning with his arms crossed over his Mindful Management polo shirt. "This is insane," he said.

"Don't blame me. This is totally not my idea."

"You could have tried to reason with her."

"There's no reasoning with her when she's like this." He kept walking toward Joe, willing him to move.

"She could fall in the shower or jeopardize her healing, and her being alone...it isn't good for her mental state. And he's still out there, which I tell her and myself not to worry about, but it's at least a little bit of a consideration."

Ethan stopped. "Man, I *know* he's still out there, okay? I know it. But what can I do? The locks are changed, and who knows what he's thinking? He could be long gone or on to fresh quarry or think she's dead, and that's the end of it."

Joe stood so still the only sign he was alive was the writhing of the muscles in his jaw and along his arms.

"All I'm saying is if she wants to go home despite all that, I'm sure as shit taking her home. Besides, Maddy...come on, man, you know her. She's impossibly adult—aside from the once in a blue moon when she's really pissed. Then—and only then—I look good in comparison. But when she burns through this bug up her ass, she'll do whatever's best. She's hardwired that way." Though, when he said this, he silently acknowledged that the attack had clearly scrambled her circuits.

Joe gazed down at his forearms. "I don't know if I believe that. Not this time."

"In a couple days, when she's calmed down and apologetic, you'll probably be hauling her right back here."

For a cringeworthy second, Joe looked about to cry, but then he said, "Well, go ahead and get her things. Do you need a hand?"

"Nah, I got it."

He went inside and gathered up the bags. Joe was still in the doorway when he came back out. They walked to the elevator together, and Joe hit the button for him. "I worry about her."

"Join the club."

"She needs help. I've been trying, but she's shutting me out more and more. Just, please, make sure she's okay. Call me if you need anything."

Ethan met his gaze. "She's my sister. My only family. Give me a little credit."

UPENDED

ON THE RIDE TO HER APARTMENT, MADDY WAS A BUNDLE OF danger seething silently in the passenger seat. Ethan's number-one priority was not to trigger her rage again, which meant he took the long way around to her apartment to avoid where she'd been attacked. He drove the curves of the Jamaica Way then the Arborway and, due to his zeal (and the swirling rotaries), almost ended up in Forest Hills Cemetery. This car, an anonymous dark gray sedan with the radio set to NPR, was so middle of the road it didn't feel like his sister in the least. It was tidy and smelled faintly of coffee—though that could be his own nose—and its quality construction and relative newness insulated them from road and city noise so much that he could hear the modulations in Maddy's slowing breathing.

When he pulled in front of her place, they both gazed out the window at the three-story, boxy building, its gray shingles peeling in small, leper-like patches. A half dozen rust-tinged concrete steps led up to the dark front door, which added to its already foreboding look.

To delay the inevitable, he said, "What's up with this car? It's totally not you."

"I know," Maddy said without diverting her attention from those stairs. "I was in an ultraresponsible mood when I bought it."

"As opposed to your normal irresponsibility?"

"It was when Jane and I were starting to unravel, and somehow I thought being unbearably grown up might save us."

Sister Jane didn't seem like a very safe topic, so he killed the engine and said, "You should sell it and get a ragtop. A VW or Mini or something. Either that or a half-ton pickup."

Maddy laughed, clearly despite herself, and pressed a hand to her right side. "These damn ribs. I don't think I'd be able to get into a pickup right now."

"Still, you totally should. You'd need some aviator shades to go with it. And those mud flaps with the pinup girl silhouette on them. Hat Trick, A-1 dyke." But what would have been funny any other time was somehow exactly the wrong thing to say right now. Maddy turned from him toward the window again, her lips twisted to the side. He asked, "What did I say?"

"Forget it."

"But—"

"I was lucky for twenty years."

"What does that mean?"

"Nothing. Just that I was...unscathed."

"Except when those bitches in high school cracked a rib."

"Stop," she said softly.

He shut his trap for a minute, letting the rest of his confused questions go unvoiced. When it was safe, he said, "So...I'll take the bags up and come down for you?" But they both just sat there.

Finally, she said, "Hey," and touched his arm. "I know this is a mistake."

"You want me to take you back?"

"No. Have you ever known the total wrongness of something but still had to do it?"

He forced a smile. "You just described my entire life."

She chewed a thumbnail and whispered, "I'm scared of going up there. If I could stay mad, everything would be easier. I don't think when I'm mad. It's wonderful. But temporary."

"Well, you did a bang-up job of it this time. I thought Joe was going to disintegrate under your fury." He thought about stopping there but said, "Maybe if you talked to the police—"

"No." She shook her head, the hand at her mouth following its movement.

"Don't get mad, but I don't understand. I've really been thinking about it, too—"

"Don't start. Not now."

"But—"

"Assault cases go nowhere."

"But you—"

"I said not now!" She hummed out something between a growl and a sigh. "My ribs hurt, and I'm tired of arguing."

UPENDED

Ethan said nothing, just got out and popped the trunk for the bags. But when he was partway up the stairs, Maddy opened her door and called his name. He stopped.

"Were you serious when you said you'd stay with me?"

He squeezed the handles of the plastic bags and felt the strap of her briefcase dig into his shoulder. He wanted to shake this broken person until his sister fell free of its unrecognizable shell. Did he believe the police would catch the bastard? Not really, but if Maddy came clean, he would know she would make it through this reasonably intact. She felt like a stranger now, but he was in this for good. Bound. "I don't know. Do you still have a couch? Because all I saw in your living room was a pile of books yea high and long." He made sofa-size gestures, the bags crinkling at his movements.

She smiled a little. "It was there last time I looked." She indicated the building's door with a tilt of her chin. "Don't forget me down here."

As if, he thought.

CHAPTER 12

ZOE WAS STILL GETTING SETTLED ON HER STOOL AT THE CAFÉ when Rosemary accosted her from the swinging door to the kitchen. "Where have you been?" She moved closer, drying her hands on a small white towel. "Just because your date with Madeline didn't materialize doesn't mean you had to avoid us."

"It wasn't a date, and it wasn't even that long ago." Ten days, not that she was counting. "Besides, if I ate here any more often, I wouldn't be able to button my pants."

"Pshaw, you could use some more meat on your bones. But Zoe"—she leaned half across the counter, her gray hair sparkling under a pendant light—"I've been dying to tell you: a man came in not long after you left that night. *Very* starched-shirt."

"What, did he order a side salad and mineral water? Do you even serve mineral water?"

"He ordered the Salisbury steak, not that it matters. He was from out of town and had a whole song and dance about the unsung glory of neighborhood restaurants. A real talker, believe me, and the one thing he couldn't shut up about, besides my gravy—"

"Of course." Rosemary's gravy *was* delicious—rich and herbaceous without being too greasy.

"—was your painting." Rosemary nodded at where it hung over a booth on the right side of the dining area.

Zoe had given Rosemary the four-foot-by-six-foot canvas the year before to commemorate the café's tenth anniversary. At the time, celebrating Rosemary's mastery of food and ambiance with a gift of her own art had felt like a burst of genius—but now Zoe made a point of pretending it wasn't there. Not only had Rosemary hung it in a place that didn't provide the right framing or vantage point, but it had become unsettling to look at.

Though it had been years since she'd painted it, she could still recall how the process had been thrilling yet frustrating enough to make her want to hurl her brush across the studio. When she accidently noticed it now, she was shocked (and shamed) at the sense of insistence, almost fury, in its composition: abstracted, crystalline forms of various reds that pushed out toward the viewer from a point just left of center. These days, it was hard to believe she'd ever gotten so worked up over anything.

Rosemary said, "The man *loved* it, Zoe, even tried to buy it off me."

She laughed. "How much did he offer?" She shifted her hips around until her ass found the stool's sweet spot.

"I would never sell it, and I told him as much. Then he said he'd settle for your name and number."

"You're pulling my leg." One of Zoe's hands drifted to the back of her head, the short hair there soft against her fingertips.

"Absolutely not. I think he's serious *and* that he's got some kind of relationship with the art world."

"What does that mean?"

"Like he's a buyer or dealer or, I don't know"—she twirled her towel around one hand—"one of those rich people with a private collection that gets loaned out to museums."

"And you gave him my name?"

"I would *never*." She traced an X over her heart. "A promise is a promise." Zoe had given Rosemary the painting on the condition that she not tell anyone who had painted it—especially the other regulars. "But I did tell him I knew you and would pass along his interest." She pulled a bent business card out of her apron pocket with a flourish and held it in front of Zoe.

Zoe hesitated before taking it and reading the raised black lettering aloud. "Bernard Collins, Consultant. That's it? 'Consultant'? No way is this guy for real, but thanks anyway. What's on special tonight?"

"I'm telling you he's for real, at least in some sense. He was very specific when he talked about your painting and the techniques you used. All Greek to me. Or was it French?"

Zoe slipped the card in her worse-for-wear wallet between her money and a Blick coupon that was probably long expired. "I'll take it under advisement."

"You're talented, you know."

"Rosemary, seriously. Talent is way more common than most people think, and it doesn't mean much. Though if I had your very practical talent in the kitchen, I could make my own"—she made a small production of sniffing the restaurant's fragrant air— "chicken parmesan instead of coming here and bothering you for it."

Rosemary settled her hands on her hips and stared Zoe down. "Bothering me? *Bothering* me? I ought to turn you away hungry for that." She made a tsking sound. "You want the parm or meatballs? It's Italian night, and it's on the house."

"I'll have the parmesan, and I'm paying."

The phone interrupted the faux spat they were going to playact through. The one where Rosemary would get her way because, hell, the woman owned the joint. "This conversation isn't over." She went to answer, leaving Zoe free to pull that business card out of her wallet and examine it under the shadow of the counter. She was sure it was nothing. After grad school, she'd gotten her hopes up over a few things like this, but the initial tease never turned

UPENDED

to seriousness. Besides, any further conversation with Rosemary about this red herring would inevitably bend around to the question of why Zoe hadn't painted anything in almost two years (and not much the year before that), which wasn't something she was eager to contemplate.

Talent maybe wasn't quite as common as Zoe claimed, but it was certainly complicated, and she felt caught between the rock of squandering it and the hard place of trying to live up to it. Except in extremely rare, savant-type cases, talent required heaps of work to amount to anything. Painting was an exercise in near-constant failure that, while engrossing and perversely satisfying, asked something huge from her that she didn't have to give.

Rosemary still had the phone clamped between her shoulder and ear, but when she turned to Zoe, her gaze was as pointed as a finger. Zoe shoved the business card back in her wallet, feeling like she'd been caught watching porn. Rosemary smiled and said something into the phone, and Zoe thought for one stupid, blissful moment that the person on the other end of that call was none other than the mysterious "consultant." Maybe selling a painting would wake her artistic fire from its cold, dead ashes.

Rosemary hung up and slid back over to Zoe. "Guess who that was?"

Zoe stopped herself from admitting her silly hope. "The Heath Department calling for their annual bribe?"

"No. Your girlfriend."

"No offense, but have you been huffing fumes back there in the kitchen? You know how monumentally single I am."

"I mean Madeline." She winked.

"Madeline is not remotely my girlfriend." Rosemary gave her a look saturated in accusatory disappointment, which made Zoe think that as nice as surrogate mothers were, there were limits to their benefits. "What did she want, anyway?"

It turned out Madeline was laid up with a wrecked knee and a burning desire for a serving of Rosemary's mac and cheese. "My

106

delivery girl is out on a run to West Roxbury then Brookline, so Madeline will have to wait a little while."

"You know how she grooves on your mac and cheese. It's probably her desert island food. I'm sure she'd wait hours for it."

"Indeed."

"Knee surgery, huh?"

"That's what she said."

Let it go, Zoe told herself, but she didn't.

Zoe walked up Green Street away from Rosemary's toward Madeline's apartment, a paper bag full of both their dinners nestled in the crook of her arm. The sidewalk was dappled with evening light filtered through trees that had finally leafed out. Forsythia and azaleas dotted her progress, but the foliage thinned out after the Green Street T, proving that the other side of the tracks really *was* the other side.

The same three-flats were everywhere, but here they sported vinyl siding or haphazard paint jobs and lurked behind scrubby, postage stamp yards or chain link fences. Madeline's building, though larger than the ones around it, was no exception. Zoe shifted their takeout from one arm to the other (it was still warm enough to cook her skin) and realized she had no clue what she was doing. She crept up the porch steps and examined a bank of buzzers before pressing the one marked "Sawyer." While waiting for an answer, she glanced down at her pink button-down shirt that hadn't seen the business side of an iron lately and sniffed at her right armpit. This was not her brightest idea.

"Are you delivering from Rosemary's?" The words jumped and crackled through the all-weather speaker.

"Yeah, but—"

"You can leave it there on the porch. Thanks."

She was tempted to do just that, but not only was Rosemary sure to demand all the details of this fiasco, Zoe couldn't deny her desire to see Madeline again, especially since this injury and her subsequent surgery might very well explain how things *hadn't* gone down between them since that night at Club True. Maybe, finally, she could find out if that kiss meant anything. *Silly girl,* Troy would say, and he'd be right. She cleared her throat. "It's Zoe. From IDK Designs? I was at the café when you called, and since the delivery girl was out, I offered to bring this by. I have my dinner, too, in case you want some company."

That was a lot of information to cram through a call box, so she wasn't surprised when Madeline didn't answer immediately. Still, the seconds dragged on long enough for Zoe to notice all the litter caught in the bottoms of the fences around her and wonder what Madeline was doing in a dumpy neighborhood like this.

Finally, Madeline said, "My place is a fucking disaster."

"I'm sure it's not that bad."

"It's beyond that bad, but I guess you can come up anyway."

"Okay. Buzz me in?" Zoe asked, her heart adding a bounce to its usual staid beat.

But the buzzer was broken, and Madeline was on crutches, which made getting upstairs a small logistical conundrum. After some negotiation, Zoe set the takeout bag down on the porch and picked her way around the building through gravel and weeds to retrieve the keys Madeline tossed down from her window. "3C," she said after they landed several feet away.

There were seven keys and a car fob that was bigger than all the rest combined. Zoe tried four of them before making it into the dim, brown-carpeted stairway inside. Upstairs, Madeline's door was still closed when she approached it, and she knocked. "It's me," she leaned in and said.

"One second. I'm coming."

After much longer than a second, Zoe heard a thump and a scrape and the thumbing of a lock before the door cracked open to reveal Madeline, balanced on crutches and backlit by warm yellow sunlight streaming through two big windows. She wore loose gym shorts and a ripped sweatshirt, and her hair was pulled back in a ponytail. The room was close with heat from the sun and smelled like Zoe's bedroom after she'd slept in: a staleness redolent of exhales and warm, tacky skin.

Madeline said, "You really shouldn't have done this. I could have waited for delivery. But come on in."

"Fucking disaster" was a shockingly appropriate description of the apartment. The good-sized living room could pass for a ransacked library home to squatters. Ground zero of the mess was a deep dent in the couch opposite the front door—an empty spot of blue tweed upholstery flanked by short, uneven stacks of books and magazines. A laptop teetered on a pile of paper and binders on the coffee table, and that theme of accumulated literature extended to the floor and windowsills and two hulking bookcases stuffed to straining. Sprinkled throughout were wadded tissues, dirty dishes, and a few articles of clothing, sleeves and legs deflated. Not one piece of art hung on the white walls.

Zoe stood in a horrified stupor until she spotted the kitchen off to her left and its relatively clear countertop. "I'll...let me get plates and stuff." She hurried from the doorway and past Madeline, so distracted with relief at this movement that she ran right into a straight-backed chair sitting in her path, nowhere near any table.

She rested the food on the counter and turned back to Madeline, who had closed and locked the door. Madeline said, "Please. Sit down. The least I can do is serve." The sunlight that had turned her into a murky silhouette in the doorway now illuminated a map of multicolored bruises across her face.

"Dang," Zoe said, "What happened to you? Rosemary said knee surgery, but..."

Madeline ducked her head. "Nothing. An accident," she mumbled while creaking into a jerky walk in Zoe's direction.

"You need to sit way more than I do. Don't worry about it." Zoe found two plates in the first cabinet she tried, then opened drawers one after another until she happened upon an empty silverware tray. The desolation of that tan molded plastic made it clear that she shouldn't be here, that she was witnessing something unbearably private.

Madeline said, "I'd apologize for the mess, but I know it's beyond that."

"You sure have a lot of books."

"Getting anyone to help me move is impossible."

Zoe scouted around in the kitchen for forks before locating a couple soaking in a bowl of cloudy water in the sink. Madeline stood by the coffee table, her breath audible from across the room. Zoe said, "Let me wash these and then we can eat." She unbuttoned her cuffs and rolled up the sleeves of her shirt.

"Actually, I think you should probably go."

Madeline's voice was so low and thick and sad that Zoe's crush expanded and solidified, settling in her joints like a delicious flu that brought with it a feverish surge of confidence. "If it's all right with you, I'll stay. It seems like you could use some help."

Madeline's face tightened, and her eyes cast up to the ceiling. "I guess I do, but you didn't sign up for that. Besides, things between us..."

Zoe hurried to distract Madeline from that thought. "Well, I doubt you signed up to be in an accident, so we're even." She squirted dish soap on a sponge and started the water to drown out whatever Madeline was going to say. Now was most definitely not the time to talk about things between them. After washing the forks and the rest of the dishes in the sink for good measure, Zoe plated their dinners, saying, "No offense, but how were you planning on getting downstairs if I'd left this on the porch?"

"I had some ideas. None of them very good."

"You look like you should be in the hospital." She glanced over in time to watch Madeline half ease, half drop down on the couch.

"If you're not in danger of a heart attack, brain damage, or suicide, they kick you out pretty quickly. I'm much better than when they released me a week ago."

The thought of this being seven days more healed than she used to be shut Zoe up. She walked into the living room, handed

Madeline her meal, and spun around, scouting for a place to sit. An upholstered armchair adjacent to the couch was clear save for a sweatshirt puddled on its seat, but when she picked it up with her free hand, she stared at it, confused at its voluminous size.

Madeline noticed her hesitation. "Oh, that's Ethan's."

Zoe draped it over the back of the chair. "Who's Ethan?" She tried to keep her interest from her voice.

"My brother. He was staying with me before…sibling shit, to put it mildly."

"Ah, your *brother*," she said in a drawn-out way that reeked of relief. "You thought I was him last time we talked. Were you in the hospital then? Why didn't you tell me you were in an accident?"

Madeline held a fork suspended over her mac and cheese. "I…It's complicated. It's been complicated." She took a bite, then another, and swallowed practically without chewing. "Sorry. I'm starving. I haven't eaten all day."

"That's okay. I'm pretty hungry myself."

But eating in companionable quiet at the counter at Rosemary's was very different from this. At the counter, they were accompanied by the burble of background conversation, not to mention interjections from Rosemary herself. The Madeline one stool over from her had been loose, easy, and had possessed a smile Zoe couldn't get enough of: wide and bright and capable of transforming her face all the way from her eyes (a gold-flecked topaz that matched her hair) to her chin (with an irresistible hint of a cleft). The imperfection of her large, crooked teeth pulled everything else together the same way introducing one small grotesque element in a painting, whether aggressive texture or a spot of unexpected, sour color, could make the beauty on the rest of the canvas snap into perfect focus.

This Madeline was shuttered off behind her mottled bruises and ate with a grim determination. Her quiet left Zoe plenty of time to wonder what she was doing here. Really. Madeline hadn't invited her, and it was far from the right venue to discuss their time at the club, so why stay now that she'd helped Madeline scratch this itch of craving? No reason at all. And yet...

Zoe wanted to be here, albeit under wildly different circumstances. For over a year, she had basked in the bloom of warmth radiating from Madeline's conversations with Rosemary, had even managed to weasel her way inside it for those wonderful minutes on the dance floor, and Zoe wanted to claim it for herself. Not just that, but she wanted to reflect that warmth back at this bruised and troubled Madeline. She just *wanted*. Something different. Something more. She thought about the uselessness of Bernard Collins's business card in her wallet and how easy it would be to waste energy hoping for that instead of trying something, here and now, that was rooted in reality.

When the refrigerator's hum rattled to a stop, highlighting their stifling silence, Zoe broke and succumbed to small talk. "How long have you been going to Rosemary's? You were already a bit of a fixture when I started up." If Madeline were as monogamous with her romantic partners as her food, she should've been happily married for at least a decade. The woman had a pathological devotion to the mac and cheese.

The question broke Madeline's food trance. She flicked her tongue across her lips before answering. "On and off for six years. I started going with Jane, my ex, but I guess you could say I got Rosemary's in the split."

"What'd you have to give up for it? When I ended things with my fiancé, I made a bad deal, trading most everything for, I don't know, some kind of freedom?"

"I was considered the bad guy, so I gave up a lot of our friends."

"Join the club. I was socially radioactive for dumping Sebastian like I did."

"Sebastian." Madeline's eyebrows crept up toward her hairline, compressing a yellow-green bruise and faint abrasions.

"For a while, I convinced myself my cold feet were because he assumed I would change my name, like it wasn't a question at all. Mind you, it was hardly a farfetched idea, seeing as how it caused me no end of trouble growing up. Doolittle." She muscled the edge of her fork into her chicken cutlet. "I should've jumped at the opportunity to change it."

"I like your name, but when I give updates to Joe on the project, I call you Zoe Do-Lots."

She tried to hide her pleasure at that. "Well, anyway, coming out at twenty-five is...uncomfortable. For years, I'd been easy around attractive women, but then I felt myself ogling." She felt heat rise under her collarbones and cleared her throat. "Anyway. When did you come out?"

"I was fourteen." Madeline lost the small smile Zoe had succeeded in drawing out of her.

"No shit."

She nodded and toyed with what remained of her dinner. "No shit, indeed."

"The guys in school had horror stories. Being an art fag has to be the absolute worst in a normal high school. At least artsy girls get to be eccentric, smoke cigarettes, and wear paint-smeared overalls. You might not get many dates, but people generally steer clear more than harass."

"You paint?"

Zoe wanted to avoid answering that question in any serious way, but she was also desperate for Madeline to know her. "I used to, yeah. Pretty seriously. But, hey, breakups and high school abuse and discarded dreams? I mean, really. Shouldn't I be trying to cheer you up?" She popped a bite of chicken in her mouth.

"Why did you discard your dreams?"

She wished for an equally uncomfortable question to fire back at Madeline, one designed to shut down anything remotely like this line of conversation. Why did the universe work like this—picking a sore spot and hammering on it from every unexpected direction? Yes, she wasn't painting. Enough already. She chewed slowly, buying time.

Madeline said, "I ask because I think my brother did the same thing. He's a musician, had a band and a couple albums, then he

gave it all up and moved here right after our dad died. A year ago."
She impaled some macaroni. "Today."

Could this visit get any more fraught? "I'm really sorry."

"Ethan's had a hard time, not that he'll admit it. Isn't that the
thing with anger? It's so pure and hot that it doesn't leave room
for anything else."

"Is that why he's not here? He's angry?"

Madeline set down her pasta-laden fork and ran fingers along
her eyebrows and down the bridge of her nose. "No. I am."

"Were you close with your dad? Aren't dads generally easier
than moms? Or they're distant, which at least removes direct
confrontation from the menu."

"He was...I loved him. He hated that I was gay. He hated that I
was *open* about being gay. But we'd gotten closer. After Jane left
me, I guess. Ethan thinks it's a badge of honor to treat the man
like the devil on my behalf, but he doesn't know what he's doing.
Nothing's as black and white as he thinks. He claims he's taking a
page from my playbook, but how can he think that this is the right
time to get stubborn and insistent with me? *Now* he wants to tell
me how to run my life? Judge me?"

The farther each sentence got from where Madeline had started,
the louder it became, and Zoe found herself leaning away, making
herself as small and inconspicuous as possible. The hard frame
of the armchair pressed into her side, and she was gathering
gumption to say something, anything, when Madeline's cell phone
rang.

"Christ on a motherfucking crutch." Madeline glanced at her
phone where it rested within easy reach on the arm of the couch
and picked it up. "Joe." After a moment, she said, "Stop. Just stop.
Don't you get it? This isn't about you!" After another pause, she
shouted, "Joe. Please! Leave me alone!" The exclamation ended in
a groan, and she dropped the phone and hugged herself, her eyes
closed, her forehead growing shiny with sweat.

Zoe was in so far over her head that all she could do was hold
her breath and stay very still.

Madeline's grip on herself loosened. "I'm sorry," she whispered before opening her eyes. "I appreciate your coming by, but I think you should go."

Zoe couldn't quite bring herself to move. Madeline's eyes were glassy and bloodshot. Those tissues scattered around were not for a cold or allergies.

"I can't seem to stop these outbursts. It's like all the years I've been calm and accommodating have backed up on me, and I can't swallow it anymore." Her voice grew strident again, and she closed her mouth tightly, sniffing in a breath. "Sorry."

"You've got a lot to deal with."

Madeline leaned forward crookedly, her arm straight against the couch, propping her up. Her sweatshirt, the Harvard lettering worn through in places, swung loosely in front of her chest. Her posture and unwavering gaze made her look both poised for flight and reluctant to let either of them escape. She said, "I wasn't in an accident."

Zoe found enough volition over her muscles to put her fork down. "What happened?"

Madeline swore. "I shouldn't have said that. See? My moral compass works fine," she said to the ceiling before moving to stand but dropping back onto the couch with a whoof. "You should go. I mean it. You should go."

"I—"

"I'm not who you think I am," she said loudly.

"I don't think you're anything," Zoe lied. "Someone needs to be here."

"Probably. But not you." She covered the bottom of her face with her hand. "The locks are changed. I'm safe. You should leave." The words were muffled by her fingers.

"I don't want to," Zoe said, though she kind of did.

"I can't feel helpless like this right now. I just can't. *Please.*"

What was she supposed to do? Stage a sit-in? Stay parked in this uncomfortable chair against Madeline's will—no matter how misguided?

UPENDED

Zoe set her dinner on the coffee table and walked to the door, the area rug squishy under her suede wingtips. She had her hand on the knob when she saw the straight-backed chair that had originally tripped her up. Madeline wasn't thinking clearly, and she should definitely stay, but the two of them weren't anything to each other, not by the largest stretch of the imagination, so she opened the door and stepped out into the hall.

When she turned back around, Madeline's hands covered her face. Zoe whispered her name, but Madeline said, "Go."

"You have my number," Zoe said and closed the door. But she stood there, her ear close to the seam between the solid wood and the varnished jamb, and after a while, she heard the creak of crutches coming closer. Then, finally, the sound she'd suspected would follow: that wayward chair being jammed under the knob.

What was she supposed to do? Break down this now-fortified door? Find the brother, Ethan, and tell him to take care of his sister, mourn their father together? Madeline was right. No matter how it might have felt for a moment, Zoe didn't know her at all, didn't even know what she was so afraid of.

The thought of going home to Troy was far from a salve to this biting reality. After talk of breakups and bargains, her life with him amounted to another abject failure. The two of them were a farce, albeit a comfortable (though increasingly stifling) one, but Bernard Collins and this conversation and her inability to do anything for Madeline made her sensitive to the smallest wrongness in her life, and it itched and ached while she made her slow way down the musty, poorly lit stairs.

CHAPTER 13

Joe squeezed the blue stress ball Beth had forced on him after he'd cracked a molar from grinding his teeth. He'd used it fitfully over the last year, but after this soulless week without Madeline, his left hand was redolent of rubber, and its fingers twinged with nascent cramps. His other hand clamped his phone against his ear while he negotiated (pleaded) with Clive over at Grasshopper. "I've told you before, I'm sure, but remember that cost and scope are flexible. We could do a pilot with one of your teams to prove the benefits to you." Squeeze, squeeze, squeeze.

Clive rambled on about how they were interested but didn't have the bandwidth, that everyone there was asked to do too much with too little already these days. But how busy could they be if he had time to say no at such length?

Joe said, "Believe me, we're in the same boat here, but we've seen a minimal time investment have a remarkable effect on productivity, quality, and, most importantly, employee satisfaction. I've been hearing horror stories about how hard it is to find qualified technical hires. It would be an investment in your business." Squeeeeze.

UPENDED

Clive wasn't listening. He talked about being a start-up as if Joe had no clue what that was like, which was a joke that flew in the face of their decade of mutual regard.

Joe strangled his emotions like the rubber ball. "I can't say I'm not disappointed. I still see this as a great opportunity for both of us, so expect a call from me next quarter to check in."

After they hung up, Joe slammed his stress ball onto his desk with a satisfying bang and swore, channeling Madeline. Trash talking was the closest he could get to her these days. Ever since that irresponsible brother of hers had taken her away, she had refused to talk to him—not counting her outburst the night before. She'd practically singed his ear hair off when he'd just been trying to offer condolences on the anniversary of her father's death (and, yes, find out how she was). He tried not to take it personally, but everything about Madeline felt personal these days.

He swiveled around so his back was to his desk and pumped the stress ball, watching tendons rise under the thin, pale skin of his wrist. If it were a year ago—three months, even—Madeline would have the just-right thing to say about Clive, something like, "Well, that rat bastard's off our holiday card list, but he won't resist forever. If you could convince me to join you—"

"I could convince the Pope to go Jewish."

"Or a vegan to eat bacon and eggs."

"Or Katie to like broccoli."

"Or Ethan to shave his beard."

The worst of it was that she was up there alone. Ethan had called him not twenty-four hours after he'd spirited Madeline away, saying that she had forced him to leave, screaming at him until he'd thought a neighbor might call the cops. Joe had spent that evening and the next camped out in his car in front of her building, keeping an eye out in the quiet glow of dim streetlights and his laptop screen.

He gave the stress ball a rest and was gazing out the window without seeing the uninspiring alley view when a knock on his door made him jump and look over his shoulder. Bridget stood in the doorway. "Sorry. I thought you heard me come in."

"What're you doing here?"

"Well. Hello to you, too."

He pinched the bridge of his nose. "I meant I wouldn't put it past myself to forget if we had an appointment these days."

Bridget sat down without waiting for an invitation. Her blouse was open to midway down her chest but starched stiff, which made for a compelling juxtaposition he'd seen on Madeline before. "No appointment, but Katie begged me to bring you something since she didn't get to see you last weekend." She dipped into her briefcase and produced a thin sheaf of paper. "It's a drawing and quasi book report about that series she's devouring, and she wanted you and Madeline to have it. I'm beginning to think she considers you two an item." She smiled without showing her teeth—exactly the opposite of Madeline.

"Fantastic. Wonderful." Joe layered on the sarcasm and took the offered papers.

"Oh, it's fine. You know little girls: hearts and rainbows everywhere. How *is* Madeline by the way?"

"She's...Katie's not right about us, you know. We're business partners and good friends. Besides, you're well aware that she's a lesbian."

"Sure, sure. But what does Katie know? Madeline's affectionate, and that's what she notices. Anyway, my secretary tells me everything's gone fluid these days."

"Not Madeline."

"This is just Katie's overactive imagination. Don't take it seriously." She looked pointedly at Joe's hand, which was working at the stress ball again. "What's wrong?"

He put the ball aside with as much reluctance as the last cigarette he'd stubbed out ten years before. "We lost the Grasshopper contract." Even airing this particular piece of bad news was better than talking about Madeline.

UPENDED

"Ah, I'm sorry. You were really counting on that one, weren't you?"

"It would've been helpful, but we'll survive."

Her head dipped to the right then returned to center, a tic Joe had witnessed countless times, and he would bet her hands were sliding down her slacks from midthigh to knee. Sometimes he wished he didn't know her so well. He waited for her to articulate whatever it was she'd decided. Finally, she said, "I can always put you in touch with people at the firm. IT, finance, library services—all those back-office departments are as wildly dysfunctional as the practice groups but more open to change."

She'd offered this before, but even after closing their joint checking account and selling shared property, they were already too impossibly entangled for Joe to consider it. Madeline wouldn't be pleased with his passing over this potential opportunity, but she wasn't here.

"No thanks, but let me ask you something. Your IP attorneys probably deal with venture capitalists, right?"

"Somewhat, sure. Why?"

He explained his latest idea, which had come to him after Madeline had accosted him over the phone the night before. He'd sat at this desk, despondent and heavy, desperate for something to rock him out of this rut of failure. Madeline needed help, and so did the company, which was a hard thing to admit. Not just any help but money. And who had money and loved software products with fat subscription fees? Venture capitalists, that's who. With a small amount of outside investment, it wouldn't matter that they'd lost these contracts and that Madeline was on the bench. They could focus on finishing the Mindful Management app, lining up early adopters, and designing a marketing blitz. With enough money, Madeline could even do some of the pro bono consulting for nonprofits she'd been talking about wistfully for months.

After Joe gave the full pitch to Bridget, she sat back, crossed her legs with a soft swish of fabric, and hummed. "You really needed that contract, huh?"

"Can you put me in touch with someone or not?"

"I didn't mean what you think I meant, and you know it. I'd be happy to ask around and see what I can find out."

He planted his hands on the desk. "Being flexible isn't failure."

She sat back. "Joe. I'm completely on your side. Even when I'm blunt. *Especially* when I'm blunt. When did you forget that?"

He rubbed the rough stubble on his cheeks and chin. "I'm under a lot of pressure. And you know your 'bluntness' was always a problem."

"You and Madeline are a much better match than we were." She pressed her lips together and released them with an apologetic pop. "That was the wrong thing to say. Or at least the wrong way to say it. You're good partners. You complement each other."

"Can we...can you just let me know if anyone at your firm has a contact who might be interested? If it's too much trouble, don't give it a second thought."

"I think it's a good idea. Maybe a bit of a long shot, but it's great that you're looking at other options. Most people refuse to change direction when they get to a roadblock."

"The original plan isn't dead yet."

She blinked, long, slow, and deliberate. "You're not going to take anything I say in a good light, are you?"

He dropped his arms in defeat. "It appears not."

"Fine." She checked her watch and got up. "I need to run, anyway. Darrin's got a call soon, and he asked me to keep Katie occupied."

"This late? Someone on the West Coast?"

"Yeah, a company in Palo Alto that wants his advice or a referral or something. He's being a bit vague about it. It's probably a huge waste of his time, which is already in short supply." She walked to the door, her briefcase swinging. "Give Madeline my regards. I hope to see her up and about soon. And try to get some rest. You look exhausted."

"I'll call Katie before she goes to bed."

UPENDED

When Bridget was gone, Joe spun the stress ball around a few times and fought the urge to call Madeline again. He couldn't believe (despite loud evidence) that she was still angry at him. Prior to the showdown at his apartment, he would have sworn he would never bear the brunt of her occasional temper, but the attack and now this radio silence made him question everything.

Squeeze. Squeeze. Squeeze.

The more he thought about raising funding, the more he was convinced it was the just-right way out of their tight spot. Madeline would push back, citing horror stories of investors coming in and whittling companies down into their vanilla blueprint of success, snuffing out all the unique cowlicks and character along the way.

"Growth isn't everything. It's not even close to the most important thing," she'd say.

But nothing was more important than survival. He had enough money in his personal account to go for a few months without drawing a salary, which might be just the cushion they needed to get them through this rough spot, but they desperately required a long-term solution to survive, then stabilize, then flourish.

Before calling it quits for the night, he removed Madeline's access from their banking site and accounting software. He was going to have to do some unorthodox things with money, and he didn't want her to stumble across it without an explanation. She generally left their finances up to Joe and their accountant, but assuming she wasn't lying lifeless in her apartment (how could he even imagine that?), who knew what she'd be driven to do out of boredom or desperation? The only way he could drive this plan to success was to have no questions, no doubts. He had to believe that everything would come together. Believe it would all work out in the end.

CHAPTER 14

ETHAN HAD MESSED UP SO MANY TIMES THAT, WHEN TAKEN together, his mistakes flowed in an indistinguishable stream the length and breadth of his life. But letting Maddy bully him out of her apartment was such a mountain of a screw-up that it overshadowed everything else. She'd gotten red-faced and verbally violent when he'd broached the topic of fixing her story with the police (a bone he admittedly couldn't stop picking), but instead of rising to the unfortunate occasion as he'd done, he should've backed down and taken care of her.

For the seven nights since, Ethan had suffered through the same iffy relationship with sleep as Maddy, lying awake for hours after being disturbed from his slumber by the least disturbing things: the patter of shower water, the refrigerator door's gentle slap, the creak of someone walking upstairs. He didn't need a shrink to tell him the psychic root of this insomnia: guilt, pure and simple. Well, that and the cringing certainty that Joe had to consider him a fuckup of the absolute highest order after seeing how he'd left Maddy. He hadn't even put groceries on the shelves, not that it was Joe's place to judge. Joe wasn't family. Far from it.

UPENDED

This morning, he was up at the ungodly hour of 6:30, a time he hadn't witnessed since senior year in high school and two-a-day football practices. He lay on his back on his futon—a deluxe model with layers of foam inside the cotton batting—and tried to coax his eyes closed again. But they kept popping open to snapshots of his Spartan but still messy room: cinderblock shelves holding a small amp and tangle of cables, his TV, and a shot glass collection that felt both juvenile and necessary; a pile of dirty clothes in a corner; a poster from one of his old bands' concerts.

For a while, he occupied himself by tracing his roommates' stumbling progressions through their morning routines, but then, in order to escape the reverberating quiet of the apartment after they left, he cozied his ears inside the leather cups of his headphones and tried to let himself be taken by music. Anything to escape the reality of the Maddy who had gone a little mad, of his father's deathiversary, of his echoing, ineffectual aloneness, even of Nettie, whose constant inquiries into his sister's recovery hinted at an unvoiced distrust of his vague answers and the regular, even excessive, hours he put in at Fuel.

Despite the music, he couldn't stop replaying the last stupid crescendo of his fight with Maddy—about their father, of course, and Maddy's refusal to give up her claim that she didn't hate the man.

"Love doesn't depend on liking everything about the other person. There are plenty of things about you that drive me crazy."

"As if you're perfect."

"I never said that. I'm just—"

"I know what you're saying, and I'm calling bullshit on it. The man effectively wanted you to be miserable. Him not liking the dyke in you isn't nearly the same as you not liking how I'm twelve credits short of my degree."

"Believe me, that's the least of my problems with you."

"You know what I mean!" he shouted.

"There are other things in me more important than being gay. That doesn't define me. It's not even in the top five. Dad knew

124

that. He knew I wanted to make my mark some other way, and he supported that."

"He liked your insane start-up because it kept you too busy to even *be* gay."

"What do you know about it?" Her face and neck were splotchy with rising anger, and she wrapped her arms around her chest and closed her eyes before opening them to glare at him and yell, "You don't know the first goddamned thing." And she was right.

He turned the music up a notch and dug in. Kris Drever, M G Boulter, The Civil Wars. He listened to one album after another, finally abandoning himself to lyrics, chord progressions, harmonies, counterpoints. He felt the music fill up his flabby cells. One recording he listened to was of such excellent quality—particular yet resonant—it felt as if he were playing the notes himself. When he closed his eyes, his small room and dirty laundry fell away, and even Maddy's madness was muted. The song's chords settled in his left hand, his breathing synchronized with phrases, and his throat tightened and relaxed along with the melody.

He listened to this music with an intensity he hadn't had since the band broke up—and his father died. Even though the two weren't as related as Maddy liked to think, she was right that things were more complicated between both of them and their father than Ethan cared to admit. The old man's death had done something to Ethan, turned him too heavy to move and yet empty at the same time. He'd felt robbed of the same something essential his mother's death had knocked out of him several years before. But right now, one year and six days later, he was somehow plugged into the current moment enough to hear absolutely everything in this music: a masterful phrase, the smallest touch of percussion, an off-beat hesitation so perfect his heart crept into his throat, and he thought how stupid it was that he wasn't writing lyrics or sitting at a piano, banging keys into a wall of sound his acoustic guitar couldn't touch.

UPENDED

He hadn't always been useless. He'd pulled the band together in the first place, not to mention had written the majority of their songs. He booked gigs and got them on the local radio. Hell, he used to be someone Danika Miller would have known, not some schlub to pass over when cruising for an opening act. But now? He was tits on a bull, good for nothing except being Maddy's mute grilled cheese buddy. Because wasn't that all she'd ever wanted? The minute he disagreed with her in any meaningful way, she had no use for him. Okay, sure, hounding her about their father or her lie to the police probably wasn't the best path to her affection, but couldn't she see that all he wanted was for the bastard to be caught so she could become herself again—even if that left him sole heir to the title of Number One Sawyer Family Disaster?

For the next three hours, he played his guitar hard and fast, then slow and meticulous, exercising joints and tendons and calluses, loosening up his voice, which was rusty but not half bad, and remembering who he'd been before these last few weeks, before all this time in Boston, before his father died and made so much seem suddenly beside the point.

For better or worse, being away from Maddy made him remember the time between when she'd left Arizona for Harvard and when she'd shown up with Sister Jane in tow. He'd effectively been an only child for those seven years and had been close, in a chummy guy way, with his father: sports and oil changes and evicting a family of jackrabbits from under their house. The man was far from a prince—had dismissed Ethan's music as a fruitless distraction—but when Jane had shown up...Ethan had been instrumental in making things go to hell with his father when he'd taken Maddy's side in a big, big way. Bigger than even she had.

When he was done playing, electricity sparked along each arm from elbow to fingertips, and he felt so good he was on the verge of throwing down some push-ups and vowing to eat salad for lunch, not to mention passing on the day-old pastries at work. But then, when he reached for his phone out of blind habit to call Maddy and tell her about this turn of events, the delicious fog of music cleared from his brain. He put his cell down without dialing, not wanting to fight with her, which they surely would.

In the shower, a surplus of negative ions made him eloquent and convincing when formulating arguments he could use on his sister, inspiring, air-tight words that would no doubt convince her that she didn't have to be afraid of the douchebag who'd almost raped her, that the man was nothing more than a weak degenerate who would never touch her again after having failed to achieve his original objective in such an embarrassing way. She would understand that if she just gave the police the right leads, they would catch the perp and put him away for good, and she'd be safe, no doubt about it. Besides, she was impeding an investigation, and didn't that carry some kind of penalty? But outside the shower, his brilliance would fade, and when face-to-bruised-face with her, his arguments would crumble under her withering glare, seething anger, and irrational but mighty fear.

He had just enough time before his shift at Fuel to stop at the diner for a burger and fries (that salad idea had been delusional), so he parked himself on a stool at the counter with his back to the row of booths he and Maddy usually sat in and ate with one hand while jotting down lyrics in a ratty pocket notepad. With the band, he'd written ballads and anthems about love and choices and manly, hairy-chested broken hearts, but he'd always thrown in at least a little hope. It had been a trademark of his underlying feel-good vibe. Today, though, he wrote about Maddy, and it was terrible gloom and doom and violence.

He dragged his last steak fries through ketchup and burger drippings, leaving his chunky white plate looking like a crime scene. That, combined with the darkness of his writing, scared him into slapping the notebook closed. When he looked up, Darla stood opposite him with the check.

"Where's that sister of yours?"

"Indisposed." He tucked his notebook in a pocket and glanced at the time on his phone. Fuel and Nettie awaited, which would've been a pleasant thought if she would refrain from asking about

Maddy. Or dump her Neanderthal boyfriend, who seemed to call expressly to criticize her once a week. Ethan wasn't unreasonable—one or the other would be fine.

Darla said, "You've missed two breakfasts."

"Aw, hey, I didn't know you cared."

"Not so much about you, but Madeline's a doll."

He pushed his plate away. "Yeah, yeah. I've heard that before. But, believe me, she can be a real pain in the ass. You know"—he plucked the check from between Darla's fingers—"I used to have my shit together. She likes to forget that."

"I have an older brother who lives off superiority like you seem to survive on grease."

Ethan dug in his pocket for his wallet. "Any advice from a fellow younger sibling?"

"I only serve food, not advice. But since you asked, I'd lose the hair."

"The beard, you mean?"

She motioned around his whole head. "All of it. Who knows? You might be good-looking under that scruff."

"Unfortunately, not so much." He fished out a twenty and handed it to her with the check. While she went to get his change, he called Maddy.

She started apologizing as soon as she answered, going on about how she shouldn't have driven him away, how she was an emotional wreck, which made him feel like shit. She bulldozed him with her words, and the more she talked about needing his company, craving his quiet presence, saying things about him "not doing anything, just being there," the more uncomfortable he got.

He said, "I know I should suck it up and lay down for you like the person I've always been, but I can't. Maybe I don't understand, at least not completely, but I understand enough to know when I'm right and you're wrong."

He heard a rustle of breath, then, "We need to agree to disagree."

"I can't do that."

"Ethan, please."

When was the last time he'd said no to her? Was anyone able to do that without feeling this squirming wrongness? Maybe Sister Jane, who had kicked Maddy like a bad habit. "I'm not being an asshole, okay? I'm not. You just— Hey. Let's make a deal. You tell the cops, and I'll shave my beard."

She didn't even laugh, which felt horrible but was maybe actually a good thing, considering he was serious. "I'll think about it."

"Think hard, as usual. Maybe I'll come by Joe's tomorrow to visit, okay?"

"I'm not at Joe's."

He got cold, clammy. "But you were, right? I mean, I called him after—"

She was quiet.

"What's wrong with you? You need help."

"I needed to be alone."

"What're you talking about? You hate being alone!"

"I know!"

"Then what the hell are you doing? Who are you? Because I don't know anymore."

"I don't know, either! Everything I feel is wrong, but I can't stop feeling it. It's like the attack broke open something in me, and now everything's a problem. *Everything*," she said so loudly he was forced to put space between his ear and the phone. "I know you think telling the truth is going to magically solve my problems, and it sounds so much like something I would have thought *before* that I want to believe you, but I just don't."

"Don't get mad, okay? But maybe you're overthinking this a little bit. A smidge. A hair. Half a hair."

Nothing.

"Are you mad?"

Nothing.

He made his tone light when he said, "So, what do you say? The beard for coming clean?"

"I said I'll think about it." She hung up.

129

UPENDED

He ran his hand over his whiskers and through his admittedly shaggy hair. What was he supposed to do now?

CHAPTER 15

A WEEK AND A HALF AFTER SO DRAMATICALLY SHOWING ZOE THE door, Madeline woke from a snippet of nightmare and couldn't fall back to sleep. The room breathed with gray light, the street lamp's glow patterning the wall opposite her with stripes from her blinds. It was too bright to be dark and too dark to read, and this good-for-nothing atmosphere echoed the impossibility of comfort. She shifted her unwieldy body around, trying to find a position that would allow her to relax her back and hips and shoulders, but her back and hips and shoulders weren't the real problem.

She felt insane. Certifiable. Her mind was an unruly, alien force resistant to reason or soothing. It whispered nonsense about the malevolent motives of those closest to her, which made her question her own murky, suspect decisions. How much of this internal misery was created by her own hand? How much worse had she managed to make the damage her attacker had already done?

She was hiding out, but there was no escaping herself. She'd never been able to do that, had only succeeded in burying what she didn't want to face under an avalanche of outside stimulation.

But now here she was, rejecting the world—more specifically anyone who cared about her, because they might have something to say about the attack or her current behavior or, even worse, who she had been (or who they thought she'd been) *before*.

Before belonged to another life—one that now felt equally charmed and misguided. Before taunted her with might-have-beens and mistakes, but after that conversation with Zoe, she couldn't keep herself from reliving the ancient history of her coming out. She'd suffered through months of relentless consideration and doubt and deep but surreptitious reading before being able to put the right words to her particular brand of otherness. But once she felt that vocabulary settle in her as an undeniable truth, she understood that knowing herself was only the first step. What good was a resonant self-truth if other people harbored an idea of her that was a lie?

Despite the potential consequences she'd read about, she braced herself and proclaimed the defining, unmistakable words into a muted moment during a family dinner. The quiet deepened, compounded by a sudden stillness—except for Ethan, who was occupied with corralling his peas. After a paralyzed moment, her mom said, "You're far too young to know..." But long ago, Madeline had elected herself to the role of unofficial third parent to Ethan, and she'd been more adult than child for years.

Her father put down his knife and fork and wiped his mouth with a napkin that made a faint rasping against his mustache. "I hope you're wrong, I really do. I hope you'll consider not being stubborn about this idea. It's a disruption. A burden. But if you end up sure, you'd be smart to keep it to yourself."

"It's the truth."

"I don't care if it's the word of God." His words were clipped and a little too loud.

At this altered tone of the conversation, Ethan glanced up from his plate at Madeline, then at their father, then at Madeline again. Just when it seemed like he was going to say something, their mother excused him from the table, which must've felt like a minor miracle since all that was left on his plate were vegetables.

When he was gone, Madeline asked, "You want me to lie?"

"What I *want* is for you to give up on the idea, but what I *said* was that you should keep your lips buttoned. Inviting other people into this business is just asking for trouble." The worst part was how calmly reasonable he sounded despite the irritation Madeline read in the way he picked up his water glass but put it down without drinking from it.

"I'm not going to lie." She tried to match the steadiness in his voice, but it trembled like the fingers she held curled into fists in her lap.

He said, "You're a smart girl, and you should act like it. I don't want to hear about this again." He got up and left the room.

Her mother watched him go. "He's right. It'll be better if you don't tell anyone else. It may not be the way you want things to be, but it's how they are. Understanding that is part of intelligence. It's part of being an adult."

But Madeline rejected that completely and insisted on being known, understood, transparent, living with nothing up her sleeves. This defiance was what made it imperative to take Jane back to Arizona once their infatuation had given way to a deep but everyday love. If her father witnessed the solid realness of what they had together, maybe he'd finally acknowledge all of her, not just the parts he approved of.

But, of course, he didn't. He greeted Jane with a handshake and the minimum set of questions that would qualify as polite, but he adamantly didn't treat them as a couple, never once turning the conversation to their life together—even going as far as excusing himself from the room in an obvious, pointed way when such allusions came up.

The morning after they arrived, when Jane left the house for an early run to beat the heat, Madeline padded down to the kitchen in search of coffee. She found her father at the table in his traditional seat, wearing his regular weekend outfit of a polo shirt and shorts.

UPENDED

He had the paper open in front of him and a bowl of half-eaten bran cereal at his right elbow.

She was about to confront him when he smiled. "There's coffee in the pot. Grab a mug and have a seat. Have you seen this?" He pointed at an article in the paper about radical salary transparency. "I've been wondering what you think. Is it something that will go mainstream?"

"I...I don't know," she stuttered, the surprise of this massive non sequitur cracking the foundation of her hurt and anger. His interest in her intellect was always tantalizing, and despite her resolve to avenge Jane, she succumbed. "Compensation can be a complex issue. But I would tend to agree that a culture of secrecy around it can contribute to the kind of chronic inequality we see in pay between men and women or whites and minorities. Or even C-suite versus other employees."

"Do you think transparency alone will fix it?"

She leaned back against the Formica counter. "Anyone who's trying to sell an easy, one-step fix to something so complex is ignorant or misguided."

"What would you do?"

She made herself breakfast, using mugs and bowls and silverware taken from positions in cabinets and drawers as permanent as her father's seat at the table. In a small rebellion, she sat in Ethan's chair instead of her old one while she talked to her father about how biased salary negotiations were, how bonuses and other discretionary pay complicated equality, how psychology affected if people did or didn't compare their compensation. While he engaged with her, trading anecdotes and asking questions and valuing her insights from school and direct experience, she felt solid and real, and the aspect of herself he refused to recognize was small in the face of everything else.

But then Jane came back from her run, ending that closeness with her father, and Madeline hated the part of him that hated this part of her but loved the rest of him that loved the rest of her. Away from him, she was as radically transparent about herself as that tech company was about its salaries—MBA and lesbian and everything in between. As her mother might have said, she paraded her many sides right up through that TEDx talk and the resulting YouTube video, which Ethan had thrown at her during their interminable, far-ranging fight the morning after he'd sprung her from Joe's.

"You stood up there and outed yourself, which was one thing, but you dragged me right into it. Or dragged *your idea* of me into it, and you can't be wrong about me, now, can you? But your truth isn't always *the* truth, no matter how fucking compulsive you are about it."

He wasn't entirely wrong about that, and maybe he wasn't wrong when he claimed he didn't know her at all. How could Ethan know her when she baffled herself? She had always been so in control, so confident, so self-consistent, and now? She would laugh if it wouldn't spark an ache in her ribs.

But this morning, when the sun replaced the streetlights and she could read if she wanted to, even her addled mind recognized that cowering here wasn't sustainable. She dragged herself out of bed and scoured every square inch of her skin twice in a scalding shower, stopping only when the water lost its hot, antiseptic sting. After emerging, flushed and moist, she wiped fog from the medicine cabinet's mirror and examined herself.

Her broken nose had healed a few degrees off from normal, and it snagged her attention whenever she caught sight of it. It was reminder and souvenir, and she vacillated between wanting to rip it from her face and appreciating this undeniable, visible proof of her internal transformation. She blew dry her hair for the first time in more than a month and checked herself from every possible angle, searching for any hint of bruising. Some faint yellowing remained at her hairline, but concealer made quick work of it, and she applied the rest of her makeup on top of it with excessive care.

When she sat on her unmade bed to rest, she played her fingers over the curves of her ribs, pressing on the healing fractures, raising a fuzzy-edged ache that no longer caused her to gasp or seize into a tortured stillness. She whispered her client cover story to herself again (wet road, dark, caught in a multicar pileup), even though she'd practiced it a dozen times in front of the bathroom mirror, adding in all the right expressions—including an eye roll at her insurance company. It turned out she was, against all odds, a very good liar.

She perused her closet of suits but rejected them all; her skirts would expose her knee brace, while her slacks were too narrow to fit over it. After admitting to herself that she'd probably just hunker down in the office for the day, she opted for the polar opposite—her oldest, baggiest jeans that sighed with holes and a long-sleeved T-shirt she'd gotten as a gift from the Coop in Harvard Square for being such a profligate customer.

With her briefcase slung across her chest and crutches wedged in her armpits, her full-length mirror showed an image of herself as off-kilter as her new nose, a strange woman hurled up out of the hectic flow of her life-as-it-had-been to a gut-clenching perspective she'd give anything to be rid of. But she couldn't be rid of it, not now that she'd seen it. Denying it would be a bigger lie than what she'd told the police.

Nearly an hour later, after removing the straight-backed chair from under the door handle, picking her way down the stairs, finding a position in her car that would allow her to drive, fighting traffic, struggling back out of the car, and lurching the block from the parking lot to the office, she backed her way through a wood-and-frosted glass door bearing the Mindful Management logo and right into Joe and Beth, who were hunched over the reception desk's monitor.

"Oh, hey," she said. "What're you guys looking at?"

"Madeline!" Beth stood up so fast she almost knocked Joe over. She sported a gray pinstriped skirt and white blouse, and Madeline wished she'd decided to wear a suit. Wool armor. "Where have you been? We were worried," Beth said before blurting out a high, tight laugh. "Duh. Understatement."

Joe stood with his hands in the pockets of his slacks, quiet and still, and Madeline moved away from the door just enough to let it close behind her. "I should've called, I know."

"Don't get me wrong. I'm not criticizing. Far from it. Just this past Friday, I was telling Joe that a character in my book—" She stopped, rolled her lips between her teeth, and tugged at each sleeve of her blouse. "Anyway. Here you are!"

"You told him about the book?"

"It was nothing. Listen, you look great."

Madeline brushed hair from her face while trying to come up with something to say that might vault them past this stuttering awkwardness. This was not how coming here was supposed to go, not at all. It was supposed to be warm, familiar. It was supposed to be a haven of sanity and peace complete with neutral tones and the greased movement of business as usual. She said, "I caught up on some of my emails already, but maybe you guys could help me get a handle on the details?"

In a voice half an octave higher than usual, Beth said, "Absolutely. Conference room or your office? Do you want coffee? We have those granola bars you like."

"How about a shot of whiskey?" Madeline joked, but no one laughed. "Okay. My office?" She crutched across the brown carpet she'd walked over a thousand times before, only now noticing its nauseating psychedelic pattern. When she pushed open the mostly closed door to her space, she froze at the mess inside—a somewhat less desperate version of her apartment—and it all came back to her: working that night, the toppled piles of shit still strewn about as if this were a sealed crime scene, how she'd thought of Jane despite herself, Madeline Mismanagement. "What the fuck is wrong with me?" she whispered before realizing Joe had followed her close enough to be within earshot.

"Let me clear a path," he said. "Just a minute."

While he bulldozed through the disarray, she suffered the prickly feeling of Beth hovering behind her. She'd made it out of her apartment and across town only to have her cosmic disorientation follow her. Disorientation. What a pale approximation of the right word, but how else could she describe the certainty that nothing would ever be the same—not her nor the world she moved around in?

Joe backtracked through the swath he'd made and gathered her in a trembling hug. "Don't cut me out like that again," he said close to her ear. Even after he opened up some space between them, he gripped her arms and examined each of her eyes in turn. Her insides shriveled away from her skin under his scrutiny.

When he let her go, she released a pent-up breath and made her way into the office, dropping into her chair with an involuntary groan of relief and residual pain. Joe closed the door and sat across the desk from her but fidgeted instead of settling in, straightening a stack of paper, crossing his arms with a soft, starchy sound she knew so well, but then uncrossing them right away. He scooted forward to rest his hands on her desk, his fingers entwined, his watch reflecting the overhead light. When he dragged his gaze to her face, she had to remind herself that any bruises were hidden under concealer. "How are you?" he asked.

Then, on top of everything else: a wave of crippling shame. "You got my text, right?"

"You mean the one that said, 'Stop calling me. I need some time alone'? That one?"

"I just—"

"The one from over a week ago? That you sent when I was ringing the bell to your apartment?"

"I'm sorry. I am. I just couldn't—"

He got the tight, stern expression she'd seen him wear while disciplining Katie, his eyebrows crowding his eyes, his chin playing the role of an accusatory finger. "You know what? That's not good enough. You can't just *do* that, Madeline, turn your back on me. On the *company*. That's not how this works."

"What do you want me to say besides I'm sorry? Tell me, and I'll say it. What will make you believe me?"

He pounded his fist once on the desk, then got up and made a circuit of the room, keeping his face from Madeline like the dark side of the moon. He stopped with his back against the closed door, his head hanging down, his shoulders sagging. "Tell me...are you okay?"

"Yes. I just needed some time to adjust." Even she didn't know what that meant—adjust to what?—but the gulf between those words and the muddled truth (she was too scared, too ashamed, too angry at herself and everyone else) made it almost easy to say. Adjust? Far from it.

Joe's head bobbed up and down a few times, and he peeled himself from the door and sat across from her again. His face had lost most of its pinched tightness. "Your bruising's gone. How are the ribs and your knee? Have you been to the doctor?"

She would have fled at his concern if she were physically able—and if it didn't feel so good to be sitting down after her crosstown journey. "Could we just work like nothing happened? I've been locked in my head with my own shit for way too long. I'd be crazy grateful to think about other people's problems for a minute, okay?" After he nodded, she said, "I didn't see anything in my email about Grasshopper, which seemed like a bad sign."

"You must not have been copied on the latest exchanges. They haven't signed yet, but we're dotting the i's and crossing the t's." He directed the words somewhere over her left shoulder. "They probably can't schedule the bulk of the work until later in the summer, but that's perfect because they're interested in being guinea pigs for our software-assisted approach. Mention automation to a tech company, and I guess this is what happens. Needless to say, we have to get the app done. Have you heard anything from IDK about the designs?"

She was flooded with the image of Zoe standing in her kitchen, washing dirty dishes, bearing witness to everything she'd dragged herself here to escape, but she told Joe merely that she had no news.

UPENDED

He said, "I need you to bring that home. I'm telling you, Grasshopper absolutely jumped at the idea, no pun intended, and it's not just about the potential cost savings. It's new and different, and having the app always available gives people more control over the process."

She flashed back to lying on Joe's couch, a helpless grub he and Beth hadn't known how to handle, and anger growled inside her like hunger. It was amorphous and useless—or at least inappropriate—but it blocked out everything else: the ache of her ribs, her chagrin at having driven Joe to such worry, the vast swathes of her life she'd been hiding out from. She bit her bottom lip with more force than necessary to temper her rage, then said, "More control sounds suspiciously like self-service, and we never agreed to that."

"I hear you, I do. This is Grasshopper spitballing. A trial is just that—we need to supervise their use, yes, but we also need to leave room for experimentation."

The old her would've fought against this change in strategy, but she swallowed her trepidation along with the paranoid suspicion that Joe was lying to her. "I can usher the development through, but Joe, I came here partly to tell you that I want to see clients. I'm *ready* to see clients, even with the crutches. I know exactly what to say about the leg and everything. I need to get out there, but it sounds like maybe you don't want me to?" Her desperation was sour at the back of her throat.

Joe reached over a pile of paper to grasp one of her hands in both of his. The move was so forceful she had to grit her teeth in order not to jerk away, but he didn't seem to notice her stiffen when he pulled her closer. "That's not what I mean. I want nothing more than for you to get back to client work. I know how much you love it, and Madeline, no matter how it might have seemed before, I'm under no impression that I hold any kind of final say in anything. We're partners, Madeline. *Partners.*"

Something about the passionate yet wishful way Joe said this, how he was constructing the pipe dream of her happiness over

140

a vaporous foundation, made Madeline recall the last gasp of her relationship with Jane, when she willed Jane to be satisfied in the same ultimately ineffective way. His grip on her hand was hot and viselike, and she wished she were home until she remembered how intensely she'd wished to be here. She said, "Okay. I'll work with Beth to put a couple client meetings on the calendar for Wednesday, and I'll get the software project moving today. I owe Zoe at IDK a call."

"Great," he said loudly and relinquished her hand. "This is incredibly exciting. We're poised right on the precipice of something tremendous. Now that you're back and ready to get at it again—I'm telling you. Chills. I'm convinced these last few years were just growing pains, a long runway perfecting our techniques just so we can take off." He made a matching upward motion with his hand, and his smile was wide and manic.

If this were the only strangeness of today, this month, this post-attack existence, she would feel no hesitation calling it out by reaching across the desk to check Joe's forehead for a fever. But everything felt twisted in some fundamental way, which meant it was she who was altered. She was the source of this madness, filtering everything through a nefarious lens that she could only hope would change focus in time.

CHAPTER 16

ZOE HAD IGNORED FOUR TEXTS FROM TROY IN THE LAST HALF hour. He'd always been a borderline fag-nag, but that tendency had hardened into habit after he'd hatched this marriage plan. Since her cousin's wedding, he'd been on her like white on rice, subjecting her to a constant, trickling pestering about lunch plans and shopping and going out with his fey friends. He kept saying he wanted to "talk," but every time she found herself alone with him, he dished gossip or snuggled with her on the couch in front of the TV like an adolescent boy too afraid to make a move.

But Troy's unsavory behavior wasn't the only reason she was avoiding him. After being expelled from Madeline's catastrophic apartment, her whole life felt like it had been thrown in a hot drier and had shrunk a size. The sight of Troy's name on her phone, his handsome face, the home they'd made—where her art supplies communed with dust bunnies under her lonely bed—sparked a seam-straining regret at everything she wasn't doing with her life. Even worse, it wasn't only Troy who induced this constriction; every time Kimberly called her, Zoe squirmed at conversations heavy with talk of the wedding, love, anxiety, excitement, and the insanity that was their mother.

Here was Troy again, calling her mere minutes before Madeline was arriving for a do-over of their aborted meeting. Zoe snatched up the phone—if only to keep him from calling again during the proceedings. "I can't talk. I'm still at work," she said and wondered how she was supposed to be professional with Madeline after what had gone down between them, what she'd seen, what Madeline had kept from her.

"Well, hello to you, too. I just wanted to know if you were coming home for dinner."

"I don't know."

"Are you going to Rosemary's?"

"Why, are you jealous of a sixty-year-old woman?"

"Ha-ha, you're too cute. Why don't I make something for us?"

Zoe swept her mouse in slow circles and watched the pointer move across her large, high-definition monitor. "What, a frozen pizza? Don't bother. I have a meeting soon that might take a while."

"Who are you meeting with at six at night?"

She imagined Troy in a tidy A-line dress, an apron tied around his skinny waist. "Do you need to get laid or something? You've been all up in my business for weeks."

"Is it Madeline?"

"Yes, it's Madeline, as a matter of fact, and if all goes well, we'll embark on a torrid affair, so don't wait up."

"We need to talk."

"So you've been saying. Just not now, okay?"

"So *you've* been saying." He mocked her uninterested tone.

She shoved her mouse away and reared back in her chair. "Troy, really. I love you, but you're not my mother, so you need to take it down a notch. We'll talk. Later." She rested her eyes on her print of Winslow Homer's *The Red Canoe*, which she'd always found the perfect combination of mellow and exhilarating, though tonight the canoe's titular color amplified her annoyance.

"Zoe, I think your uncle knows."

Though Troy wasn't effeminate, he could get dramatic with the best of them. Zoe sighed. "Knows what?"

"That we're not really together. That we're gay."

She grew cold and sat back up. "Why do you say that?"

"See? That's why I wanted to talk. But no, you said, not now. Later, Troy, later!"

"Why do you think Uncle Mike knows about us?" She spoke slowly, as if to a foreigner or a small child. Or a drama queen.

"Because at the wedding he said, 'I know all about you two,' totally sneaky and semidrunk."

"Are you bullshitting me?" she said in a screeching whisper, then groundhogged out of her partitioned space to see if anyone was around to hear. Luckily, the cube farm was as empty and still as high noon in the desert. She sank back down. "Why didn't you tell me then?"

"I thought that, maybe, if you'd just agree to get married..."

"That's not a solution." Zoe put a hand to the back of her neck under her shirt collar and squeezed. "What else did he say? Did he rub his nose when he said it? Because that means he's lying."

"How is getting married not a solution?"

"Troy, wake up. If he knows, he knows, and some fake marriage facade won't convince him otherwise."

"But it'll convince everyone else."

She shut her eyes. "Maybe them knowing wouldn't be as bad as we imagine."

"It'll be exactly as bad." He said this softly and with undramatic seriousness, and he was surely right.

Her monitor blinked with a reminder for her meeting. "I really can't talk about this now. When I get home, okay? I promise."

Zoe hung up and went out front with her laptop to wait for Madeline, but she couldn't move past that conversation. Mike was close enough to her in age to be more cousin than uncle, and while they'd been tight growing up, things had soured when she'd thwarted her parents' wishes (pursue something, *anything* practical) and enrolled at Mass Art. Mike had turned into a frustrated lawyer and a closet artist (he was pretty good with charcoal), and she could picture him smarming those words to Troy, could imagine him hoarding the knowledge for the right, worst opportunity.

She couldn't marry Troy. Not only was it a ludicrous idea that wouldn't even solve this problem, but these days she was swollen with unspecific, undirected desires. She craved a weighty satisfaction, the kind of thing that accompanied love or accomplishment or even the unredeemable failure of a large painting. She wanted to try hard at something dauntingly difficult.

From one of the gray, bean-shaped couches in the reception area, Zoe watched Madeline back her way through the glass door of the suite and thought: something difficult, indeed. The knobs of Madeline's knees were shadowed behind sagging holes in her jeans, the left one obscured by the black straps of a brace. Her hair drifted to her shoulders in soft curls, she had dark circles under her eyes, and the sleeves of her T-shirt were pushed to her elbows, bunching over her biceps like they were caught by the pads of her crutches.

Zoe scrambled to her feet, vexed at being so affected by the sight of Madeline that she'd failed at the most basic courtesy of holding the door open for her. "Hi," she said. "It's really good to see you."

"Thanks for agreeing to meet me so late."

"Of course. Absolutely. I was worried about you. I wanted to call, but—"

Madeline's chest rose and fell in a deep breath. "You were afraid I would treat you like I treated Joe on the phone."

"It was an effective deterrent, though it shouldn't have been."

"I'm sorry. For that whole night."

"You don't need to apologize—for that or anything else. I mean, in case you're so inclined." Zoe tucked her hands into her pockets and pressed her shins against the oblong coffee table in front of her. Both her shirt and pants were wrinkled this time; the universe seemed intent on not giving her proper notice for these encounters. She wanted to offer excuses for her appearance but managed to choke them back.

"That's usually the message I give to other people—especially women."

"I learned it from my first art teacher. 'Art needs no apology, Zoe, but so help me God, if you're late to another lesson...' Needless to say, I became bold and punctual."

"That's right, you're an artist. Discarded dreams." Her gaze was direct on Zoe, her face neatly made up and impassive.

The words landed with the force of a slap, but she made herself maintain eye contact with Madeline and pretend she didn't want to crawl under the nearest rock. "The conference room is this way, right around the corner."

"I didn't mean that. Not in that way, at least. I'm...will you let me apologize for that? It's been a long day, and—"

"Sure, of course. You probably need to sit down. Follow me."

Retrieving her laptop from the reception desk gave Zoe a welcome excuse to turn her back to Madeline. It was her own damn fault, taking every offhand comment so personally. Zoe led them into the conference room: The Fishbowl, they called this one, too big and decked out for just the two of them, full of monitors and whiteboards and enough soft leather seats for an army, and she felt stupid for trying to impress Madeline this way. She pulled out a chair for Madeline and set up opposite her.

Business, Zoe told herself. Stick to business. "We've got a lot to cover, so we should probably get started. You must be anxious to get home," she said before remembering the state of Madeline's apartment.

"Anxious isn't quite the word I'd use." Madeline settled into her chair with a grimace and soft groan and leaned her crutches against the table next to her. "But yes, let's get started."

Delving into work was initially a relief, but over the next hour, while Madeline maintained a total focus on the designs, tilting her head this way and that, nibbling at her thumbnail between bouts of note-taking, Zoe couldn't tame her own distraction. She kept stealing long glances at Madeline while she was otherwise occupied, Zoe's varied memories of Madeline layering on top of each other like oil paint on a reused canvas.

With her makeup and hair done, she looked remarkably like the Rosemary's Kitchen regular Zoe had admired across the vast acquaintance divide, but the stretched-out neck of her T-shirt kept evoking that night in Madeline's apartment, the night of the grand dismissal, and Zoe wondered yet again what had happened to her. Not an accident, she'd been clear, but what was the absence of accident if not intent, as another one of her mentors had taught her? Intent meant nothing remotely good in this case, just like there was nothing remotely good in Mike showing his hand to Troy.

When they'd covered the last of the material, Madeline asked, "Sergei over at Pinskey is okay with all this? Does he anticipate any problems in the final implementation?"

"They've approved it all. Is it true you guys give them management training?"

"On and off for the last couple years."

"Well, Sergei likes you, and he doesn't like anyone."

"What makes you say that?"

"When he talks about you, he sounds less like the Terminator than usual." Madeline's mouth softened into a half grin at that, and she settled her gaze on Zoe, who felt a surge of the same feverish confidence she'd experienced that night at Madeline's. "I shouldn't have left you like that."

Madeline closed her laptop and sat with her hands gripping its sides. "I don't recall giving you much choice."

"You said it wasn't an accident."

She scrunched up her face, and her knuckles whitened. "Can we...let's just leave the whole thing at my not being my best self that night."

"I hate that phrase. Are we supposed to walk around being our best selves day in and day out? What's 'best' about that?"

UPENDED

This came out way more forcefully than Zoe had intended, her insistence leaving her leaning over the table.

"Fine. I was well below average. Still am, if you want to know the truth. It's been a long day, and I left my medication at home, not that I want to go back— Hey, are you hungry? I'm hungry." She checked her watch, which was loose and so far up her wrist that it crowded her hand. "How about Rosemary's? You and me?"

What the hell was that? An hour of business-only freeze-out, then a dinner invitation? She wanted to be offended, but she was tempted to surrender, forget Troy waiting at home, and go have dinner—*with* Madeline, not just next to her. Instead, she asked, "Will you tell me what happened to you?"

"Forget what I said that night," Madeline said to the darkened monitor at the front of the room.

"I can't. You were scared, you needed someone there with you, and I shouldn't have left, no matter what you said." It was a fantasy that she could have resisted being railroaded out the door, but that was beside the point.

Madeline relinquished her laptop and rubbed the tip of a forefinger over the ragged nail of her thumb before meeting Zoe's gaze. Her eyes were glassy, but underneath that sheen, her gingerbread irises were soft and inviting, and Zoe, who had always made a point of not looking too directly at Madeline, didn't want to turn away. She wanted to have known Madeline in high school, befriended her when no one else would, kissed her behind the bleachers years and years before their moment at Club True.

Madeline tugged at the collar of her shirt. "It's been a really long day."

Zoe nodded but didn't budge. She didn't know where this wave of ballsiness came from, but she was going to ride it as long as it lasted.

Eventually, Madeline started to talk, but instead of a coherent story with a defined beginning, she came out with a number of seemingly disjointed comments about her ex and her office and, finally, her brother. "Ethan's right, I don't like being alone, and

I've been alone a long time even though I'm always with clients or Joe. So I went to the club, as an escape, and I danced with you, as an escape, and you kissed me…I really had had too much to drink. I wasn't lying. I didn't lie before, not intentionally, at least. And I took the T home even though it was late and I shouldn't have, but a car would have gotten me there too quickly. Then, a block from the train…"

She was looking right through Zoe, unblinking, her eyes wide. Zoe could see her pulse working in her neck and watched the top of her chest rise and fall with her breath. She thought Madeline was going to stop there and leave her hanging again, but after a long moment, Madeline went on, her voice low and husky, telling Zoe the horrible truth.

"He dragged me into an alley, called me—" She cut herself off and held her breath for a moment before going on. "He was going to…rape me, but he couldn't, you know, do it, and he freaked out about it. He was furious, totally lost it and beat me instead. Tried to kill me." She took a breath, held it, then said, in a low voice, "He called me a dyke. Again and again. Blamed me for—" She shuddered and winced, pressing the back of a closed fist against her mouth. Her eyes slowly focused on Zoe, and they sat in a quiet made thicker when the office ventilation system shut down. Zoe felt unequal to what had just gone down, but at the same time, she was saturated, vibrating, and she let this fullness guide her hand across the blond wood table between them until it settled on top of one of Madeline's.

She said, "I'm really sorry."

Madeline's shoulders jerked back, and she slipped her hand out from under Zoe's palm. "What am I doing?" The words were a thick, angry mumble. She pushed her laptop into her bag and got up with a hop, keys jangling in her pocket.

"Madeline."

"No." She slung her bag across her body, ducking under its strap, wincing when she pulled her arm through. "I can't believe I just did that. This is not your problem. *I'm* not your problem. My choices are...my fucking choices." She touched her nose and her eyebrows. "Letting you up that night..." She dropped her hands to her sides. "It was a mistake. I was stupid and desperate."

Zoe stood to bring herself to Madeline's level and maybe keep her from running (or crutching) away like she seemed about to. "Hey, I'm trying to help here. You're acting like there's no such thing as friendship."

Madeline's eyes were squeezed into a devastating squint. "Of course there's friendship. And family. And love. And it's all conditional. And transient." She settled her crutches under her arms. "And we're not friends." Then she was gone.

Well, that wasn't exactly true. Without the white noise of the HVAC, Zoe heard her crutch down the short hall, turn the corner to reception, cross the room, and pause to open the door. *Then* she was gone.

Part of Zoe wanted to leave it at exactly that: they weren't friends, they would never be friends, and she would be smart to forget everything about the last twenty minutes. What had gone down with Madeline was too heavy to add to what she was already dealing with around Troy and her uncle Mike and the low-level nagging of Bernard Collins's business card. But at the same time, she felt an undeniable connection with Madeline, and having heard the sadness, maybe even regret, in her last knife-twisting statement, Zoe wanted to shoulder some of her pain, help shave off the edges of her clearly immense loneliness. She believed she could do it, given how well she understood the self-doubt behind Madeline's abrupt hardness. Discarded dreams, indeed. And complacency. Zoe had gone to art school and dumped her handsome, well-heeled fiancé, but she was wrong if she'd thought that was the end of it. That wasn't the end. It was, she realized now, just the beginning.

CHAPTER 17

Katie called Joe Saturday morning with an invitation to come over and ride bikes that afternoon. The cadence of her voice, her intonation, and the vocabulary she used were eerily adult, though they rode on a childlike enthusiasm, and the dichotomy haunted Joe through the rest of the morning, reminding him how much of her childhood he was missing. He observed her maturation in (admittedly rapid) stop-motion—a film that lurched forward at random, unexpected moments. While he had it better than most divorced dads, he was also the founder of Mindful Management, where good enough was anything but.

For the past three years, imaging difficult things before turning them into reality had consumed his business life, and in the desperate weeks since Madeline had fled his apartment, he had elevated this practice to an art form. His plan to rescue the company through outside investment by pushing toward the efficiency, scale, and cold, hard cash that software would give them underpinned his every breath. He sugared his morning coffee with positive intentions and spread thick layers of self-affirmations on his sandwiches. He set goals about reaching out to three venture capital firms on Monday, cold-calling four midsize technology companies the day after. He focused on his physical proximity to Madeline and put aside the lingering emotional distance that persisted between them. He pushed forward despite the burden of failures and the weight of his lies. He would succeed, and Madeline would recover. They both needed time, but time was the one thing out of his control.

KATIE BUMPED UP ONE DRIVEWAY, CRUISED ALONG THE SIDEWALK to the next, and catapulted back down to the street. Her chatter was as constant as the turning of her pedals. "I only have two more books in the series, then I'll have to wait for another one to come out. Mom said that might take a while." Astride her bubblegum pink bike, wearing a short knit skirt over rainbow leggings, Katie was, once again, wholly a little girl.

Joe basked in her company, coasting next to her on Bridget's dusty three-speed that weighed more than he did. He'd turned his jeans up to midcalf to keep them from catching in the chain, and he felt the breeze against the hair on his legs. "Are you going to savor them? Slow down and make them last? Squeeze them dry of every word?"

She laughed. "I tried that, Dad. I *can't* slow down. It's physically impossible."

"They're that good, huh?"

"They're better than good. They're *fantastic*."

Joe laughed. After Katie pulled ahead and couldn't see, he took his hands off the handlebars for a few pedal strokes in a burst of exuberance. He loved how she emphasized words, adding in whole syllables painted with swooping intonation. She was the freshest breath of air.

When he caught back up to her, she asked, "Why didn't you bring Madeline with you?"

"Why would I?"

"She's with you a lot."

"Well, you only invited me. Besides, her knee's still healing, so she wouldn't be able to ride with us."

"Did you give her my book report?"

"I sure did, Ladybug. She loved it," he said, though he'd done no such thing.

"Are you going to marry her?" She drifted dangerously close, and he opened up a bigger buffer, checking around for cars. "It'd be okay if you did. She could be my other mom like Darrin is my other dad."

He tightened his grip on the handlebars. "Madeline and I are just friends. We're friends, and we work together. That's all."

"But she stayed with you when she was hurt."

"That's what friends do for each other."

He braced himself for more questions, but she said, "Hey, watch this. Are you watching?" When he convinced her his eyes were peeled, she sped ahead and hit her brakes, making a short skid mark on the asphalt.

"Wow, when did you learn to do that?"

While Katie demonstrated her new skill a few more times, Joe imagined Madeline riding next to him, drawing close enough to bump shoulders. He'd never seen her on a bike before, but in his mind he put her on a beach cruiser and made her laughing and relaxed like she got after long work sessions, when she threw off hours of effort and spun amusing anecdotes. The beautiful late-spring day (the middle of May already!) and light exercise would send her hair fluttering behind her and bring color to her cheeks, a rouge of well-being he hadn't seen since the attack. She'd stand up and pump the pedals to chase after Katie if she got too far ahead—healthy and whole and his.

He'd almost given Katie's book report to Madeline several times, when she had smiled or said something recognizably her, but those moments were inevitably followed by a return of the cautious, shuttered look she'd worn since the attack. He wanted sharing Katie's creation to mirror the intimate scene of his imagination, which was full of a common pride and laughter, and the fear of how far that was from reality made him slip the stapled papers in the bottom drawer of his desk. Sometimes it felt impossible to be sitting next to this hesitant, withdrawn Madeline while his vision of her future was so clear in his mind: wholly their Chief Consulting Officer and brimming with vitality and renewed affection for the company and him. Even as he felt a sickening shame at his romantic desire for Madeline, it fueled him through late nights and long hours, and he couldn't quite convince himself it was impossible—not that he tried all that hard.

He and Katie cruised around the neighborhood's side streets, talking about school and the new summer camp she would be starting in June, why traffic stayed to the right (Joe didn't know), and how the gears on his bike worked (he had a decent handle on that one). They passed parked cars covered in a thick haze of green pollen, and he wondered, in a demented fit of fancy, if it might be possible for him to get custody of Katie. He hadn't lobbied for it at the time of the divorce, but if he and Madeline got married, things might be different.

Marriage? Too much oxygen and momentary happiness made his already precarious state of mind tilt even farther off balance, but when he bounced over a curb onto Bridget's driveway, reality reasserted itself at the sight of his ex-wife leaning against the bumper of her car in the open garage. She wore a yellow sundress at odds with her dour look. He ignored her expression and said, "Beautiful day!"

"Perfect for a walk."

He said, "Don't let me stop you." Bridget's walks were not pleasurable affairs. During their marriage, they'd been a symbol of the relationship's ultimate dysfunction, a keeping-the-peace device that forced a placidity to the surface of their interaction while everything underneath remained churned up. The air between them would gather the charge of a brewing emotional maelstrom, but Bridget kept it from sparking in release by blowing out the front door for one of these walks, powering around the neighborhood instead of working things out with Joe.

Katie skidded up the driveway, leaving a foot-long black mark on the concrete.

Joe said, "*Nicely* done."

Bridget said, "Katie, honey, can you go inside or play in the yard? Your father and I are going to take a walk."

"We are?" Joe asked, but he dismounted, deposited his bike in the garage, and closed the overhead door behind him, not sure why he was obeying Bridget like this. They started down the block, and he tried to take charge by maintaining a staid stroll and saying, "Katie's the absolute best. Are you and Darrin considering having another kid?"

"At my age?"

"You're not forty yet. Besides, there's always adoption. Darrin seems to really like being a father."

She glanced over at him. "We have a problem."

"One of the perks of divorce is that ex-husbands aren't typically involved in current marital disputes." He smiled. "The rhododendrons are incredible this year. The ones in front of my building have so many blooms they've been declared the town's bee sanctuary."

"We need to talk."

Madeline never said that, always left it up to Joe to realize that they weren't just talking but "talking." "Is this about Katie? Because I thought we settled the summer camp–slash-soccer situation, and I've already blocked out my calendar for the two weeks I'll have her in July."

"Do you remember that call Darrin had the night I stopped by your office? The company in Palo Alto?" He didn't but motioned for her to go on. "Well, it turns out they're intent on hiring him as their CTO."

"The Palo Alto in California?" He made a dismissive sound. "No way." She took a few steps without commenting. "No way, right?"

UPENDED

"They pursued him, not the other way around. They weren't on his radar at all, but now it's"—she gave a sharp, one-shouldered shrug—"complicated."

"It seems simple to me." He kept his voice calm, though he felt his nerves start to tingle; they were on perpetual high alert since Madeline's attack. "We live here, not in California. Case closed, right?"

Bridget was usually vocal in her hatred of that phrase, but her quiet fizzed in the soft spring air between them. Finally, she said, "He's flying out to talk to them on Monday. Just to talk, he said. No promises or expectations."

"What? He has no place 'just talking' to a company in California."

"He had no intention of getting tangled up in anything out of the area, but by every measure, this is beyond his dream job."

Joe stopped, but Bridget took a few more steps before turning to him. She looked relaxed, her stance easy, her hands still, but he knew years of debate and court had trained her to appear calm even when she wasn't. *Especially* when she wasn't. He folded his arms, his T-shirt pulling across his shoulders. Adrenaline trickled through him. "This isn't about him. This is about all of us."

"I know that. That's why we're talking about it now when it's still just a vague idea."

"How in the world does flying out there qualify as vague? If they're serious, which they clearly are, they're going to woo him hard—this job and the package they offer and the neighborhoods and the sunshine, it's all going to be plated in twenty-four-karat gold and studded with diamonds. You've hired enough rainmakers at your firm to know how it goes."

"I've warned him about what they'll say."

He laughed through a throat constricted with anger. "Fat lot of good that'll do. This isn't going to happen, so letting him fly out there is a mistake."

Bridget looked away from him to a yard across the street that crawled with purple phlox, an evasion that chilled him despite the warm sun. "Maybe it's a mistake, but can you blame me for wanting the best for him? How could I deny him that when I have everything I want? And my firm was already considering opening an office out there. If this happened, they would make me the anchor partner."

"You've talked to the firm about this?"

"Just to understand options."

Joe's arms felt fused together. "There *are* no options. You want to know how to deny this to him? Just say no. Making sacrifices is part of life, certainly part of being a parent. Have you even thought about Katie in this? I'm not going to roll over and be one of those fathers who only sees their kid on major holidays."

"Joe, hey, you need to calm down. You're about twenty steps ahead of reality. I'm not taking Katie away from you! Do you think I want to move to California? No. I don't. I'm just trying to get the lay of the land, so don't get emotional."

Joe started back to his car, firmly in the grip of his fight-or-flight response.

Bridget caught up with him. "Don't walk away from me."

"Why not? You did it to me for years."

"You're overreacting."

"Oh, really? Why are we even talking about this? You want the lay of the land? Here it is: if you try to take Katie away from me, you'll be hearing from my lawyer." He pointed a shaking finger at Bridget.

"It's not like that."

"Not yet, but after he goes out there Monday?"

Her hesitation was so strong her steps slowed, and she had to hurry to catch up to Joe again. "Let's be reasonable."

"Not this time. I've been reasonable my whole life, and look where it's gotten me. You said it yourself: you have everything you want. *Everything.*" He surprised himself by punctuating the word with a punch against a nearby fence picket, then had to swallow the resulting pain to say, "You always have, so why not now?"

"Do you think I wanted things between us not to work out? For Katie not to have both her parents under the same roof?"

"Forgive me if I don't feel bad for you, Bridget. I stand to lose everything in this, and you'll lose nothing. You could even be better off, and you can't even see it for how lucky you've already been."

"We're in this together. I swear."

"Yeah. Keep telling yourself that." He walked faster, and Bridget finally dropped back. He vibrated like a string pulled just short of breaking. His arms and legs felt swollen with adrenaline, and his can-do, climb-any-mountain attitude of this morning was blown apart into a mist of useless fragments. The only thing keeping him from whaling on anything within reach was his already throbbing hand—and the threat of Bridget behind him.

When he finally got back to his car, he threw himself in the driver's seat and pulled several g's in a rough, squealing U-turn. It took a few blocks for rational thought to break through his anger and fear, but when it did, he remembered that this was a neighborhood where there were kids, that he shouldn't be driving in this state. He pulled over but kept his death grip on the steering wheel while he started to tell his Bluetooth to call Madeline.

Then he stopped. His hands shook when he relinquished the steering wheel, and he curled his fingers into fists to quell his trembling. If he called Madeline, and if she miraculously answered as the woman she'd been before all this happened, he'd speed over to her and tell her what Bridget had said. She'd lay her hand on his arm, look at him with naked affection, love, even, and he would tell her *everything*. The only reason he could deceive her was because she wasn't herself. But who was these days? He sat with the engine idling until he was calm enough to drive home.

CHAPTER 18

ETHAN WAS SCHEDULED TO OVERLAP HALF A SHIFT WITH NETTIE, and he'd been looking forward to it with zero reservations for the first time since the attack. For weeks, Nettie had been relentless with her demands for the Sister Status Report, but she'd blissfully dialed it back after Maddy had returned to work. The time with Nettie behind the counter was again a pleasure that balanced out the creaky twin tortures of song writing and his visits with Maddy, which comprised long, tense hours of him not asking and her not volunteering.

He put Maddy out of his mind, turned off his music, and even stowed his headphones in his bag while crossing Davis Square so he could be totally unencumbered for an appropriately exuberant Nettie greeting. But the atmosphere inside the shop was so palpably morose it stopped him in his tracks before he even made it past the threshold. Nettie was working the bar instead of her usual customer-facing post behind the register, and she buried herself behind her hair at his arrival.

Though they worked shoulder to shoulder, they barely spoke to each other before Ethan took his long break, so instead of bringing his sandwich back to the shop and keeping Nettie company like he usually did, he aggravated himself in an entirely different way: by reviewing the lyrics he'd written during a marathon session the day before. They were worthless, as his first drafts always were—so insipid and dull that by the time he walked back to Fuel, he was in complete harmony with Nettie's foul mood.

She wasn't behind the counter, which was strange, but when he slipped into the back to pick up his apron, he found her crouched in a corner, crying next to their industrial water filter. He put his hand on her shoulder, and she whirled around, her face emerging from behind her hair, red and splotchy. "Go away," she choked out.

He considered it because, frankly, the last thing he needed was to feel ultimately useless yet again, but he said, "What's wrong?"

"Nothing. Forget it." But she got up, slithered into his arms, and cried against his chest, which made up for her cold shoulder earlier. She said, "Eric came in while you were out, and he—"

The Boyfriend. Ethan pulled back. "Did he hit you?" He searched her face and arms for evidence.

She shoved him away. "No. *God*, Ethan. He just, he just," she stuttered and started crying again, turning her face to the corner she'd just been in, her hair obscuring his view.

"He just what? You know, it doesn't matter," he said too loudly for the space, but it was either yell or do something else way more destructive like pulling a baker's rack of supplies down on their heads. "That jackass has no business treating you like he does, and you *excusing* him like you do makes me—" He was going to say "sick" but stopped himself and dialed it back a notch. "It makes me crazy, okay? I would never treat you like he does. *Never*. He should be drawn and quartered, just like the guy who went after Maddy, but both of you—"

Nettie had stopped crying during this tirade, which should've been a good thing but really, really wasn't, not with her mouth clamped closed and her nostrils flared in an expression he'd seen plenty of times before, when a customer got his panties in a wad over some imagined slight and pulled out the I-want-to-talk-to-your-manager card. Her eyes were slitty and swollen, and he backed away from their glare until his ass hit the stainless steel sink behind him.

He said, "I didn't mean that like you think. I'm not saying you're to blame or anything."

"Like hell you aren't."

"Nettie, come on. All I mean is I can't stand guys like Eric who think they can do whatever they want to whoever they want. I'd give my left nut to be with you, but instead you insist on choosing some asshole who makes you cry."

"Get out of here," she said quietly.

"Nettie, hey. I'm trying to help."

She pulled her hair away from her red, inflamed face. The fury he saw convinced him that, yes, his left nut was nothing compared to her and that his anger wasn't just because The Boyfriend was a flaming prick but because he was The Boyfriend. She said, "Leave me alone. Like, permanently."

"But—"

"Go away," she screamed, and he stumbled from the room, through the swinging door, and out past Neal, who said something about Ethan's shift and getting in trouble. He flipped Neal the bird and was through the front door and into a light rain that hadn't been there a few minutes before. His hatred of The Boyfriend was undermined by his embarrassment at having told Nettie the left-nut thing, at having fucked up at being the supportive friend. His screw-ups tangled his feet like untied shoelaces, and he was incapable of doing anything but stumbling in the vague direction of his apartment.

He passed small shops and two- and three-family houses—all normal enough besides being made dreary by the rain. By the looks of things, it was impossible to tell that the world was going insane, but it was wildly tilted on its axis, and all he could do about it was write some songs that just possibly were starting to get good. What use was that? Perfect lyrics and a sparkling melody

UPENDED

wouldn't make Nettie dump The Boyfriend or convince Maddy to go to the police with the truth. It would not erase the attack or resurrect his parents or even help him pay his rent.

He covered several blocks, the motion of his body and the unspooling of the sidewalk under his feet the only things he fully understood. He had to do something, wrestle some nugget of sense from this madness, but what? He stopped in the middle of a block on Broadway, ducked under an awning out of the drizzle, and fumbled his phone from his pocket.

Maddy answered on the second ring. "I'm heading into a meeting in a few minutes."

"Have you told the cops yet?" he asked, ostensibly extending the benefit of the doubt she always gave him but really baiting a trap. Just a couple days before, they'd sat in her apartment that looked like a certifiable nutjob lived there and shared a pizza with extra cheese and a side of soft sighing from The Mad Hatter. "Just being," she called it, but every time he saw her, she drifted farther from his memory of her.

She said, "I can't talk about this now. Tonight, okay? Maybe you can come over?"

"Have you told them?"

"Have you shaved your beard?"

He shoved his free hand deep in his pocket. "I'm not going over there tonight."

"Why not?"

"Or tomorrow night. Or the night after."

"Can we talk about this later?"

"There's nothing to talk about. I'm not going to be your dumb teddy bear and pretend everything's fine. If you want to see me, tell the cops the truth. Or, like, get some therapy. Or even a cleaning lady. Make some kind of effort."

"Let me call you after this meeting. One hour. Then you can tell me why you're being such an asshole."

"Hey, everyone else gets to be an asshole, so why not me? Why do I always have to be the nice guy if you can be someone entirely

162

different now? It's not just the lie, it's everything. That's all I have to say. I'll see you when I see you. Maybe. Over and out." He hung up. He hung up! On Maddy! "Holy shit," he said. "Holy shit."

He was still as jumbled as before, but for the first time since their father had kicked it, he felt released from whatever had been weighing him down. He was finished with going along with whatever was happening, *accepting* shit like Nettie did, maybe even like Maddy. He was going to make changes, find some way to work these songs into something meaningful, important, transformative. Maybe doing so wouldn't change the course of the world, but it would change *his* course, which was enough. In fact, wasn't it practically everything? There was an open mic at Fuel in a couple weeks, and if Danika Miller showed up, he was going to give her a show that would knock her socks off.

CHAPTER 19

MADELINE WAS UP EARLY THIS SATURDAY. AFTER A PERFUNCTORY stop in the bathroom to brush her teeth and wash her face, she poked her head out the back door to size up the weather. She recoiled from the heavy humidity and swore. The morning was already disgusting, heading quickly toward oppressive, but she pulled on shorts and a T-shirt, plucked her cane from where it hung off the breakfast bar, and stood at her apartment door, psyching herself to leave.

This was her first weekend free from her knee brace, and she'd promised herself she would go on a walk—specifically one around Jamaica Pond. The pond was a mile away and a mile-and-a-half around, but despite her atrophied ass and compromised gait, the length of the round trip wasn't the real challenge; the most direct route to the pond passed within spitting distance of where it happened, the brick that had busted open her head, the ground that had soaked up his vitriol, the dumpster she'd lain next to for hours before being found.

She didn't *have* to walk around the pond. The area was full of appealing places to put one foot in front of the other. Short drives could deposit her at the Arboretum, or along the Charles, or even near that nice little reservoir out on Route 9. But Jane was sure to be at the pond, running her habitual three or four laps. Jane, who had dogged Madeline's thoughts since that first night in the hospital. Jane, whom Madeline fervently hoped hadn't moved away. She just wanted a glimpse, and walking past the alley was her self-imposed price.

First she had to get out of her apartment, but her feet felt as if they'd grown roots deep into her hardwood floor. "Everything's fine," she told herself. She'd been sleeping without the chair wedged under her door handle for days, and the frequency of her nightmares had decreased significantly; wasn't confronting the scene the next logical step? This cold rationality didn't budge her, so she tried calling herself a fucking pansy and told herself she wasn't allowed to be scared if she, as Ethan put it, wouldn't participate in the possible incarceration of the perpetrator (he got flowery when he'd been drinking). Hadn't Jane called them two strong bitches when they'd gotten together? She'd claimed her physical brawn plus Madeline's "intestinal fortitude" made them an indomitable pair. What would she think if she saw Madeline now?

This combination of carrot and stick was potent enough to propel her out the door, and she trundled down the gloomy stairs in a concentrated rush. Outside, she tried to occupy herself with her physical therapist's instructions: walk with even intention, feel the push and pull of balance and support, focus on not favoring her recovering knee. But this higher order thought was a pale distraction, and each block she covered squeezed her ribs and tightened her diaphragm until her breaths were ineffectual sips of air. Her attempts to walk faster so the alley would pass in a blur were hampered by her knee and her lungs, and she had to make do with keeping her sightline fixed across the street from well before the scene to far after the Orange Line station. Her hands didn't stop shaking for long blocks, and by the time she actually got to the pond, sweat dampened her T-shirt and trickled down her forehead, and her leg was already tired.

The grip of her cane was slippery. Every bench she passed crooned at her to sit, whispered that sitting still would allow her to scan the other people moving around the pond and find Jane if she were here (surely she was here, *had* to be here), but the thought of engaging in such intentional surveillance made her squirm with shame. She pressed on, her lungs full of saturated air, the drumbeat of her steps playing rhythm to a melody of unsavory musings, like how his calling her a dyke remained a horrible mystery. The pond itself looked thicker than usual, its dense placidity reflecting the sluggishness of the morning runners and walkers, none of them moving with Jane's distinctive stride. The trees were indistinctly green in the humidity, and even the dogs looked weighed down, their tongues lolling from their mouths. This outing, she admitted, was ill advised. A touch desperate.

But then she heard, "Mad?" and there, to her left, wearing a sweat-soaked tank top, shorts, and a mile and a half of legs, was Jane. "Well, shit. It *is* you." She stopped running.

Her standing just a few feet away was impossibly real, and Madeline felt a sob burble up from her gut. She pushed it down, but it left her throat tight and her voice unruly when she said, "Jane."

"Wow, right? What're you doing here?" Jane asked, then laughed. "That's not what I meant, but what're you doing here?"

I'm here for you, Madeline thought so strongly that not saying the words was nearly impossible. An acceptable half-truth came only after a gaping pause. "I...exercise. Physical therapy." She raised the cane in punctuation. Madeline hadn't seen Jane in the three years since she'd vacated their apartment, which just went to show how well they'd divided their assets—friends and favorite haunts included—or, maybe, how wrecked Madeline had been but had pretended not to be, how very well she'd hidden out.

"What'd you do to yourself?"

"Tore my MCL."

Jane waited.

"Long story."

Jane shifted from foot to foot on the asphalt path and popped both her forefingers, pulling them toward her palms with her thumbs—a nervous habit. Why was she nervous? She was tall and broad-shouldered and ridiculously strong, and Madeline had to keep herself from drifting closer and tucking herself under a protective, finely muscled arm.

Jane finally said, "I see. Well, you look good. The cane really works for you."

"Better than the crutches I was on. I didn't handle them nearly as well as you did when you had that ankle sprain."

"Mm," she grunted. Everything was so intensely familiar: this vocal tick, the knuckle cracking, the way she squeezed one eye shut and thumbed sweat away from it. Her hair was still short and tousled, sweat-spiked around her ears and neck. She said, "I cannot believe you're here."

"I'm intruding, I know. This is your place."

"That's not what I mean. This heat...are you sure you're not a mirage?" She gave Madeline a half grin and glanced at her watch—the same one she'd had when they'd been together. Old faithful, she'd called it. "Saturday? 8:30 in the morning? Shouldn't you be working?"

"I'm turning over a new leaf."

Another grunt.

"I was stir-crazy, couldn't stand the apartment anymore."

"Are you still in the same place?"

"I downsized two years ago, and the books have taken over. You'd hate it."

"I bet I would." She wiped sweat from her other eye.

They both spoke at the same time, Madeline saying (with regret), "I'll let you get going," while Jane said, "Should we walk?"

Madeline said, "I don't want to keep you."

"The run was a hot mess, anyway." Whether that was true or a polite lie, she didn't know, but they fell into step together, Jane modulating her long strides to match Madeline's shorter ones, just like she used to.

Jane said, "Madeline Sawyer."

"Jane Gunther."

"How's the company?"

"Busy."

"But you're turning over a new leaf. How many hours have you worked this week?"

Madeline cleared her throat. About sixty, she didn't say.

"Come on." Jane nudged her with an elbow. "I'm just giving you a hard time."

"You were always good at that."

"I was, wasn't I? You liked it, though."

"Mostly."

They walked without talking for a while. *Seven years* they'd been together, which was, as Ethan would say, a chunk of change. Seven years, most of them pretty happy—at least until Joe and The Great Distraction, as Jane called it. She must be with someone else now, and Madeline didn't want to hear about it. She'd made it all the way through their breakup officially not knowing about the affair Jane had been carrying on at the end, and any similar sort of information wasn't welcome now.

"How's Joe?" Jane finally asked, the words coming out in a blurt, breaking the atypical quiet they'd maintained for a quarter of a mile to the shady west side of the pond.

"He's fine. We're...how about we not talk about work?"

Jane stopped short and slapped a hand to her chest.

Madeline couldn't help laughing. "Drama queen."

They started walking again. "I'm the subdued one in my relationship now." Ah, there it was. "Sometimes I wonder what I've gotten myself into but then decide to go with the flow. What about you?"

"Still married to my job, I guess." Jane probably had a lot of things she could say to that, but before she could come out with any of them, Madeline asked, "Are you coaching yet?"

"High school, which is *insane*, those girls, and I picked up a summer program. I'm playing masters now and beach half the year." She glanced sideways at Madeline. "I'm getting old, though. I keep thinking I'm one bad landing away from serious injury. I've been too lucky. Someday I'll find myself the ace of the rec league."

"I'll bet you're good with the high schoolers. They probably all have crushes on you."

"They think I'm ancient. Besides, they're busy screwing their pimple-faced boyfriends."

"Even so."

Jane elbowed her again. "*Anyway*."

"Yeah, anyway. How's your family? Have they successfully absorbed your girlfriend?" There had been moments over the last several weeks when Madeline had missed Jane's parents almost as much as Jane herself. They were warm, welcoming, easygoing—the exact opposite of her own, when she'd had some to compare them to.

"Absorbed. How perfect. They're good. The same, pretty much. Mom's retired and causing no end of trouble, Dad's at the jumping-off point, and the sibs have started popping out kids to my parents' great delight." She pulled at the hem of her tank, flapping it away from her body a couple times.

Madeline nodded for quite a while before she could get herself to swallow her sadness and stop. "Good," she said. "I'm glad." They had been the first real family she'd had, or at least the first family that was like how she'd always imagined a family being, which was another thing she couldn't say.

"They didn't take our breakup well. It was months before they stopped asking when we were going to get back together. How about you? Is your dad still...your dad?"

"He died a year ago. Stroke. It was unexpected. Ethan took it so badly he moved up here right after."

Jane's voice was quiet and genuine when she asked, "How did *you* take it?"

UPENDED

Her proximity tugged at Madeline, making her want to capture Jane's long-fingered hand in hers. She resisted, barely, squeezing the grip of her cane, but the effort it took meant she couldn't summon a lie—something at which she'd become increasingly, alarmingly adept. "It was...difficult. We'd gotten pretty close at the end—the last six months we talked at least every week. He was making an effort."

"I'm sure his amenability had nothing to do with the fact that I was out of your life."

"He was—"

Jane flicked her wrist, interrupting Madeline. "I shouldn't have said that. I know you always wanted a relationship with him, and I'm really sorry you lost him like that."

"It's over. It's been over for a year, so thanks, but I'm okay."

"Yes, you're good at being okay." She grunted. "Hey, do you still drive that car?"

"Ethan wants me to get a half-ton pickup."

Jane laughed. "I'd pay good money to see that."

"It's not like I'm in love with the sedan." Madeline reached up and grabbed a leaf from a branch hanging over the path. She twirled it by the stem and crumpled it in her fist before dropping it.

"You can't help that you're addicted to doing the responsible thing."

"I'm not— I made choices. I've made lots of choices."

"Yeah, and you chose your job and your father over me."

"And *you* chose that bartender at Swing." Why did she say that? Why were they talking like this? Jane wasn't friends with her exes and didn't sleep with her friends and, in those ways, was a questionable lesbian. So what was going on here?

Jane cracked her knuckles and glanced over at Madeline. "You knew about that?"

"You came home reeking of smoke for a month straight."

"Why didn't you say anything?"

"I almost did. But as much as I blamed you, I couldn't blame you, and then you dumped me anyway, so what did it matter?" Her knee ached, and the cane clicked when she ground its tip onto the path.

"Wow, I sound like a real asshole."

"And I sound like the long-suffering wife."

"Good thing we broke up, then," Jane said.

"Good thing."

They crept along the north side of the pond, the sun direct and unrelenting. Madeline was sweating like a pig, and she slowed as they approached a bench. "I need to take a break. Don't let me hold you up." She collapsed on the sun-warmed wood slats with a sigh.

But Jane didn't move on. She stood in front of Madeline, *looking* at her, and in that gaze, Madeline felt small and damaged and unbearably lonely.

"Mad," Jane said. "Is everything okay?"

"The knee's just aching."

"How did you hurt it? The MCL's not a common injury."

"I told you. It's a long story."

Jane sat down next to her, leaving less than a foot between them. "Car accident?"

Madeline spun her cane around on its tip.

"Icy stairs? Have you taken up skiing?"

She examined her right thumbnail.

"Fall out of a tree? Full-contact Scrabble? What?"

"You really don't want to know." Madeline stared at her, unblinking, deadly serious—a look that usually made Jane relent.

This time, she returned it in full. "Yes, I really do."

Madeline glanced out over the pond, imagining the placid surface hiding a similar boiling turmoil to what she felt under her sweaty skin. In a lie bigger than the ones she'd laid on the police, she had told herself for weeks that Jane would know what to say, would drape her in understanding, would hold her hand in the perfect way. She'd feel safe with Jane around; why not, since Jane had always felt safe above everything else? But now even as Jane was here, in all her glory, she was actually less "here" than Zoe was, and telling Zoe the truth of the attack, even more of the truth than Madeline had told Joe and Ethan, had been absolutely the wrong decision. She gripped the top of her cane, then relaxed, then did it again before saying, "You should get back to your running."

"What happened?"

Madeline met Jane's gaze, trying to determine if this interest was serious. She saw affection and concern in how Jane leaned toward her, how her hand was planted close to Madeline's leg. She'd been so dear once. With her this near, it was hard to think of her any other way. But Jane wasn't hers. Jane's family had spit Madeline out and incorporated a new member. So she pressed hard on her right eyebrow and said, "Forget it. I'm not your problem anymore."

"Don't do that."

"Do what? Be honest?"

"No, dismiss me."

"Let's be realistic. We haven't talked in three years." She got up, wincing both at her knee and this truth.

"Then why'd you have to think so hard about it? You're so in love with the truth, but back then you lied to me. You lied about the important things. And you're lying now."

Madeline sniffed away ready tears, glancing down at her pale legs and finally back to Jane as steadily as she could manage. "I guess I can give as good as I get." She walked away with an effort way more emotional than physical.

"Hey." Jane followed her.

"Don't," Madeline said.

"Don't what? Keep you from having the last word?"

"You're the one who left."

Jane's hand clamped on her shoulder and spun her around. Her anger squared her jaw, sharpened her cheekbones. "Only when there was nothing left to leave! Only when you redirected every last bit of your attention to your job. And your *prick* of a father. I loved you, and you shit all over that."

"I know," Madeline yelled. They faced each other, both puffed up with emotions, and Madeline felt the gravitational pull of her ex, the heavy truth of how stupid she'd been to drive her into the arms of that chain-smoking bartender. She repeated, softly, "I know. And because of that, you need to drop this." She gave in and reached out to capture Jane's forearm and squeeze it. "I was wrong then, but believe me, I'm right about this." She let go.

"You broke my heart."

She nodded, not trusting herself to speak.

"Just because it was a long time ago doesn't mean I don't want to know what's going on, but if you need me to let it go and leave, I'll leave."

Madeline gathered the dregs of her self-control and said, "It's for the best. I'm sorry. For everything."

"For Christ's sake, Mad," Jane mumbled and gathered Madeline in a crushing hug. "You don't make things easy."

After a thick dollop of time, Jane released her, turned, and ran away, her strides both long and quick. Madeline made it to the next bench before sinking down and crying until she felt hollowed out. For two months, since that horrible morning after, this was all she'd wanted, this encounter—or not this exact encounter but a chance to go back in time and have Jane with her. Even if the attack was inevitable, even if her father had to die the way he did, even if she had to lose Jane first, to have this one part of her life reset to a glorious "before" would make this "after" somehow manageable. She'd wanted this so much even though she'd known there was no going back, but this future she stepped inexorably farther into every day, this life she'd somehow chosen without choosing...it was a mistake, she thought. It was all a terrible mistake.

CHAPTER 20

WHEN ZOE CAME FULLY AWAKE, A SICKENING WAVE OF disorientation greeted her, regret snapping at its hungover heels. The woman next to her was asleep, her mouth inched open, a drool-induced darkness to her pillow. She seemed perfectly harmless—blue polka-dotted sheet slipping down her tattooed shoulder and exposing the top of a freckled breast—and Zoe considered putting an arm around her, going back to sleep, and seeing what happened. Maybe this wasn't the disaster it appeared to be. Maybe they had more in common than just loneliness and desire.

But that possibility wasn't enough to keep Zoe from slithering out from between the sheets, reuniting her glasses with her face, and scouting around the floor for her clothes, which were evenly distributed on both sides of the bed. One of her socks had made a break for it and was all the way across the room by the door, and when she bent down to pick it up, a snippet of memory from the night before distracted her from her mission: the woman on top of her, her thigh between Zoe's legs, their laughter turning to seriousness when Zoe reached up to gather the woman's hair away from her face.

She blinked it away and took her bundle of clothes out to the living room, easing the door closed behind her. Above the couch was a framed print of Monet's sunset haystack that Zoe had studied more than once where it hung in the museum here in Boston, and she hesitated, letting the color seep into the rods and cones of her eyes, recalling the glinting texture of the brushstrokes on the original. Lots of people had these on their walls: *The Kiss, Starry Night*, the haystacks, and why not? They were reprinted endlessly for a good reason. Just because she could stare at one of Monet's originals for an hour that went by like a minute, or that there had been a moment in their sex that had vibrated with a false intimacy, didn't mean this woman was her soul mate.

Zoe dressed quickly and left a short note (without her number). She felt a pang at not being able to lock the deadbolt on her way out of the apartment but dismissed it and padded down a flight of stairs to the building's front door. When she sat on the concrete steps outside to put on her shoes, heat enveloped her, beating down on her back while also radiating up from beneath her. Her glasses fogged, and sweat prickled on her forehead. She ran a hand through her hair, knowing it had to be an unruly disaster but not really caring.

She needed to go home, drink some water, take a shower, and find something to occupy her mind, which clearly shouldn't be left to its own devices. But she'd gone out the night before (to the very club she'd been avoiding since that kiss with Madeline) and put herself in this position of tying her shoes on someone else's front steps because she couldn't stand to be in her apartment.

She and Troy were at an angry impasse about her uncle in particular and their semicloseted existence in general. The key to Troy's entire self-image was his rejection of unseemly desperation, which manifested either with the pretense that he didn't actually want what he wanted or with an impenetrable patina of confidence that getting what he wanted was a foregone

175

conclusion. In his mind, marrying Zoe would put an end to the undeniable desperateness of their situation, and he was at least as angry that they both knew it would never work as he was that she refused to just give in. He would *never* come out to his family, and if she pulled out of this charade (even though it was careening toward disaster), what then?

She glanced up and down the street, not sure exactly where she was. Somewhere in Brighton, but they'd taken an Uber here, and she hadn't been paying very close attention. The last thing she remembered clearly was the woman upstairs nodding to a man across the street from the club and saying, "What a creeper." He stood half in the shadows, a cap pulled low over his face, watching them. "Let's give him a show," she said and kissed Zoe thoroughly before pulling her into the car's back seat.

Zoe hauled herself upright in this humid-ass morning and summoned a ride to Rosemary's and blueberry waffles with a side of easy conversation. The café was blessedly cool and dim in this first slap of summer, and Zoe hovered inside the door, waiting for her eyes to adjust and the mirage of Madeline at the counter to fade away. But the vision only got sharper and clearer until Zoe remembered her morning breath and last night's clothes and the unknown state of her hair and took a step back, then another. She was about to escape when Rosemary called her name.

Busted. Doubly busted when Madeline turned and spotted her.

"Hey," Zoe said and took her usual place at the counter one stool over from Madeline because it would have been weird not to. She glanced at Madeline's plate, half expecting to see mac and cheese despite the hour, but it held part of an omelet oozing provolone and a biscuit with a perfect bite missing.

She felt both Rosemary and Madeline checking out the wrinkled chinos and little tank top she'd worn to the club the night before, but neither said anything. Rosemary slid a steaming cup of coffee in front of her. "Waffles?"

"And a side of sausage. And a big glass of water."

176

"Ah, I see." Rosemary winked at Madeline as if to a coconspirator. "One hangover cure coming right up."

Maybe Rosemary was right that Zoe needed a hangover cure, but Madeline looked pretty trashed herself. Her eyes were puffed and face pale, and she had sweat patches under her arms and at the small of her back. Even more anomalous was that she didn't have a book or magazine with her for company—all of which made Zoe want to demand what the fuck she was doing here and what the fuck was wrong with her and why the fuck she kept opening up to Zoe before shutting her out. Instead, she put her elbows on the counter and cradled her forehead in her hands, waiting for her fucking waffles.

She hefted the thick ceramic mug Rosemary had given her and took a gulp of coffee that scalded all the way down to her empty stomach. "Hot hot hot hot hot," she said in a rapid whisper.

Madeline glanced over from her breakfast.

Zoe said, "You may have gotten this place in your last breakup, but you're not getting it this time. I don't care how long you've been coming here. Or that we were never together. You know what I mean."

Madeline put her fork down on her plate, and Zoe was sure she was going to slip off the stool and hobble right out the front door. Instead, she assaulted her eyes with the heels of her hands. "I've behaved badly."

Zoe refrained from agreeing verbally but couldn't keep herself from a single, curt nod.

"If I could take back what I told you, I would."

"But, see, that's the thing. I don't want you to take that back. I want you to take back what happened next. Just because we're not necessarily friends now doesn't mean we can't ever be." Truthfully, Zoe wasn't sure they could, not with how she couldn't seem to settle on whether to hate Madeline or long for her.

"It may not seem like it, but I'm trying to do what's right. How can I possibly start a friendship with anyone right now when I can't trust—"

UPENDED

Rosemary interrupted with Zoe's waffles and water. She plunked the plate down and hovered across the counter from them, wiping her hands on her perennial white towel even though Zoe suspected they were already dry. "It's been an age since the two of you were here together. My favorite regulars."

Zoe said, "You say that to all your regulars."

"You're like my children. I never would have gotten over my empty-nest syndrome without you guys." Her features darkened with an out-of-character frown, her lips pursed as if at a burned batch of lasagna. In a wild non sequitur, she said, "Rich was in last night"—another regular—"and he said the new exhibit at the MFA, the one about woodblocks and printmaking, was more interesting than he expected. Have you seen it, Zoe?"

"No, not yet. There's a sweet spot for going to those. Both too soon and too near the end, and you can get herded along in the crowd like cattle."

"I haven't been to the MFA in years," Madeline said.

Yeah, probably not since her breakup with the infamous ex. "You can use my pass if you want. I'm a member." Zoe didn't know if she was being nice because Rosemary was there or because she was absolutely hopeless.

Rosemary leaned into the counter, her forearms—meaty but shapely—pressing against the worn wood. "My daughter was artistic. Like you, Zoe. Not paintings but small carvings or wire sculptures. Trinkets, I thought of them at the time, but now that I look back, they were quite fine."

Madeline said, "I didn't know that about Susan. Does she keep it up?"

"Not Susan. Rebecca."

Even after all these years of sopping up conversations with Rosemary like gravy with a crust of sourdough, Zoe had never heard that name, but the way Rosemary said it, softly but firmly, reminded her of how she used to tell people she was gay: a forcefulness undermined by fear or timidity or just the strangeness of it all.

178

"Rebecca?" Madeline asked.

"My youngest. We don't talk."

Rosemary had always seemed perfectly nice, but secrets lurked everywhere. What had gone down between her and this mysterious daughter to make Rosemary kick her to the curb? The closer Kimberly's wedding got and the more Zoe talked with her sister, the heavier the lie of her life with Troy got. Zoe realized she was white-knuckling her fork, but she couldn't relax her grip.

Rosemary gazed at a spot halfway between Zoe and Madeline and made a dismissive motion with her hand. "It's...Wood blocks seem like the kind of thing she would have gotten into."

While waiting for Rosemary to go on, Zoe felt aligned with Madeline for once, both of them humming in the indigo of morbid curiosity. Neither of them moved.

Finally, Rosemary said, "She stopped talking to me when she was sixteen. Ran away, really. Long time ago and long story." Her eyes regained their focus, and she straightened back up and clapped her hands together. "Anyway, she's been on my mind." She glanced over at the register, where a couple loitered, probably waiting for a fix of Rosemary's cinnamon rolls, which were so dangerous Zoe'd had to swear off them. "Whoops. Back to work." Rosemary pushed off into business as usual.

Zoe finally looked at Madeline, who said, "Did that just happen? Or was it some kind of hallucination? Heat stroke, maybe?"

"I'm afraid my family will disown me if I come out to them." The words tumbled from Zoe's mouth before she knew what was happening.

Madeline's eyes went wide, and she reached out to touch Zoe's bare arm, but Zoe moved away.

"Forget it. We're not friends because apparently you've got trust issues." A snap lurked in Zoe's voice that she didn't try to hide. It felt good. Real. And Zoe liked that very much.

"Not about you, about myself."

Zoe laughed. "We've totally skipped the relationship and gone to the breakup. It's not you, it's me?"

UPENDED

"Will you stop? I mean that I don't trust my motives for confiding in you, for wanting to be around you. I'm spectacularly damaged and completely alone. Hell, I went to the pond this morning specifically to run into my ex. How desperate is that?"

"Did you? Run into Jane?"

"Yes, and it proved how fucked up I am. Believe me, you do not want to get involved with me."

Zoe gripped her thighs under the counter. "Stop telling me what I want! You don't know me. You don't know anything about me. Like, like, right there"—she pointed behind her to her painting—"I made that. And besides, I *own* all the mistakes I've made, including whatever mistakes I might be making right this very minute. I'm clear about who I am, and even after all this, I still want to know you. I'm sick and tired of people trying to manage me into their version of safety." She took a deep, shaky breath. "Now if you don't mind, my breakfast is getting cold."

She cleaved off a too-large bite of waffle and shoved it in her mouth, at least partly to shut herself up. She narrowed her vision to her plate and mug, but she couldn't quite avoid seeing Madeline twist around to look at her painting, putting a hand to her ribs at the motion, her breath catching a little.

Madeline said, "I think it's wonderful."

They ate for a while, the murmur of the dining room accompanying their quiet. Rosemary stayed by the register, and it was as if round one of this match of intensely personal revelations was over, and they'd retreated to their corners to lick their wounds.

Zoe wiped up syrup with half a sausage link and was reaching in her back pocket for her wallet when Madeline said, "Can we start over? Go back to being two Rosemary regulars who happen to be working on a project together?"

Before answering, Zoe made herself stop and think. She dug around in her memories of Madeline before all this happened, trying to recall what had provoked such an intense crush. It was her warmth, yes, and her ease with Rosemary, but more than that, it was this undeniable sense of "what you see is what you get," of forthright honesty and an immensely appealing integrity. Was that still in Madeline, or had the attack made it a historical fact?

Zoe said, "No. I don't want my life to be about lies anymore. There's been too much of that already. But, Madeline," (oh how she liked saying that name despite everything), "that doesn't mean we have to talk about it all the time. There *are* other topics we can cover, like the weather or woodblocks or your unhealthy relationship with cheese." She indicated Madeline's nearly empty plate.

"You've noticed, huh?"

"Seriously, what is it with the mac and cheese?"

"It's comforting. If I didn't have cheese, I'd probably be a raging alcoholic."

"Oh, well, here's to cheddar, then. I like it sharp enough to curl your toes."

That teased a smile from Madeline, wide and bright and maximally appealing. "Love it," she said.

"See? This is nice. Normal. You need to stop thinking so much. You should do what I do: go look at art. Immerse your eyes in color. Dip your brain in pattern and texture." Or, she supposed, have sex with a stranger.

"I don't know anything about art."

"Literature is art, and you're quite the reader—unless all those books at your place are for show. Art is communication on all sorts of levels. Painting and sculpture just do it without words—at least mostly."

Madeline used a tine of her fork to tease some provolone from a lingering fold of omelet. She nibbled it before saying, "Will you show me? At the MFA?"

She said it softly, shyly, and Zoe melted just like that cheese. She was such a sucker, which she decided was better than becoming closed off, unmovable, though sometimes not by much. "Sure, of course."

"Soon?"

UPENDED

"I'll make you a deal—you get the last of your comments to us on your design, and we'll celebrate at the museum."

"Deal." Madeline wiped her hand on a napkin and presented it to Zoe. After they shook, Madeline's grip lingered on Zoe's fingers for a tantalizing extra few seconds.

CHAPTER 21

AT JOE'S DIRECTION, IDK HAD DESIGNED A TWO-PAGE advertisement to launch the Mindful Management app, and it surpassed even his inflated expectations: dynamic and slick as if they were a company ten times their size, a *hundred* times their size. He and Beth huddled in front of her monitor so he could point out little touches here and there on the screen. She followed along for a while before asking, "What does Madeline know about this?"

This had been Beth's refrain since she'd caught him lying to Madeline about the two lost contracts, and though he expected the question by now, it still needled him. She'd become such a master at this particular brand of torture that he was convinced she'd missed her calling as a CIA agent. He answered without actually answering. "She's going to love it. Divide and conquer, right? She's making sure the software does what it's supposed to do, and I'm selling it. She was crystal clear about not wanting to be in product sales."

"She's not going to like being this out of the loop, and you know it."

He straightened out of his stoop and stepped back to lean against the white wall behind him. "What does it matter? She's not in a place to be strategic and aggressive right now, but strategic and aggressive is exactly what we need."

Beth swiveled a quarter turn toward him, crossing her legs neatly, her pump swinging inches from his shin. "Joe, listen."

"No, *you* listen," he said with a snap and sighed. "I need you to get this ad placed in these journals"—he leaned past her and tapped the list he'd written—"so it runs as soon as possible, and that's the end of it. Please."

Beth looked at him over the tops of her glasses. "How bad is it?"

"How bad is what?"

"Listen, I'm not a total idiot. You haven't let me touch the books in a month. We lost those contracts, and now you're being..."

He folded his arms across his chest.

"...like this." She motioned at his stance.

All the things he was plotting and juggling pinged around inside him, which was equally exciting and terrible, but he needed to keep a lid on them until the first pieces of his plan ticked over from to-do to done. Everything would be different when he could point to a signed software contract or a round of funding (no matter how small), when he could use tangible success as both springboard and justification. His cell phone buzzed in his pocket, but before he checked it, he said to Beth, "If there are any problems, it's only because we haven't pushed hard enough. We haven't had the manpower for it, but with this software..." He pulled out his phone and saw it was his lawyer calling. "I have to take this. Please get that ad placed, and we'll talk later."

He answered the phone on the way to his office. "Terry. What's the news?" He shut the door behind himself.

"Let me repeat that I don't think a suit is a good idea."

"You were clear about that last time we talked."

"First, nothing's even happened. It's all very theoretical."

Joe leaned against his desk, too agitated to sit. "Darrin's out there right now, meeting the board of directors. It's becoming less theoretical by the minute."

"Even so, I think mediation would be the best approach. It worked wonderfully with your divorce, and if you're thinking of this suit as a scare tactic, knowing Bridget..."

He scanned the surface of his desk for his stress ball but didn't see it. "Terry, seriously. Mediation worked because whatever we disagreed about wasn't important. Besides, what would be the middle ground between Boston and Palo Alto? Chicago? It doesn't work that way."

"Okay. I understand. I'm prepared to file, but I want to make sure you're clear on what happens next. Suing for custody isn't an easy process, especially when you're up against the biological mother, and especially when that mother is a very successful lawyer."

Joe rifled through his drawers and finally found the stress ball behind his stapler, amazed he'd experienced a moment of calm long enough to put it away. He pumped it a few times. "Are you intimidated by Bridget? Why? She wouldn't be representing herself."

"It's not that. I'm talking about stability. She's been at the same firm for a decade, and you run a start-up. They're going to dig into your finances. That and your working hours. You'd be a single parent going up against a two-parent household. An *ideal* two-parent household."

"Not ideal. They both work too much."

"Yeah. Don't we all. I'm telling you this is going to be long and expensive, and the outcome is not likely to be in your favor. Also, and I know you've considered this so don't get angry, you need to focus on what's best for Katie."

He pressed the stress ball flat against his desk and held it there, his arm shaking, but a knock on his door interrupted his fury. He muffled the phone against his chest. "One minute," he called out, then raised the phone back to his ear. "Terry, she can't take Katie to California. She just can't."

UPENDED

After a long pause, Terry said, "I understand. If I can't find any better options, I'll file."

Joe hung up, sank into one of the chairs he reserved for visitors, and tried to muster the will to finish the day. Whenever he accidently lapsed into stillness like this, what started as rest descended into a paralyzed contemplation of all the screaming problems in his life, the slow-motion prelude to a terrible wreck. Sometimes surrender felt like the only possible response. Forget heroic evasive action, let go of the wheel, and watch unchecked momentum do its worst. But surrendering would mean the end to everything worthwhile in his life: the company, his partnership with Madeline, his ability to realize his own vision of the future— even being the kind of father to Katie he'd always imagined. It would mean lying down to be flattened by everything out of his control. Impossible.

The knock came again, and thinking it was Beth wanting to continue their argument, he snapped, "Yes, what is it?"

The door swung open to reveal Madeline, leaning on her cane and wearing a gray suit paired with a pale pink shirt. The sight broke down the flimsy barrier that held back the secret fantasy of him and Madeline together with Katie; their daughter coming to the office in the afternoons, doing schoolwork at the conference room table, Madeline or Joe popping in with snacks and help; the three of them walking home in the evening, a two-parent family even better than what Bridget and Darrin provided.

"Bad day?" Madeline asked, and that beautiful vision deepened with her unmistakably concerned tone.

"Darrin's being aggressively wooed by a company in Silicon Valley." Saying the words was an immediate relief, and he hoped she wouldn't somehow make him regret it.

She closed the door and walked to the chair next to him, limping a little. "Tell me," she said and listened to him exactly how she used to, with her gaze never wandering from his face, her hand moving to touch his knee then retreating, her attention focused so sharply it landed an inch or two under his skin. He felt so at home

186

in her intense interest that he leaned back in his chair and became expansive with his gestures. He forgot the filter he'd been using with her since the attack and spoke to her as to a friend—about his dismay that things with Bridget had turned sour, how he wished he had more time with Katie, how seeing Madeline negotiating her relationship with her father had made Joe adamant that he would be such a solid presence to Katie that she would take him for granted.

Then he heard himself say, "Now Terry's telling me Bridget's lawyers are sure to look into my finances—well, mine and the business's—and that's not something..." He stopped before he let slip what he'd been so careful to hide. "He's insinuating it's going to be ugly and that a judge will always pick the mother over the father."

"I'm surprised she's let Darrin get so far down this road. It doesn't seem like her."

"Apparently love is exception-making. At least that's her excuse."

"Fucking love." She said it while looking down at nails even more ragged than usual, her voice soft but firm.

"That sounded...somehow specific."

"It was. I— Forget it. Tell me if there's anything I can do to help."

"What were you going to say?"

She nibbled at a thumbnail and shook her head a degree or two each way, surely about to shut down the conversation like she'd been doing these last couple months. He braced himself for it, but she said, "I saw Jane recently."

"Jane Jane?"

"The one and only." She dropped her hand to her lap.

"How'd that go?"

Her eyebrows drew together and mouth curled down. "Ultimately terrible. More terrible for how not terrible it was at certain moments. She..." This time she shook her head nearly shoulder to shoulder. "The whole thing reminded me of dead desert mosses that come alive at a little rain. I swear I could see it in her, didn't even have to look very hard, I mean she practically said it, and"—she covered her mouth with her fingers but talked through them—"let's just say it was icing on the cake."

"Insult to injury?"

"Salt in the wound, definitely."

They sat amid the wreckages of their separate recent histories, contemplating each other and the carpet and the uninspiring art he'd been meaning to update. (An aerial view of Fenway Park? What had he been thinking?) The money he'd just transferred out of his savings to pay for the magazine advertisement and Pinskey's latest bill wouldn't go over well at a custody hearing. All they needed was a million to do it up right with no skimping and minimal stress. Maybe even only a half million. If he could secure that piece, everything else would fall right into place. Would moving their operations to Silicon Valley make getting funding easier? Would Madeline go with him? Not that he wanted to give Bridget an inch of satisfaction, but maybe what he and Madeline both needed was a major change, a great escape from this place and everything that had gone wrong here.

Madeline heaved an audible breath and propped herself up on an arm of the chair, getting comfortable. "By the way, it seems our clients talk to each other."

"Why, what are they saying?"

"I was just over at Ropes and Gray, and they asked me when they were going to get in on the software trial they've been hearing about. They were pressing for all sorts of technical details, which is a little crazy, since the app's not going to be done for at least another month, assuming only minimal things go wrong, which is probably overly optimistic."

In fact, Joe was pushing hard to sign up a couple of his accounts to start a trial in just over three weeks, and he had promised Pinskey a hefty bonus (which would also come out of his savings) if they delivered the software in two. Assuming, as Madeline said, that *some* things went wrong, he still expected them to come up with the goods before the trial was supposed to start. Next week, he would go back to Grasshopper and Bates and pitch the software approach at a fraction of the cost of their usual services. Getting those two on the hook might open up some venture capital pockets.

While all this went through his mind, he said, "I'm not sure where they're getting their information, but something's clearly garbled in translation."

She examined him for an uncomfortably long time, her eyes narrowed and steady. He kept his features relaxed and his hands at his sides, trying not to give anything away even though it felt like she could see right through him to the too-rapid beat of his heart. It wasn't just the lying he had to hide but the churning sadness of its necessity in the face of how they'd just been talking: open and honest and deeply personal like before the attack.

She blinked and shifted, her jacket falling open, revealing its silvery lining. "Okay…"

"I know you're anxious to get out from under that project, so you can forward any questions you get about the software to me."

"There are lots of things I'm anxious to get out from under. Not that she believed me, but I told Jane I'd turned over a new leaf and didn't work as much. When I said it, I wanted it to be true, but what's the point? If I'm honest with myself for once, I've made it so work is all I have right now."

"What do you mean honest for once?"

She got up and took her cane from the back of the chair. It both matched the steely gray of her suit and clashed horribly with its grace. "Let's not have this conversation, okay? This is exactly why Ethan and I aren't talking. It ends up becoming an unfair comparison between who I am now and a version of me that wasn't even real to begin with. Forget I said anything because I can't handle alienating you, too." She walked to the door and stopped with her hand on the knob. Her jaw flexed then relaxed, and her shoulders dropped. "I'm sorry about this California thing. Really. Anything I can do to help, let me know. And thanks for being here. I know 'difficult' barely scratches the surface of my behavior, and your putting up with it and hanging in means a lot."

When she left, he moved back behind his desk, thinking that putting himself in the right position would make it possible to get work done, but he hadn't managed to start on anything when Beth walked in. She leaned across his desk and whispered, "The ad's placed. Did you tell Madeline?"

"We had other things to discuss."

"Listen. If you don't come clean with Madeline, I'm going to quit. Not today, but soon."

"I get it."

She straightened up and smoothed down her skirt. "Don't make me regret telling you about my book and giving you those excerpts."

He was penned in by the truth and his lies and necessity and fantasy, but even as the path ahead grew increasingly claustrophobic, retreat was impossible, not after he'd just reconnected with Madeline when she'd listened to him about Darrin, when she'd told him about Jane. The absolute, unavoidable reality was that he was all in, which might (he admitted) end in disaster, but anything less would certainly leave him with nothing. Nothing at all.

CHAPTER 22

ON HIS SHORT WALK FROM THE BUS TO FUEL, ETHAN FELT individual air molecules play along his newly bare cheeks and thread through the quarter inch of hair he'd left on his head. This cut, which he'd accomplished with a set of clippers he'd discovered under the bathroom sink in a cabinet he'd never opened before, brought him back to his childhood in Arizona: hot sun on his scalp, head under a knit cap on cold desert nights, Maddy there then not there, his parents ubiquitous and alive. This surge of memory, coupled with how shaving had left his face raw and exposed, was fitting, seeing as he was on his way to sing two of the most personal songs he'd ever written. The process to get them into shape had been wrenching enough on its own without the chafing, ever-present absence of both Nettie and Maddy. After that storeroom altercation, Nettie had changed her shifts around so they never worked together, which had been a relief for the first few days but quickly became untenable.

And Maddy. The longer they didn't talk, the more guilt clogged his arteries. So many mornings, he woke up wondering why he was being such a dick with her. Her head had literally been beaten against a brick wall, and here he was, acting like another one. She was probably right that going to the police and fixing things might not do any good, but that didn't matter anymore.

This wasn't about the lie, had never been about the lie, to be honest. It was about how her sea change of personality had broken the age-old thrall she'd held him in, and how, without that, her rejection of his opinion (of anything he had to offer, actually) cut him to the quick. How could she refuse to consider his totally reasonable request that she tell the truth while at the same time admonishing him to grow up, already? And yet, he'd suffered a spasm of this requested maturity yesterday and sent her the info for this open mic, and this morning he'd shaved his beard, and now, even though the thought of singing one of these songs in front of her was terrifying, he wanted very much for her to appear.

Nettie was behind the counter when he got to Fuel, and the sight of her and her curtain of blond hair sent a charge through him made up of loneliness and regret. She wouldn't meet his gaze, and he parked himself in a corner after putting his name in the third slot on the open mic sign-in sheet. Some espresso would be nice. Maybe even a latte. But getting one required approaching Nettie, who was doused in a thick coating of Ethan repellant. He yearned to fix that, but the path to redemption was as muddy as a red eye with a splash of cream—Maddy's favorite drink.

He was nervous, which was silly over a stupid open mic, but even though he'd had some modicum of success down in Texas, this was different. He'd *lived* in the words and notes of these songs, even in the spaces between notes, maybe especially those. For weeks, he'd molded them into shapes that were clear and hard and like nothing he'd produced before, and cracking the lid on them was almost as scary as thinking he'd lost Maddy that night. Scary yet undeniably compelling, and this was something he knew she would completely understand. Or at least would have, before.

The spring she was eighteen, she'd obsessively checked the mailbox for responses to her college applications. Some afternoons, after their grilled cheese ritual, they would sit at either end of the living room couch and do homework, Maddy reading books dense with text while Ethan chugged through multiplication tables or marked capital cities on maps. She'd steal his art supplies to make drawings in her notebook and talk to him, interrupting them both. One day, when she was swiping pencils one by one to build up a thick rainbow across the corner of a paper half filled with notes, she said, "Maybe it's best if I go to ASU. It's a good school and cheap. No scholarship required. And I'd get to see you more often." She put the pencil down and sighed. "It's just, have you ever wanted something so much you think not getting it will actually maim you?"

"Like playing shortstop?"

"Yeah, like that. Only less specific." She put the orange pencil back and dug around in his case for the red. "Like wanting something super delicious for your birthday and not knowing what. But the idea of that something delicious teases you. It haunts you. And it'd be better for everyone if you knew what you wanted, but you don't. You just...want."

What did Maddy want now? For it not to have happened? For everyone to forget? Ethan could only guess. But tonight, he wanted to feel proud of himself. He wanted to surprise people. Delight them. Maybe even move them.

Nettie plunked a to-go cup down in front of him. "Latte. Three shots."

"Hey, thanks."

"You can pay at the end of the night," she said and turned away.

He was still cursing into his drink when the first person on the list—a tiny woman with a scary-powerful voice—took her place behind the mic at the same time Maddy came through the door, using a cane she didn't appear to need. His breath stilled inside his lungs. In fact, everything stopped except the rise of heat from his chest to his face. What had they been doing to each other? How stupid to hang on to their anger. Ethan watched her scan the room. In her work clothes, she looked so different from the last time he'd seen her—vastly more different from that night at the hospital. He closed his eyes against the memory (as if that would help). When he opened them again, she was halfway to his table, and she jumped when the tiny woman started to sing.

Then she was sitting next to him, leaning into him, saying, "Someone told her she had a wonderful voice when she was eight, and she never forgot it."

She was so cool and collected, and Ethan wondered how he was ever going to sing that song about her, about the her he'd seen at the hospital, the one she'd apparently sloughed off in the last few weeks. For years, Ethan had felt behind the times, had one foot in the game and one foot way, way out, and this had to stop, already.

Before he could say anything, she pressed lightly on his thigh and went over to the counter, leaving her cane hanging from the table. The tiny woman gave a long-winded introduction to her second song, and Ethan watched while Nettie and his sister tilted toward each other and had a conversation he suspected had nothing to do with coffee. In fact, they talked through the rest of the tiny woman and most of the willowy guy who came on after her, and Ethan had his guitar out and ready by the time Maddy returned to the table, carrying a tea. Mint, by the smell of it.

He asked, "Who are you, Grandma Ruth?"

"I read somewhere that caffeine causes insomnia, night sweats, and bad dreams. So, you know." They sat and listened to the willowy guy—or at least pretended to listen. Ethan tried to get any performance jitters out of the way by psyching himself out ahead of time to exhaust his adrenal system—an exercise that took no effort at all when Danika fucking Miller snuck in the door and slid into a free seat near the entrance. He'd wanted her there, had imagined impressing her into a deep acknowledgment of his existence, but now that she was actually here, he wanted to disappear into the back, to the space between the syrups and the extra paper cups he gravitated toward in times of crisis, and hide there until everyone left.

Well, maybe everyone but Nettie, though she'd probably just make him pay for the latte he hadn't even drunk and turn her back on him. That thought and the hopeless anger it prompted enabled him to ignore Danika Miller and the nothing Maddy had said about his newly naked face, march up to the microphone after the willowy guy, and dive into his first song without introduction or explanation.

Partway through the chorus after the first verse, he saw Danika Miller nodding along, and he cared but didn't at the same time—the exact something delicious Maddy had talked about so long ago, the perfect combination of savory and sweet, of heavy and light, of familiar and new, and it made him sing with a firm confidence. He loved it so much right then he didn't care how messed up everything else in his life was.

He almost didn't care about the applause, which was downright raucous for the small crowd. When it died down, he said, "This one's for my big sis, who hauled herself all the way up here from J.P. tonight."

And he was off, eyes drifting closed from the get-go—to concentrate, to block out the people looking at him, to forget Maddy was out there. This one had some gnarly chord changes, a brush of percussion in the choruses. And the lyrics, of course.

Bones bent, smile broken
Harsh words she'd never spoken
Beaten, bloodied down that day
Still, she'll somehow find her way.

When he was done, he was sure there'd been a moment of silence before the applause, a moment during which he continued to leak breath from the last phrase. When he opened his eyes and saw Maddy, his throat clenched tight, making it hard to swallow.

Her arms were folded, and her chin was tucked against her chest. Ethan's heart pounded while he untangled himself from the chair and mic chord and walked over to hear the surely damning verdict, but Danika Miller intercepted him, giving him a hug and some whacks on the back. "Awesome, man. Really. You didn't play stuff like that before, did you?"

"I guess not." He looked at Maddy, who hadn't changed position. "I got inspired."

"No kidding. Do you have more like that?"

"A couple, but those are the best."

"I'd love to hear them."

"Oh, they're not ready."

She laughed. "Now's not the time for modesty, man. I'm serious. Let's get together soon."

Maddy got up and put her hand on his shoulder. "I should go. Early meeting tomorrow. Walk me out?"

"Sure. Of course." He ducked out from under his guitar strap and tried to decide where to set the instrument. "Let me get this put away."

Danika Miller gave them a heavy, meaningful look. "I'll hold it. Go ahead."

Just outside the door, Maddy stopped and turned around. Her ears were so red they were fluorescent in the summer evening sunlight, but she said, "That was awesome, Ethan. Really incredible."

"But you're mad."

"How could I be mad when you've never written anything remotely as good as that?"

"But you are."

"Goddamn it, I'm not mad!" she yelled. "I'm— I'm— Fuck." It came out in a growl. "How could you sing that about me? Not only sing it but call me out before? What were you thinking?"

"I don't know, maybe that you'd actually listen, that you'd hear the hope in it."

Her face squeezed in pain, and he wondered about her ribs and shoulder. But she said, "Sometimes, for a few minutes or an hour, I can forget it happened. I can succeed in forgetting, which is *really hard*, Ethan, and now you've set remembering to a perfect melody! What am I supposed to do with that? What am I supposed to do with how damaged you think I am?"

"Nothing, okay? I wrote what I felt, and you weren't around to consult. I didn't even know if you were going to be here tonight."

"You're the one who took off."

He shoved his hands in his pockets. "What do you want from me? I try to be responsible—or get you to be responsible—and you come down on me. And when I'm regularly irresponsible, you let me get away with it. 'There's Ethan, my fuckup of a younger brother.'"

"I don't think that."

"*Sure* you don't. You know, just because Mom and Dad dying didn't faze you doesn't mean something's wrong with me because I had a hard time. I was *really* upset, Maddy, and your being calm and collected and above it all didn't help. There's Maddy, all forgiving and accepting and mature. Showing us up just by breathing."

"Are you shitting me with that?" She started to walk away, but Ethan ripped a hand from a pocket and grabbed her arm. She whirled around. "I can't believe you just said that."

A couple passed by, eyeing them with suspicion as if deciding whether to intervene, or maybe call the cops. Wouldn't that be rich. He dragged her around the corner to a quiet spot. "You're right that I left things with Dad badly, and I really don't want to do that with you, but I can't be this rag doll of a person anymore. I'm not going to accept whatever you say, nod my head like a jackass when you're absolutely fucking wrong."

"I don't expect—"

"Yes you do, Maddy. Yes you do!"

Then it was like someone slapped her or flipped some hidden panic switch, and she was crying. Ah, shit, he thought and pulled her into a hug, partly so he wouldn't have to see her crumpled face. Ah, shit.

She tried, mostly unsuccessfully, to talk through her tears, saying disjointed things like "I can't be—" and "He knew I was—" and "I don't f-f-fucking care if—"

UPENDED

Finally, she pulled away from him, assaulting her eyes and nose with the heel of one hand while the other choked the life out of her cane. "You think you know me, but I don't even know myself, so how could you? Everything is either a mystery or a mistake."

"Which one is the lie you told?"

"*The* lie?" She barked out a laugh. "Like that was the only one. Or the worst one. I know you're making some kind of statement or plea by shaving that shitty-ass beard, but you've *got* to let this police thing go. Please. Drop it."

"But—"

"It was a stupid mistake, okay? I told you. I slipped up, said the wrong thing, and the way they jumped on it, pushed me about it, I didn't want to tell the truth for once. I didn't want for it to have happened. I didn't want to have had the evening I had leading up to it. I didn't want to admit that to anyone. I made a mistake at first, but I *chose* not to correct it. I don't care if it's a terrible choice, because it's the only thing I hold in my hands about any of this," she said, hitting herself way too hard in the chest. "Don't you see?"

He didn't, particularly, but he tried not to show it.

Apparently he was unsuccessful because she made an annoyed noise. "He got to me. Inside me. The smell of his breath, the sound of his voice, the feel of his hands. I was invaded and then the police...they wanted to march right into that opening and do it again, and I couldn't let them. I *wouldn't* let them. I needed to own myself. Tell a story that wasn't the real story."

"Maddy—"

"Why did you come to Boston when Dad died? Why did you drop out of school when Mom died?"

Then, like a major chord creeping from the darkness of a minor one, he felt a glimmer of understanding. He'd needed to *do* something, to take some kind of control, to put intentional distance between the before him and the after him.

She watched him, then said, "And by the way, fuck you very much for thinking I cruised through their deaths. You think you

198

had regrets? I practically didn't have parents after I came out—at least until the end with Dad. I was crushed."

"You sure hid it well."

"I had to take care of things."

"The world won't end if you lose your shit for a while. Maybe you should try it."

She snorted, wet and snotty. "I lost it pretty well recently, and you didn't seem very happy about it."

"Well, what do you expect? I'm the immature, inconsistent one." She smiled at that, and he had to hug her again so she wouldn't be able to see the enormity of his relief.

When he let her go, she looked at her shoes, business all the way to their high shine. "I know I don't make sense and you don't understand and are probably right, but it doesn't matter, not really." She took a deep breath that lifted her shoulders and face, then gazed at him and tilted her head to the right a bit. "You look almost handsome without all that hair." He struck a glamour pose, and she laughed. "I said almost. By the way, what happened between you and Nettie?"

"None of your beeswax."

"You should ask her out."

He laughed. "Very funny. She hates my guts."

"She's crazy about you, and she broke up with the cretin she was dating."

He looked back toward the shop as if catching a glimpse of Nettie would make this information sink in.

Maddy touched his arm. "I'm sorry, okay? For disappointing you."

"You didn't—"

"I know when you're lying."

"No, you don't. You didn't disappoint me. You scared the hell out of me, then confused me, then made me crazy."

"Yeah, well anyway, I'm sorry. And that song was beautiful. Just don't ever sing it in front of me again. It made me want to go back and barricade myself in my apartment."

"Noted."

They talked for a couple more minutes until Maddy started yawning, and they agreed it was the mint tea at work. She hugged him and left. He heard faint applause from inside the shop and knew he had to go deal with Danika Miller and maybe Nettie, too. But for a moment longer, he stood and felt the air against his face.

When he went in, he sat next to Danika Miller, who had taken Maddy's vacated seat, and she handed his guitar to him without a word and barely a glance. But when the current song wrapped up, signaling the ten-minute break in the middle of the lineup, she leaned closer and said, "I've been thinking. Can you put together a twenty-minute set of that quality by July 5? Jeff Horton was supposed to open for me at Somerville Theatre, but he got an offer he couldn't refuse, and I've been looking around for a replacement."

Opening for Danika Miller was nothing in the face of the rest of his experience, but he knew very well he was starting over, and a break was a break. "Twenty minutes? Sure, I can do that."

They coordinated a time and place to get together again, then she disappeared—first from his table then the shop. He itched to leave, too, but what Maddy had said about Nettie kept him from going anywhere through another half dozen open mic participants, men and women, young and old, decent and horrifying, until it was just him left languishing at his table while Nettie and Justin, a new hire who was too good-looking for Ethan's taste, hurried through their closing tasks.

He took his guitar case up to the counter and laid four dollars in front of Nettie. "Keep the change."

She swept up the money. "Thanks." Without looking at him, she said, "You did great."

"Does that mean you're talking to me again?"

"No."

"Why didn't you tell me you broke up with The Boyfriend?"

"What business is it of yours?"

"Or that you liked me?"

Then Nettie did look at him, and he wished a curtain of hair still hung between them. "Get out of here, Ethan. Just...leave."
Okay, so he didn't have quite everything figured out yet.

CHAPTER 23

ADELE HAD ZOE PINNED DOWN WITH A STREAM-OF-CONSCIOUSNESS monologue about Kimberly's wedding, but that didn't stop her from touching on such topics as the dismal state of road repair in and around Albany, the ins and outs of global warming, and how impossible it was to keep the entryway grout clean. Zoe listened with half an ear, tuned to pauses that called for some kind of response while she perched on the couch, reminding herself not to get comfortable since she had to extricate herself soon or risk being late to meet Madeline at the Museum of Fine Arts. She alternated between flipping through a *Men's Health* magazine (that Troy "read" for the articles) and checking her watch.

Adele said, "Don't forget, your final dress fitting is in two weeks. Then don't gain an ounce until the big day—not that that's ever been a problem for you. You and Troy are always so slim. Too skinny, almost, though who in their right mind would complain about that? And, please, nothing drastic with your hair. For what the photographer's charging, these pictures had better last forever."

"Unless Kimmy and Devon get divorced," Zoe said, which proved her ultimate distraction. Divorce ranked right up there with death in her family's scale of tragedy. The choice between divorce and, say, a felony conviction was a real toss-up, though she suspected some of her more distant cousins would prefer jail time to their marriage. About her split with Sebastian, Zoe had once heard her mother say, "At least she did it before the wedding," which Zoe knew was about more than nonrefundable deposits or mailed invitations.

She held the phone away from her ear while Adele elevated her divorce lecture to a level of excruciating detail. Eventually, Troy appeared from the hall and leaned over the back of the couch to whisper into Zoe's ear. "Still Adele?"

"I accidently said the 'D' word in relation to Kimmy."

"Why would you do a thing like that?" he asked. Then he called out, "Hi, Adele!"

The sound of Troy's voice disrupted Adele's tirade, and Zoe handed the phone over to him so she could finish getting ready. In the bathroom, she ran her hands through her hair, shaping it into something styled (but not obviously so) while trying not to look at her nose and cheeks and chin, knowing how easily she could cascade into criticality about how all her pieces didn't quite fit together. At least her ears were nice: small but not freakishly so, hung at just the right height, and sleek against her skull. Out in the living room, Troy's amiable voice didn't soothe her like it did Adele. Kimberly's wedding was looming *large*, and Zoe couldn't stand the thought of taking Troy as her fake date. A cousin's wedding was one thing, but her kid sister's?

Troy laughed, and it sounded so genuine maybe it actually was. He and Adele actually got along quite well, no matter how much Troy pretended he was humoring her. Zoe put away hairspray and product and abandoned any more sprucing up. No matter how much her stomach dropped in anticipation each time she thought of seeing Madeline today, this wasn't a date. Not. A. Date. Even so, she refused to be late, so she went to give Troy a signal to get off the phone.

He was lounging on the couch with his bare feet propped on that *Men's Health*, saying, "Of course I'll wear the blue suit. Didn't we decide that when you girls finally picked your dresses? And so you know, I plan to bend my knees and stoop a bit so I don't stick out in the pictures too much."

Those pictures of a studied homogeny were forever, Zoe thought and felt a flare of panic. She took the phone from Troy and interrupted Adele's laughing. "Mom, I've got to go and meet a friend soon. I'll call you during the week, okay?"

It took a few more minutes to free herself from the conversation, but when she did, Troy said, "See?"

"Yeah, you've got the golden touch with her, all right."

"It's Madeline, isn't it? This friend you're meeting?"

"Yes, it is."

He sat up and twisted around, putting his arm over the back of the couch to face her. "Things were fine between us before her."

Zoe slid her phone in a back pocket of her jeans and took a half step to the door, glancing back at the tangle of shoes just inside for the loafers she was planning on wearing. "That depends on your definition of 'fine.' Besides, since when did fine become the ultimate goal? Don't you want more than fine? Don't you want more than me?"

"It's not that simple, and you know it."

"I don't know if I do, actually. I mean, if you expand your scope of 'it' enough, complications are inevitable, but that's life. If you look at just you and me, it's simple." She kept easing toward the door, feeling the seconds slide by.

"She's not even good for you, but you'll puppy-dog around her until she's had enough and breaks your heart. And where will you be then?"

She shrugged with a jerk. "I don't know. Hurt. Sad. But alive."

"Alone."

"What's so bad about being alone? Maybe that's exactly what I need to get desperate enough to paint again." She finally made it past the threshold between living room and entryway, past the big gap in the hardwood floor that had snagged practically every sock she owned.

"God, Zoe!" Troy said so loudly it stopped her short. "It's like you think I'm responsible for your every disappointment. I *want* you to paint. I think you're awesome, and arguing like this— I want everything to be okay and us to be happy." He sighed and made a complicated, dramatic motion with his hands. "But if you're so upset with how things are, stop fighting with me about it and leave."

Everything happened at exactly the worst time. She had to get going or be late to her next sticky complication, but she made herself stand still and feel the astute truth of his words and the many layers of her hesitation. "You're right. It's not that simple."

"I love you, Zoe. You're my best friend."

Her face scrunched up, and she turned away from him to their shoes, where her loafers were tangled with his sandals, her oxfords with his wingtips. "I have to go. I really do. But I'll be back this afternoon. I promise. We'll talk then."

DESPITE HOW INTENTIONALLY ZOE HAD LOWERED HER expectations about this afternoon, "not a date" was laughably apt. For an hour, she dragged Madeline from gallery to gallery, plumbing the depths of her companion's total ignorance of art. The woman didn't even know the basics covered in the first week of a freshman survey class, and Zoe swallowed a disappointment made bitter by Troy's prediction and gave a rambling lecture about composition and perspective, color theory, and what she'd picked up about restoration techniques.

Madeline offered up virtually nothing of substance in return. She talked about the weather (unseasonably warm), about the freedom of finally being rid of her cane, and about the minor insanity of Rosemary having an entire child neither of them had heard of. In between, she asked on-point questions about the concepts Zoe presented as if this visit were, above all, an academic field trip. But she also wore a diaphanous blue blouse that begged to be touched, and she stood a few inches too close to Zoe at each painting.

To cope with this boggling dichotomy, Zoe let her mind drift during each bout of lecturing, which was easy enough to do, given that she was regurgitating concepts drilled into her twenty years before. But that, too, backfired when her thoughts turned to Troy or Kimberly or her own painting at Rosemary's and Bernard Collins's business card, which reposed on the top of her dresser along with a spray of spare change and crumpled receipts, gathering more than dust.

The more exhibit rooms they visited, the more Zoe wondered what she was doing here anyway. With Madeline around, it wasn't as if she could sink into a painting like she usually did on these visits. This was nothing more than an antiseptic walking tour of the thing that had once been vitally important to Zoe. She should've stayed home to work things out with Troy. She should've called Bernard Collins weeks ago and seen that through to its inevitable nothing. She should do just about anything other than stand next to this woman who couldn't possibly be worth this amount of angst.

But she guided them along to the Japanese area, saying, "I have to admit I don't know much about this kind of art, but I find it fascinating. They have an incredible collection here, and I always make time to look at a piece or two when I visit."

"I took a class in business school about Japan, and their culture is..." Madeline gazed over Zoe's head as if searching for the right word.

"Foreign," Zoe supplied.

"To say the least."

They turned a corner into the exhibit, and there, as the latest chapter in this labyrinthine bad dream, was Charlotte Devine, an old Mass Art classmate of Zoe's. She spotted Zoe immediately and was all over her with hugging and cheek kissing and introductions to an awkward husband.

Zoe inclined her head toward Madeline. "This is...Madeline Sawyer. Madeline, Charlotte Devine, an old friend."

Charlotte reached to shake Madeline's hand. She was still as bottle-blond as ever but had rounded out her figure with a few more pounds, which actually suited her plus-sized, pinup-girl personality. "Devine, Doolittle," Charlotte said. "Not only practically next to each other in the alphabet but equally as..."

"Notable," Zoe said.

"Exactly. Destined to be friends, but it's been years."

"Six. No, seven."

"Don't. You're making me feel old. How's Sebastian?"

"I wouldn't know. We split a long time ago."

"Oh! Well, to be honest, he was easy on the eyes, sure, and loaded"—she fanned herself, prompting a stink eye from her mute husband—"but you were, too, I don't know...free-spirited for him."

Madeline eased closer to Zoe and captured her hand from where it had drifted up to the back of her head. She then entwined their fingers in a way that surely looked natural, was meant to look natural, but was so shocking Zoe was hard-pressed not to stare at Madeline in disbelief.

Charlotte flicked her focus from their hands to Zoe's face. "And there's that."

Emboldened by the feel of Madeline's warm fingers between hers, Zoe said, "Yeah, it turns out he wasn't my type."

"I can see that. How long have you two been together?" Charlotte glanced down at Zoe's left hand, which was bare of any rings. "Is marriage in your future?"

Madeline was so smooth, turning questions back around to Charlotte and her husband without giving anything away. She

207

drove the conversation deftly, leveraging Charlotte's tendency to babble. In the world Madeline projected by her very ease, *of course* she and Zoe were together. Why wouldn't they be? All the while, Zoe's hand lay deliciously paralyzed in Madeline's grasp.

When Zoe feared Charlotte was going to attach herself to them for the rest of the afternoon, her husband leaned in and whispered something, which sparked a flurry of parting hugs and promises to stay in touch. Zoe savored the last moments of physical contact with Madeline while she craned her neck to watch Charlotte and her husband walk from the exhibit, turn a corner, and disappear. Then Madeline let go of Zoe's hand—not dropping it but disengaging so lightly, almost reluctantly (in Zoe's imagination), that their fingers dragged across each other when they came apart.

Zoe considered pretending the last quarter hour had never happened, talking about lacquer and folded steel—folded everything with the Japanese—but she said, "I guess some people didn't get the memo about me."

"Were you two close? Besides alphabetically?"

"We were the kind of school friends who are close until graduation. Or, I should say, until I had enough doubt about my engagement to Sebastian that I opened up distance between us. And not just Charlotte, but pretty much everyone."

Madeline smiled a little bit, not even showing her teeth. "He was easy on the eyes, huh?"

"Yes, extremely. And funny. Even people who knew I was gay before I did thought I was crazy. My art friends especially, since I could have painted as much as I wanted without the pressure of ever having to be successful—at least in a monetary way."

"Sounds nice."

"Doesn't it?" She felt herself pulled in by that imagined relaxation but snapped out of it and adjusted her glasses. "But it would be a lie, though a more comfortable one than what I'm living now."

"You mean by not telling your family?"

"Among other things."

Madeline cocked an eyebrow in question, but Zoe shook her head out of loyalty to Troy and their private mess. Madeline said, "I'm beginning to think everyone's living a lie to some degree."

"You're probably right, but that's a bullshit excuse. All this art in here? It's honest, or it wouldn't be hanging on these walls. It would be in hotel lobbies or some unfortunate mother's living room. That doesn't necessarily mean the artists were always honest with themselves, but I don't believe they could make this if they were completely disingenuous."

Madeline looked away from Zoe and bit at one of her thumbnails. "My brother's a musician. A good one. He laid some of his honest art on me the other night, and it was uncomfortable as hell, which I guess is an accurate reflection of my life right now."

"Sometimes discomfort is necessary to shake you out of complacency and give you fresh eyes. I wonder if I could've painted at all if I'd stayed with Sebastian. I mean, even without his support, I managed to drown myself in easy acceptance, and my art went down the toilet. If you want the truth, I stopped painting because I was disgusted at how fake it had become. At least at IDK, when I'm putting together an ad for your software, it doesn't pretend to be something it's not."

Madeline's gaze snapped back to Zoe, and she dropped her hand to her side, her blouse settling to rest around her arm in a soft drape Zoe wanted to reach out and touch. "What ad?" she asked.

"You know, the two-page spread with the mobile display rendering?" Madeline didn't even blink in recognition. "The one with the bar chart? In Mindful Management green? I delivered it to Joe last week."

"So he asked you to design it? When did he do that? Did he say what it was for? When he wanted to run it? Where?" Questions tumbled out of her too quickly to answer, and Zoe took a half step back, then another, from the craziness unspooling in front of her.

When Madeline ran out of steam, Zoe said, "Hey, what's going on?"

"He did this behind my back. That mother*fucker*," she said forcefully but softly. "I knew he was lying to me. I *knew* it. But why?" Madeline's lips clamped into a thin line that she twisted back and forth. Then, as quickly as the anger came in, it dissolved into a loose despair. Her hand drifted upward again but this time to her eyes, and she turned her back to Zoe.

Zoe was as clueless about what was going on as Madeline was about the mad genius of Van Gogh's perspective, but she felt Madeline's suffering nestle deep in her stomach, right up against her angst about Troy and her family. She closed the gap between them and embraced Madeline from behind. They were so close Zoe could feel when Madeline took a deep breath and held it. And held it. And held it some more. Zoe tightened her arms and whispered, "Breathe, Madeline."

The air finally came out with a hitch and a moan, but Madeline made no move to pull away. "I trusted him even though I knew he was lying. I trusted him absolutely, thought he was the one stable thing...What am I doing? Really, what the *fuck* am I doing?"

In grand contrast to Madeline's confusion, Zoe knew exactly what the fuck she was doing: she was holding someone she wanted to hold. Was this the perfect scenario? No, not by a long shot. But at the same time, it felt perfect in its imperfection. Madeline's outward distress matched Zoe's inner disarray, and while the combination might be the ultimate recipe for disaster, Zoe was okay with that. The huge potential of getting hurt was an acceptable cost for experiencing this feeling of being resonantly alive and herself.

Madeline reached up and squeezed one of Zoe's arms before turning around. "You should be painting, not designing advertisements."

"And you should maybe tell me what's happening."

Madeline nodded until it seemed less agreement than muscular impairment. "Is there a place to sit down around here?"

In the museum's café, they perched across a small table from each other, cradling paper cups of tea while Madeline talked about Joe's recent strangeness and his single-minded insistence on the completion of this software project, acting like it would save them. But save them from what? Themselves? Pressures in the marketplace?

"He's frantic about pushing us forward, and I don't know why. We've talked about expanding, mostly by investing in this app and automation, but it was never really what I wanted...I thought maybe I needed to let go of my doubts and recommit myself, but I was fooling myself as much as Joe's trying to fool me. This job was supposed to bring people together, you know?" She looked at Zoe as if it weren't a rhetorical question, but she went on before Zoe had to come up with an answer. "If I'm really honest, I hoped it would lure my dad fully into my life so I could have both Jane and him. And it was working, too, on my dad. He saw me. Most of me, at least. But it pushed Jane away, then he died, and now it's a cosmic joke." She rotated her cup one quarter turn and shrugged.

Despite the mention of that persistent ex, Zoe wanted to reach out and comfort Madeline by touching her hand or arm or even her knee under the table—something simple and genuine like Madeline would do without even thinking about it. The problem was that Zoe wasn't Madeline, and the hug she'd given her in the gallery was already a move so out of character it couldn't be repeated for the rest of this day, if not the whole month. Madeline telling her she should be painting was easy: *of course* she should be painting, all she'd done recently was whine about not painting. But what could Zoe possibly say about anything Madeline was going through: the attack, her father, this job, not to mention the ever-present ghost of Jane?

If she couldn't say anything useful or touch Madeline or satisfy her sudden, overwhelming desire to paint (which she hadn't felt with this kind of urgency in years), the only other avenue left to release this rolling boil of emotion was to spit out something so honest and pent up no one in her right mind would ever say it. "I'm falling for you, Madeline. Or maybe have already fallen. I'm

UPENDED

not exactly sure, but they're essentially the same thing, right? Or end up the same thing. Gravity, you know."

Her gaze slid away from Madeline's face to the steam coming off her tea and the perpetual motion of her thumb rubbing back and forth and back and forth over the cup's recycled cardboard sleeve. Time spun out sickeningly, her thoughts spiraling right along with it. Things were over with Troy; their friendship would never survive the breakup of their fake relationship. She'd have to find a new place to live, maybe one with the right light (or right enough) and room to paint, though her canvasses had always been too large to deal with at home. How much was studio space going for these days?

She'd almost managed to forget what an ass she'd just made out of herself when Madeline said, "I..." She was a collage of pinched eyebrows and glossy, red-rimmed eyes.

"I know. You're unavailable. Want to be Rosemary buddies. I get it."

"I didn't say that."

"I know, but you don't have to. I understand."

"No, you don't understand."

"Or you're *damaged*," Zoe said, prying her hands from her cup long enough to make finger quotes.

"Yes," Madeline whispered.

"We're all damaged in some way. It's called being human. It's called having skin in the game. Before this shit went down, I had a silly crush on you, but now that you're totally real to me, it's so much more. It may sound stupid, masochistic, but it's true. People who haven't been through something hard, whether voluntarily or not, are shells, and I want more than that. I know it's inconvenient, but it's true, and isn't that what you keep talking about? The truth?"

"I can't do this right now."

"No, you just think you can't. If you want to, you can. If you don't want to, that's something else. But I'm guessing you're so tangled

212

in your own brain that you can't even get down to deciding what you do or don't want."

"You don't know the first thing about me."

"Come on, I know plenty about you. At *least* the first thing. I'd like to know the second and third things, too, if you'll let me." Her heart was pounding, and she stood up before she knew what she was doing, full of an overwhelming energy, a certain badassery she hadn't felt in years. "We're all confused, you know, making it up as we go along. I've been lying to myself and everyone else for ages, running around, convinced I had it figured out. I thought I was making choices with my eyes wide open, but I wasn't. Not until you came around and woke me up."

After all that, she wanted to crawl under the table and give in to embarrassment, but Madeline interrupted her chagrin by saying, "I didn't do anything, though. I'm just trying to deal with my own shit."

"Yeah. I know. And this probably doesn't make it any easier, so I'm sorry about that. I need to go, but maybe you should stay here awhile, enjoy the museum, and call me when you want to talk again. *If* you want to talk again, now that you know how I feel." She left without waiting to hear how Madeline might respond.

She walked through the museum to the exit, shaking and horribly exhilarated. She wasn't at all sure what she was doing, but the doing itself felt terrific. After emerging into the sunny summer afternoon, she headed into the Fenway with long, hurried strides. The trees were emerald green, the sky behind them cerulean blue, and when she couldn't see the MFA anymore, she sat down on a bench and let her eyes drink it in and become reacquainted with color.

CHAPTER 24

AFTER ZOE LEFT HER AT THE MFA, MADELINE SAT VERY STILL, HER gaze affixed to the white plastic top on her cup of tea. In her peripheral vision, she saw people move to and from the tables around her, but she didn't budge—certainly not to go look at paintings, which had to have been a joke. Madeline was, aside from some lingering aches, physically recovered from the attack, but her skin felt as thin as tissue paper. If she moved too quickly from her seat, the holes that had already appeared at the revelation of Joe's subterfuge and Zoe's feelings would snag on the museum's soft air and rip wide open.

She wanted to go back to that Japanese gallery and stand with Zoe's arms around her, not to relive her reaction to Joe's lies but to sink into that physical contact, to receive a simple instruction to breathe and to follow that and nothing more. But there was always something more. When she finally unfroze herself enough to take a sip of her tea, it had cooled to room temperature. Tea was bad enough, but lukewarm tea? She got up, tossed the cup in the nearest trash bin, and went home.

From the permanent depression she'd made in the couch since the attack, she logged in to her laptop and pored through project documents and contracts, shared folders and cloud drives, but she found nothing out of the ordinary until she realized she was locked out of their accounting software. Digging more deeply, she failed to find the agreements with Grasshopper or Bates that Joe had told her should be there. In fact, she found no contracts executed since the attack. Instead of the hot, queasy anger that had come to her so easily lately, she felt a cold dread, and she retreated, picked a book off her shelf—a whodunit she already knew the who-what-why-how of—and read that and another book for the next twelve hours straight before succumbing to sleep. When she woke, she read even more and more, not stopping until her eyes refused to focus.

Monday morning, when she pried herself out of bed for a meeting at Pinskey, she felt heavy with undigested words and her own unsavory history. She wanted to abdicate it all, slip out from under the burden of hurt and disappointment and stifling regret and start fresh, but what would it mean if she tried to refuse her past? If she attempted to outrun the echoes of it that reverberated into the present, wouldn't it still be defining her direction as much or more than any free will she might still have? The past was never gone. It knitted itself into the warp and weave of life's fabric despite any attempt at eradication, so what was left but to accept it?

Just as the trauma and fear of her coming out had long ago become an objective fact, so would this new shitty situation. Time would compress the attack and her fear and anger and lies into hard nuggets of indivisible, formative information—dates, times, milestones that could be set out in a dry sequence of events. It would be her history, no matter what she felt about it.

She'd tried to convince Ethan she owned the lies she'd told the police, and if she owned them, didn't that mean she owned the lies she'd told Jane? That she'd told herself? And where did that leave lies of omission—everything she hadn't told people about the attack? She'd paid homage to the truth for most of her life, but now she was pretzeled up in her own deception and had to figure out how to untangle herself. Zoe had made moving forward sound easy, but right now nothing was easy or normal or obvious, and Madeline could barely remember who she'd tried to convince of what, least of all herself.

WHEN MADELINE ARRIVED AT PINSKEY, SERGEI WAS WAITING IN the Spartan reception area, leaning against a bright white wall and watching her with his usual broody expression. She set her face in a smile—pleasant but not overwhelming, the one he responded to the best—and felt queasy at this kind of effortless deception that had greased the wheels of her whole life.

This was not the time, she told herself, not in front of Sergei, of all emotionally tone-deaf people. She remembered the task at hand and said, "Ready to get started? I'm looking forward to seeing IDK's elements in the app."

His head ticked to his left like a clock's second hand. "There's nothing to get started on. It is finished." He presented a DVD in a slim case, holding it between his first two fingers like a cigarette.

"What do you mean it's finished?"

"I mean finished. Done. Complete. All boxes checked, and bug count equals zero. See? Finished. Source code, documentation, manual. Everything like you requested. Also"—he crossed the room and slid a piece of paper toward her along the top of the receptionist's desk—"the waiver."

Madeline squinted at him as if that would put his words into understandable focus. He wagged the DVD with a flick of his fingers until she snatched it from him. What she wanted to say was *What the fuck?* but she managed to keep it to, "I understand 'finished,' but I don't understand how it happened or who decided on these deliverables or...what waiver?" She picked it up from the desk and skimmed it enough to understand it was assigning all intellectual property over to Mindful Management. She said, "I thought it would be another month."

Sergei shrugged. "Overtime. The big boss said, and we delivered. I always deliver." He winked. "You'll want the new app on your phone." He held out his hand for her device and fiddled with it while he talked. "You're feeling better. That's good to see. Pain clouds the mind unless you're trained to handle it."

"And you're trained?"

He looked at her with complete seriousness. "Vodka," he said, pronouncing it with a 'w' instead of 'v.' "Every Russian knows this."

She let out a short laugh. "My mind's clouded enough without pain. Or vodka." That was both true and completely manipulative.

His attention was back on getting the app installed, but he said, "You have a fine mind. An A-plus mind. You have trained me well, or so this software says. We use it here—to work out the bugs, you know. You Americans call this 'eating our own dog food,' as if we're animals. It is a bit, how do you say, psychedelic, but effective. The code runs like clockwork and tells me my meetings are productive. Gold star, right?"

"Productive still indicates room for improvement. It's two steps away from 'indispensable,' so don't get ahead of yourself."

"Ahead of myself is the only place to be." He held out her phone. "All set. The DVD has instructions on how to load the app until you put it in a store for your customers. Okay?" He held up another piece of paper. "Receipt. It says we give you what we give you. You need to sign." She signed. "And your final invoice." He passed along an envelope she took as gingerly as a ticking bomb. "*Now* we are finished. Celebratory drink tonight?"

She shook her head with a half smile. "Still a lesbian."

"Can you fault a guy for trying?"

"Sergei, for the last time—"

"Yes, yes. Da. You Americans and your fickle harassment."

"Not fickle."

UPENDED

He waved her off. "Is it harassment to say it was good to work with you? No. And if you change your mind about the gay thing..."

"Sergei."

He held up his hands. "Kidding. Okay, then." He turned and went back into the main office without another word.

"Okay then," she said to herself.

MADELINE MADE THE MISTAKE OF LOOKING AT PINSKEY'S INVOICE on the train ride out to Brookline. The bottom-line figure made her swear a blue streak, and by the time she arrived at the office, she was so angry it actually felt good—strong and unambiguous. Being pissed was a hell of a lot easier than all that understanding and forgiving she'd done for most of her life. Screw understanding. Everyone was a complete mystery in the end.

She flung open the door to the office suite, making Beth jump. "Is he here?" Without waiting for an answer, she walked to Joe's office and looked inside. Empty. She went back to the kitchenette. No one. When she turned around, Beth was standing right behind her. "Where is he?"

"Madeline, listen."

"Is he signing up someone else for our software trial? Commissioning another ad from IDK? Hm?"

"He said he'd be in soon, but Madeline—"

She took Pinskey's bill from her bag and shook it at Beth. "Did you know about this? The rush on app development? Did you? They charged us an arm and a leg for it. Joe and I will be eating ramen for months to pay off this premium."

Beth backed away from her. "Listen, you need to calm down."

She was probably right, but Madeline said, "What the fuck, Beth? How long have the two of you been lying to me?"

"You have to talk to Joe," Beth said while walking back to her desk, her high heels stealthy across the carpet.

"I'm talking to you."

"No, you're not. You're yelling, and I'm going out for some coffee. Maybe you'll be yourself again by the time I get back." She slung her purse over her shoulder and hurried out the door.

Her exit both inflamed and shamed Madeline. Herself again? Beth sure had high hopes. She paced back and forth across the office, her rushed, thunderous steps burning off her anger despite herself. Her heart eased back from its previous pounding racket, and the flush of her temper receded from her face. Finally, when her pacing started to feel neurotic rather than necessary, she went into her office, sat behind her desk, and tried, mostly unsuccessfully, not to think.

CHAPTER 25

Joe encountered Beth in the atrium of their building, where she was drinking a coffee from Peet's. Though she looked calm, when she spoke, her words were sharp as knives. "This is all your fault. I knew you should have told her what was going on weeks ago. But you went behind her back, and she nearly took my head off for it."

"What happened? What did she do?"

Beth briefed him on Madeline's rage in such a merciless way he expected to look down and find blood. He fell on his sword as hard as he could, apologizing until she sighed and said, "Don't use up all your groveling on me. Go work things out with Madeline."

He went upstairs slowly, girding himself for an onslaught of Madeline's temper—but, at the same time, relief lifted his shoulders. He had hoped to be farther along with his plan, but one of Mindful Management's tenets was that reality could not be wished away. He braced himself before opening the door to their suite.

"Beth?" Madeline asked.

"No, Joe." He walked to her office, stopping in the doorway.

She sat at her desk, still as a mannequin, her face pale, not flushed with rage. This waxy version of her was unnerving, and he was glad when she finally blinked and spoke. "I was at Pinskey this morning for a review meeting we've had on the books for weeks, and it turns out they're finished. Funny that I didn't know about the overtime you authorized. Or the ad you had IDK design. Or the contracts that were never closed. Or the software trial you lied to my face about."

He moved some papers from the chair across from her and sat down.

She asked, "How many clients have you signed up for the trial?"

"Only two, though I think Grasshopper might come on board this week. It's cheaper than our conventional consulting."

She put her forearms on her desk and leaned over them. Her eyes narrowed in a squint that pulled her eyebrows together. "What's going on?"

"I have a plan."

"Did Pinskey tell you how much that rush was going to cost? *A lot*, that's how much." She picked up an envelope from in front of her and tossed it over to him. "And I'm sure that ad wasn't cheap— forget about the bill for actually running it. I doubt we have the money to cover it, but what do I know, since you locked me out of the accounting software? I trusted you absolutely, but for the last two days, I've stumbled across one deceit after another." She raised her hands in a what-the-fuck gesture. "And by the way, I was blindsided by this last lovely surprise in front of Sergei, no less. Sergei! I want an explanation. No bullshit. What are you doing?"

Madeline's rekindled anger made the truth (or at least most of it) easy for Joe to admit. He started with the loss of those two key contracts and went on to the cost of the software project so far—not particularly eager to look at the last bill she'd thrown at him—and the per-user subscription fee he thought they could work up to charging after the trial period. He pulled out his laptop to show her the revenue projections he'd worked up for potential investors. The growth numbers were aggressive but achievable with some help and would put them back in the black in eighteen months to two years with an investment of a million dollars.

Madeline paid silent, unwavering attention through it all.

"This assumes our current baseline of customized consulting, which you'll direct, of course. I know we've fallen off that mark this year, but with some additional staff, we could grow in that area as well. Call it the 'Sergei' package." Finally he buttoned his lips, sat back, and waited.

She placed her hands, palms down, on the top of her desk and closed her eyes in a long blink. "Jesus Christ, Joe."

He fought the urge to justify what he'd done: pointing out it was what they'd agreed on before the attack, only accelerated; indicating that serious decisions had to be made when she was incapacitated; or even, desperately, by explaining his desire to present her with the culmination of his vision, to give her everything she could want all at once.

"I don't even know where to start on how fucked up this is." She leaned back in her chair and cast her gaze around the room, her fingers rising to press on one eyebrow and feel down the length of her nose. She eased forward and zeroed in on Joe again. "How are we paying for all this until we *maybe* get funding? That Pinskey's bill alone was the definition of sticker shock."

Joe looked away from Madeline despite himself, a rookie move that she read right into, exactly the way she used to be able to.

"You used your own money? Are you insane? What possessed you to do such an irresponsible thing?"

"What did you want me to do, Madeline? Let the business go under because of a momentary cash flow problem? I'm not going to do that, not when so much is riding on it."

Madeline got up and rested her hip against the credenza behind her desk, reaching down to rub the muscles above her left knee. Joe watched a stack of journals shift but stay intact. "Will you close the door?"

"I don't think Beth is here."

"I know. I ran her off earlier, but she'll be back."

Joe closed the door and stood by it, staying eye level with Madeline. "Say whatever you want. Don't spare my feelings. You have every right to be upset."

"This whole time, I trusted that you—that this would be the one stable thing I had—whether I wanted it or not." She gave up massaging her knee through her tan slacks. He remembered when she'd stopped wearing skirts around Sergei and wondered how he hadn't known about her meeting with Pinskey that morning, not that it mattered now. The damage was done—though how damaging could it be if it let there be truth between them again? "Aren't you tired? Don't you ever want to run away?"

"No. And what do you mean whether you wanted it or not?"

Her mouth made the shapes of words, but instead of speaking, she clamped her lips tight and huffed out a breath.

"Please," he said. "I thought we were being honest with each other again."

"The other night, Ethan accused me of being unaffected by our parents' deaths." Before Joe could voice his outrage at that, she went on. "I know. Believe me, I wanted to knock his block off. But my dad's been on my mind a lot. He wanted this company like you want it. He wanted it for me, but I wanted it for us. For him and me. It gave us a relationship. It's stupid, I know, to have wanted that so much at my age, after all those opportunities he missed, but—"

"It's not stupid," he said. He didn't know what he'd do if Katie didn't want a relationship with him. The idea of it twisted him with loss.

Madeline made a sound of disgust, crossed her arms, and knocked back against the credenza, sending those journals scattering across the top, one slipping to the floor next to her. She didn't seem to notice. "When he softened after Mom died...yes, stupid. How desperate! I had this little-girl fantasy of how I'd build a real family—not just blood but love and affection—and now he's dead, and here I am, in a life that's cost me *everything* and is all wrong."

Joe forced his hands into his pockets to hide his trembling fingers. By "everything," he knew she meant Jane, and he gave that idea a wide berth, saying instead, "Surely not all wrong. Because working with you, watching you do wonderful things with clients…"

She sat down with a clatter and a momentary grimace of pain. "Of course it's not all wrong! That's the worst part, and it paralyzes me. I tell clients to embrace complication and complexity while outright denying it in my own life. I'm like a therapist with a drug addiction or uncontrollable panic attacks."

Joe sat across from her. "I wish you wouldn't be so hard on yourself, especially given all that's happened lately."

She groaned. "You know what? The beating wasn't the worst part. The worst part was how it made it so I can't even trust my own perception. I worked so hard to spin things to myself. To lie to myself. The only thing I know for sure right now is that I'm not who everyone thinks I am—or even who I've always told myself I was. How am I supposed to let that go and move on? Do I do it by pretending what I see now isn't really true? Or do I say hey, I got my head split open by a guy who somehow knew I was a big dyke, and that trumps everything else?"

Joe felt an otherworldly stillness. "He knew…"

"Fuck," she said and covered her face with her hands.

"It was a hate crime? Is that—?"

"Leave it alone. Please." Her voice was muffled.

"But…I don't understand. Are you saying he knows you?"

She said nothing for so long that he finally leaned over the papers and books stacked between them and pulled her hands from her face. She opened her eyes with seeming reluctance. "I don't know. Maybe he thinks all women are dykes. Maybe he saw that stupid TEDx video. Maybe it's like six degrees of professional separation. I don't know, and you need to leave it at that. I'm serious."

"You haven't seen him again, have you? Has he been around your house? Has he—"

"Joe, stop."

"But do you think—"

"*Stop.* I don't know what he looks like. I can't live thinking it's something personal, that he might be lurking around every corner. I have to let it go or it'll drive me insane, it really will. So you need to leave it."

"I don't know if I can do that."

"Sorry, but you have no choice. And for Christ's sake, you've got to stop using your own money for the company, Joe. There has to be a better solution. Bank financing or something. Give me a few days to ask around, get some options. Have you looked at cutting costs? Or collecting on those outstanding invoices we've been way too nice about? Never mind. I'll comb through the books and come up with ideas. What else do I have to do when I can't sleep?"

Her change of subject was emphatic, and Joe didn't have the guts fight it, though the thought of her seeing how bad their finances were made his heart thump in panic. Still, he said, "I'll have to give you the new passwords, but okay."

She heaved a deep breath, her gaze never wavering from his face. "We'll figure it out."

"So you're not quitting? The way you were talking, about this being a mistake..."

"There's a lot I need to think about, but you told me not to make any rash decisions, and I'm taking your advice. Or trying to. It's...everything, every single thing, is hard these days."

"It'll get better."

"If it doesn't, we're all in for a world of hurt—although with the way I yelled at Beth earlier, my deep shit is going to start the minute she's back."

UPENDED

THAT EVENING, HE SAT IN A BAR IN THE FINANCIAL DISTRICT, waiting for Bridget to show up for their parley. The place was dim and upholstered, muting the post-work crowd to a dull rumble and enabling both festivity and intimacy. Joe and Bridget used to meet here during their early marriage before having dinner out, sitting in the corner booth whenever they could get it. A young couple was there now, holding hands between their cocktails. Bridget's selection of this venue for their meeting didn't bode well, not with the way it seemed designed to evoke warm nostalgia.

A burst of summer-evening sunshine preceded his ex-wife into the bar, and she powered toward his table without even stopping to order a drink. "Thanks for meeting me. It was time we talked without lawyers involved."

"Easier said than done with you around."

"I left my attorney hat at the office." She got herself situated on a stool across from him. "We used to be able to talk, remember? We were always the world's most civilized divorced couple. Now's when we need that the most."

"No, now's when you tell me Darrin got an offer he can't refuse." Joe drank a third of his draft, wishing it were something considerably stronger.

"We can figure this out." Even though he'd been certain this was the reason behind Bridget's request to have this conversation, her thunderous lack of denial was tough to accept. "We can set things up so you see Katie as much—or even more—than you do now. Believe me, I've counted the days, and that doesn't even include video chats or trips you might be able to make out there while she's in school. Besides, there are a million dysfunctional companies in Silicon Valley that need your services. You guys could go bicoastal. You see? We can work this out." She was pitched forward and talking quickly, the very picture of desperation, not at all the courtroom shark he knew too well.

All at once, he bent under the tiredness Madeline had spoken of, the weight of it causing a deep deflation. "My business is here. All my contacts are here."

"We can help with that if you'll let us. With us and your software—"

"I'm telling you, you don't understand." He paused and said, "Madeline's here. You're asking me to split myself in half."

"Does she know how you feel?"

Bridget's response was so immediate, so unthinking, that Joe was surprised, offended, and relieved. He'd been desperate to tell someone. That the recipient of this knowledge was Bridget was...appropriately unfortunate, but it was acknowledged now, which gave him a sort of freedom. "How am I supposed to tell her? It's impossible. I can't stand to lose Katie, but if not losing her means losing Madeline..." The words brought a thickness to his throat.

Bridget's brow furrowed, and her hand went to her cheek, then mouth, then chin before dropping back to the table, her engagement ring sparkling even in the bar's dim light. "I suspected, but I hadn't guessed how much..."

"She thinks what you're trying to do is horrible, by the way."

Bridget shrugged. "I don't doubt it. She's a good friend to you. You should tell her."

He laughed. "Do you think this is some after-school special where the moral of the story is that the truth always wins out? She's a lesbian, not to mention still hung up on her ex." He drank more of his beer. "And it wasn't a car accident that put her in the hospital."

"I know. You're a terrible liar, but I didn't want to pry. What was it?"

He told her about the attack, and she made appropriate murmurs of distress and sympathy. Even though this was Bridget, the very woman intent on spiriting his daughter to the other end of the country, talking to her about Madeline's difficult recovery—her anger, fear, remove—was like shrugging off a suffocating weight. Finally, when he caught up to Madeline's still troubling disclosure of this morning, he said, "Hypothetically..."

"Is that my signal to pretend the following has nothing to do with you or Madeline?"

"*Hypothetically*, if the victim of a crime withholds information about that crime from the police, could that person get in trouble? Legally?"

She folded her fingers together. "What has Madeline gotten herself into?"

"If she would let me take care of her, this would be a totally different situation! She needs a change. She needs distance from where this maniac attacked her, from the persistent ghost of Jane—who up and deserted her, not that Madeline will ever admit that...She's so myopic, but she won't take anyone's word for what's right in front of her."

"California's a lot of distance," Bridget said.

He pointed at her, his fingertip shaking. "Don't think I've forgotten how hard you're trying to screw me right now." But he had—at least for a moment. He'd let himself see this mess as an opportunity in disguise. Yes, if they could get away, start over. But that presupposed a status of "they" that wasn't real.

"Joe...how long can you stand to work so closely with someone you're in love with?"

"I've handled it this far, and don't change the subject."

"Handling is not a life."

"It's nice that you have the luxury of saying so. You stand to lose nothing, while I'm this close to losing everything—Katie, Madeline, the business. You have no idea, Bridget. Really."

"Maybe, maybe not. But I know you, Joe. The divorce didn't change that, and neither does this situation. I see it in your face. You need to tell her and see if it's possible between you two, and if it's not—and don't get mad at me for saying this—you have to move on."

He finished his beer. "Bridget, don't take my daughter away from me."

"I'm not taking her away from you."

He stood up. "Yeah. Keep telling yourself that."

CHAPTER 26

WHEN ETHAN AND DANIKA MILLER HAD GOTTEN TOGETHER, she'd revealed that she'd listened to some of his old songs from Texas. He didn't know if he should be pleased that she knew he wasn't an inexperienced open-mic junkie or mortified that those soulless songs were attached to him like a jail record. But then she said, "This stuff is so much better. Really," and he felt confident and accomplished—at least until now, when he was still one kick-ass song short for his opening set in a mere three weeks. He had no trouble coming up with songs that were okay. Half-baked. Near misses. *Workable.* Was there anything worse? Workable was the toe-tapping fluff he'd written down in Texas. Workable was what came before the real effort, the gnawing, sweet torture he hated and loved in equal measure.

This Friday, on the late shift with brownnosing, son of a bitch Neal, he stood at Fuel's concrete counter, waiting for nonexistent customers and making a forest of slashes, scribbles, and Xes in his notebook over potential but ultimately shitty lyrics for this last stubborn song. Neal was in the back, organizing stock no one had asked him to organize, and Ethan relaxed into this dereliction of duty and tried to uncover a sparkling chorus on this mess of a page.

Neal pushed through the swinging door behind Ethan and surprised him at this impossible task. His sigh needled into Ethan's ear and shot down the nerves of his arm to his hand, which choked the life out of his pen. Better than Neal's neck, though that left him with breath to say, "Plenty to do on the closing checklist. Or maybe I'm the only one interested in being thorough and leaving on time."

"Actually, Neal, you *are* the only one interested in that. You're interested in it enough for both of us." But he shoved his notepad in his pocket and grabbed a broom from the corner. "Fucking pissant," he said, not nearly as softly as he should have, which felt terrific.

"I heard that."

"Good for you."

God, he missed Nettie, the way she ducked her head behind her hair when he complimented her, the random crazy / awesome stuff she came out with, the way she hugged him when the shit went down with The Mad Hatter. In the weeks since he'd made an ass out of himself, he was consumed by the idea of vaulting past redeeming himself with Nettie and catapulting directly to being ultimately worthy. Swoon-inducing, if that were at all possible. But Nettie hated grand gestures, so whatever he did had to be subtle. Cool. He swept and plotted his next move with her, dragging his broom back and forth across the shop floor, keeping his back to Neal.

ONCE FUEL CLOSED, HE CROSSED DAVIS SQUARE TO J.P. LICKS, THE ice cream parlor where Nettie worked, but things did not go well. After a long wait in line (why were so many people getting their dairy on at ten at night?), he stood face-to-face with her across the freezer case, but before he could even open his mouth, she glared at him, said, "Shut up," and went at a tub of chocolate ice cream with palpable force. "Go down to the register and pay," she said, and he obeyed even though he didn't want any ice cream and had no idea what Nettie was concocting for him except that it contained a truly massive number of scoops.

An hour later, he could only be described as a creepy stalker, watching Nettie work while he remained planted on his seat at a sticky table. The towering (and exorbitant) hot fudge sundae that he had been forced to buy had incapacitated him, though Nettie was the real reason he couldn't move. Her hair was pulled back in a ponytail, and when she dipped into the freezer case to scoop out ice cream, the muscles in her arm tensed and flexed. She most decidedly did not look at him.

She came over at closing, her hands on her hips, her face set in an impressive scowl, and what was left of Ethan's confidence and determination drained away, pooling beneath him like the melted dregs of his sundae. So much for swoon-worthy. "You need to go now," she said.

"Can we talk?" The words came out in an emasculated whine.

"No. We're closing, and you have to leave."

"Nettie, please. Are you going to be mad at me forever?"

"That's the current plan."

"No offense, but that's a terrible plan."

She laughed a short yip. "I just got rid of one asshole. What do I need with another one?"

She was serious, not to mention right—not that he was an asshole (though he had his moments), but that her say in whatever was or wasn't or might or might not be between them was as important as his. He left the parlor but sat on a bench outside with a clear view of the front door.

The night was cool but comfortable, and plenty of people roamed around, taking no notice of him. He thought about pulling out his notebook, but he wasn't remotely in the right frame of mind. He just sat and waited, a little sick from the sundae, which, despite being mostly liquid, sat like a rock in his stomach. Don't fuck this up, he told himself, as if he were in control of what would happen next. When Nettie came out a nerve-racking half hour later, he said, "I'm sorry, Nettie. Please." He kept his voice calm and quiet.

He saw her sigh more than heard it. "You're only here because you've been working with Neal."

"Seriously. What an insufferable prick. He makes it easy to see how awesome you are, but I already knew that."

For a while, she stayed as far from him as the sidewalk would allow, but then her shoulders dropped, and she walked over and sat next to him, freeing her hair from its ponytail.

He said, "I like it better up."

"Tough luck. I liked your beard better."

"Really?"

"No," she said with a laugh. "It was horrible."

He pressed his hands against a worn wood slat of the bench beneath him and took a deep breath. "I'm sorry but glad you broke up with the cretin." She just hid behind her hair, and he let the quiet between them spin out for a while before saying, "I shouldn't have been such a jerk about him or about your being with him. It wasn't my business."

When she didn't respond, he despaired of ever resurrecting their previous blissful ease. He waited for her to leave, wondering what he would do then, but finally she said, "He never hit me."

"I totally shouldn't have said that."

"Shut up, Ethan, I'm trying to tell you something."

He made a locking motion at his lips.

"That day at Fuel, when I was so upset, it was because I finally saw him for what he was—or saw that who he was really was who he was, and that he had no hidden cache of caring that only my love and patience would unlock." She tucked a drift of hair behind an ear and looked at him. Her eyes were shadowed by her brow, and the streetlights made her skin look soft in an otherworldly way. "We were together for six years, and that whole time, I willed myself into blindness about him, about his habit of discounting me and how I let him take charge because he was so confident, but the thing he was best at was making me feel inferior."

"I should get in shape just so I can kick his ass."

"Maybe a beating would get through his thick skull, but don't I have the same exact problem? Why couldn't I see what was going on until what happened to your sister? I'm more mad at myself than anyone else. I feel like a total idiot." Despite those words, she didn't hide herself from him, which felt like a minor miracle that emboldened him.

"Join the club. We're all total idiots, including my brilliant sister, and the more you think you know, the more deeply idiotic you're probably being."

"Word." She knocked her shoulder against his.

He propped an elbow on the back of the bench, swiveling to face Nettie. "Hey, I'm serious."

"I know! When you told me about Maddy and made that jump to Eric and his temper, I got so angry I tried to convince myself I was mad at you, but really I was furious at myself, at how hard I'd worked to not let myself acknowledge what you saw." She ducked her head down, and her hair escaped to shield her face. Her hands hung loosely between her knees. "I pissed away the last six years of my life."

"I know what you mean." He told her about his mom dying, how he'd felt emptied out, adrift, how everything had seemed pointless, how angry he'd been at Maddy and his father for what he saw as their callousness, how caring about anything after that seemed explosively dangerous. Until, at last, music. It filled him up, gave him a feeling of solidity that counteracted the strange transparency his mother's death had shocked him into. He felt *seen*, felt like a part of the world despite how estranged he really was from his father and Maddy.

"Then my dad died, and it was obvious how unbelievably stupid I'd been. No matter what I thought I wanted, the only thing I was capable of doing was coming here—to Maddy. Back to what was left of the fold." That phrase resonated, but he willed himself

233

to remember it rather than pulling out his notebook and jotting it down. "Besides, being a driftless fuckup around Maddy is comfortable. She practically expects it, and I aim to please her, always have."

"We're quite the pair."

"But now..." he said.

"Yeah. But now."

"Is your ass numb? My ass is completely numb. Want to walk?" He got up and stood in front of her, shaking out each leg in turn.

"I'm staying with a friend a few blocks away until I can find something permanent and move my things from Eric's place."

"I'll walk you there," he said, but she didn't move from the bench. "Believe me, I live in a shithole, too, if that's what you're worried about."

"That's not it. I lost almost a quarter of my life to one guy. Getting involved with someone else right away seems pretty stupid." She sat back, her arms crossed over her chest as if daring him to dispute her.

No matter her challenge, he couldn't help but conclude that she was interested, but he hid the bump of excitement he felt. "I'm offering to walk you home, not proposing."

"But you meant it, right? What you said about your left nut?"

"I'd never lie about one of my nuts. If you need time, that's okay. We can be friends. I like being friends with you—especially if it means I don't have to work with Neal."

"Ah-ha. I *knew* this was all about him." She pulled her hair back into a ponytail (victory) and snapped a band around it. The streetlamps gave her face a Halloween cast, which made him irrationally happy. "Those songs you did at the open mic were really good. Powerful, you know. Danika Miller was all over you."

"I'm opening for her at Somerville Theatre in three weeks."

"Really? That's awesome, but...she's really pretty."

"Eh. She's all right."

"What does your left nut have to say about it?"

He dipped his head down and squinted as if listening. "My left nut expresses no desire," he said, which while not *entirely* true was true enough, given the circumstances.

She finally got up from the bench and eased closer to him. "That beard really was awful. Without it, you're, I don't know, kind of beautiful." She was inches away. "I promise both of us that I'll leave you at the slightest provocation."

"Well, I often need several chances, so this will clearly never work."

She touched his cheek. "Maybe I can be flexible."

"Maybe I can be better."

"This is a terrible idea," she said right before she kissed him.

CHAPTER 27

THE WAVE OF DETERMINATION THAT HAD CARRIED ZOE RIGHT UP into Madeline's face then directly out of the MFA had fizzled almost immediately, leaving her sitting in the Fenway for hours, unable to make herself go home and talk to Troy. In an act of the most fundamental cowardice, she decamped to a friend's place and texted Troy that she needed time to think. Then, to top off that old, stupid, and untrue cliché, she braved dirty underwear and the judgment of her manager at work by only sneaking back to the apartment for clothes and a toothbrush during the week, when Troy was sure not to be there.

But now, after six days on her friend's piece-of-shit couch, her back ached, and she was exhausted—with herself and the situation. Today was the day. End things with Troy and start painting or...or nothing. There was no alternative. Later today, she had an appointment to check out some shared studio space in North Cambridge, which was a haul from her office in the Back Bay but at least somewhat affordable. She'd tried to convince herself that she didn't need studio space, that she could hedge her bets around this sudden desire to create and start small. Literally.

Pieces that wouldn't take too much paint or cost too much for the canvas. Pieces she could work on in her bedroom. Dip her toes until she knew her resolve was serious and long-term.

The problem was that starting small would doom the whole endeavor. Her mind worked in life-size, large, busy canvases. Murals! She'd had a long love affair with her three-inch brush. Anything less didn't feel worth it, and so here she sat with her checkbook in her pocket, her balance memorized, and nothing between her and this jumping-off point except Troy, the last tether to the person she no longer wanted to be. He was due home from his morning workout soon, and she laid in wait on his couch, which faced her TV. The TV was next to his bookshelf that complemented her coffee table. This place was a vortex of ease and companionship, and the intimate knowledge of how easy it would be to get sucked back in hardened her resolve but also made her nerves grow so unruly they became their own entity, vibrating red where they perched next to her.

When Troy finally arrived, his hair still damp and cheeks flushed, he stopped just inside the door and dropped his bag. "That was a lot of thinking. You must have your PhD in figuring things out by now."

"I don't take what I'm doing lightly."

"What *are* you doing?" He said it angrily, but his eyes were downcast. Sad.

"I'm moving out as soon as I find a place, and I'm going stag to Kimberly's wedding." She should've said she was breaking up with him, but that was admitting too much for comfort.

"What about Madeline? Aren't you moving in with her?"

"She has nothing to do with this. I'm not even sure we're friends anymore."

"But you want to be."

She turned her hands palms up and shrugged. "You want to make this about her? Fine. I want to be more than friends with her. Isn't that the point? I'm a lesbian, Troy, so I can't be with you the way you want me to. Or the way you've convinced yourself you want me to."

"I'm not the one who needed a week to think about this. But, hey, if you want to be true to your lesbian self"—he pulled out his phone—"I'll call Adele and let her know that they should change the place cards at Kimmy's wedding to Zoe Doolittle and Madeline…what's your fictional lover's last name?"

She was up and across the room in a rush, grabbing for his phone, which he held above his head and out of her reach. "You wouldn't dare." She stretched up for it.

"What's the big deal? Once you're rid of me, isn't it all truth and art for you?"

"Why are you being such an asshole?" She gave up on the phone, the immediate danger past.

"Why are you ruining this for both of us?"

"Because it was already ruined! We've been over this a million times. What you claim to want is a fantasy. It's not a future, not for me. If I end up not finding something more, fine, but I need to try." That was more bravado than she actually felt, but she went on. "Besides, I'm going to tell my family. Soon. But you never, ever will, and I don't know why. Do you?"

He dropped his phone on his gym bag and rolled his eyes. "Of course I know. I saw it happen to my uncle. They removed every trace of him from family history. I mean *gone*, Zoe, so gone that sometimes I think I actually imagined him. That's what happens. I'll become invisible, passed over, discarded. I've seen it—not only with my uncle but at work. When people know a man is gay, they…" He shook his head, his eyes widening. "It's like he almost becomes a woman." He said this without a hint of a smile.

Zoe's mouth hung open in shock. "What do you think *I* am?"

"That's not what I mean. I'm talking about how other people—*stupid* people—think. I mean—"

"You know what, Troy? I don't care what you mean. You're off your rocker, and I was nearly as bad to stay with you for so long.

What you want is way more perverted than any crazed perception of what being gay actually is."

"You don't have a leg to stand on, criticizing me."

She frowned and walked back to pick up her bag from the couch. "You're right. But not for long. I'll be out by the end of the month, and I'll give you an extra month of rent for your trouble." She was out the door before he could respond and hauled ass to the train—not because she was late but to outpace the small truth of what he'd said. She had to tell her family. If she didn't, she might as well retrace her steps and grovel for Troy to take her back.

LATER AND SEVERAL HUNDRED DOLLARS LIGHTER, SHE STOOD ON A sunshiny sidewalk outside the studio space she'd just rented and called her sister. When Kimberly answered, Zoe said, "Where's Mom on the crazy-o-meter?"

"God, Zoe. It's like she's the one getting married. No, it's like this is the first and only wedding the world has ever or will ever know. Why didn't you do the decent thing and get hitched before me? You *are* practically ancient by now."

"Funny. You could have eloped. Still could."

"Hell would hath no fury, and you know it."

"Indeed." She walked back and forth across one square of sidewalk, placing her feet heel to toe, then turning and doing it again. "Hey, I was calling at least partly to tell you that Troy won't be coming with me to the big event."

Pause. "*No.* Tell me you didn't."

"Didn't what?"

"Break up with another perfect man."

Zoe groaned.

"Don't pretend you don't know what I'm talking about. First Sebastian and now Troy? What do you want, some ugly brute who beats you for sport?"

"Whoa, hey, there's a lot of room between a supposedly perfect guy and a monster."

"But why even explore the middle ground when you've already gotten the best—twice?"

"Your fiancé isn't chopped liver. I've seen the man's abs, and he adores you."

Kimmy said, "All I'm saying is that the supply of really great guys is far from endless."

"I've got it under control."

"I'm not so sure about that. Mom's going to shit a brick. She *loves* Troy."

"I know. That's why I'm telling you and not her."

"Great. Thanks so much. Seriously, Zoe. What happened?"

"I..." She scanned the sky for an answer that was neither the truth nor a lie. The best she could come up with was, "I met someone else."

"Well, of course. Why not. I want the details, I do, but I have to ask: are you not the marrying type? Not that that's necessarily a bad thing. I have my own doubts."

"You and Devon are going to do great, and I'm totally the marrying type. I just—"

"Haven't found the right, beyond-perfect guy. But maybe this new one? When did you meet?"

Zoe stopped her pacing and sat down on the curb, her feet in the dry, dusty gutter. "A while ago, actually. It might end up going nowhere, but I couldn't stay with Troy, not when I feel like this about someone else."

"Troy's a lot to give up for a maybe."

"He and I had some fundamental disagreements." To put it mildly. And to avoid the clear, definitive truth. "Anyway, I'm starting to paint again. I just put some money down on studio space." She took her glasses off and cleaned the lenses with the hem of her T-shirt.

A sigh rustled through the phone. "I don't know how you do it, go along and not care what Mom thinks. Or what anyone thinks, really. How do you stand people telling you to get a real job all the time?"

"Believe me, Kimmy, no one's interested in what I do with my time. Besides, I have a real job. Forty hours in an office for the last four years. A girl's got to eat."

"Oh, you know what I mean. It's like you didn't get the news that adults are supposed to give up on their passions."

She almost came out to Kimberly right then so she could show her what a weakling she'd actually been for so many years. Kimmy had her on a pedestal for being the defiant black sheep, and she couldn't stand how untrue that felt on so many levels. Wait until after the wedding, Zoe told herself. Wait until they got through that day with everyone happy—even if out of blissful ignorance. "I care what Mom thinks. Too much. Being a couple hundred miles away helps, though. You need to get out of Albany."

"I don't know. I like it here—most of the time, at least. You're coming out next weekend for the dress fitting, right? I'll pick you up at the bus station. Tell me when you're getting in."

They chatted for a while longer, but Zoe couldn't quite relax into it, not with being distracted by the question of whether keeping the truth from Kimberly was cowardly or loving. Cowardly, she finally decided. And loving.

THAT NIGHT, SHE CALLED MADELINE WHILE WAITING FOR HER ride outside Club True. She'd had too much to drink, it was way too late, and she assumed, with single-minded ferocity, that Madeline wouldn't answer. So when she did, Zoe didn't know what to say.

"Zoe?" Madeline asked.

Fuck. Caller ID strikes again. A girl couldn't drunk dial in peace and anonymity anymore. "Hi. I promised myself I wouldn't call first. Now you know how much my promises are worth."

"I've—"

"Hey, hey. I'm not trying to guilt trip you. I just like you a lot, a stupid amount, really. And I wanted to tell you that I ended my pretend relationship and rented studio space and *almost* told my sister. And I wanted to see how you were. I'm sorry and not sorry I was so hard on you."

"I wanted to call."

"You should have. You should!" A car pulled up. "I've had too much to drink but not quite enough, so I should go."

"Where are you?"

"Club True, but I'm leaving." She had one foot in the back seat of the car when she heard yelling behind her and turned around.

"What're you staring at, man?" A woman shouted across the street to a shadowed figure who started walking away, keeping out of the streetlights. "That's right, perv. Get the fuck out of here."

Zoe heard her name and remembered her phone and Madeline. "Sorry," she said. "That creepy guy was here again, but someone ran him off. He *really* needs to get a life. I'm going to go, but call me. Seriously. Don't just want it, do it. That's my motto now. Don't just want it, do it." She closed the door behind her and sat back for the ride to her friend's apartment and that uncomfortable, lonely couch.

CHAPTER 28

INSTEAD OF SPEEDING PAST THE ALLEY WHERE SHE'D BEEN attacked with her eyes averted like usual, Madeline stopped and surveyed the scene from the relative safety of the sidewalk. Her gaze traveled over broken-up asphalt, a dumpster with its lid thrown back, and the brick wall she'd been held against, slammed into. She took it all in until the gut punches of her memories made it hard to breathe. A half mile later, she still held her takeout bag of udon soup too tightly to her chest and had to focus to bring in more than shallow sips of air. She tried to slow her pace as she got closer to home, but she couldn't—at least not until she saw Jane sitting on her front steps.

Jane raised her hand in greeting. "Not so much with the new leaf, huh?" She tapped her watch in a move that seemed rehearsed. "Home at seven-thirty on a Friday night?" She was in workout clothes, but they were dry, and her hair was suspiciously tame—both unlikely conditions, given the mid-June warmth.

"I...what're you doing here? And how did you find 'here,' anyway?"

UPENDED

Jane cracked her knuckles, got up, and stretched. How long had she been parked there, waiting? "I called our friend and former landlord. He tried to ransom your forwarding address for a date."

"Ah, Chuck."

"Yeah, the retiree with an eighteen-year-old's libido."

Madeline stopped in front of her and shifted the bag of takeout from one hand to the other. "You shouldn't be here."

"Probably not, but here I am. And here you are. Late."

"I didn't know I had an appointment."

Jane's grunt was short and matter-of-fact, that vocal tick Madeline used to know so well. "Right. You and your calendar."

"If you came here to criticize me—"

"I didn't," she said quietly. "I couldn't stop thinking about you. I tried, but I can't leave it alone—especially not when I know something's really wrong." She popped her knuckles again and glanced to the side. "I was so good at putting you out of my mind, but I guess you can still get under my skin."

"Your kryptonite?" It was how one of Jane's friends had described Madeline at the beginning—though Jane had managed to build up a tolerance.

"Undeniably."

Madeline slipped her heel out of a pump and curled her tired toes. "I *want* to turn over a new leaf. That must count for something."

"Close only counts in horseshoes—"

"—and hand grenades, I know." It was Jane's favorite saying when a spike of hers hit just out instead of in. Madeline looked at the front door then back at her interloper. "I suppose you want to come up."

"It would be more comfortable than these steps."

"I know the place is kind of dumpy. Wrong side of the tracks and all." She walked past Jane and up to the porch. "But you're going to absolutely hate my apartment."

"Books. I'll brace myself."

Madeline led the way upstairs. When they used to climb the steps to their last apartment, Jane would goose her all the way up. Madeline shook off the memory and unlocked her door before making a beeline to the kitchen, not waiting for Jane's inevitable disapproval. Luckily her place was in better shape than when Zoe had come by all those weeks ago—at least the dishes were clean and put away. She set down her briefcase, dug a spoon out of the silverware drawer, and freed the container of soup from its paper bag.

Jane was staring at Madeline—not disgusted, as she had anticipated, but frowning and shifting from foot to foot, her calves tensing and relaxing with her movements. "What happened to you?"

"I'm fine."

"Sorry, but no. You're not."

"I told you not to get involved." Madeline walked to the couch, set her soup down on an empty window ledge, and cleared cushions of books and files before curling up in a corner, her skirt pulled across her thighs.

"Despite what your job may lead you to believe, your word is not the be-all end-all. Mad, this place looks like a crazy person lives here. Like, certifiable." She kicked off her shoes and sat on the couch in the opposite corner from Madeline, spreading her arms out along the back of the cushions, taking up space.

"It's not that bad." Madeline spooned soup into her mouth, slurping at a noodle.

"Yes. Yes, it is." Jane leaned forward and put a hand on Madeline's arm, stopping another spoonful halfway to its destination. "I'm here. I'm involved. So tell me."

Madeline moved her arm out of Jane's reach, and even though she really, really didn't want to, she asked, "Where's your girlfriend tonight?"

"Don't do that. This is between you and me."

"Does she know you're here?"

"Let me worry about my business. You've clearly got enough on your mind already."

Madeline ate her soup quickly while casting around for something to say that would blunt the hard needle of Jane's attention. She thought about her day, of the line of credit application in her briefcase from their bank, the one the loan officer was clearly pessimistic about approving. She thought about her resolve to call Zoe and catch her before she went out to Club True, like she had the week before, and...what? Kissed someone else like she'd kissed Madeline that now-ancient night? Instead of all that, she said, "Something's going on with Joe."

"Joe didn't cause this." Jane swept her long arm in an arc.

"I'm not saying he did, but if someone's going crazy at the company, it's him." She told Jane about the software project, their precarious finances, Bridget's move to California. "I think he's cracking."

Jane asked, "Did he finally fully succumb to your charms?"

"What do you mean? You're the one he had the hots for—like everyone else."

"Mad, the man's been the slightest nudge away from being in love with you since day one."

Madeline put her spoon down, its head half submerged in the dregs of her soup. A montage of Joe over the last couple months projected in her brain, and she said, almost to herself, "No. He wasn't. I know he wasn't, but then...at the hospital, Ethan told me Joe said...but that surely didn't mean—"

"The hospital?"

"Ah, fuck." Madeline rolled her eyes at her own loose lips. This was heading toward another set of lies she was going to have to keep straight.

"How long were you hospitalized? Your knee would have been outpatient, right? But your nose is different, too. Did you break it? What else? What happened?"

Madeline tucked hair behind her ears and pressed hard on her eyebrows, consciously not touching her nose, which had become habit. "This is impossible. I shouldn't have let you up. You shouldn't be here."

"But I am. I'm here, and I care about you." She examined the fabric of the couch, seeming almost small. "I love you."

"Don't say that."

"Hell, Mad, sometimes leaving doesn't have anything to do with love."

Madeline jerked her head away from Jane, though that didn't keep the words from setting up residence in her. She felt her face grow tight and her eyes burn. "I was attacked. Back in April, down by Washington Street."

"Mad." The nickname came out a half octave lower than Jane's normal voice, and she reached out and took Madeline's hand. With that comforting touch (exactly the touch she'd imagined in the hospital), Madeline's resolve crumbled, and she told Jane everything: Ethan's too-pointed teasing over breakfast, the loneliness of this apartment, the kiss at the club, the attack, him calling her a dyke in a hundred different ways, the lie, all the lies. The whole time, she kept her attention latched to their hands, which were clasped together on the couch between them.

"And now," she said, "everything looks different. I've read a dozen survivor stories and books on recovery and, yes, I see a menace in the world I didn't see before, but mostly I see a menace *in me*. Lies and a willful blindness. Jesus, Jane. I used to be so sure about everything, but it turns out I didn't know anything. *Don't know anything*." The words escaped before her mouth twisted into a tight curl of despair.

Jane drew her close into her firm warmth, her easy strength, the expansion and contraction of her breath, and the slow, even beating of her heart. The familiar comfort of this embrace kept Madeline from crying but heightened her distress, sharpened the edge of her loneliness, shone a spotlight on her mistakes.

Finally, she sniffled and sat up. Jane said, "I'm sorry."

"Don't look at me like I'm broken."

"How am I supposed to look at you? You *are* broken, and rightfully so. It's horrible beyond belief. How did he know you were gay? Did he see you at the club? Do you think he targeted you because of that?"

"I don't know. I really don't. It felt personal, but how could it not feel personal when someone takes control of you like that? I have to believe it was random, that he would say that to anyone, that he hasn't been out there stalking me, that he isn't waiting around to finish the job. No matter how much I try to remember him from somewhere in that night before the attack, I can't. But..."

Jane watched her expectantly.

What had Zoe said on the phone about a "creeper" outside the club? Was that him? Had he been there that night and followed her home? Kept her in his sights on platforms and trains without her seeing him? "Nothing," she said. She'd think about it later, when Jane wasn't here. She got up and took her soup container to the kitchen. "I'm tired of dwelling on how horrible it was. It's become this thing that gets between me and everything else. Besides, sometimes I think the attack was just a catalyst for all the shit that's come to the surface since it happened. Do you want something to drink?"

"No."

She filled a glass of water and gulped it down, thinking she really wanted something stronger, but she'd eschewed alcohol since that night, not trusting herself to keep from becoming slobbering drunk. Back in the living room, she stopped behind the armchair instead of going to the couch, afraid of falling into Jane's gravitational field. "I'm so messed up. I mean, just now I'm strategizing how to save the company I regret even starting."

"Don't ask me to express an opinion about that job."

"I screwed up. I know." She lifted a thumb to her mouth and clipped off a corner of her nail. Jane was watching her and hated this habit, but Madeline didn't drop her hand. "Good intentions aren't worth anything. I know that. I've always known that. I should've had it engraved on my dad's headstone for as often as he said it, and yet I'm so guilty of it." She squeezed the back of the chair with her free hand. "You were right. Ethan was right. But I couldn't stop wanting to have a relationship with him. I just couldn't accept his not accepting me."

"But wanting a relationship with him *was* accepting it, in a way."

"You don't know what it was like."

"We've had this argument before."

"I know! But, no, I'm not saying the same thing this time."

Jane crossed her arms. "Until you say that he made you ashamed of who you were and that you've carried that shame around ever since, I don't want to hear it."

Madeline's hand drifted down from her mouth and hung at her side. "I..."

Jane grunted. "It drove me crazy to see that shame in you. And to see you being blind to it. And so *contradictory* about it—out but in denial at the same time."

Madeline looked away from Jane, who had her stern game face on, but seeing her crowded bookshelves was no comfort. They were suffocating. The pile on her nightstand Ethan had long ago said was going to fall on her in her sleep was nothing. She was dying a slow death in here. She glanced at Jane. "I thought I'd moved on from Arizona, from feeling so isolated. I thought I just needed connection to put those years behind me. And I did. Need connection. I do. I'm desperate for it, really, but you're right. I chased something stupid—the job, my dad—because I thought it would fix me. However much I lied to you, I lied to myself a hundred times more. I had so many excuses, but the truth is I did this to myself. And now that I know that, I feel it all the time. I can't escape it. I can't work my way out from under it."

Jane's features softened, and her shoulders relaxed. "Sweetheart, things are going to get better. You'll deal with all this and come out the other side. I believe that completely. But taking the blame for everything is as bad as not taking the blame for any of it. You have to stop being so hard on yourself, and if I'm saying this, it has to be true, right? Your town and your parents would have screwed anyone up. And now the attack? I guess just accept the fact that what happened has made you different. Maybe even in a good way? And move on from there."

The rest of Jane's words should have overshadowed the term of endearment that started it off, but it reverberated inside Madeline. "I don't want to be different—at least in this way."

"Want has nothing to do with it."

She knew what Jane meant, but right at this moment, all she could do was want: to figure out how to move through this, or if that were impossible, to go backward, reverse the choices she'd made and change the course of her life enough so that instead of being out that night, making such an easy target, she'd have been in bed with Jane. Her hand fluttered up to her eyebrow, her nose.

Jane was up off the couch and in front of her in two large strides, and she took Madeline's wrist and pulled her fingers from the futile exploration they were pursuing. She stepped closer, then a little closer, tall and strong and irresistible. Madeline snaked her arms around her and tightened them.

"You shouldn't be here," she made herself say into Jane's shoulder.

"And yet here I am."

"I should make you go."

"Try it."

Madeline had wanted this exact comfort for months, and she felt her heart rate slow and her breathing deepen and ignored the thing in herself that knew regret would follow. Jane was not her friend or her lover, but Madeline let herself pretend. How many times had they stood like this, and how many of those had she taken for granted? She was reminded of Zoe's embrace in the MFA, the unexpected and achingly welcome feel of someone holding her (finally), a closeness she'd been missing for so long.

She heaved out a shaky sigh and relaxed into Jane, feeling their breaths synchronize. Time slowed and warmed, and she could forget...just about everything. A hundred things to say floated through her mind, but she swallowed them all, not wanting to break this spell, not caring if it were right or wrong, real or a lie.

Whether she or Jane started it, she couldn't tell, but their hands became unmoored, roamed each other's backs and shoulder blades. Jane's fingers made her skin come alive through the thin fabric of her blouse. She couldn't possibly justify what was happening, but that didn't stop her from allowing the rest of her morals to crumble under the pleasure until, finally, all that was left for her to do was let Jane pull back enough to lean down and kiss her.

Madeline came a little to her senses. "I don't want to be the bartender. I can't be the bartender."

"I never loved the bartender."

"Don't talk about love."

"It's true."

"Don't." But she didn't unwrap her arms from around Jane, just turned her face to the side, searching for clear air, perspective. Jane kissed her neck, and they were at it again. "This is so complicated," Madeline managed to say.

"Don't think about it."

"You should know that's impossible."

"Try. Hard."

Things crossed the line into serious intent, and Madeline remembered the way Jane breathed when she was aroused, the fan of hot exhales against her cheek, the mounting pressure of her hands against Madeline's back that, while familiar, became suddenly too aggressive, confining.

"Not too tight. It—"

"Okay. I won't. Don't worry. I won't hurt you."

"I want you." Madeline admitted the obvious.

"Bed?"

"Couch." It was closer, which was imperative, but after Jane lay back on the cushions and reached up for her, Madeline hesitated. "I didn't stop wanting you back then, when things got bad. I somehow forgot what it was like, let it get buried."

UPENDED

"Let's not talk about that."

She didn't want to talk about that either, but she was paralyzed with the enormity of her want, the harsh, animal nature of it. Years of pent-up desire, disappointment, and regret. "I'm afraid to touch you," she said.

Jane leaned forward, captured Madeline's hand, and slid it up the bottom of her tank top and under her sports bra to a small but pliable breast. Breath whooshed out of Madeline, and sweat rose on her forehead and upper lip. She pressed Jane into the couch, wanting to crawl right into her skin. Her kisses turned rough, and she pulled hard at Jane's clothes, frantic to get closer.

They were naked, tight together, and she found a groove, a rhythm, a subsumation into this place where she didn't think, just breathed and felt her skin expand. She closed her eyes, put her mouth against the side of Jane's breast, and reveled in being out of the reach of words, of the past and dreaded future, of the weight of unending questions.

But then Jane's hand slid down Madeline's arm, settling at her wrist, pulling lightly. "Mad," she said, then again, more loudly. "Mad. Madeline, please." She held her wrist more tightly.

Madeline said, "Wait. I can do this. Let me do this."

"I can't."

"Wait, just wait. Let me."

"Mad, no." Then Jane pushed her hand away, strongly. Madeline's eyes snapped open, and she sat up with a lurch.

"What?" she said. "Did I...did I hurt you?"

"No, no, no." Jane shifted as if to get up, but Madeline was on her leg and had a hand splayed on her flat belly for balance. "You're right. I shouldn't be here. Shouldn't be doing this. I'm *with* someone. Really with her. This is a mistake."

The words froze Madeline's insides solid, but her free hand drifted up to her hair, to her mouth, to her eyebrow. And then, as if they'd been waiting in ambush all along: tears. She covered her face with her hand, but that gesture hid nothing when a keening cry escaped her.

252

Jane pulled her leg out from under Madeline, who listed to the side and curled into herself, putting her curved, naked back to Jane.

Jane's hand settled along her spine, a warm press covering what felt like acres of skin. "Mad. Madeline." Jane's voice filtered through an overwhelming sense of violation. "Hey, please don't cry. I got caught up. I should've..."

"Go away." Madeline managed to choke out the words.

"I'm—"

Before Jane could finish whatever useless thing she was going to say, Madeline dropped her hands and turned to glare at Jane, though so much of the anger and hatred she felt was self-directed.

Jane stood it for a moment before pulling her hand away, shifting her eyes, and popping her knuckles. "Mad," she whispered.

"Get. The. Fuck. Out."

Jane got the fuck out, clearly couldn't get the fuck out fast enough. Madeline even heard her thundering down the stairs, taking them two or three at a time. When the sound faded, Madeline dragged herself to the bathroom, turned the shower on as hot as it would go, and let it scald her. She scrubbed hard with a soapy washcloth, eliminating the memory of Jane's touch, evidence of her deluded desperation, her utter weakness. She scrubbed until she was raw, until she realized that what she wanted to wash away was herself, erase her existence, relieve herself of the necessity to figure out what she could possibly do next.

CHAPTER 29

ZOE'S PHONE WOKE HER AT THE BUTT CRACK OF DAWN. THE TIMING would have normally disqualified the call from the remotest consideration, but she happened to unstick her eyelids enough to read the caller ID. Madeline. She answered.

Madeline sounded like she'd had about twenty espressos: fast, loud, and nonsensical while proposing several contradictory things. Breakfast at Rosemary's (which wasn't even close to open yet), a walk in the arboretum, driving out to the Cape, maybe all the way to Provincetown. Zoe dragged herself upright, her back beseeching her to give up on this couch surfing, but she had over a week until she could move into her new place and still couldn't face Troy. "Hey, wow, okay. All of that sounds really good, but I can't today. I'm getting on a bus to Albany to do some things for my kid sister's wedding. What about tomorrow? I'll most likely spend the night, but I'll be free in the afternoon."

Instead of acquiescing like Zoe expected, Madeline now insisted on driving Zoe to Albany. Zoe tried to dissuade her, but Madeline wouldn't budge. "Getting out of town sounds heavenly. I won't be any trouble. Consider me a chauffeur. I'll drop you off and make myself scarce, but you don't have to sit in the back. If you *want* to sit up front, of course. I won't presume."

She wouldn't presume where Zoe wanted to sit, but going with her to Albany wasn't up for debate. What kind of cruel world would present her with the gift of hours alone with Madeline in a way that made it undesirable in almost every respect? Not only were her mom and Kimberly at the end of the journey, but Madeline was just using her, which she might roll over and accept despite herself if Madeline weren't unpleasantly hyper. Zoe couldn't quite rouse the energy to continue arguing, so she gave in and coordinated a time with Madeline, then lay back for another hour of sleep that ultimately eluded her.

While she turned this way and that, searching for a cool, comfortable position that didn't exist on this couch, she kept catching faint whiffs of turpentine on her fingers from her session in the studio the night before. Going there felt like life and death, with stakes so high it was hard to breathe, let alone paint.

She knew what she wanted to paint: a representation of the present muddled feeling that was gathering, creeping, yearning for the light of expression and direction. She could almost see that luminous destination in her mind, but it was too diffuse to depict, and the rest, well, "muddle" was an apt description. She'd been at the studio until late, in front of a literal blank canvas, sketching one bad idea after another in her notebook. But they were ideas, and she was sketching, and she even painted a little bit at the end on a different, hand-sized canvas she'd bought on an impulse when stocking up on supplies.

The truth was, no matter how difficult or frustrating her time in the studio was, she felt alive in those hours, her senses heightened and precise—not only in her vision of color and shading but in how she noticed the smell of the space, the scratch of pencil against her sketchbook, the texture of brushes and canvas, even the taste of the summer night when she hurried from the studio to catch the last T from Alewife. Some people might call it an escape from her life and its problems, but it had never felt that way. To her, the incredible difficulty of this kind of expression was the highest, most real problem she could solve, and tackling it, day in and day out, shored her up inside and was the only thing that made it possible to face the rest of her life head on.

OVER AN HOUR INTO THE DRIVE, MADELINE WAS ASLEEP IN THE passenger seat, puffy eyed and red nosed. She'd talked nonstop through the glut of suburbs in and around 128 until she'd run out of steam close to Worchester and pulled over, begging Zoe to take the wheel. Something was terribly wrong with her, and as usual, she talked about everything but it: dry heat, rhododendrons, udon soup, the perfect cheese to eat with coffee.

Whatever was going on between them was officially impossible, but Zoe couldn't stop herself from taking her eyes off the road to drink in the sight of this infuriating woman. Asleep, Madeline looked harmless, peaceful, tantalizing, her wavy hair draped over a rounded, pliant-looking cheek. The sight made Zoe want to try portraiture again, despite how terrible she was at it, how lifeless she made her subjects. In the undulating stretch of the Mass Pike between Worchester and Springfield, the hills on either side of the road verdantly green and soft looking, Zoe promised herself that if they didn't make progress toward something real today, something that didn't include habitual lying and desperation, she would let go of the wisp of hope she clung to and shut this whole pseudo relationship down. She drove on, trying to relax into the smooth ride of this unassuming sedan, which required her to pretend she couldn't detect the creamy yet spicy scent of Madeline's soap.

When they were well past Springfield, Madeline's cell phone rang, and she jerked awake. "Call from Ethan," the car's Bluetooth said, and Madeline replied, "Son of a bitch." She disconnected the phone from the car speakers and answered. "Where *were* you. I called you like ten times." Ethan spoke for a while; Zoe could hear his angry tone. Madeline grunted. "You and Nettie, huh? Well, bully for you." He talked more, and Madeline turned to her window, as if privacy were possible in such close quarters. "I...yeah, spectacularly shitty. Shitty to end all shitty...No. Don't come over. I'm not there. Listen, I'll call you later...I know how I sounded in those messages, but it was a long night, and things have changed...I'm a big girl...Yeah, fat sagging ass and all. Maybe tomorrow. The diner. I gotta go." She ended the call, sat up straight, and pushed hair from her face. "Where are we?"

"Getting close to the New York border."

She leaned forward to the glove box and took out a pack of gum, folding a stick into her mouth before offering one to Zoe, which she took. Spearmint. Madeline said, "I'm sorry I was such a freak. I was a freak, right?"

"You could say that."

"I had a rough night."

"Spectacularly shitty."

"To say the least." She passed a hand across her eyes. "I've behaved so badly with you, not even including this craziness."

"It *is* better than riding the bus. What happened last night?"

Madeline's face twisted into a grimace. "Rock bottom? Maybe? Hopefully, at least." Then, miracles of miracles, before Zoe could even breathe in to ask more, Madeline said, "Jane, my ex, came by, just showed up, and it..." A sound a lot like a whimper escaped her. "Went really badly."

"I'm sorry."

She dug the heels of her hands into her thighs where her shorts left off. "I've been a total fucking idiot. Right to this very moment, to be honest."

"I'm only a little bit ahead of you on that. I mean, I'm still drunk dialing people."

"I guess we're even, though I wasn't exactly drunk this morning. Sleep deprived with a thick layer of caffeine over alcohol. Listen, I meant what I said—or at least what I think I said. I'll drop you off to do your family stuff and turn right around. What family stuff are you doing?"

Zoe told her, leaving out all the potential angst, and found out Madeline had never been roped into wedding party duties. "Lucky you. Troy made all these weddings bearable."

"And you and he...?"

"Done. As of the morning of the infamous drunk dial." She couldn't seem to stop herself from bringing it up. "In my defense, I really didn't expect you to answer."

"Sleep refuses to bend to my will. Have you told your family?"

"About Troy? Yeah, mostly. I mean via Kimmy, who has a really big mouth. The gay thing has to wait until after the wedding, which my mom's certifiable about. Besides, it's supposed to be joyous, not to mention all about Kimmy and Devon, and it would be incredibly selfish to ruin that."

"You don't have to justify yourself to me. For not coming out or calling me or anything."

"Unfortunately that doesn't keep me from trying to justify all that to myself."

"I hear you." Madeline sighed and dropped her head back. "That's enough seriousness. It's a beautiful day, I only feel a little like puking, and we're out of the city. Enough. I'm done. Stick a fork in me, as Ethan would say."

"Amen." Zoe took her hands from the wheel and shook them as if at a revival. They *were* out of the city and into a whole different palette—motion and topography and a time that flowed with a smooth continuity.

Madeline twisted in her seat so she was mostly facing Zoe. "I wish I could see you in your dress."

"I look so femme, especially when I do my hair and makeup and everything. No wonder no one's guessed."

"I like femme. At least sometimes."

"Are you flirting?" Zoe asked without looking away from the road.

"It sure sounds like it."

258

Zoe lowered her voice. "Don't, please. Not unless you mean it."

Madeline faced forward again and clasped her hands in her lap. "I mean it. I'm just not sure—"

"It's fine."

"No, don't. I mean it. The thing is, I need to start making different choices now instead of focusing on the different choices I wish I'd made before."

"Choices are..." Zoe blew out a breath in lieu of the right, elusive word.

"Really fucking hard, yeah. But you're doing it, and I'm using you as inspiration. I think you're...being around you...I meant the flirting, but I'll stop until I'm in a position to back it up."

Zoe drove for a while before saying, "Screw it. Keep flirting. A girl can dream, right?"

Zoe pulled over behind the Albany bus station. "I'd say thanks for the ride, but since I drove the majority of it..." She winked.

"Why do I get the feeling you're going to hold that over me for a while?"

"Probably because I'm going to hold it over you for a while."

"I guess I can live with that. Listen." Madeline unbuckled and faced Zoe. "Would you have dinner with me after you get home tomorrow? Rosemary's at seven?"

"You know she always takes Sunday night off."

"Exactly."

This shared knowledge and Madeline's seriousness that was neither angry nor sad made Zoe feel a zing of electricity in her fingers. "It's a date. I mean, it *is* a date, right?"

Madeline covered Zoe's hand where it lay on the on the gear shift and squeezed. "It's a date."

Zoe pried herself from the car and floated into the bus station, where she sat as far away from other people as she could. The station was scuzzy in the way of every bus station she'd ever been in, which admittedly wasn't that many, and she had almost a half hour to marinate in its institutional gray-green paint and echoey atmosphere of tired crankiness. All the other times she'd passed through here, she'd literally *passed through*, hoofed it from the bus, through the station, and out to where someone was waiting to pick her up. Now, the griminess in the corners of the room and the other passengers slumped on benches, faces buried in their phones, stood in silent judgment on this subterfuge of her pretending to take the bus to keep Madeline from her family's radar. In different circumstances, would Kimberly like Madeline? She'd thought Sebastian and Troy were the perfect men, and Madeline was not only a woman but one whose imperfections currently lived right on her surface, which was ironic, given how Zoe had made an art form out of the just-right facade.

Only a few more weeks, she told herself. Just until after the wedding and the honeymoon and the reassertion of the dreary daily routine. She had no illusions about the likely aftermath of her revelation, and it seemed prudent to avoid making it worse by adding in a direct contrast to the elevated happiness of very public love and commitment. She'd waited so long already; she could wait a little longer.

When the bus from Boston finally arrived, she wandered outside to wait for Kimberly, who was already idling at the curb in her little blue coupe. Zoe felt caught out even though she knew Kimmy couldn't have seen her sitting inside. She lowered herself in the passenger seat, stretched out her legs, and gave her sister a once-over. "You look great."

"Three months with a personal trainer will do that." She flexed a shapely bicep.

"Wow. Good for you."

"Necessity is the mother of...sweat, I guess. Wedding dresses are *not* slimming, and you got the skinny genes in the family." Kimmy pulled away from the curb.

"Seriously. You're, like, incandescent with health."

"Thanks." She grinned and glanced at Zoe. "You look...too skinny. The breakup? I don't know how you don't drown your sorrows in ice cream like everyone else."

"That would probably be healthier than the ulcer I'm working my way up to."

"Any news on the new guy front? I want to hear all about this man who dethroned Troy."

Zoe's palms and chest itched with her deception. "This is your day; let's keep my drama out of it."

"Are you kidding? I've been living vicariously through your drama for years."

"I don't know whether to be dismayed or honored at that."

"Honored, totally. No one has a sister remotely like you." And she only knew the half of it.

They talked about the wedding and their mother for the rest of the short drive to the bridal shop, where Adele was waiting for them—bottle-blond and on the thin end of her perpetual battle with her weight. The pictures *would* be forever, after all. They hugged hello, and Zoe braced herself for whatever criticism Adele would come out with first. "How's Troy, that poor baby?"

"I don't know. He's not particularly eager to talk to me." Or her to him, for that matter.

"This'll pass. You two are so good together." Adele examined Zoe from her combed hair to her V-neck T-shirt down to her best jeans and newest sandals—an outfit she'd picked out for Madeline despite herself. "You look like an exhausted vagabond. Anyway"— she clapped and smiled—"let's see these dresses. I wore my cry-proof mascara for the occasion."

Kimberly and Zoe rolled their eyes at each other behind her back, but Adele was happy, and it radiated out, infectious. Here, today, with them, Zoe was content enough to put aside her lie for the time and participate fully in the event.

The bride was appropriately stunning in her ivory-and-lace dress, her hair pinned up messily to get the full effect. Maybe it wasn't slimming, but it showed off her work at the gym—her shoulders and arms were long and graceful, and the bodice of her dress revealed curves in all the right places. Zoe "cleaned up beautifully" in her own dress, which had to be taken in an inch at the waist after this season of stress. While the seamstress circled her and pinned, Adele frowned. "Are you going to wear those glasses at the wedding?"

"I was planning to, given that I can't see without them."

"Surely you can take them off for the pictures. Or get contacts!"

"Mom, I've worn glasses since I was nine. I don't think people would recognize me without them. And, no offense, Kimmy, but I'm not about to start sticking my finger in my eyes for the sake of some pictures that aren't even about me in the first place."

Adele sighed. "Suit yourself. But it *is* time to update those frames. Have you considered rimless? It might be nice to actually see your face."

Zoe laughed. "I'll keep it in mind."

Adele looked poised to say something more—almost certainly about Zoe's hair, which she'd always made a point of taming for family events—when Zoe's phone rang from the front mesh pocket of her overnight bag. Kimmy looked at it. "Madeline?"

The name was such a pleasant surprise that Zoe said, out of pure reflex, "Oh, yeah. Give it here."

The seamstress said, "You need to stay still."

"I'll hold it to your ear," Kimmy said.

"It'll just take a second, I swear." Zoe took the phone. "Hey, what's up?"

"I just realized you left your sweatshirt in the back of the car, and I wasn't sure if you needed it tonight." Madeline's voice hummed over a background of road noise.

"Oh, thanks, but I'm okay. I can just get it tomorrow."

"Are you in your dress?"

"Yeah."

"What color is it?"

"Admiral blue. Between cobalt and navy."

"I bet that looks great with your hair."

"I have to go. The seamstress is getting impatient, and she's got a whole lot of pins at her disposal."

Madeline laughed. "What I wouldn't give to be a fly on the wall. But I guess I'll be with you tomorrow. Seven o'clock. Rosemary's."

"I haven't forgotten. See you then." She hung up and handed the phone to Kimberly, who gave her a searching look.

Zoe consciously refrained from glancing at herself in the mirror or touching her cheeks, afraid to find evidence of the surge of happiness she'd felt at that low-key flirting. She should've let the call go to voice mail, not exposed the smallest bit of that part of her life to this family-charged atmosphere, but she couldn't resist. Luckily, Kimmy seemed to forget all about it during the following excessively detailed conversation about the serving platters she'd registered for that no one had purchased yet. Zoe filled the time trying to visualize the painting she wanted to make for their present, which didn't technically have to be done by the wedding but probably should be. The colors of their dresses would ground it, and being here made her excited to start sketching ideas once she got back to the studio.

When Zoe turned over her position with the seamstress to Adele, she was still thinking about the painting, feeling it take shape in her mind, when Kimmy pulled her into another room out of earshot from their mother. "Who's Madeline?" The wall behind her was gauzy with veils ranging from a brilliant white to an ecru with a putrid yellow tinge. Zoe gravitated to it out of a morbid fascination.

"She's a friend. My company does some work for her company, and she lives in the neighborhood."

"Does she have something to do with the new guy?"

"No. Why? What do you mean?"

"You looked all cat-that-ate-the-canary when you were talking to her."

"I did not." Zoe scowled and plucked at the offensive veil. "What's up with this one? Who could wear this without looking like they have a liver condition?"

"Don't change the subject. Why are you blushing?"

"I'm not blushing."

"Why haven't you mentioned Madeline before if you guys are friends?"

"I haven't?" Zoe let the veil fall back and settle among its brethren. She was angry and afraid and hard-pressed but determined not to show it. "I guess we got closer while working together. It was a gradual thing. What's with the interrogation? Is it to get your mind off the insanity that is Mom and this wedding? Because she's totally the stuff of reality shows right now."

Then Kimberly gasped, just like she used to when she was surprised as a little girl. She clapped a hand over her mouth. "No." Her voice was low and breathy. "She *is* the new guy, isn't she?" It came out in a whispered hiss. Her frown was instant and complete, her eyebrows brawling over the bridge of her nose.

Zoe moved away from the veils and took her sister by her upper arms with a grip that was too firm on her bare flesh (she really did look tear-worthy in this dress). "Now is not the time. We should focus on you and Devon and your day."

"Don't do that. You always deflect like that. I'm right, aren't I, about this Madeline person?"

"We're just friends."

Kimberly twisted away. "I'm not an idiot. People have been wondering about you since high school."

"I didn't even *know* in high school," Zoe said before realizing she'd just tacitly admitted that Kimberly was right.

"But Sebastian, then Troy." She gasped again. "Does Troy know? How long have you been pretending to be normal?"

"Normal? Really? What does normal have to do with it?"

"Come on, you know what I mean. Have you been playing at being straight this whole time?"

"Don't talk like you know what you're saying. It's complicated. I was ignorant for years, and then I was afraid. Of exactly this."

"You think 'this' is because you're gay?" Zoe winced at the word and its volume and glanced at the doorway in involuntary damage control. "You think I'm that backward? *This* is because I revered you, and now you're telling me you've been a lying sack of shit for, what, years? I don't even know who you are." Her hands were at the corseted waist of her wedding dress, and her face was stormy with anger, even the twist of her hair bristling with it. The juxtaposition was jarring.

"I'm exactly the same person I've always been. It's just a label."

"No, it's not! The person I thought you were wouldn't have stopped with saying, 'I'm a painter, this is what I love, so deal with it.' She would have said, 'Oh yeah, and I like to get down with women, too!"

"Those aren't remotely the same thing." She was finally more angry than afraid, which was both good and bad.

"Sure they are."

Zoe huffed out a breath. "Don't be naïve. My painting is hidden away from everyone, but what do you think would happen if I brought a woman to your wedding? How well do you think that would go over?"

"Who cares what people think?"

"I do! And you would, too, if it meant maybe losing everything."

Kimberly dropped her hands from her hips, and her face relaxed a notch, but Zoe didn't have time to press the point because Adele appeared, still in her dress. "What are you two arguing about?"

"Nothing," Zoe said. "Sister stuff." She shot a look at Kimberly, daring her to disagree.

She muttered something that sounded a lot like "Pants on fire" and walked away.

Adele asked, "What did you say to her?"

"It's between me and her, okay?"

"Whatever it was couldn't wait until after the wedding?"

"Believe me, I tried. Just leave it alone. We're big girls; we can handle it."

"You're not giving her any ideas, are you?"

"What kind of ideas?"

UPENDED

"Oh, I don't know, about not getting married? God help her, she sees you as a role model, and the way you go through men..."

Zoe took a moment to beat down the urge to shove that ecru veil down her mother's throat. "Mom, I love you, I do, but you say terrible things to me all the time." She reached behind her, trying to find her dress's zipper. "I'm going to take off, okay?" She felt at her back and turned a little and felt and turned like a dog chasing its tail. "Can you unzip me?" she finally asked.

"I'll do no such thing. What in the world is wrong with you?"

Kimberly revering her. Madeline using her for inspiration. Making things right at long last. None of these things overlapped at all with wielding the truth as a weapon, but she said, "Nothing's wrong with me. Not a single goddamned thing, not that you'll believe it once you know that I'm a lesbian. I didn't realize it until I left Sebastian, but that still means I've been lying to you for a long time."

"You're—"

"Gay." She practically spit the word at Adele. Nothing like making a bad situation worse.

Adele's frown melted away, leaving behind a mask of neutrality that was infinitely worse. "Yes. In fact, I think you *should* leave."

This was not a suggestion but a cold, angry command, and Zoe hurried to the dressing room where her clothes were, scrabbling at her back for the damn zipper.

"What're you doing?" Kimberly asked.

"Taking off."

"Fine by me." She crossed her arms in a shadow of her six-year-old self.

"I told Mom the truth, and she asked me to go. Ordered me." She contorted her arm in the right way, snagged the pull, and struggled the zipper down.

"Wait. You told Mom?"

"I'm sorry, okay? That I told her like I did and that I've been a disappointment to you." She stepped out of the dress and yanked on her jeans. "This isn't how I wanted things to go. Not by a long

266

shot. I was planning to tell you after the wedding. You've got to believe me."

"You told Mom? Just like that?"

"Yeah." Zoe ducked into her T-shirt. "And now she's wearing her poker face, which means when she says leave, I need to leave. I know this is...I'm sorry, okay? I have to go." Zoe ran a hand through her hair and started toward the front of the shop, hoping to God she wouldn't encounter Adele on the way out.

Kimberly stopped her, pulling her into a hug. "I'm really mad."

"I know."

"And I can't believe you're leaving me with Mom like this."

"I'm sorry."

"But I still think you're kind of awesome."

Tears stung Zoe's eyes, and she squeezed Kimberly tight enough to cause some damage to her dress. "Love you," she said and took off, staring straight ahead until she was a block away, where she leaned against a parking meter and took several slow, deliberate breaths.

She felt sick and forced herself to walk another block to open up more distance from the scene of the crime. A hard ache set in below her solar plexus at her mother's look and the sinking suspicion that she shouldn't have let herself get run off like that. But she couldn't go back, not now. At the same time, she was aware of the soft summer sunshine and how it illuminated the leaves on the trees that arched above her, how the rays that made it past the canopy warmed her face. It was color and feeling and a glinting texture that was made more sweet and tantalizing by the bitter taste in her mouth.

She realized she was walking away from the bus station, which had to be her destination now, given her mother's banishment of her. Buses ran to Boston all the time, and at least whatever wait she had in that unpleasant station for the next one would be honest. She looped back, edging around the bridal boutique and the mushroom cloud of what was hopefully her last deception to her family. That thought both deepened her despair and made her feel a shade of lightness, as if the sunshine were penetrating below the top layer of her skin—the same way Madeline's gaze did when she got unwaveringly serious.

Zoe fished her phone out of her bag and called Madeline, who answered on the first ring. "I had a feeling you might change your mind about the sweatshirt." Her voice was soft and stuffy sounding, and the road noise that had accompanied her last call was gone.

"Where are you?"

"Outside the library on, uh, Washington Ave."

"What are you doing there?"

"I...wasn't ready to go back home."

"Stay there. I'll come to you." Zoe turned toward the library's main branch and quickened her pace.

"What about the fitting?"

"I accidently-on-purpose came out to them. Under duress and of my own volition. It was a disaster. My mom told me to leave."

"Zoe."

"Don't say anything more. I can't handle it. I'll be there in fifteen minutes. Don't move." She tried not to think of anything on the walk—not Kimmy's disappointment in her, not her mother's freeze-out, and especially not how her taking Madeline's earlier phone call had started this whole horrible fiasco. She reminded herself this was what she ultimately wanted, that the truth was a priceless thing. She hurried more, chasing green lights and walk signals until she turned the last corner and saw Madeline sitting on the steps of the library, her face tipped to the sun. While Zoe approached, she wiped one cheek, then the other. If anyone looked like an exhausted vagabond, it was Madeline, hair flyaway in the breeze, dark circles under her eyes. When Zoe was close enough to be heard, she said, "If you wanted to avoid Boston, Mount Tom between Springfield and Northampton would at least have given you a better view."

Madeline swiped at her cheeks, rubbed her nose, and sniffed. "Mount Tom doesn't offer the distraction of literature."

Zoe sat down next to her. "You live in words, and I live in color."

"That's a nice way to put it. I would say I bury myself in words like an ostrich with its head in the sand."

"I'd say that about color, but I've been doing a bang-up job of not painting for years." The thought of Kimmy's wedding present, of Kimmy in general, made her put a hand to her eyes, then drop it in defeat. "I shouldn't have been aggressive with my mom, but she pushes my buttons so hard."

Madeline snaked her hand over to Zoe's and entwined their fingers. Squeezed. "Zoe, you can't second-guess. Or regret. It'll kill you. You need to forgive yourself your mistakes."

"I think that's good advice for both of us."

"Mm." Madeline turned her face away. After a moment, she wiped at her cheeks with her free hand.

"Why are you crying?"

"I don't know." Then, lowly, "Change is hard. Especially when it means letting go."

"What are you letting go of?"

She took a shuddering breath. "Everything, it seems like."

"Jane?" Zoe asked with an inward grimace. The most potent four-letter word ever. A truck rolled by them, giving Madeline time to respond.

"Yes, but more like everything that might have been but isn't. Old habits. My books. The family experience I never had. The bad choices I made. My fear. Everything."

"How about maybe take one thing at a time? I'd say books seem doable, but remembering your apartment, I'm not so sure."

"I actually started on that last night but only made it through a couple shelves before I got disgusted with myself. I spent half my life reading to hide from reality, and then, after last night, I still pick a library as the perfect place to hide out from my apartment." She motioned behind her and shook her head.

"Okay. You *really* need to cut yourself some slack."

Madeline laughed, weakly, and pushed away more tears. "Yeah, maybe. But now I can't believe I'm going on about this when you just came out to your family."

"Talking about that will only make me anxious. Anyway, I know I said that books seemed the easiest to let go, but they wouldn't be my first choice."

"No?" Madeline looked at Zoe. "What would that be?"

Zoe's bravado cracked under Madeline's gaze, but she managed to say, "I think you can guess."

After a while, without glancing away, Madeline said, "I didn't like thinking of you at Club True that night you called. And it wasn't because I was wallowing in sleepless loneliness at home. I behaved badly about what happened between us, but it was the last place I went before..." Madeline frowned, and her fingers tightened around Zoe's. "I forgot. I totally forgot, what with Jane and all. You said something on the phone when you called from the club. Someone ran off a creepy guy. What did you mean by that?"

"Oh, him? He's some perv peeper. I saw him across the street from the club both times I was there, lurking in the shadows."

Madeline took her hand from Zoe's but leaned closer. "Did he wear jeans? A dark windbreaker?"

"I don't know. Something like that. Why? You're kind of freaking me out."

Madeline stood, muttered something Zoe couldn't hear, and pinched her nose. But then she took Zoe by the shoulders, her fingers digging in. "Don't go there again."

"Why, are you jealous?" Zoe said in a lame attempt to diffuse the situation.

"Promise me you won't go there again." Madeline's face was scrunched up, and she looked near tears again. "He's not just a perv. I think he's the one who attacked me. Followed me home somehow, without my seeing him, and...Stay away from there."

"Okay. I promise."

"Good." Madeline let her go. "Let's find the car and head back." She turned and started walking, not waiting to see if Zoe was following her. Zoe scrambled to her feet, but before she had taken more than a couple steps, Madeline glanced back over her shoulder. "Don't go back there."

CHAPTER 30

THE OFFICE PRINTER'S BUZZ WAS ACCENTED BY PLASTIC CLICKING sounds with the production of every page. It whispered productivity in Joe's ear while he was anything but. He'd been at his desk, but everything he latched on to do slipped through his grasping fingers like sand. At times like these, Madeline would say to take a break (yes, even if it were before you really got started), walk around the block, get a coffee—anything but sit and get nothing done while frustrating yourself about getting nothing done.

He scooted back in his chair to do just that even though Beth was here, was the one who'd queued that print job. Before he could get up, she strode into his office, cream-colored slacks swishing around her legs, and held a sheaf of binder-clipped papers out to him. "Chapters four through seven, as requested."

He reached across his desk to take them. "Hot off the presses, literally." He placed his palms on the warm pages.

"Now you know where all your printing stock has been going, though I guess Madeline's still in the dark." She made a sour face and sank into one of the chairs across from him. "And has to stay that way, at least about this little experiment."

He slipped the chapters into his briefcase on the floor next to him. "Says the woman who's been giving me the worst time about just this for weeks."

"That's business. This is..."

"Somewhat inexplicable."

"Listen, it makes total sense. Madeline's practically a professional reader. Exposing these chapters to her would be *way* too scary." Beth tugged sharply on the cuffs of her crisp white shirt—first the left then the right.

"I see."

"I'm saying sometimes you need a critic and sometimes a cheerleader."

"I get it. Rah rah sis boom bah." Joe waved imaginary pom-poms. "Well, I loved the first few chapters. Very rich, very noir."

She crossed her legs and sat back. "My point exactly."

"I'll have you know, my taste is not only impeccable but also critical. I hired you, after all."

"And saved me from life as a starving artist. I was only too happy to give up my New York City waitress experiment."

"Do you think Boston is your permanent home now?"

"Why do you ask?"

"Just curious. Some people have more wanderlust than others." And, if so, might be interested in following him and the company to California. After the last two months of upheaval with Madeline, Joe felt Beth's indispensability acutely, which made it even more agonizing to wonder how he was going to pay her salary next month.

She tilted her head and looked at him over her glasses like a strict schoolmarm. "This is an odd conversation. Too chitchatty. Too idle. There's something you're not telling me."

He wasn't telling her any number of things: that he'd failed to sign up enough software trial clients to meet their baseline costs; that his lawyer had convinced him he would lose a petition for custody of Katie in dramatic, expensive fashion; that he'd been stupid enough to cash in part of his retirement savings to keep the lights on and was burning through it at an alarming rate. He stopped himself from reaching for his stress ball. "I'm not sure about your main character's name. Lucy seems, I don't know, too young and hip for the person you're portraying."

Beth laughed. "Ever heard of Lucille Ball? My grandmother's name was Lucille. Classic in every way."

"Still, I don't know. Maybe something more weighty. Agatha. Brunhilda."

"You're lying, and you know it. You're doing that thing with your hands."

He glanced down to find his fingers in a church-and-steeple configuration, which, as Beth had pointed out to him, was a surefire sign he was being less than truthful. He flattened his hands on his desk, thinking he should've gone for the stress ball when he'd had the chance. "You're right. I love the name Lucy. It was a contender when we had Katie. And it perfectly suits your character."

Movement behind Beth made him look up and see Madeline step into his doorway. "Your character?" she asked.

Beth practically broke the sound barrier getting to her feet. "Hi. Happy Monday. I was going to make some coffee, not that you're drinking any lately. Or have you started again?"

"Your character?"

Joe wished Madeline would look away, as she did so often lately, but she was slack-faced and sad. He said, "I convinced Beth to give me a small preview. Badgered her until she relented." He caught Madeline staring at his hands and quickly dismantled his finger church.

Beth started to the door, saying, "I'll let you two talk and eavesdrop from outside, as usual." Her escape was arrested when Madeline put a hand on her arm.

"I'm not going to badger or guilt-trip you, but I think you're the best and just want to experience this wonderful, creative thing you're doing."

Beth spoke to her high heels. "When it's ready." Then she stepped out.

Madeline closed the door and took Beth's place across from Joe, the chair surely still warm. "The book, huh?"

"What did the bank say on Friday?"

"They have to run the numbers, but it doesn't look good. The book?"

"Let's go to the branch together this afternoon. Bankers are always in a better mood on Mondays, and I can compile some very convincing information. Tweak my projections."

"Fine. We're changing the subject." She settled into the armchair, wedging her back into one of its corners and slumping a little. "But I can't go to the bank today; I have an appointment with Detective Henderson later."

"The detective on your case? Do they have a lead? Have they found him?"

"No." She looked too relaxed for this topic—too relaxed to actually be relaxed. "I'm going to tell him what the man said to me. And where I was before the attack." She told him about what Zoe from IDK had said about Club True over the weekend (Joe had always wondered if Zoe was gay), and Madeline's suspicion that the "creepy guy" there was her attacker. The more she spoke, the more forced her relaxation appeared, her hands crossed on her knee just so but seeming to be welded in place.

"You think he's been targeting women at that club?"

"Yes." The word was clipped. Tight. "I didn't know...was sure he hadn't followed me. I was so stupid, really." She squeezed the bridge of her nose. "It's another thing I'm not sure how I'll live with. But at least I can help stop him now."

He leaned forward. "Is it going to be an issue that you've withheld this information?"

"From what I've read, they can charge me with something like evidence tampering. But if I can be a good liar one more time, I can probably convince them not to. Assault victims lie to police for all sorts of plausible reasons: fear, intimidation, self-incrimination, the expectation of disbelief."

"What was it for you?"

She cast her gaze to that Fenway Park picture. "Complicated. But that's not much of a defense."

"Do you want me to go with you?" he asked softly. "I think I should go with you."

"No. I'm taking responsibility for cleaning up all my messes right now."

"What does that mean?"

"Just what it sounds like." The words were easy, but the glance she nailed him with was hard, serious.

He motioned around him. "Is this one of your messes?"

"I started this for the wrong reasons."

"That doesn't mean the venture itself is wrong."

"No, but—"

"Move to California with me," Joe said, too quickly and loudly. Madeline stared at him, her mouth open an inch, revealing the bottoms of crowded front teeth. Chiclets, he thought, and hurried on. "Bridget's taking Katie, and I can't do anything about it. But she's right that there's incredible opportunity out there, not to mention money. I think we could be really successful."

Madeline frowned, uncrossed her legs, and finally looked ill at ease. "What do you mean move 'with' you?"

"I mean that to be the father I want to be, I need to be near Katie no matter what harebrained schemes Bridget comes up with. You and I could try to run this as a bicoastal thing—might have to in the beginning—but Silicon Valley is swimming in VC money, not to mention companies right in our sweet spot. I've done some research, and we could hit the jackpot out there."

Madeline braced her hands on the arms of her chair and pushed herself up and back. She blinked rapidly as if his words were dust in her eyes, a surprising irritation. "Whoa. That's…"

"I'm being proactive, visionary."

"No, you're being more harebrained than Bridget. Have you even considered me in this fantasy?"

Now was the time. Now or never. He hurried around his desk to her side and was halfway down on one knee before he realized what he was doing. He straightened up. "You and Katie are the *only* things I've considered. All I want for you is happiness, Madeline. We make such a fantastic team, and if we move to California, not only will you get away from all the bad memories here, but you'll be able to do what I think you're meant to do."

Madeline pressed on one eyebrow until her fingertips turned white. "Move *with* you. If *we* move. What are you really saying? Because it sounds like I've been recruited into something I never even knew about, let alone agreed to."

He took her free hand and squatted down. "Maybe this sounds crazy, but I love you. When I saw you in the hospital and thought I might lose you, all these feelings were overwhelming, undeniable. You've been my best friend for years, but we're perfect together. Just perfect. You must see that."

Madeline pulled her hand from his and leaned as far away from him as the chair would let her. Her mouth worked at words, but before she could say anything, he went on.

"I'm sure this is a surprise. I've been trying to hide it, but hear me out. I know you care for me, even though things between us have been difficult since everything happened—"

"Difficult?" Madeline got up and moved across the office from him. "And you think this declaration of yours is supposed to make things easier?"

"That's not what I mean. I know this is anything but straightforward, which is why I've kept it to myself so far, but now…"

"What, you think because you've concocted some fantastical way to align the elements of your life, I'll— I'm not a chess piece, Joe. You can't just move me where you want me."

"I know that."

"I'm gay! What am I supposed to do with this?"

He made a calm-down gesture, which, instead of calming her down, made her ears glow red. He said, "Just...try to consider everything the way we do at clients."

"This is my *life*, not some management exercise." Her words were as hot as her ears, and he felt the air molecules in the room grow unruly and sharp around him.

He tried to slow things down with a long breath. "I know you love me, Madeline," he said softly. "We make a great team."

"Of course I love you, but that's— Building a company together isn't the same as building a relationship. Or, what, a marriage? For fuck's sake, Joe. I can't believe this."

He grew warm under his shirt, and his heart pounded. "I don't think you're something to be manipulated. I've never thought that. My feelings have been so overwhelming, and so many things have been unraveling—please, the thought of losing you is unbearable."

She covered her face with her hands for a moment, then dropped them, slapping them against her thighs. "Relying on me for your happiness is a terrible idea. I can't even rely on myself right now."

"I'm not—" he started but knew she was uncomfortably on target. "You and this company brought me back to life after my divorce."

"Joe." Her voice was calm, as he'd requested, and he didn't like it one bit. "I can't be that person anymore."

"I know. Change is the only constant. But maybe we can change together?"

She pushed her shoulders against the wall and whispered, "Everything is just *impossible*. All these years, I've been clinging to the idea of Jane, punishing myself for fucking things up with her, and the minute I decide to let go of that, the *very* minute, Joe, you do this. This!" Her face crumpled and twisted. "I can't. I just can't, no matter how nice and easy it would be if your fantasy could come true, no matter how little I want to disappoint you."

"You don't have to— I mean, we don't have to be together like that. We can—"

"No, I can't. I came in here to tell you I want out. I can't reverse course on that, not now. And shit, Joe, I couldn't be with you in the company when you want more. Not just more but *everything*."

She sounded absolutely reasonable, and he wanted to rip the words from his ears before they solidified into the truth. "Madeline," he whispered. "Can we...what if we reorganize things? Completely split responsibilities, still have a common goal but not—"

"No. Not that either of us should be making decisions for the other, but you need to take the company to California and be with your family."

"You're as much my family as Katie."

"No, I'm not. We've both put expectations and desires on this company it can't withstand. No company could. I need to walk away, and you need to go to California. If I sign over my part of the business to you, you can make a run at things out there. The software's done, the methodology is solid. You have a great chance."

Joe took Madeline's vacated chair. "You're just trying to make yourself feel better."

"Of course I am! I'd do a lot to feel better right now—except keep lying the way I've been."

He felt a tightness in his chest he might have thought was a heart attack in ordinary circumstances.

She said, "When is Bridget moving?"

"Two weeks," he croaked out on thin breath.

"Then we'd better get this wrapped up quickly."

Instead of responding, he turned away from Madeline and tried to beat down a huge, choking sadness that took up all the spaces between his cells, all the space *in* his cells. When he felt her hand on his shoulder, he closed his eyes against everything that touch didn't mean.

"I'm sorry," she said. "You know I don't want to hurt you. You've been—"

He cut her off. "I'll call our lawyer to put together a separation agreement. If we give notice this week, we'll only be out an extra month's rent. Will you take care of that?"

She took her hand from his shoulder after a long beat. "Sure. Of course. What about Beth? We need to decide what severance we can afford and tell her the news. We should also call around to see if any of our clients can use her."

"I'll put a figure together, and we can discuss it."

"What message do you want to give to our clients?"

But he couldn't speak anymore, just opened his eyes and let his gaze rest on a corner of the office away from Madeline. Bits of random detritus on the carpet spoke volumes about the cleaning crew's half-assed efforts.

"Joe?" Madeline's voice was soft and intimate.

He shook his head.

"I'm sorry."

But it didn't matter how much she said it or how heartfelt it might be. No amount of apology or remorse would ease this suffocating loss. He heard the door open and close behind him. What now? Try to make the company a success without her when every single part of it was patterned with her fingerprints? How could he move on if she continued to be all around him yet out of his reach? Tears muscled past his eyelids, which he'd squeezed shut against the release of crying, knowing it would make all of this undeniably real.

CHAPTER 31

THE LAST STRAGGLER OF THE AFTERNOON RUSH AT FUEL NURSED his four-shot latte until Ethan was sure he was going to lick dried foam from the inside of his mug. Ethan and Nettie watched the college kid take miniscule sips of his drink while alternating between looking out the window and crouching over his phone. In whispered coordination, they agreed to stare at the same spot on the back of his neck and waited for him to squirm under the combined power of their intention—or maybe even combust. He didn't flinch. Ten minutes later, when he finally vacated Fuel and left Ethan and Nettie alone, they kissed with pent-up seriousness behind the espresso machine.

"I thought that guy's ass had become one with the chair," Ethan said when they came up for air.

"You know, if we get caught, we'll never get another shift together again."

He snatched his hands from her hips and glanced around, eyes wide. "Do you think Neal's got hidden webcams?"

"Only because he's jealous."

"He should be. Who knew you were such a good kisser?"

UPENDED

She snapped a coffee-stained towel at him and went back to her post behind the register. Even after spending every night together for the last week and catching up for lost time in the whole sex department, he couldn't believe what was happening. He was so elated he couldn't finish any of the serious songs he had in the works, so in the short hours he and Nettie were apart, he tried to write a kick-ass happy song full of truths about love and the surprise of pleasure after both pain and friendship. Forcing himself from warm Nettie bliss into the cold, self-critical mindset necessary to create anything halfway decent was a trial, but this, he thought, was one problem he didn't mind having.

He was concentrating on perfecting new latte art—a treble clef this time—when Nettie nudged him. "Your sister's here."

The Mad Hatter stood across the counter from Nettie, looking decidedly worse for wear: her hair in disarray, her blouse coming untucked from her slacks, the paleness of her skin highlighting her imperfectly healed nose and a raw redness around her eyes and nostrils. For a moment, he felt bad for feeling so good.

"Hey, Hat Trick. This is a bit outside your usual territory. Client meeting?" A *really* bad client meeting, if so.

"No. I wanted to see you. Can you take a break?"

He and Nettie surveyed the currently empty shop. Even the street signs on the walls looked lonely. Nettie said, "I think I can handle things for a while. Do you want something to drink?"

Before Maddy could answer, Ethan said, "Don't even with the mint tea. Sit down, and I'll make you something."

When he had her red eye with just the right amount of steamed cream, he sat down across from her at a table in the corner. "Drink," he said, sliding the mug toward her.

She took a deep sniff of the coffee and sighed. "I was caffeine free for a month until poisoning myself with Red Bull Friday night. Fuck it. Nothing's helped me sleep any better. Or made me sleep any worse."

"That caffeine-slash-sleep thing is a total and complete fallacy. But Red Bull, really?"

"Desperate times." She took a sip, then another. "Oh, so good. I'm sorry I bailed on the diner yesterday. I needed time to sort things out."

"Things?"

"I just came from the police. I told them everything. I think the guy who attacked me is hanging out by lesbian clubs to find victims."

"Whoa. Wait. What? You came clean?" He replayed what she'd said, trying to parse it for information that wasn't there. "Start from the beginning, will you?"

"What beginning? The one where you threatened to disown me if I didn't tell the truth?"

"Now, wait a minute."

"I'm kidding." She lavished some more quality time on her drink before saying, "Zoe's seen him, I think. Outside the club I went to that night."

"Zoe?"

"A friend."

"A friend?"

"This is going to take forever if you play the echo game."

He got serious then and listened to all the details: her telling the cops where she'd really been that night, what her attacker had said (which was news to Ethan), and her suspicions about his methods, given the man lurking around the club. The police kept her for hours to give her entire statement again, multiple times, and had reacted harshly to what she'd said.

Do you know how many people you've potentially put in danger?

How are we supposed to believe anything you say now?

Can anyone corroborate this? Are you even taking this seriously?

While she recounted all this, she touched her eyebrows, her nose, her hair, and her throat in agitation.

He said, "Why didn't you tell me you were going there? I would've gone with you. Everything I've read says assault victims need to have advocates. No way would they have fucked around with you like that if I'd been there."

283

Maddy's face was stiff with surprise, her mug hovering a couple inches over the table.

"What? I read."

She put her mug down and covered his hand with hers, her fingers coffee-warmed. "Playboy, right?" He was an instant away from getting mad when she cracked the kind of smile he hadn't seen in months—since way before the attack. "This coffee's going right to my head." She raised her mug, with its gas-pump-shaped handle, in emphasis.

"I'm serious, Maddy. I could've helped. I would've been useful."

"I know. I had to handle this myself. Some kind of redemption. Oh, and I quit the company this morning."

He made his eyes go wide and scraped his chair back from the table. "Nettie? Call 911. My sister's delirious."

Maddy said, "Ignore him. I'm more sane than I've been in months." She turned back to Ethan. "Maybe years. I have no idea what's going to happen next."

"Welcome to my world. Drinking helps. Not Red Bull, though."

"All tips and words of wisdom are appreciated." But then, as if she suddenly remembered she was supposed to be miserable, her face went ugly and twisted, and she passed her fingers across her eyes and wiped them on a napkin. "I'm all over the place. This woman, Zoe, she just came out to her family, and I could see it was hard for her and she was anxious about them not accepting her, and I kept thinking about how it was for me, how stupid young I was, how I tried to convince myself that being honest was the thing that mattered the most. What did I know? I was fourteen. I was desperate to put things in a comprehensible order, but I was only honest because I wanted to pull other people into the same strange world I'd ended up in so they could see and validate me somehow. But Mom and Dad didn't really want to know or understand. If I hadn't been so young, maybe that wouldn't have meant so much, but I was, and it did, no matter how much I tried to convince myself it didn't, no matter how much recognition and comfort I found in books. It wasn't the same. It wasn't nearly the same."

"You know, Mom and Dad were just people. Fucked up like the rest of us."

"I shouldn't have said what I did about your having unresolved issues with Dad. I'm the queen of unresolved daddy issues. I told Zoe she can't beat herself up or regret any mistakes she might have made, but if there's anything I'm expert at, it's that."

Ethan rubbed his chin and cheeks out of habit, raising a rasp of stubble rather than the soft swish of beard. He knew what this would look like to Maddy—some combination of frustration and concern—so he relished the idea of her reaction when he said, "Hey, Hat Trick, you can't keep mentioning this chick without telling me if she's hot or interested or anything."

He was awarded with an eye roll/smile combination. "Just because you're finally getting some doesn't mean sex is on everyone's mind."

He shrugged. "Hot or not."

Maddy's ears got red, but so did her cheeks and neck. "Hot." Then, before he could ask, she said, "Totally different from Jane. But, really, who am I to get into a relationship right now?"

Ethan leaned forward and lowered his voice. "What, and you think I've got my shit together? I smell permanently like coffee, which is wonderful in small doses but is nauseatingly indicative of my poor socioeconomic position in the long run. I have very few prospects except that I'm singing down the street in two weeks— you're coming, by the way, with this hot Zoe. But I don't have enough songs to fill my opening set. Yet somehow, Nettie still digs me, and I dig her, and it works."

"It's not nearly all that bad, and you know it. Hey, if you're hard up for material, maybe you can write something about Mom and Dad. A memorial like we talked about before."

"Yeah, and maybe you can make the moves on Zoe."

"Still with the bargaining."

He wagged a finger at her. "It's negotiation, and I learned it from the best."

"You used to call it manipulation."

"I used to be an immature asshole."

"And I was the know-it-all bitch."

"Finally, firm proof that we're actually related, though you know that's bullshit."

Maddy smiled and tilted her head. "I love you, and that's very nice, but for better or worse, I've rediscovered the truth." She sipped her drink again. "And coffee, thank you very much."

"Oh, great. Here we go again with honesty-is-the-best-policy Madeline. Maybe ease back into it. I've started to appreciate this shitty version of you."

"I'll throw you some curve balls every once in a while. Like, I don't know. You look really good in that T-shirt."

He squared his shoulders and batted his eyes, smiling when she laughed. He thought about the line that had come to him that night with Nettie, the idea of returning to what was left of the fold, no matter how little that might be, and with those words—and with Maddy right across from him, being the sister he remembered, the sister he'd come running to a year before—he felt full and vibrant, suffused with a happiness made even deeper because of its higher purpose.

He felt for the notebook and pen in his pocket. "I have to jot something down, but don't go anywhere."

"Believe me. I'm not leaving."

CHAPTER 32

ZOE TOOK A COUPLE STEPS BACK FROM THE CANVAS SHE'D BEEN working on for the two weeks since that disastrous visit to Albany. She pushed her glasses up with the back of a hand and squinted at the easel. Something was wrong with what she'd just laid down, but she couldn't see it yet, not that this was unusual. For her, painting was about navigating the great divide between the atmospheric perfection of the idea in her mind's eye and the dull imitation that ended up on the canvas. Sometimes the difference was tantalizing, sometimes demoralizing, but it sat as a metallic taste in her mouth and an itch at the back of her neck. Luckily, oil paint stayed wet and workable for a while, which allowed her a complicated, slow dance with her vision, inching closer and backing away, scraping off or layering on in attempts at fidelity to that sublime mental model. Watercolor, on the other hand, was one harsh mistress.

Today, she'd changed this and tried that, circling the image defined by the taste in her mouth and the colors behind her forehead. But then she mixed a little more white into the amber on her palette, and a soft bloom of inspiration took hold. Her senses narrowed on the canvas in front of her, the weight of the brush in her hand, the shadows of light caught in the dips and swirls of her paint. Nothing came close to the focus that stole over her when chasing down an image with brush and oil. It was electric and total.

So total, in fact, that she wasn't sure how long Madeline had been standing next to her when she finally heard her name.

"Hey!" Zoe said. "What time is it? Am I late?"

"I'm early. I wanted to catch you in action. That's really different from what's hanging at Rosemary's. I love it."

She looked back at the canvas. It was incomplete but particular, with shifts away from pure abstraction into something tantalizingly close to realism. A shadowy ghost of herself was right there at the bottom of the painting, reaching up toward enlightenment. "Well, I'm kind of a different person, so I guess that's good."

Madeline ran her fingers along the dry tips of brushes that stuck out of an old plastic container that probably had held wonton soup in a former life. "I could ask you a million questions about what you're doing, but I don't want to interrupt. Or at least not too much."

Despite part of her mind being stuck on the painting, Zoe couldn't help noticing the relaxed drop of Madeline's shoulders and the softening of the lines around her mouth that she'd begun to think were etched in place. "What happened?"

"What do you mean?

"You look...relaxed. Really good."

Madeline gave a half smile. "I was tired of being a mess every time I saw you, so I took Ethan's advice and starting drinking *a lot*." She winked. "The reintroduction of coffee to my diet may have worked some miracles." Madeline rocked back and forth on her feet, slipping her hands into the pockets of her blue shorts. "And I've been making some changes." She wore a pale orange shirt that brought out the gold in her hair and eyes.

"Good ones, it looks like."

"Well, at least drastic. I really don't want to distract you. I have some calls to make, so I'll be outside when you're ready. No rush." She touched Zoe's forearm and was gone.

Yeah, right. How could she possibly not be distracted after the feel of Madeline's fingers, her smile, this seismic shift to the person Zoe vaguely remembered falling for at Rosemary's so long ago? The canvas still pulled at her with the shimmer of possibility, but she checked her watch and saw there really wasn't time to get involved. She had to get cleaned up and change her clothes and generally prepare for what was, finally, their first real date. There'd been no dinner at Rosemary's without Rosemary—no nothing for days after their quiet, nerve-racking drive back from Albany, during which Zoe couldn't stop replaying the scene in the bridal salon and berating herself for answering Madeline's call. But then, a few days ago, Madeline had extended this invitation to her brother's concert, and now here they were.

After covering her canvas with an old bedsheet and cleaning her brushes, she scrubbed her hands in the studio's utility sink. She was still scraping under her nails, having abandoned her cuticles, when her phone rang, vibrating against her leg in a front pocket. Madeline, she thought, and hastily dried a hand as much as she could on her paint-crusted shorts before answering.

"Zoe," her sister said.

"Hey! Hi. Why haven't you been answering my calls?"

"Because it's been an absolute shitstorm since you ran off."

She shut off the water and dried her other hand. "I didn't run off; I was run off. Maybe if someone out there would pick up their phone or call me back, I'd be able to do some damage control."

"You have no idea what it's like. If Mom found out I was having this conversation...She's scary silent about you but also so far up my ass about the wedding I'm choking on her. Why'd you have to do this right now?"

"Hey, you bullied it out of me. *And* thought I was awesome for it."

"Yeah, well, that was before Adele went on the warpath."

Zoe paced back and forth in front of the sink. "Tell me what I can do."

"Nothing. I'm only calling to insist that you leave it alone."

"For how long?" she asked after taking a steadying breath.

"I don't know, Zoe. A long time."

"And the wedding?"

"What do you think? You didn't consider anyone else, and now everything is poisoned under this manic happy facade."

"Kimberly."

"I gotta go. Don't call us, we'll call you. Maybe." She hung up.

After the last two weeks of radio silence from Albany, Kimberly's words weren't really a surprise, but Zoe felt the sting of them anyway. Her sister was right about one thing, at least—Zoe shouldn't have let Adele scare her off that day. It would've gotten ugly, but at least it would've been real. Now it was the worst kind of irony that her masquerade had become theirs, an outcome of truth telling she never would have anticipated.

She walked back to her area, glad her painting was covered because she'd surely see it from a different, muddied perspective now. She leaned down to pick up her backpack, and there, right in front of her on her plastic tub of supplies, was Bernard Collins's card. Dog-eared and wrinkled, it was supposed to be inspiring, but it mocked her instead.

If only she really could compartmentalize her life the way she'd tried to for so long, but colors bled across boundaries, images resonated, and the truest truth caught in oil one minute could become irrelevant in the next. Everything informed everything else, and pain was unruly and absolute. She slung her bag over a shoulder and went to the bathroom, angry at herself and her family.

She locked herself in a stall and tugged off her T-shirt, turning it inside out to contain any paint that might be on it, and stood half naked in this aggressively air conditioned bathroom. No phone, no painting, no Bernard Collins, no Madeline, and almost no clothes, given the sorry state of her shorts. Just her. At her deepest core, the Zoe-est part of Zoe, which she imagined as an impossible combination of dense as diamond and light as helium, wasn't there stillness? Even certainty? Wasn't this center of herself as much a valid input to her experience as everything that bombarded her from the outside? Wasn't it this infallible center that had withered under her lies?

She stood, shivered, closed her eyes, and called on this Zoe-est Zoe. "This is you," she said, "No matter what." Kimberly was Kimberly and Adele, Adele. Ditto Madeline. But if she let them drown her out, she was the only one to blame for her own internal chaos. She stood and listened, and only when her shoulders started trembling in the chill did she let herself move again.

Back by her easel, she dropped her bag, pulled the sheet away from her painting, and contemplated it for a while with cool reserve. It was different, yes, but was it any good? Could it be any good? She gave her eyes time to do the work they were trained to do. Then she picked up her phone and Bernard Collins's card and dialed.

CHAPTER 33

THE LAST TIME JOE HAD PACKED HIS THINGS AND MOVED, IT HAD been part and parcel of the divorce, just another thing to do in a long blur of wrenching yet ultimately freeing tasks: untangling finances, selling their place, changing health insurance plans— unraveling all the knots they'd tied themselves together with, one deliberate yank after another. This time was a different experience entirely. He wandered through his apartment in a haze of inefficiency, tripping over jagged edges of memories. Beth had volunteered to help him pack (and a boon like that from Beth was not something to dismiss lightly), but he couldn't stand to be seen like this. Even though the moves and mistakes leading up to his and Madeline's demise had unfolded in the same inevitable-feeling subsecond stop motion that preceded all bad wrecks, he still reeled from it.

He closed the last box in Katie's room, the bare twin mattress behind him evoking images of his daughter's hair flying when she jumped up and down the bed's length and then of Madeline, woken by nightmares, bruised, battered, and so dear, her hand in his, both of them illuminated by the clown lamp now wrapped in newspaper and tucked in the box under his hands. He sealed it closed with tape that screeched off the roll and tried not to think about that post-nightmare intimacy.

Still, in not thinking about the end of things, his mind drifted back to the beginning, when they'd started Mindful Management during long evenings at his dining room table. He'd been avoiding that room, which was now crowded with the boxes he'd brought from their hastily dismantled office. The first time she'd come over to strategize, they'd talked over plates of beef and broccoli spooned over sticky white rice, and Joe had been captivated. Those first months before they'd taken on any clients had been thrilling: working together in spare hours squeezed from their evenings and weekends while honing techniques in their respective companies. He'd drawn power from Madeline's boundless enthusiasm, her deep well of ideas and innovation. The onset of exhaustion had been gradual, but when he thought back, he'd first seen it in her on the afternoon he'd helped her move from the apartment she'd shared with Jane. The sag of her shoulders he'd attributed to sadness had almost certainly been a manifestation of the first payment she'd made toward the true cost of this endeavor.

Joe was paying it now. He sat at the head of his dining room table and sifted through boxes from the office, one of them full of steno pads he'd accumulated over the years, each of them host to nuggets of wisdom, painful lessons, contacts, client kickoffs, hash marks tallying positive and negative comments in team meetings, and more. The last two weeks had been a frenzy of closure with Beth bossing them around, wild with power for the last time, and he'd dumped the steno pads into this box without looking through any of them. They called to him now, but reading them would be like perusing old love letters—always a terrible mistake.

After they'd told Beth the news and were reviewing separation papers from the lawyers, Madeline had said, "This is an opportunity, you know. You can decide everything all over again. Your way. With all the wisdom of the last three years." But he'd already decided once, and he didn't want to start over again. At the same time, he had to stop looking to Madeline for direction. For anything: support, warmth, commiseration. Love. He'd put his whole life outside Katie and Bridget in her hands, and while she hadn't abused the privilege, she'd just given it all back, and he didn't want it, had nowhere to put it, was already running out of boxes.

Later, in his bedroom, he was packing winter clothes he should go ahead and donate when his phone rang. Madeline. For three rings, he considered not answering until he realized that soon, one of these calls would be the last.

"Are you packing?" she asked.

"About halfway through, maybe more."

"Mm." He heard the air brakes of a bus in the background and wondered where she was. "I know you didn't ask me to and might not appreciate my butting in, which this isn't, not really, but I made a few calls to business school friends, asking if anyone knew of potential clients out there."

Out there. That's how he and Bridget referred to Palo Alto, as if it were a foreign country. Or deep space.

"I'm still waiting for some folks to get back to me, but I heard about a couple companies and a position I thought you might like. Do you want me to send you the information?"

One thing that had come from the disaster of his declaration of love was a return to truthfulness between them, painful though it was, so he said, "I was thinking about the first time you came over here. Chinese food."

"Beef and broccoli."

"I've been wrong about a lot of things. A lot. But throwing my future in with you…I'd never been more sure of anything. I would give so much for this not to be what you want. But I know it is, and all you've left for me to choose between is giving you what you want or not, and that isn't much of a choice, is it?"

Madeline's breath made a windy sound over the phone. "If what happened hadn't happened, I might have gone on for years with you, thinking I was happy enough until maybe things were too late. I know someday you'll see that you didn't really want me, that I was just in the way. It's been too hard to say it, and maybe I shouldn't say it now, but you know that I love you, Joe."

That might be the very worst part, and suddenly he could see how this was going to play out: sliding into a possible success facilitated by Madeline, trading weekly then monthly then seasonal emails with her, clinging to that wisp of transcontinental connection, always looking back, always tied to her through sheer force of will, through news of a new girlfriend, through regretfully declining an invitation to her wedding, through communication dwindling to birthday and Christmas check-ins. He saw this with a lurching clarity, and he said, "I think maybe I'll say no to those connections. And to us being friends. You said this is my chance to decide, so this is it. If you need a reference, of course, but—"

"I get it." Her voice was clipped, almost mean.

"I'm not saying this to be the bad guy or because I don't want—"

"I get it, Joe. Just...don't."

"Okay." His heart thudded, but he didn't succumb to the lure of taking it all back.

"So, I'll say good-bye, then."

"And I'll say good-bye, too."

Several more moments passed, and Joe wanted to reach through the phone and pull her to him in a way he'd never, ever done, convince her of his feelings to the marrow of her bones, but it wouldn't change anything.

Madeline said, "Good-bye, Joe."

"Good-bye, Madeline." He hung up the phone, his fingers shaking, set adrift and uncomfortably free.

CHAPTER 34

THE ATTACK, MADELINE HAD COME TO REALIZE, COULD NOT BE neatly construed as an isolated event, a momentary aberration of her personal safety, a bump in the road soon lost to the rearview mirror. Instead, it was the violent big bang of a new, raw universe. In those short but desperately long minutes in that alley, the laws governing nature, behavior, and morality twisted away from the ones she'd previously known, and these last three months had been a negotiation between waiting for normality to reassert itself and learning how to navigate this perverted world: walking in gravity that pushed instead of pulled, interpreting fun-house-mirror reflections of herself, reckoning with time that stretched and contracted on a whim. She'd grown to expect the lurching, biting unexpected, so that now, when Joe's resounding good-bye left her feeling untethered, she didn't panic—or at least not much. Instead, she lifted her face to the strong July sun, felt the chain link fence she leaned against press its crisscross pattern into her back, and thought about cause and effect. Choice and consequences. So many consequences.

Leaving Joe and the company, which was somehow simultaneously rash and long overdue, had launched Madeline into an abyss that wasn't a bottomless cavern below her but an unbounded expanse above. The stomach-clenching lightness that resulted had peaked this afternoon, when she'd donated all but two hundred of her dearest books to a good cause. She watched, holding on to the back of a chair for support, while two burly men hauled away twenty boxes and left her apartment barren, leaving her with no plan, no lover (not even the ghost of one), and only the tattered remains of friends from before the madness of Madeline Mismanagement—precisely the situation she had spent a considerable amount of energy ensuring would never happen.

Untethered, yes. She reminded herself that this was a good thing. This was a good thing. She stood and breathed, still and warm and calm, until the sound of a door opening made her turn, and she watched Zoe come out of the studio building and walk toward her. She wore a short-sleeved blouse, pressed khakis and sandals, her dark hair wild and free, and Madeline peeled herself from the fence to meet her halfway and lean in to kiss her on one soft cheek.

Zoe turned her face and tapped the unkissed side. "Got another one right here."

Madeline obliged. "I'm sorry about interrupting, but I was curious."

"You're forgiven, especially since I never really finish a painting session. It's more like I'm forced to abandon it for one of a dozen reasons."

"That's how I used to feel about work."

"Used to?"

"As of yesterday at five, I'm officially unemployed."

Zoe cast her gaze around, her hands out as if feeling for something. "I need to sit down."

"You can lean on me; I've had a whole twenty-four hours to adjust."

She stepped closer to Madeline but hesitated, examining her toes. "This is a date, right? Officially?"

"I haven't been on a date in ten years."

Zoe looked at her with narrowed eyes.

"Yes," Madeline said quickly, "it's a date."

"Well, then." Zoe pulled her into a hug. Before Madeline could absorb their closeness, sink into the feeling of Zoe's arms (so different from Jane's, positively ephemeral in comparison) or connect this embrace back to their first that night at Club True, Zoe let her loose.

Madeline said, "I need to tell you something."

"Oh, no. Not serious Madeline. Is serious Madeline going to come with us on all our dates?"

"Maybe not all of them, but despite my recent track record, I have a thing for honesty, and I need to be honest with you about my previous dishonesty."

"If you insist, but let's at least walk and talk." She took Madeline's hand and pulled her into motion toward Davis Square.

Movement made talking easier—or maybe it was not having to look Zoe in the eye as she recounted her lie to the police and how they now thought they could relate at least two other attacks to her revised version of events, one before hers and the other a month after. "I'm not sure how I'm going to live with that one, but I have to somehow. And don't say that I wasn't the one who attacked that woman, because I'm complicit."

"I wasn't going to say that, and you *are* complicit."

Hearing it from Zoe made it even worse. They walked a few steps, from the shade of one tree to the next, before Madeline admitted, "I know."

"But that doesn't mean you shouldn't forgive yourself."

She glanced over at Zoe. They were the same height, which was disorienting after seeing Jane so recently. "That sounds so easy, but..."

"I know. It's kind of audacious, isn't it? Owning something you deeply regret? I have to do that with my family, and my time in the closet, and I'm not sure where to begin except with the idea that pretty much everyone deserves forgiveness. Even me."

"Someone told me that forgiveness is necessary for growth." Jane had, in relation to volleyball, but she'd insisted sports was a microcosm of life. Madeline forcibly put her out of her mind.

"And yet it's still hard." Zoe smiled, then sobered again. A bus trundled by them down Mass Ave. When its roar had abated, she said, "Thanks for warning me about the club. I told some friends of mine, too."

"I think the police will find him now that they've narrowed down where to look. When they do, I'll have to testify, and I have no idea what that's going to be like."

Zoe squeezed Madeline's hand. "You'll be okay. It'll be a kind of horrible I can't imagine, but you'll be okay. I'll help you be okay if you'll let me."

"Oh, I don't know. That's a lot to ask." Madeline laughed at how absurd and yet true that was.

"At the very least, I can offer distraction."

"Distraction is good."

"Great! If you're looking for some soon, what do you think about driving me out to Albany again? Maybe next weekend? I'll show you some sights this time. Or we can stop and climb Mount Tom, which is both quiet and distraction in one big package."

"Still handling fallout from the family?"

"If you call a freezing-cold shoulder fallout, then yes, and I don't have much confidence in being able to do anything about it. I shouldn't go within fifty miles of them right now, but I have a selfish and pressing motive: there's a stash of paintings stored at my parents' that I should get if my mom's serious about not talking to me again. There's a possibility I might have a buyer for some of them, not that I'm holding my breath—or at least I'm telling myself not to."

Zoe spent the next couple blocks recounting what she knew about this mysterious, Salisbury-steak-eating "consultant" who had happened into Rosemary's. One thing that became very clear was that the art and business worlds couldn't be farther apart. It all sounded vague, subjective, and absolutely uncertain.

Zoe said, "One of my photographer friends once told me the difference between scrapbooking and fine art was the willingness—insatiable drive, even—to endure the burning discomfort of public opinion, even the microscopic subset of the public who are serious about your particular form of expression."

"So right now you're walking along in burning discomfort?"

Zoe adjusted her glasses. "Discomfort doesn't even come close."

"Lately I'm beginning to wonder if queasy anticipation is the most definitive sign of sentient life." Madeline felt again the enormity of the decision she'd made to leave Joe and the company and knew the implications would continue to evolve and ripple out, fueling both regret and freedom—the seemingly inevitable by-products of choice.

She and Zoe talked about painting and family and the delicious trepidation of change. It was how they should have talked before everything happened, sitting so close to each other at Rosemary's, wasting time and opportunity. Their conversation, their proximity, was strange and comfortable and created a warmth inside of Madeline that pushed out and met the heat of the sun on her face and arms.

She wasn't ready, was going to fuck this and other things up, was still too afraid of being alone to be with anyone else, but she walked and held Zoe's hand and moved inexorably closer to Ethan and that song he warned her he would sing, and it was okay in its not-okayness. Gravity pushed, and uncertainty pulled, but this was true, honest, and Madeline wondered what was going to happen next.

ACKNOWLEDGMENTS

THIS BOOK TRAVELED A LONG AND DIFFICULT ROAD TO PUBLICATION. Over five years, I wrote and discarded drafts, structure, points of view, even entire characters. I'm still not sure whether I should thank or throttle Mike Magnuson for viciously disemboweling an early version. Three years into the proceedings, at the Vermont College of Fine Arts Postgraduate Conference, Xu Xi opened my eyes to the fact that I still had no idea who Madeline really was. Amy Merrick and Karen Ackland were additional readers I tortured with drafts not nearly ready—thank you for your kindness and feedback. Tim Hillegonds commiserated with me at several different coffee shops when I admitted it was back to the drawing board again. Mike Levine's editorial eye helped me focus my way to the final draft and what really mattered.

Deep gratitude to Mary Ann and Ruth at Brain Mill, who always find things in my work that I didn't even know were there and have been a champion of my writing from the start.

Thanks to my parents, who tell me about every bad book they read, indignant on my behalf. Finally, of course, Anna. You've talked me off more ledges than I can count, reminding me that the worst will pass and that I do this for a reason, no matter how inscrutable. Thank you for sacrificing your time (and sometimes your sanity) to this compulsion of mine.

ABOUT THE AUTHOR

AMANDA KABAK IS THE AUTHOR OF *THE MATHEMATICS OF Change*, a novel. Her work has appeared in the *Massachusetts Review*, *Tahoma Literary Review*, *Sequestrum*, and the *Laurel Review*, among other publications. She has been a recipient of the Al-Simāk Award for Fiction from *Arcturus Review*, the Betty Gabehart Prize from the Kentucky Women Writer's Conference, and the Lascaux Review Award for Fiction.